Father Mac

Father Mac

Mike Rafferty

IGUANA

Editors: Lisa Sparks, Greg Ioannou
Book layout design: Greg Ioannou
Cover design: Jane Goodwin

Library and Archives Canada Cataloguing in Publication

Rafferty, Mike, 1933-
    Father Mac / Mike Rafferty.

Issued also in electronic formats.
ISBN 978-1-927403-14-3

    I. Title.

PR6068.A27F38 2012   823'.914   C2012-905749-5

This is the original print edition of *Father Mac*.

FOREWORD

In this book I have scattered a few thoughts around under the headings of theology and science. Why do I rush in where angels fear to tread? Because in both disciplines many aspects remain imperfectly understood and invite scope for speculation. And who is to say that a layman should not attempt to fill in some of the acknowledged gaps? And I do have an axe to grind. I believe the time is long overdue for Man to come to terms with the sort of events recounted in my story. They're surely going to happen one day, anyway. Indeed, they may already have happened.

Some of the action in this book is centred around a Signals Intelligence agency tasked with doing something quite different from its normal remit, but where else would the appropriate mix of skills be found? Although this is a work of fiction, former colleagues nevertheless took the time and trouble to read and offer their advice on draft versions, and for this I am most grateful. I also owe a debt of gratitude to Dr Bob Marriott for his advice on various medical matters, and to Dom Damian Sturdy, OSB, of the Benedictine community at Prinknash Abbey, for stimulating, and always amusing, conversation on matters both sublime and ridiculous. I welcome in particular his guidance on certain matters of Church protocol.

Phil Mawdsley of the Gloucestershire Constabulary provided helpful background information on police matters in general, my friend Marie Carroll was kind enough to suggest a few textual refinements, while Charles Mossop, with his professional eye, explored the book for structural deficiencies, and I have been more than happy to accept his advice. Finally, I am vastly grateful to members of my family who, in their own different ways, have provided the love and encouragement a writer needs to stick to the task in hand and see it through to the end-product.

I hope you will read and enjoy this book as an entertainment with a serious message. Oh, and by the way, love one another. I mean really love one another, however unlovable some blighters are.

Mike Rafferty
Winchcombe 2012

FATHER MAC: LIST OF MAIN CHARACTERS

Father Donald McNulty, parish priest of St Nicholas Roman Catholic Church, Bourton-under-Wychwood in the Cotswolds. Age mid-70s. Known to all as "Father Mac."

Sister Winifred, his sister, a nun from a convent/hospice south of Stroud. Age about 80.

Andrew, his brother, resident in Ottawa, recently retired from Canadian Civil Service, but still on-call as a "consultant." Age 62.

Chantelle, Andrew's French-Canadian wife.

Father Ambrose, priest in Ottawa, friend of Father Mac.

Norah Walsh, Father Mac's housekeeper. Age 72.

"Doc" Campbell, retired GP, great friend of Father Mac. Recently retired. Age early 60s.

Megan, wife of Doc Campbell.

Tim Sullivan, parishioner, recently retired from GCHQ. Age 62.

Lucy, Tim's wife.

Mike McGuire, parishioner, builder.

Brian Jenkins, journalist with the *Cotswold Regent*.

Hugh Frobisher, former head of cryptanalysis, GCHQ. Just retired. Part-time "consultant." Age 60.

Nick Watson, current head of cryptanalysis, GCHQ.

Kathy Webb, senior cryptanalyst, GCHQ. Age 39.

Debbie Faulkner, member of Joint Intelligence Committee's assessments staff in the Cabinet Office. Age mid-50s.

Professor Alan Lewis, senior scientific advisor to the government. Age fifty-ish.

Father Danny and **Brother Simeon,** members of the Benedictine Community at Prinknash Abbey.

Monsignor Jim Brogan, SJ, Vatican staff.

Misha, Stepan, and **Feliks**, foreign agents.

Mary, former hotel receptionist, working for the foreign agents.

Kevin and **Dave,** teenage hoodlums.

Lennie Gill, small-time crook.

Colin Gill, Lennie's teenage son.

Assorted government officials, intelligence officers, clerics, scientists, police, and medical staff.

PART ONE

GENESIS

PROLOGUE

Saturday 21 May 20

The untidy man behind the wheel of a large, grimy SUV swore in frustration. He snatched up his cell phone.

"Слишком поздно!" he roared. Yes, it was too late, much too late. There were already troops at the scene. He saw a cluster of military helicopters on the ground, beside the lake. Police cars were also arriving, RCMP and Ontario Provincial.

"Уже прилетели, войска. Полиция тоже здесь," he growled. How could they expect results when they had given him such scant guidance? He'd been told that the precise time and location could not be specified until the last few minutes. That meant that he and no doubt others had had to patrol a wide area before they could zero in. That was OK on major highways, but his beat had been mainly old logging tracks that were still as narrow as when they were in use for their designed purpose. He'd been on the road, jolting about, since before dawn. And this wasn't the first time.

Some troops emerged from the forest and began working with the police to set up barricades. A uniform approached him.

"I'm sorry, sir, you'll have to go back. We're closing the park."

"Why what's happened?" His face showed innocence and curiosity.

"There's a fire in this part of the forest. We have to contain it with all speed. Now please move."

He wondered if they and the troops knew what was really going on. He started the SUV and, as he turned, he noticed a grey VW emerging slowly from the trees. The back seat was stuffed with what was obviously camping gear, hastily thrown in by the look of it. The driver was an old dedushka who, despite his age, clearly enjoyed the outdoors. He must have been there when the ... incident occurred. It probably woke him up. How the hell could anyone sleep through it? Even he, over 30 kilometres away, had heard something – faint, but clearly discernible. So the old man might even have got up close enough to ... to what? Recover items of interest? The sort of things he himself was hired to get hold of? Yes, it was possible. It was definitely possible.

As the untidy man slowly moved off in his SUV, he saw the old man with his window down, talking to the same police officer who'd just ordered him to go back. The officer made the old man get out of the car, and gave the contents a cursory examination before nodding.

The SUV driver found a scrap of paper, scrawled down the VW's plate number and sped off to wait for the old man in a side lane. He'd like to examine the contents, too, but he would be much more thorough. Some coercion might be necessary. Well, that was within his remit. It had been all his working life. No grievous bodily harm this time. Just scare the "ровно" out of him.

Tuesday 7 June 20

The old priest woke in a sweat. That recurring dream. Every night now he relived the three times they'd tried to kill him. Twice in Canada and once back here. Or did they just want to force him off the road and then question him? And that girl calling at the presbytery, pretending to be a book-buyer. It was all very worrying. Was it all related? He really must get some thoughts down on paper. The story of his time in Canada. He'd been so busy examining all those bits and pieces. He knew he'd been burning the candle at both ends and to what effect? What had he actually achieved? Very little, beyond developing a wild, wild theory and an appreciation of the enormity of the task that lay ahead for someone with an extraordinary range of skills. Sounded like a team job. Who would have thought that with all those fragments, one single badly charred sheet he'd tossed aside to start with might be the most important. The stone the builders had rejected might become the keystone, assuming of course he was right about the orthography. Dear God, he felt drained. Mental exhaustion merged with feelings of deep anxiety. He wouldn't call it fear. That was to deny the love and protection of God, who had kept him from harm and would continue to do so. And, of course, of his angel. He knew he had an angel looking after him. Was it the same one he'd seen? Or was that one not an angel – or not quite an angel? Were there such things? He took up the small crucifix he kept on his bedside table and felt comforted. He spoke to God.

Monday 13 June 20

Thank God he'd finished the record of his recent experiences, the horrifying air crash near his campsite in Algonquin, the amazing meeting few would believe had occurred or even could occur, the fragments he'd been given and the others, many of them charred, he'd plucked from the fringes of the fire. It had taken several late nights to collect his thoughts, but he had it all down and now he felt exhausted. Importantly, he'd decided who he was going to share his adventures with, but would he be believed? He knew that's what he'd seen and, indeed, met. Thank God, too, he'd safely hidden...

Dear God, what was happening? Sweat was pouring from him now. Not another TIA? He groped for his crucifix.

"Jesus, Mary, Joseph, help me. Be with..."

The crucifix slipped out of his hands, slid down the duvet and on to the floor. Oblivion.

CHAPTER 1

Norah Walsh thrust out a bony arm from beneath the bedclothes and killed the alarm. She climbed out of bed pretty nimbly for a 72-year-old, closed the bedroom window and surveyed the day. It was 6:20 on a fine June morning. The garden birds were busily foraging and a pigeon on the roof opposite was stalking a female, elaborately bowing before her every few steps. Norah knelt beside the bed, made her morning offering and gave God his instructions for the day. Then, thirty minutes later, she was washed, dressed, and ready to begin her day. She locked the house and set off briskly down the road as the little Cotswold town was slowly awakening.

Norah had been looking after Father McNulty for the last seven years, since she was widowed and his previous housekeeper had become too old and frail. In a way, it was a happy coincidence that the poor dear had had to relinquish command of the presbytery just a few weeks after Norah was widowed. It put purpose back into Norah's life at a time when she might well have given in to a long, empty depression.

As she neared St Nicholas, she noticed a light on in Father Mac's bedroom. The dear old fellow must have been so tired he'd gone to bed and fallen asleep instantly. Well, he was entitled. After a tiring trip to Canada, he'd plunged right away into his Parish, Deanery and Diocesan business, jet-lag or no jet-lag. She knew he'd been burning the candle at both ends. He was four or five years older than Norah, and, but for the acute shortage of priests, would have retired a few years ago. The day of married priests was surely not too distant now. The Church would have to relent on purely pragmatic grounds. Norah was a strong advocate of married priests. Why should priests escape the beneficial influence of a good woman in their lives? Besides, the Church already had quite a number of them – disaffected Anglicans who had moved over when the ordination of women came, Deacons appointed in middle age, already married.

She let herself into the presbytery and made Father Mac his tea. She put it on a tray with two biscuits (a treat he dispensed with in Lent) and went upstairs. The light was still showing beneath the door of his bedroom. She tapped lightly on the door, then louder as there was no response. She called out, "Father, may I bring your tea in?" Still no response. For the first time, Norah began to feel a twinge of anxiety. She called again and thought she heard a noise of some sort. Tentatively, she eased the door open and peered inside the room. Father Mac lay on his back, a soft groan escaping from him every few seconds. His crucifix was on the floor. Dear Lord, what was wrong with Father? A heart attack? A stroke?

She must fetch Doctor Campbell, the retired GP and great friend of Father Mac, who lived a few houses away. She flew down the stairs and out the front door. It took no more than a minute to reach the doctor's house – a large old building set back from the road with a gravel drive leading to a glass-panelled door. She could see shadowy signs of life behind the glass, and rang the bell.

Doctor Campbell himself answered the door. A fit, sixty-something with a lined, lived-in face, he was wearing a dressing-gown and bearing a large mug of tea.

"Father Mac's ill, Doctor. He's collapsed. Can you come?"

"Of course! I'll sling a raincoat on. Have you phoned for an ambulance?"

"No. I thought you could get to him quicker."

"Quite right," said Campbell, struggling into a Burberry. "I can call them from the presbytery after I've seen if there's anything I can do for him."

He shouted up the stairs, "I'm away out for a while, darling. Father Mac's ill. There's some tea in the pot."

A few minutes later Doctor Campbell was examining Father Mac, while Norah made herself scarce. He'd known Father Mac as a patient down to his last toenail for many years, and it was just possible his immediate attention could make a difference. Besides, they were great friends – both exiled Scots from the east coast, he from Montrose, and Father Mac from Arbroath – and both keen golf and chess opponents. But Doctor Campbell soon concluded there was nothing that could be done by him. He came out of the bedroom and went to the phone.

"They're on their way," he said a minute or so later, "There's nothing much I can do here."

"Is it one of those ITV things he's had before?" asked Norah anxiously.

Doctor Campbell smiled. "I think you mean TIA. It could be transient ischaemia, but I rather think it's the real thing this time."

"You mean a stroke?"

"Yes. He's more or less conscious, but he seems very agitated. Keeps trying to say something, but nothing comes out. I've seen that many times. Patients realise there's a real danger they might not survive and immediately get concerned over some unfinished business in their lives. They try desperately to get it out, but speech is often affected, at least for a while."

"What are his chances of a full recovery, Doctor?"

"Hard to say at the moment. Though" (he smiled ruefully) "I can say bang goes our golf partnership. Someone will have to contact his family. His brother in Canada and his sister."

"I can do that. Their phone numbers are in his address book, and I know exactly where he keeps it. As you know, his sister is a nun. Sister Winifred."

"And about five years older than Father," said Campbell. "Bit of a battleaxe, isn't she? She's been here to stay, if I remember."

"She certainly is a forceful lady," agreed Norah, "But kind and caring with it. She works in a hospice attached to her convent. She's in a nursing order. I've met her, but not the brother. I think he has a grown-up family. They've never been over here, though Father Mac visits them at least every two or three years."

"Yes," said Campbell, "But he kills two birds with one stone. He's very friendly with a priest somewhere near his brother's home in Ottawa."

"Yes, Father Ambrose. Which reminds me, I'd better phone Tim Sullivan. Someone will need to tell the Dean to arrange for a supply priest."

"OK," said Campbell, "And can you get some things together he'll need in hospital? Toiletries, pyjamas, things like that for starters."

"He'll want a rosary and his Daily Missal and Divine Office book, too, for when he gets well enough to pray or read. I do hope he'll soon be on the mend," said Norah with a choke, as she felt a tear trickle down a cheek. "Oh, poor, dear Father Mac. Don't leave us, Father."

She then busied herself with packing a small bag, while Doctor Campbell went outside to flag down the ambulance when it came. She then picked up the phone.

*****

8

Tim Sullivan had just emerged from the shower when the phone rang.

"Why does it always ring when I'm naked and wet?" he grumbled, wrapping a towel around himself and heading for the bedroom extension. Normally, Lucy, his wife, would pick it up, but she was away looking after her mother following a fall by the old lady. It was Norah. Tim listened carefully.

"It was bound to happen sooner or later," he said. "I'll talk to the Dean shortly." Tim was one of the more active members of Father Mac's parish: Chairman of the Parish Council, reader, Eucharistic Minister, even altar server when needed. He'd also taken on the job of organising the various rotas. One way or another, the Church was never far away in its need of his time, but there were many other interests to keep him out of mischief. The children and grandchildren, the garden, the Bridge Club.

"Well, don't worry about feeding the supply priest. If he needs a meal," said Norah, "I'll take care of that. In the past, they've usually said Mass then gone straight back to Cheltenham or wherever."

Tim rapidly finished drying himself, dressed, and drove across town to the presbytery. It was still only 7:40 and the town was quiet. He parked in the church's tiny car-park just as the ambulance appeared. He joined Doctor Campbell and the two chatted quietly until Father Mac, now muzzled with an oxygen mask, was stretchered into the ambulance. Curtains in the houses opposite moved aside a little, betraying unseen eyes following the course of events. A car slowed as it passed by, then briefly stopped a little way further on. Ambulances always seemed to attract gawkers. Norah followed behind the stretcher with a small haversack. Doctor Campbell briefly introduced himself to the paramedics and told them he would arrange for Father Mac's list of medications to be emailed. A few moments later the ambulance sped off.

"I'll phone and find out what the position is," said the doctor, "Though there's not much point in phoning until at least late afternoon or early evening. They'll need to stabilise him first, then give him various tests. I'll let you both know what they say."

"And I'll prepare for a Service of the Word," said Tim. "The regulars will turn up expecting the usual weekday Mass. And I can tell them about Father Mac. I think I'll contact the other churches here, too. Father Mac has always been very active in Churches Together. They'd certainly want to know."

9

"I'll phone his sister," said Norah, "And I'll call Canada about mid-day. They're five hours behind us in Ottawa. I'll try his sister now." She hurried back in.

Doctor Campbell turned to Tim. "How are you managing without Lucy?" he asked.

"Oh, I can manage pretty well with the basics, like cooking. The only problem is it's an open-ended arrangement. Mama fell and fractured her arm. By the way, she's always known as 'mama.' Lucy's father was Italian and he always called her that. Their kids still do. She's not ill enough to stay in hospital, but she does need looking after. Lucy's the nearest, so, as ever, she's the one who goes there in the first instance. The others will take a turn if it goes on for more than a couple of weeks, which I'm quite sure it will. At least Lucy's mother is only about thirty miles away.

"Does Lucy's mother have any chronic condition?" asked Campbell.

"Only old age," grinned Tim. "But seriously, her eyesight's pretty awful. She's got macular degeneration but not quite seriously enough to be registered blind. That may come soon. I wish to goodness she'd move in with us, then we could keep an eye on her. She wouldn't even come to us while her arm mends. She frightens the life out of us, cooking with such dodgy vision. She's also getting very frail now. This isn't the first fall she's had. She's only had a bit of bruising before. But she's so bloody independent! Or thinks she is. In fact, Lucy takes her out every other week to do a major grocery shop. And I'm always popping over to help with little household jobs. She doesn't like asking her neighbours."

"Wouldn't she like some sort of sheltered accommodation, with a warden and perhaps a communal lounge?"

"No. She's just a stubborn old lady. She's got visions of a lot of old biddies playing bingo every night. She's confusing it with the Day Centre, which really is a social outlet for the elderly. We're going to have to be very firm from now on. Anyway, coming back to Father Mac, you see him pretty often, probably more so now you're retired. Was there any indication something like this was going to happen?"

"Not really. True, he's getting on a bit, he's had angioplasty and a few mini-strokes, and he's a Type 2 diabetic, but it's well controlled. Despite all this, his underlying health is surprisingly robust."

"I've noticed a few odd things lately," said Tim cautiously. "Nothing much you could put your finger on, just a general impression of reserve. He's usually so ebullient and has a word with everyone he sees. As I'm sure you've seen, he even shouts across the street to people. But in the last week or so, since he got back, he's been a bit – what's the word …?"

"Subdued, perhaps?" supplied Campbell.

"Ye-e-s. Thoughtful, anyway. Or pre-occupied might be nearer the mark. Mind you, I've only seen him two or three times. Have you noticed anything odd, too?"

"Well, now you mention it, I suppose I have. Ever since his holiday, he's not quite been himself. I couldn't even entice him into a round of golf. It may be nothing physical, at all. Perhaps something worrying to do with his family. Stress can build up and the body sometimes responds quite severely."

"Yes, that could be it, I suppose. Come to think of it, he didn't have much to say about his last holiday. He's usually full of the trips he made with his brother, and how his pal – Father Ambrose is it? – how he was doing. I gather Father Mac went off camping with his brother as usual. His brother and sister-in-law are mad on camping – always have been, and Father Mac has come to like it, too. Of course, Canada is so geared up for outdoor pursuits like hunting, fishing and camping. The facilities are terrific."

"Yes, he mentioned going camping," said Campbell frowning, "And I do know he actually spent the last day or so on his own. His brother's quite a bit younger than Father Mac – more our age – and though he's recently retired he keeps getting roped in as a consultant. I'm not sure what his line of business was. Some government job, I think. He had to go back to Ottawa unexpectedly, and his wife went with him, leaving Father Mac to decide whether to go back with them or spend a day or two on his own, fishing and watching wildlife. He loves doing that. He'd driven there in Andy's second car, so he opted to stay on. Ah, here's Norah. Did you speak to Sister Winifred?"

"Yes, she says she'll come as soon as she can and if Father's going to be in hospital for a while, she'll stay on and use the presbytery as a base for visiting him, provided the Dean has no objection. I'd be happy to find her a bed in my house if there's any problem. She'd like to take care of Father Mac if he comes back here for a while. As I mentioned, her convent also incorporates a hospice, and she's a trained nurse."

"Well this is all rather premature. We don't know what the future holds for Father," said Tim. "He may never come back here. Oh, by the way, Norah, we were saying that Father Mac has been unusually quiet since he came back. Have you noticed this, too?"

"Very much so," said Norah emphatically, "But not in a miserable way. Sometimes his mind just wanders off. Anyway, would you two gentlemen like a cup of tea?"

"Not for me," said Campbell, "I'd better get back and tell Megan what's happened."

"I've got a few phone calls I must make," said Tim. "And a Service of the Word to prepare. Thanks all the same. Doctor Campbell will be in touch with the hospital, Norah, and he'll keep us posted on Father Mac."

Norah went back inside the presbytery as Tim and Campbell walked off.

*****

Bourton-under-Wychwood was one of those quiet Cotswold towns where everyone knew everyone else and their business. Strangers stood out like sore thumbs. And there were plenty of strangers, especially in the summer, as tourists used the town as a base for walking holidays, or flocked there as one of their stops on the scenic tour that took in the likes of Stanton, Snowshill, and Broadway. The little town had a long and chequered history, dating back to the seventh century, when the Anglo-Saxons created it, built a royal palace there, then the first St Peters Church followed by a magnificent abbey. Down the centuries, periods of prosperity – prestige even – had alternated with famine, plague, and war. At its zenith, it had been one of the richest Cotswold wool towns. Nowadays, it served more as a dormitory town for Cheltenham, where the large employers of the area ran their affairs.

The history of the little town was far from Norah's thoughts as she bustled down the narrow streets to the main shopping area, wondering when she would next be buying food for Father Mac, or, come to that, if she ever would buy food for him again.

Norah called first at the newsagents for her paper. The shop was always full first thing in the morning. Apart from a man with a haversack, Norah knew all the customers and smiled and nodded to them as she joined the line.

"How's Father Mac?" called out Caroline, the bustling little blonde who helped out in the shop. "I hear he was taken off this morning by the paramedics."

"Yes, how is he, Norah?" enquired a woman being served.

"Was it his heart?" asked a man just ahead of Norah in the queue.

Norah took a deep breath and addressed them all collectively:

"We don't know anything yet. All I can say is that he was conscious when they took him off. Doctor Campbell will be contacting them later today."

"Doctor Campbell? But he retired a few years ago," said another woman.

"He's Father Mac's friend," said Caroline. "He'll be contacting them as a friend. He probably knows half the consultants at the General."

"Absolutely right," said Norah, "Anyway, how did you know about him?"

"How long have you lived in Bourton, Norah? There's no secrets in this town. In fact, Fred Roberts saw the ambulance from his bedroom window."

Norah's next call was at the butcher's.

"Hello, Norah," said Colin. "How's Father Mac?"

"First things first," said Norah. "A sliver of lamb's liver, please, Colin. He's in the General right now. He collapsed during the night some time. We don't know anything yet. Doctor Campbell will be asking about him tonight. And a couple of pork chipolatas."

"He'll be missed," said Colin. "He was a friend to all."

"You'll be talking about Father Mac," said a man entering the shop, followed by the man with the haversack she had seen in the newsagents.

"Yes, Mr. Parker," said Norah. "I'm sure the whole town knows all about it. The poor man's only been gone just over an hour."

"Well that's the measure of the concern we all feel," said Mr Parker. He had recently retired as headmaster of the senior school. "Father Mac was one of those rare individuals who could be accepted by people in all walks of life. He was a naturally caring man. He also had a brilliant mind. He spoke four or five languages, I believe, though he wore his scholarship lightly."

"I'm sure you're right," said Norah. "I do know that in spite of his pastoral duties, he would still set aside a short period every day for study. Church books, of course, but also foreign books. He had loads of them. Thank you, Colin." Norah paid and left.

She made her way to the Co-op, the only shop with anything like supermarket status in the town. She was again assailed with queries about Father Mac, so she again provided a collective response. Again, lurking to one side was the man with the haversack. Norah studied him. Probably late forties, short hair that had once been black, but was now flecked with grey, stocky in build, perhaps a few pounds overweight but pretty fit-looking. Oh, no! The object of her scrutiny was coming over to her. Norah quickly looked away and set off through the shop to get the milk she needed, but there was to be no escape.

"Your Parish Priest is ill?" It was a voice deep with concern, but one that had its origins somewhere beyond the British Isles. Eastern Europe? The Middle East? Father Mac would know in an instant.

"Yes, he's ill," said Norah.

"Will he return?" asked the stranger.

"We really don't know anything yet," said Nora uneasily. She felt as if she were betraying a confidence. It was all very well sharing her information with the town at large, but not with a complete stranger, who seemed to be probing unnecessarily.

"When will you know if he will return?"

"I've no idea."

"You clean his house?"

"The presbytery, yes. Why?"

"You live there?" That was the last straw.

"I'm sorry. You'll have to excuse me. I must attend a church service."

"A service for your Parish Priest?"

But Norah was on her way to the counter to pay.

CHAPTER 2

Tim entered the church with his script in his hand. The need for a Service of the Word came up several times a year when Father Mac had his holiday or was called away on diocesan business, and over the years Tim had conducted many of them, but he still took comfort in his script.

He checked that everything was to hand. Enough hosts in the tabernacle, water and towel for post-communion ablution, Weekday Missal on the lectern, together with the bidding prayers. He knelt in one of the pews to wait for 10 o'clock and to compose himself for the service. Tim rose and walked to the altar. He genuflected and moved to the lectern.

"Good morning everyone," he said, "In the absence of our Parish Priest, let us join together in celebrating this Eucharistic Service. Some of you may have arrived expecting Mass this morning. As I'm sure you all know now, Father Mac was taken ill some time in the night. Norah found him collapsed when she got to the presbytery. He's now in Cheltenham General Hospital. I may know something by this evening, so if any of you wish to hear the news please phone me after about 7 pm."

Tim continued with the service and added prayers for Father Mac in the bidding prayers. He then took the ciborium from the tabernacle, placed it on the altar, and led the congregation in the "Our Father."

"Let us offer each other a sign of peace," said Tim leaving the altar to shake hands with everyone. As he reached the back of the church, the door opened and a stranger walked in. Instinctively, Tim shook his hand and said, "Please join us." The man sat down.

Tim returned to the altar, gave himself Holy Communion then offered the host to the others. The stranger did not come up.

After Communion and the closing prayer, Tim said, "I'm sure we'll not be able to offer a Service of the Word every morning. Twice a week will probably be the limit, so please assume there will be a service on Tuesdays and Fridays. I'll post something outside the church, and provide updates in the Parish Bulletin."

After the service, people stayed talking together in small groups. The stranger came up to Tim.

"How is your Parish Priest? Is he very ill?"

"I have no idea yet" replied Tim, "Are you staying here in Bourton?"

"No," said the stranger, "We're just driving around. I like to look at old buildings, especially churches."

"I don't think you'll find this church of much interest. It's only about 120 years old. Compared with the Parish Church, that's the Anglican Church, this is almost a new building. The Parish Church goes back to the 15th century."

"I must take a look," said the stranger. "Thank you, and I hope your priest soon comes back. If he is too ill, what will you do?"

"It's not up to us. I presume the Bishop will eventually appoint a new Priest and until then we'll have a succession of stand-ins. Look, I have to go now. Have a pleasant stay here. Good-bye."

As the stranger walked away, for some reason Tim felt he had not seen the last of him.

Norah came up with a group of women.

"Who was that?" she asked.

"I've no idea," said Tim, "But for a stranger he seemed to be taking an unusual interest in Father Mac's illness. I couldn't guess his nationality, either. There was only a slight accent, but he was definitely not British."

"What an incredibly handsome man," said Megan Campbell. "He looked like a film star. I can just see him starring in something romantic."

"Megan!" said Norah, pretending to be shocked.

"There are loads of visitors at this time of year," said Tim. "Many are from overseas somewhere."

"I met someone a bit like that this morning round the shops," said Norah. "A similar accent, though more marked. He was also physically quite dissimilar, built like the proverbial barn door."

Everyone drifted away, except Tim and Norah.

"Come and have a coffee, and we can compare notes on the two mystery men," said Norah.

*****

"What I can't understand," said Tim a few minutes later in the presbytery, "is why Megan's 'film star' gravitated to our church. If he likes to explore old churches, what on Earth is he doing here, when the Parish Church is just up the road, steeped in history. Bullet holes in the door from the Civil War, old tapestries, things like that and those gargoyles are almost world-famous." He sipped the coffee Norah had just made.

"It must be to do with Father Mac," said Norah. "That was certainly what the man who spoke to me was interested in. He also wanted to know if I lived in the presbytery, or just did housework."

"That really is intrusive," said Tim, thoughtfully, "And if he's interested in old buildings in general, why didn't he ask about the presbytery. That's nearly as old as the Parish Church. I mean, he was standing right next to it."

"I'm convinced all this has to do with Father Mac," said Norah.

"Perhaps they know him," mused Tim. "Or perhaps they're not so much interested in Father Mac as a person, as in the consequences of his absence. Look, I'll tell you what, drink up and get in the car with me. I'd be interested to see what they're up to now. We might just see them. You'd recognise your man again, wouldn't you?"

"Oh, yes," said Norah, nodding. "Your man might be in the Parish church, I suppose. But I wouldn't be surprised if one or both of them are having a coffee somewhere."

"Yes," agreed Tim, "They may be out of sight. We can but try."

Tim unlocked the car and they got in. He drove straight for the Parish church and stopped outside.

"I can't wait here," said Tim. "So I'll carry on and turn round in the pub car park. You take a look inside the church and I'll pick you up in a few minutes."

The Parish Church, unlike St Nicholas, stayed open most of the day all year round. It was a handsome church in English perpendicular Gothic style, built largely with wool money and consecrated in 1470. Several wealthy wool merchants had lived in the town. There was much to be seen in the church and there was always someone rostered from the Friends of St Peters to welcome visitors and show them around, if necessary.

Norah walked slowly round the church, and nodded to the Friend, whom she knew.

"Hello, Norah," said old Mrs. Gratten, "You don't come here often."

"No, dear," said Norah. "Only funerals, weddings and the odd christening. I'm looking for someone, a friend of a friend, you might say. A man. Two men, in fact. Have you had many visitors this morning? I mean, very recently."

17

"A steady trickle, but nobody very recently. June is one of the busiest of months for visitors, but it's a little early in the day for the coach parties."

"All right, dear, thank you. I'll take a look round the town."

Norah left the church just as Tim was drawing up.

"Nice timing," he said. "Any luck?"

"No. Why don't we just crawl round the town a few times? I think it would be too awkward to keep stopping and looking in every tea shop. Wait a minute, who's that?"

Norah pointed towards the bank about a hundred yards away. A man had just used the Cashpoint and was getting into the driver's side of a BMW. Tim accelerated, than slowed down behind the car.

"That's him," said Norah. "The man who followed me around the shops."

"There are two of them," said Tim. "If he's the driver, I'll bet the passenger is our church visitor. I can't see him all that well through the tinted glass, but it's certainly a man. I don't intend to follow them, but I will take a note of the number, though that won't tell us anything. Even if we could find out the owner it'll probably be a hire firm." He became thoughtful. "You know what? I could swear this is the same car that crept past the presbytery when the ambulance came, then briefly stopped. That was a BMW, I'm certain. Come on, let's get back."

CHAPTER 3

Though no longer embroiled in the world of intelligence, Tim had many friends still involved in the work, both locally and in the collaborating agencies, to say nothing of those like himself who had given their 35 – 40 years to Queen and country and had now retired. He phoned one of them now.

"Hello, Bob, it's Tim."

"Tim, you old bugger, how good to hear you. What are you up to these days?"

"Not a lot. Gardening, helping the church here and there, giving the odd talk to retirement groups and U3As. How about you?"

"Getting under the wife's feet, mainly. I feel lost at home. It's a place I was hardly ever in and I don't really know how to behave there. I pop into the library most days, and have a regular date in a pub with some of my old crowd. I miss the buzz of operations, though I do still get called in sometimes when they need to pick my brains. They call me a consultant."

"Lucky you. I know exactly what you mean about missing the buzz. We lived in exciting times."

"We still do, though the focus has shifted. Anyway, what can I do for you?"

"I just thought you might like to know that our priest has had a stroke and is in hospital. It's amazing how quickly the word spread. We had a little service this morning. Quite a turnout at such short notice."

"Sorry to hear your news, Tim. Let's hope the old boy recovers."

"Thanks. He was very popular. We even had a tourist in church asking us about him and his illness, and a mate of his doing the same in town. You know, he's been a priest for fifty-three years." Tim continued giving him a few more facts and figures from Father Mac's alleged clerical career, laced with several mythical references to episodes involving golf in November followed by whiskey. By the time he'd finished, Bob knew exactly the registration number to get checked out. Bob also knew that Tim was worried about a stranger sniffing around a rather obscure Catholic church deep in the Cotswolds. It was from tiny fragments of apparently unrelated information that a big, and sometimes sinister, picture could emerge. Bob's agency encouraged its staff to take into retirement with them the need to keep their ears to the ground and report anything interesting they came across. Tim's former employers made no such request. Sigint was quite different from Humint.

"Well, you've certainly made my day," said Bob. "It's like old times, hearing from you. We must keep in touch."

"I'll make sure we do. Cheers for now."

Tim was in no doubt they'd be in touch, when Bob had a few answers for him. He did not see Bob shaking his head in amazement and muttering, "Well, I'll be damned. It's almost like telepathy!"

No sooner had Tim put the phone down than it rang again. It was Norah.

"Sister Winifred phoned. She'll be down this evening," Norah reported. "I must air a bed for her." Norah always thought along practical lines. "I think her hospice is somewhere between Stroud and Bristol. So she's relatively close. She mentioned coming up the M5."

"I'm not sure that whizzing up the motorway in the twilight is a wise thing for an eighty plus nun," said Tim thoughtfully. " I know it stays relatively light until quite late and I suppose she knows her capabilities, but surely she'd be better coming tomorrow. There's nothing she can do for him today."

"True." said Norah. "Anyway, if you need me again I'll be back in the presbytery if I'm not at home."

*****

Norah got herself a light lunch, put her feet up for an hour or so, and considered where to put Sister Winifred. With eight bedrooms in the presbytery, there was plenty of choice for Sister, but with so many rooms on the ground floor, it was difficult to keep more than a few rooms comfortably warm in winter. Good job it was summer, she mused. Father Mac was talking of having a new boiler. The existing one had been installed just after his arrival twenty-odd years ago, so it was getting near time for a replacement. The men were coming to service it in a few days. At least the whole building had been rewired a few years ago, and heaters could now safely be used in any room.

There was no doubt that the presbytery was a handsome building. It had been built a few years before 1500 in a two acre plot by a wealthy family as a dwelling house. Some years earlier, the same family, who were wool merchants, had helped endow the lovely Anglican Church, and in doing so had been left alone by those who might have made life difficult for people who clung to their Catholic faith following the Reformation in the 1530s. After a generation or two, the building was sold to pay a gambling debt, then it saw service as a Grammar School before reverting again to the status of dwelling house. It passed back into Catholic hands in 1870, and a few years later the owners offered Clifton Diocese some of their two acres for the construction of a church as well as use of part of the house by the Priest as his own self-contained living quarters. Following a bequest in the 1920s, it became one hundred percent Church property and evolved into a full-blown presbytery.

*****

Tim elected to kill several birds with one stone. He'd wait until Doctor Campbell had had some feedback on Father Mac from Cheltenham General and would then go to the presbytery and pass on the news to Norah and Sister Winifred. Around six o'clock the phone call came.

"It could be worse," said Doctor Campbell, "As you probably know, strokes arise from an interruption in the blood supply to the brain. This will be due to one of two causes: a thrombosis or embolism – in other words a clot – or a haemorrhage. In either case the most common effects are the inability to move the limbs on one or other side of the body, speech impairment and a reduced understanding of speech, and perhaps some visual loss. In Father Mac's case, he's suffered some loss in movement on the right side and some loss of speech, though technically, we can't call it a stroke until twenty-four hours have elapsed with no restoration of functions."

"So, technically it could still turn out to be another of those TIAs he had, whatever they stand for."

"Yes," said Campbell, "Temporary Ischaemic Attacks. But this twenty-four hour business is only an arbitrary deadline. It's most unlikely to be a TIA with the damage caused. In practice, they usually start treatment as soon as they have diagnosed the cause, in this case using clot-busting drugs. There's no evidence of haemorrhaging. Yes, Father Mac has had a stroke, but it's nothing like as severe as I have seen. In fact, some of my patients died within a day or so."

"You mentioned some loss in his own speech and his inability to understand other people. Does that mean he's lost a few marbles? Pardon my technical jargon."

"Not exactly. His speech will probably improve over time, perhaps even quickly, but he might not regain his mobility for some time, if at all. There's no question of his mental powers being affected."

"So what's the overall prognosis, Doc?" said Tim anxiously.

"It's far too early to say," said the doctor. "The poor chap was only struck down twelve hours or so ago. We really won't be able to firm up on anything I've said for at least another week and more tests. I've stuck my neck out for you, because I know you'll be discreet."

"I've told Father Mac's parishioners to phone me for news, and I'll be seeing Sister Winifred and Norah Walsh soon. I think perhaps I'd better tell them it's too early to say much. Just something simple like: Father's Mac has suffered a few of the effects normally associated with a stroke, but it's too early to say how reversible they are."

"I think that would be about as far as you can reasonably go," said Campbell. "Sister Winifred, as a nurse, will know that."

"How about visitors? Can he have any yet?"

"That's something I can't tell you. You'll have to contact the General yourself in the morning. Better still, get Sister Winifred to do it. She's family."

"Well, Doc, thanks very much indeed. At least there's some cause for optimism. Goodnight."

CHAPTER 4

Just after eight o'clock there was a screech of brakes in the presbytery drive and the banging of a few doors. Sister Winifred had arrived in a Mini Cooper. Norah went out to meet her.

"Come on in, Sister," said Norah. "You've just brought one small bag?"

"I don't intend to stay long," said the nun, breezing into the presbytery. "There's nothing much I can do for the dear man. How is he?"

"I'll phone Tim Sullivan to say you're here. He said he'd come over to let us know the latest. Then I'll show you where you'll be sleeping."

Norah phoned Tim, then showed Sister Winifred to her bedroom. The Sister looked around and nodded approvingly.

"You are a little treasure," said Sister. "I could have sorted something out."

"It's my job," said Norah. "I will still expect to come over every morning for an hour or so to keep the dust down. Apart from getting your own meals, don't even think of getting involved with housework. You're the guest of Father, even though he's not here, and he wouldn't want things to be otherwise." Her voice quavered a little, and to Norah's amazement Sister Winifred dabbed her own eyes, then gave Norah a hug.

"You're a good, good woman, Norah Walsh," she said.

The doorbell rang.

"That'll be Tim," said Norah. "Why not let him in while I put the kettle on?"

A few minutes later they were sitting round the kitchen table with mugs of instant coffee.

"It's much too early to say very much," said Tim, "All we know is that Father Mac has suffered some of the effects normally associated with a stroke. Doctor Campbell said there's some loss of movement down one side and some loss of speech. We won't know for a while yet how severe or how reversible these are."

"Can he have visitors?" asked Sister Winifred.

"Certainly not tonight," said Tim. "Doctor Campbell said we should find that out tomorrow. He suggested you contact them, Sister, as next-of-kin. You are next-of-kin, aren't you?"

"Yes," said Sister Winifred, "Our parents, of course, are long gone. There were three of us children. I'm five years older than Donald – that's Father Mac, as you call him. Andrew is twelve years younger than Donald. Mother married very young. So there was quite a spread, though I believe there were a few miscarriages. Mother never mentioned them. I learned about them from an aunt."

"And one way or another you all abandoned your native Scotland and ended up in England or Canada."

"Yes, and curiously both Donald and I trained for quite different work from where we fetched up – working for the Church. Our vocations came later. I qualified as a State Registered Nurse, while Donald thought he wanted to teach Classics at a public school. He was a quite brilliant scholar. As for Andrew, he met a delightful French Canadian girl at University, and followed her back home. He was the mathematician, and, like Donald, also very clever. His wife was an art teacher, now retired, of course, like Andy."

"And you found a way to harness your medical training to the service of the Church by working in a hospice near Stroud?"

"Yes, but before then I'd had various posts in nursing homes. I'm still able to help out at the hospice, but to be honest I'm really now just working part-time until I become one of the patients."

"Oh, go on with you, Sister," grinned Tim, "You've probably got more get-up-and-go than most people half your age. Anyway, we were talking earlier about what might have caused Father Mac's stroke. Doctor Campbell mentioned his diabetes, of course, but said it was well under control and that his underlying health was – what did say? – robust. He wondered if Father Mac was suffering from stress – perhaps something to do with the family."

"If it is stress, I can tell you exactly what caused it," said Sister Winifred emphatically. "The accident he had in Canada. In fact, the two accidents."

"Accidents?" said Tim. "He never mentioned them to me."

"Or me," said Norah.

"He might have mentioned them to Doctor Campbell," said Tim, "He and Father are quite close. I'll have to ask him. Anyway, Sister, what happened?"

"I'm not really sure," said Sister Winifred, "But I do know they both happened on the same day. Andrew had given Donald use of his second car for his holiday to give him more flexibility. When they went camping, he also drove separately, in case Andrew was called back to Ottawa. As it happened, Andrew was called back and Chantelle, naturally, went back with her husband. So Donald had a day or two there on his own. This suited him nicely, as he could just fish or study nature – two of his favourite pursuits. Just after he'd packed up and set off back to Ottawa, he was driving away from the lake on a back road when a car raced out of a side road right at him. Donald swerved and somehow avoided him, but it was touch and go. Donald decided not to stop, as there had been no actual collision, so he carried on. He was approaching the city boundary, when something similar happened. This time a car came out of a side road right in front of him, but again he managed to avoid a collision. He braked hard and his car spun round. By the time he'd got it back under control the other car had vanished. He was pretty shaken up, but otherwise unharmed."

"Good God," exclaimed Tim, "I think that would certainly frighten most people."

"But you haven't heard the really odd thing," said the nun. "Donald swore that it was the same vehicle in both cases. Both were those large utility vehicles they call SUVs, both were dark red, both were fairly old and both had the same sticker in the window. A baseball thing."

"Like some people here put football club stickers in their cars, I suppose," said Tim. "Are you saying that they were deliberately targeting Father Mac?"

"But making sure they were not hurt themselves," said Sister Winifred. "Yes, I suppose I am. It's almost as if they planned a near miss – two near misses after the first one failed, designed to cause Donald to crash, while they remained unharmed. I'm quite sure that sort of accident could be staged by experts. After all, they knew what was planned to happen, while the target would be reacting to the unexpected."

"I don't like this talk of experts planning to kill Father," said Norah with a shiver. "Why on Earth would anyone want to do that?"

"I must talk to Doctor Campbell about this," said Tim. "Surely Father would have mentioned it to him."

"Donald may not have done," said Sister Winifred. "He may have regarded this as strictly family business. He will have told Andrew at the time, then felt he ought to put me on an equal footing. He phoned

25

me the day after he got back. His stroke changes that a bit now, doesn't it?"

"I think you're right, Sister," said Tim. "Thank you so much for telling us about all this. We'll not let it go any further, apart from Doctor Campbell, and he may already know. Thanks for the coffee, Norah. I'll get back now and give Lucy a call. Find out how dear mama is. Lucy will be upset to hear about Father. I hope you settle in well, Sister. We'll be in touch tomorrow."

*****

During his working life Tim was always flying off to meetings mostly in North America or Europe. Since his retirement he had become used to Lucy being there every hour of every day, and missed her dreadfully on those rare occasions they were apart. He missed the awareness of a comfortable lump on the other side of the bed. He missed taking her a cup of tea in bed at about eight o'clock. He missed doing the crossword together with her at mealtimes. He missed hearing her engaged in one of her interminable phone conversations with one or other of the girls. They'd had a son, then twin daughters, and ever since the girls got married and had children of their own, it seemed there was always some situation confronting them that would benefit from motherly advice (chickenpox, chestnut stuffing, washing tights, you name it). Their son had never phoned for advice while he lived in the UK. He now lived in Australia. Perhaps his wife had phoned her mother. Yes, that must be it. Perhaps above all Tim missed being chided for some domestic misdemeanour ("You've lived in this house over thirty years and you still don't know where the mixer goes"). His friend, Bob, in MI5 had admitted a similar inadequacy. Like Bob, Tim found home alien territory, where he had little or no authority.

But Lucy, bless her, was always pleased to hear his voice, as she was now. She was saddened at the news of Father Mac, and intrigued to hear about the strangers snooping about. Mama was no trouble to look after, but Lucy was bored. She missed her daily routine in Bourton, and her circle of friends, and there was only so much pleasure to be had from Scrabble with mama. The old lady used a set designed for the partially sighted. The letters were about one inch tall and with the help of a magnifying glass mama just about managed. She usually won, often deploying words Lucy had never heard of, presumably from those bygone generations that fascinated her. Mama had been a history

26

teacher, and would tell them how her grandmother proudly told them that her own grandmother was born on 18 June 1815. "And what was that date famous for, Lucy? Yes, dear, the Battle of Waterloo."

Tim rang off, a little sad, but cheered up at the prospect of a nightcap.

CHAPTER 5

Sister Winifred did not like strange beds. Not that there was anything wrong with the bed Norah had prepared for her in the presbytery. If anything, it was more comfortable than her bed in the Convent. Perhaps that disoriented feeling came more the bedroom than the bed, and from the absence of some of the trappings in her little Convent room, like the statue of Our Lady on the little chest, and the crucifix above the bed. She should have brought them with her. Perhaps it went even deeper than that – to the building itself, with its alien creaks and assorted tappings at the window from twigs a little too close. All buildings had their own distinctive signature, she thought, and this one had had over four hundred years to evolve its medley of noises. She did not feel frightened or uneasy – God and His angels would take good care of her, just as they had kept Donald from harm – she just felt displaced.

She said her night prayers, read from her book of devotions, then climbed into bed with her rosary. She usually said the rosary in bed, partly as an inducement to sleep. Her own priest said there was nothing exceptionable in this, just as there was nothing exceptionable in saying prayers "on the hoof" as he'd put it. Sometimes something secular, but necessary, intruded and prayer could only be accommodated in parallel. He was a wise priest, she felt, who said that keeping up an informal dialogue with God as a friend was often the only approach in a busy world. And one of the jobs of the Holy Spirit was to turn our poor prayer offerings into something acceptable to God.

She normally got about as far as the third decade of the rosary before sleep overtook her. Tonight, she completed all five decades of the Joyful Mysteries and began again, this time with the Sorrowful Mysteries. At some time or other, she slipped away into a dreamless sleep, the beads warm and smooth in her hand.

She was suddenly wide awake. The first pale hint of approaching dawn stole across the sky and the glow of her digital clock told her it was 3:27. She heard noises. Noises that were certainly not part of the presbytery's sound signature. They were not discreet noises either. It sounded as if someone was moving furniture around, quite oblivious of the noise this made. That could only mean two things: whoever they were, they clearly knew that Donald was no longer here. And equally clearly, they had no idea that Sister Winifred had moved in. Her car on the drive would have meant nothing to them. Even if they noticed it, they would probably assume it was Donald's. Perhaps she could take advantage of their assumption that the presbytery was empty. If she crept down, she might be able to phone the police without disturbing the intruders. It registered in her mind that she had already unconsciously adopted the plural. There had to be more than one of them.

The presbytery's phone was in the hall, by the front door. She quietly eased herself out of bed and slipped into a dressing-gown. A flight of creaky stairs had to be negotiated. She timed her descent, step by step, to coincide with the thumps coming from whatever room they were in. She saw the lights were on in the study. Through a crack in the doorframe she saw two young men. Men? From the little she could see of their faces, they were probably no more than teenagers. They wore standard teenage uniform – jeans, hoods and trainers. There was a shock of red hair sticking out of the tallest lad's hood. They were grabbing the books from the shelves, briefly examining them, shaking them, then tossing them on to the floor, which by now was littered with scores of books. Book shelves covered three walls of the room, and they still had many more shelves to go. Against the fourth wall was a desk, under the window that looked out on to the back garden. The hoodies had a big bag with them, part full of something.

Sister Winifred crept down the hall, picked up the phone and keyed in 999.

"Emergency. Which service, please?"

"Police," she whispered.

"Could you repeat that, please."

"Police."

"I'm sorry, you'll have to speak up."

"Police," snapped Sister Winifred, much more loudly. "Look, there's a burglary going on in St Nicholas' presbytery, Bourton-under-Wychwood. Come…"

"Oy!" said another voice. "Look, Dave, there's an old bag on the phone. Oy, you. What you doing here?"

"I might ask you the same thing. My brother is the parish priest here. He's been taken ill and I'm quite sure his health will not improve if he hears about you. And by the way, I am not an old bag. I'm a religious sister from a convent."

"A fucking nun!" said the redhead in disgust.

29

"How dare you use such language," Sister Winifred shouted, "And, in any case, that, young man, is an oxymoron."

"She called me a moron, Dave."

"Look Sister, or Mother," said Dave gently. "Kindly put that fucking phone down. Oh, my God, everything you just said has gone over the phone. Let's get out of here, Kev, before she gets the police."

"They're on their way," said Sister Winifred.

"Bullshit," said Kev, "There's no police in Bourton at night. And no-one from Cheltenham would come over the hill at night, not even for a bleedin' chain saw massacre."

"Please go," said Sister Winifred. "Donald is a good man and he doesn't deserve to have his home vandalised. Besides, there's nothing here worth taking. Priests are not rich men."

But they were already beating a hasty retreat, Dave dragging the *bag* behind him. Seconds later, Sister Winifred heard a car engine start up nearby. She sighed in relief. At least they had not touched her.

"Why didn't you smash the fucking phone?" asked Kev petulantly, as he swung a left on to the main road out of Bourton.

"Time adds up," said Dave. "Besides, the old biddy's bound to have a mobile. Everyone does."

But he was wrong. Sister Winifred had never had a mobile phone. She'd never had the slightest use for one. The Convent had one, which was issued to anyone who had an errand to discharge that involved leaving the Convent for some time and for which some means of communication in case of problems seemed sensible. Owning an individual mobile phone would certainly be frowned upon as an unnecessary luxury or (worse) a fashion accessory. This was exactly the time she had needed one. She could then have made the 999 call from one of the more remote parts of the presbytery.

She pondered what to do. Was it worth making an emergency call now the emergency was over? She decided it was necessary, if only to show that she had followed the correct procedure. And besides, those two hoodies might be back, though she doubted it. She keyed in 999.

"Emergency. Which service, please?"

"Police," said Sister Winifred. The response was instantaneous.

"Police emergency desk. Please state briefly the nature of the emergency and its location."

"Burglary in St Nicholas presbytery, Church Street, Bourton-under-Wychcood."

"Is this incident still in progress?"

"No, they've just left. Look, it's really all over now."

"We'll still come for a statement. In incidents where there is a victim, we will always respond as soon as we can. Please stay up. We'll be with you shortly. May I have your name."

"Sister Winifred," she said.

"A nun?"

"Yes."

"I've not had a nun before," said the voice. "Say one for me, Sister. The response team is already on its way. We'll brief them en route. Oh, and could you make a note of this number. Got a pen?" He dictated a string of digits. "That's an incident number. Always mention it if you want to contact us again. You'll get a form through the post confirming the number. Goodnight, Sister."

"Goodnight, young man."

Next job: make a cup of tea, the standard British panacea.

As she sat sipping her tea, she decided to have a quick look around. She moved to the study and surveyed the scene. There was not much real damage. Books everywhere, certainly, some of which had landed awkwardly and now had folds and creases on some of the pages, but nothing actually destroyed. If there were anything valuable – first editions, say, there might be some loss in value, but she'd never known Donald to be a collector of rare books. The other feature was Donald's desk. Now there was some damage there, as drawers had been forced open, but nothing a good joiner couldn't fix.

She looked in the desk. There were the usual bills for utilities, council tax and credit card transactions. There was also a good deal of correspondence involving affairs of the Parish, the Deanery and the Diocese. Whatever filing system Father Mac had had, was now in ruins. Sister Winifred wondered whether there had been money inside the drawers, but thought it highly unlikely. In fact, she found a small wad of notes in one of the desk's pigeon holes. They could hardly have missed it, but may have planned to collect it later after concentrating on the task in hand.

Soon afterwards, the doorbell rang. There were two of them, a Sergeant and a WPC. They introduced themselves as Sergeant Thomas and WPC Henderson. They were very pleasant, taking her through the entire incident.

"So there were two of them and they addressed each other as Kev and Dave. Drove off, so obviously old enough to drive. You were unharmed. Frightened, though, eh?"

31

"Yes," she said, "But not terrified. I felt the angels were protecting me."

"I've no doubt they were, ma'am, said Sergeant Thomas.

"I'm afraid I can't give you the sort of background information other people can give you. The housekeeper, for instance, can tell you exactly what was taken, or at least what sort of things were taken. I'm sure it was nothing valuable. Father McNulty had nothing of value. She might also know the likely identity of the hoodies. Other people in the town will certainly know."

"You're sure the burglars are from Bourton, ma'am?" asked the WPC.

"I've no idea," said Sister Winifred. "But they were in the presbytery less than 24 hours after Father McNulty was taken away. So, as I was saying, why not have a word with one or two others who live in Bourton? I could give you some names."

"Yes, we will," said Thomas. "Or we'll get the Community Police in Bourton to make a few enquiries. Well, thank you very much, ma'am."

"You could call me Sister," said Sister Winifred. "It is allowed."

After they'd gone, she put the electric fire on in the sitting room and sat in an armchair. Despite the trauma of the last hour or so, she succumbed to the emotional fatigue and dropped off into a peaceful slumber.

*****

She awoke with a start. 6:35 am. She quickly washed and dressed, and made her way to Doctor Campbell's. She was relieved to see a figure drawing the curtains downstairs. She rang the bell. Campbell came to the door in his dressing-gown.

"Ah, Sister Winifred," he said with a smile. "Come on in. I was half expecting you, though perhaps not quite so early in the morning. I'm sorry to be seeing you again in such sad circumstances. I've just made a pot of tea. Will you have a cup?"

"That's very kind of you," said Sister Winifred, "I would love one. But I didn't come to enquire after Donald's health." She explained to Campbell what had happened during the night.

"Good heavens," he exclaimed, "What a good thing they didn't attack you. Look, stay here for a while until we've got a few things sorted out. You've already seen the police, and they said they may want

32

a follow-up session. The hospital can wait for a while. You'll get nothing sensible out of them until after Doctors' Rounds. We'll get Tim over here shortly. Norah, too, if you think that will help. I suppose she will know as well as anyone if they took anything of value."

"Well, yes, and she did take part in a sort of council of war we had last night just after I arrived."

"We need another one now, in light of the break-in. I'd be happy to be involved, if you think I can contribute anything beyond medical opinions."

"Oh, yes, Doctor, I'm sure you should be involved. There are one or two things you won't be aware of."

Sister Winifred filled Doctor Campbell in about the events discussed by the three of them the previous evening.

"Well, I never," said Campbell in surprise. "No, Father Mac didn't mention those two incidents to me in any specific terms, though come to think of it he did speak vaguely of a near miss on the road. I thought no more of it. Most of us have little excitements on the road quite often – a bit of unwise overtaking, people cutting in, things like that. There are so many vehicles on the road these days that driving is one continual adventure. Anyway, it's getting on for seven. Let's see if Tim's up and about. I dare say Norah will be, so I'll try Tim first."

*****

At about the time Doctor Campbell was phoning Tim, two 18-year-olds were entering the picturesque town of Broadway from the south in a Ford Fiesta that had seen better days. They turned right at the T-junction, then turned left into a nearly deserted car park. As they did so, one of the few cars there flashed its lights and moved out.

"They want us to follow them," said Dave.

"You sure it's them?" asked Kevin nervously.

"There aren't many black BMWs in Broadway likely to behave exactly as they told us," said Dave scornfully. "I just hope we can keep up with them in this old banger."

Ten minutes later, the two vehicles drew up in a lay-by on the Stratford road. Dave got out of the Fiesta, and a man in a black anorak and wearing black leather gloves climbed out of the BMW.

"You didn't tell us some old bag would be sleeping there," said Dave. "We heard her phoning the police. She may not have got through, but we got the hell out of there."

33

"The housekeeper does not sleep there, so that would be the Priest's sister. We did not expect her to come so quickly. Did you have time to search for the sort of things we are interested in?"

"We went quickly through the desk after we'd busted the drawers open. Nothing there that matched what you said, but we've brought a sample of the contents. We also found some books not in English. Some with funny letters."

"Funny letters? You mean an alphabet you are not familiar with."

"I've seen some of the letters somewhere," said Dave. "But I'm not sure where. Wait a minute. I think they use them in Maths."

"All right. It doesn't sound like you've found anything useful. Where are these books and things?"

Dave went to the Fiesta and picked up the bag from the back seat.

The man handed Dave an envelope.

"This is more than you deserve. But we can afford to be generous. One thing you and your friend must know. If you mention any of this to the police or to anyone else, we will know. And we will be back. Or some of our friends will. There are many of us."

The man turned abruptly and returned to the BMW. The interview was over. Dave returned to the Fiesta.

"Did you get the money?" asked Kev anxiously.

"Yeah," said Dave, "Or at least an envelope that should have it inside."

"Better check quick," said Kev.

"Look, mate, even if the money ain't in here, we'd be bloody stupid to chase after them. Not that we could catch them, anyway. He said not to mention this to anyone or they'd be back for us. And they bloody would!" He drew an imaginary knife across his throat. Kev shivered.

*****

The BMW was out of sight. The driver turned to the man in the black anorak.

"В порядке всё? Everything OK?"

"Совершенно безполезно," his companion replied. "As the British would say 'Fucking useless.' Probably not much more than a Grecheskaya grammatika!" He laughed uproariously.

*****

34

"OK, let's see what we've got," said Tim.

They were sitting round the table in Doctor Campbell's spacious kitchen, with tea or coffee. Megan, Campbell's wife, had joined them.

"I'll run through what we know chronologically. That seems the most sensible way. We might get a sense of cause and effect, though I don't think we can claim yet that everything is inter-connected. Chip in if there are other events you know about that you think are tied in but which I don't mention. Sister, let us know what the police have been told, and what they have not been told."

"I've not mentioned anything to do with events in Canada, the two accidents on his way back from camping. I've stuck entirely to the break-in."

"I'm sure that's the wise thing to do," nodded Tim. "Anything beyond the fact of the break-in is all speculative. If, on the other hand, the police actually solicit our views, then we can tell them what we think."

"I can't think it will come to that," said Doctor Campbell. "As far as the police are concerned, they'll think here are two young hoodlums taking advantage of the illness of the sole occupant of a large house. That presents them with a glorious target of opportunity. When they were disturbed, they fled the scene and nobody was injured. So the whole thing was a pretty negative incident, perhaps not worth chasing up when other things are competing for police time."

"You may well be right," said Tim. "Though they might think differently if we give them the full picture. But I think we're getting ahead of ourselves." He took a deep breath and looked round at them all. "Right, to start with, I'm assuming that things began with Father Mac's visit to Canada in May. OK, they could have started with some earlier event we don't know about. You're not aware of anything, are you, Doc? Or you, Norah?"

"No," said Norah. "I first noticed that change in his personality when he got back."

"Me, too," said Campbell.

"So something happened to him while he was on holiday," said Tim.

"You mean apart from those two apparent attempts on his life by a hit and run driver," said Campbell. "They could have left him rather subdued."

"I think we're again running ahead a bit," said Tim. "We have to consider these hit and run attacks as the result of something earlier.

35

Something he saw, perhaps, that he shouldn't have seen. People involved in criminal activity of some sort."

"Yes, that makes sense," said Sister Winifred.

"But that doesn't square with the nature of his personality change," said Norah. "He was certainly subdued, but in a happy, dreamy state of mind."

"Let's move on a bit," said Tim. "He returns home, and about two weeks later is suffers a stroke. No sooner does that happen, than strangers close in on the event, asking in the town and at church about Father Mac's health. They were here within an hour or two."

"Really?" said Sister Winifred. "How would they know to be in Bourton yesterday?"

"Good question," said Tim slowly. "You know," he continued thoughtfully, "I wouldn't be surprised if they'd been keeping the presbytery under observation ever since Father Mac got back from Canada, perhaps looking for an opportunity to go in and have a look around. They probably found the presbytery was occupied most of the time during the day with Father Mac or Norah there, or both of them."

"And," said Norah emphatically, "wanting to know if I slept there. Don't forget that."

"Then," continued Tim, "when they learned of Father's stroke, they apparently recruited two young yobs to ransack the house. They must have known in advance who they could approach. On balance, I don't think these two hoodlums just happened to turn up on their own initiative, as you were suggesting the police might think, Doc."

"And they didn't ransack the whole house," said Sister Winifred. "They were concentrating on the study."

"You may have caught them in the early stages of their job," said Tim. "Perhaps they planned to cover the entire house. But it does seem that they were looking for something pretty specific."

Megan spoke for the first time. "So surely that suggests that, rather than just seeing something he should not have seen in Canada, Father Mac may actually have come into possession of something he should not have."

"And brought it back to the UK on his return flight. And those two yobs were recruited specifically to find it," said Doctor Campbell.

Silence descended. Tim smiled.

"There you are. Brainstorming really does work! I'm sure you're right. Now, is there anything else to add? We really do need to find these two yobs…"

"Who, by the way, are called Kev and Dave," said Sister Winifred triumphantly. Everyone looked at her admiringly. Tim beamed.

"What a clever Sister," he said. "Now, let's draw up a must-do list – things we must at least start today."

"Phone the hospital," said Sister Winifred.

"Phone the hospital," said Tim. "I think that falls to you, Sister. Are you happy with that?"

"Certainly I am," said Sister Winifred emphatically. "You told me to phone after ten."

"So while we're waiting we need to arrive at some assessment of what, if anything, was taken," said Tim. "And that means Norah taking a look. Could you recognise what might be missing?"

"I might," she said doubtfully, "though to be honest, there was very little in his study apart from his books and the papers he kept in his desk, and he always kept that locked anyway. I might be able to remember what books were taken, if any. Or at least what sort of books, not specific titles. I dust round Father Mac's books at least once a week. He won't let me empty the shelves for a good old go at them, unless I really nag him about it."

"We also need to find this Kevin and Dave," said Tim, "But we must be very discreet about it."

"The police said they'd get the community police involved," said Sister Winifred.

"I can do something there," said Megan Campbell, "I'll look at this year's electoral register. They keep a copy in the public library, I think, and it's a public document."

"But it's not like a census. They only include those eligible to vote," said Tim.

"In some ways it's better than a census," said Megan. "It's updated every year, but the census is only done every ten years. There was one last year, but in any case it's not open to the public."

"I could probably work round that," said Tim. "I still have a few useful contacts. How old did you say these lads were, Sister?"

"It's so difficult to say these days," said Sister Winifred. "I didn't get a very good look at them, but I'd guess they're somewhere between sixteen and twenty. That should cover it."

"But don't forget the electoral register includes those who will become eighteen within the next twelve months," said Megan, "so we're only excluding the sixteen-year-olds and younger."

"We can exclude those, anyway," said Sister Winifred, "unless they're compounding breaking and entering with a driving offence, one at least was old enough to drive."

"Bingo," said Tim. "So we're looking at seventeen, plus a year or two?"

There were general nods all round.

"Look," said Doctor Campbell. "Why don't you let me also have a quiet word at the Medical Centre. Tom Martin's been head of practice since I retired. We've worked closely together for years. He can at least look at his computer records for any Kevin or Dave in, say, the 17 to 20 age group."

"That sounds like an awful chore," said Sister Winifred.

"Not these days," said the doctor. "Tom Martin would just do a word-search for the name 'Kevin.' All hits would show up within a matter of seconds. There won't be many, and by looking at individual records Tom could soon identify who might be in the running. Then do the same for 'David.' He'd probably get a few more, but not many more."

"Aren't medical records confidential?" asked Norah uneasily.

"Yes, they are," agreed Doctor Campbell. "But we're not asking for health information. Anyway, we're likely to get what we want from the electoral register. So it's academic, really. Just a fall back."

"Then finally, on our list of things to do," said Tim, "there's the visit to Father Mac, as soon as we're allowed to. Sister Winifred will do that. OK, Sister?"

"Of course," said Sister Winifred, "though I'll change into mufti. When patients see a nun enter the ward they either think she's come to discuss funeral arrangements, or that they're already in heaven."

Tim smiled. "I think I'd feel the same," he said.

"Curiously," said the nun, "it's different in a hospice. Patients there are either beyond that sort of awareness, or are looking forward to their final release."

"By the way," said Tim, "if he's allowed more than one visitor I'd like to go with you, Sister, or perhaps you could go, Doc, you're a good friend of Father Mac's."

"I think I'd better stay well clear, at least to begin with. I'm too well known at the General, and someone might just get hold of the wrong end of the stick."

"Perhaps you're right," said Tim. "OK, is there anything else to discuss, or any other actions we should be taking? No? Then let's get moving. Sister, I'd like to be with you when you phone the General."

"I'll need to go to the presbytery with you, too," said Norah, "to see if I can tell what's missing. In fact, we could have a bit of breakfast there. Are you and Mrs Campbell joining us, Doctor?"

"Yes, why not?" said Megan.

*****

"Well," said Norah, "that's about it. I knew I wouldn't be able to give the titles of any books missing, but I can say they were from the shelves where he kept all his foreign-language books. They haven't touched his books on religion or philosophy, as far as I can see. He also had loads of biographies and a few crime novels, too, and all those are still there."

Norah, under strict instructions not to disturb anything before the police got there, had spent the last half hour or so crawling around the floor and contorting her body to find the titles, or at least the nature, of the missing books.

"So all his foreign-language books have gone?" asked Tim.

"No, no," said Norah, "Not by any means. Only those in different alphabets. Books in French, German, Spanish, and Italian, for instance, are still there. I think that's what the languages are. I do know a little French."

"You mean books using the Roman alphabet were not taken?" asked Tim.

That's right," agreed Norah.

"What scripts were the books in, then?" asked Tim. "Greek, for instance?"

"Yes, and Acrylic," agreed Norah.

"I think you mean Cyrillic, the Russian alphabet," said Sister Winifred with a smile. "There would also have been some books in Arabic, including the Koran. Donald studied several languages. He has many grammar books, but he only used them when he got stuck, and that wasn't very often. He mostly read literature. He would say so much is lost in translation, it's far better to read the originals if you can."

"There's a lot to be said for that," said Tim, "but I'm surprised he found so much time for languages when he was studying for the priesthood."

39

"Oh, that came later," said Sister Winifred. "He'd already graduated in Classics before he had his calling. In fact, after graduation he still had to do his National Service. You mentioned Cyrillic. In fact, Donald spent his two years learning Russian."

"Good heavens!" said Doctor Campbell. "It's amazing how little we know of each other's lives. I mean Father Mac is a great friend, and although I knew one of his languages was Russian, we've never really talked about it."

"So after National Service, he began his studies for the priesthood," continued Sister Winifred. "He may have been lured down that route by the prospect of surrounding himself with Latin, and to some extent Greek, though I like to think I had something to do with his decision. Whenever I saw him, we'd have long discussions about vocations. Anyway, he took the plunge, and it was the right decision. He's been a very good priest. Everyone says so."

"Going back to the Russian business I know several people who spent their National Service learning it, or in some cases Eastern European languages or Chinese," said Tim thoughtfully. "Some of my former colleagues did. I'd no idea Father Mac was involved in it."

"Why did they do it?" asked Norah. "I mean, why was this language training considered necessary?"

"World events," said Tim. "By the late 1940s the Cold War had begun. The Soviet Union was becoming a major threat to world peace. There was the blockade of Berlin, then the Korean War. This could so easily have escalated into an even more major conflict with Russia joining in. Things like that underlined the need for a trained body of linguists, like we'd had in the Second World War, though then, of course, the emphasis had been on German. To some extent Japanese, too, though the Americans looked after most of that side of things."

"So how many were there? Trained, I mean?" asked Doctor Campbell.

"There must have been a few thousand altogether," said Tim. "But there were two sorts: those they called translators, who could deal with captured documents or monitor communications, and an elite group of several hundred, who were trained to interpreter standard. That was seen as their main job: interrogating prisoners – especially officers, who were more likely to know about military objectives. These had longer and more intensive training at Cambridge or London University."

"So, having trained all these people, did they find jobs for them after they were demobbed?" asked Campbell.

"Not in the least," said Tim. "The training ran through much of the 1950s, but most of the interpreters already had plans to go on to university, or join the family firm, or …"

"Take Holy Orders," said Sister Winifred.

"Yes," said Tim, "In fact, you'd be amazed how many of these people reached eminence in their chosen fields. Academics, certainly, professors of this and that, ambassadors, QCs, bishops, playwrights, actors, novelists, a Governor of the Bank of England, you name it. These people were the intellectual cream of the National Service recruits, and they were only too happy to pass two years in the congenial atmosphere of academe. I only wish I could have been involved, but they had finished the courses before I was called up."

"I must get breakfast ready," said Norah.

"Please let me help you," offered Sister Winifred.

"No, I wouldn't hear of it," said Norah. "I'm not doing anything elaborate, just boiled eggs, and toast and marmalade."

*****

They sat round the table, reminiscing fondly about some episode or other in Father Mac's priesthood, until Sister Winifred pointed to the clock. "I'll phone them up now. All right, Doctor Campbell?"

"By all means," said Campbell.

"Oh, good morning. I'm phoning to enquire about my brother, who was admitted yesterday morning with a suspected stroke. Father Donald McNulty…" She drummed her fingers on the table. "They're connecting me to the ward. Yes, the Catholic priest. I am his next of kin." She was looking puzzled. "Well, I'm surprised. They had no authority. I've no idea who they might have been. I suppose it could have been a parishioner. He's very well-liked. So, how is he? He's stable and he passed a comfortable night. Can he have visitors? Oh, good. Normally, three till four-thirty and six to eight, but only a brief visit today at about two-thirty, so as not to tire him. And can two of us come? We can. Thank you very much. If you see him, tell him Sister Winifred and his friends were asking after him. Will he understand that? Probably, but we mustn't expect him to be all systems go. No, I understand, it will take time. Very well, thank you. Thank you. 'Bye."

41

"I suppose you caught the drift of that," said Sister Winifred. "Someone phoned earlier, saying they were a close relative. What a cheek!"

"It's probably our friends," said Tim. "They don't give up easily, do they? Anyway, he doesn't sound too bad. At least that's a blessing."

"Most of the damage with a stroke happens right at the time," said Doctor Campbell. "It then becomes a matter of how much gets reversed and in what time frame. Then you're down to how long is a piece of string."

"Yes, so I believe," said Sister Winifred. "Donald will be in a part of the ward reserved for the most recent arrivals, so he'll be sheltered from the stampede of visitors. We're to go before the main visiting times anyway, and a ward sister will be available to discuss things."

"Well, I don't think there's much more we can do for now," said Tim. "I'll pick you up about one-thirty, Sister. Thanks for the grub, Norah."

"We'll pursue the identity of Kev and Dave," said Doctor Campbell.

"I'll tell the Dean how Father Mac is, and see if he's thought about a stand-in," said Tim.

The little party disbanded.

CHAPTER 6

Cheltenham General Hospital is a vast complex of buildings located near the famous Boys' College.

Tim picked up Sister Winifred as planned, and they managed to park near the College Road entrance. The Stroke Unit was in St Luke's Wing in the West Block. They soon found Father Mac. He was at the far end of the ward, lying on his side facing them, a network of tubes delivering a cocktail of goodness knew what into his system.

They approached him tentatively. He registered their arrival with a faint, lopsided smile.

"He recognises you," said a nurse who suddenly materialised at their sides. "He's already made some progress with his speech – just the odd word comes out, when he needs something. Though I must say I'm surprised at a couple of the words he uses."

"I'm not," said Sister Winifred, "I nurse in a hospice. Why use a long word like 'urinate' when there's a perfectly good monosyllabic alternative available. Especially if he's struggling with his speech."

The nurse smiled. "I think he'll recover much of his speech. The main problem will be his general mobility. But even there, we can get him walking with a stick in a few months, even weeks. We'll be assessing him for physio in the next day or two."

"You don't hang about," said Tim.

"We try to show the body who's boss," said the nurse. "By the way, I'm Nurse Bingham, but call me Lynne if you wish."

Tim introduced himself and Sister Winifred. The nun knelt down at the bedside. She grasped Father Mac's hand. "Donald," she said, "You know me, don't you?"

One word, "Wiffie," came softly but clearly from Father Mac's lips.

"Yes, Donald, it's Wiffie," she said. She turned to the others. "He's always called me Wiffie since the time he first learned to talk. It was the nearest he could get to Winifred when he was about two. He's stuck with it ever since."

"Wiffie," he said again.

"I'll leave you with him," said the nurse. "I'm just outside at the desk if there's anything you need."

"Thank you," said Sister Winifred, "Well, Tim, I'm very encouraged. Donald, you're looking pretty well. I think you're a bit of a fraud."

Father Mac gave another lopsided smile. "Ay-je," he said.

"What was that?" asked Sister Winifred.

"Ay-je," he said again, "Ay-je. Ay-je."

"What are you trying to tell us, Donald?" asked Sister Winifred gently.

A look of intense concentration came over his face. "Ay-je," he said, "Ay-je. Sore ay-je."

"I can't make it out," said Sister Winifred. "Can you, Tim?"

"No," said Tim, shaking his head.

Sister Winifred brightened. "Look, I'll tell you what; let's say a prayer or two very quietly round the bedside."

"Good idea," said Tim. "It'll put Father Mac into familiar territory, and it may help with his speech. I suppose it's all right. Political correctness and all that. Come to think of it though, I often bring Holy Communion to hospital, as do other special ministers, as well as members of the clergy."

"Absolutely," said Sister Winifred. "Let's just say one decade of the Holy Rosary. We're going to think about the first Joyful Mystery, Donald. The Annunciation."

They knelt, and Sister Winifred took the lead. Father Mac's lips moved, though little sound came out.

To their astonishment, faint echoes of their prayers came from a patient a few beds away.

After the ten Hail Marys, the nun said, "We'll say the Hail Holy Queen now."

"Why not do it in Latin?" suggested Tim. "It's the one prayer he prefers to say in Latin. *Salve*, Regina, *mater misericordiae…*"

Father Mac could be heard mumbling an approximation of the prayer. At the end he looked at them both and said, "Ay-je. Ay-je. Ay-je. Sore ay-je."

"What is it, Donald? Are you saying you're sore?"

Father Mac strained to move his head. He then blinked his eyes.

"I think he's disagreeing with you." said Tim. "He's not saying he's sore." Suddenly he smiled. "I know what it is. That eye movement. He's trying to tell us he saw something. Is that right, Father?"

Father Mac gave another lopsided smile. "Ay-je. Sore ay-je."

"Bingo!" exclaimed Tim. "In fact, he's saying he saw an angel. Right, Father? You saw an angel?"

Again the smile. Father Mac noticeably relaxed. Sister Winifred took his hand.

"Where did you see the angel, Donald?" she asked gently. "Was it here?"

The nurse was suddenly back again. "I'm sorry, but we'll have to finish now," she said apologetically. "I'm afraid you'll be taxing him too much."

"We're very encouraged," said Sister Winifred. "We've actually seen signs of progress even in the short while we've been here."

"Well your presence here provided the stimulus for that," said the nurse.

"We also said some prayers with him and he tried to join in, with some success. In fact, another patient also tried to join in with him."

"Prayers do seem to help in speech recovery," said the nurse. "Obviously for the power the believers place in them, but they are also useful as pure therapy. There's a Muslim on the ward, who holds the Koran all day, and prays."

"Eess," said Father Mac with his lopsided smile.

"You're a little mischief," said the nurse. "He was reminding me to make sure the patient's bed is facing east. He hasn't been here five minutes and he's telling us our jobs."

"Thank you so much for all you're doing," said Sister Winifred. "'Bye Donald, be nice to this lovely nurse and we'll see you tomorrow."

"Wiffie," he said. "Wiffie."

"'Bye, Father," said Tim. "Don't worry about a thing. Everything is being taken care of."

They left and drove back over the hill.

*****

Tim found two messages waiting on his answer phone: one from Doctor Campbell and one from his friend Bob at Box 500. Neither left a message other than a request to phone back. Tim tried the Campbells first.

"Thanks for calling back, Tim," said Doctor Campbell. "How was Father Mac?"

"Not too bad," said Tim guardedly, remembering he was speaking to someone who had seen hundreds of stroke victims in his career. "I can't comment on his general mobility. He's apparently lost some sensation down one side, but you knew that. His speech is also affected, but the signs of recovery are there. Also, on the bright side, he recognised us and seems to have escaped any major brain damage. And he also seems to be in control of his bodily functions."

"Hmm," mused Campbell. "About what I expected. Perhaps a little better. Now the other reason I phoned is that Megan's been busy and we have something to show you. It's pretty interesting. Can we pop over?"

"Yes, please do," said Tim. "Give me about ten or fifteen minutes to return another call, then we can get down to business."

Fine," said the doctor. "Oh, and by the way, the library doesn't hold a copy of the electoral register. Only the Borough Council has the full listing, but the local Town Council holds a copy of the Bourton electorate. So off we went to the Town Hall. Anyway, we'll tell you all about it."

"Thanks, Doc. See you soon."

Tim phoned Bob. "Thanks for getting back so soon. As we suspected, the car is hired – one of the smaller companies, Rent-a-Limo, near Terminal 3 in Heathrow. Hired by an employee of a company – a fictitious company, in fact. I won't bother you with details. So all this adds up to something fishy."

"There's been something even more fishy," said Tim. He outlined the previous night's events at the presbytery, including the involvement of a Kevin and a Dave.

"What do the local police say?" asked Bob.

"At the moment they've no reason to think this is anything but two local bad boys taking advantage of the absence in hospital of an old boy who happens to be a priest, not realising his sister had moved in. They've not been told about the two strangers sniffing around. They said they'd follow up later when we know what's missing. I was going to phone them after two of my friends had done some research in the electoral register."

"Looking for Kevins and Daves?"

"Yes."

"You don't waste time, do you? It's like old times, forming those ad-hoc working groups in the Cabinet Office – you, us, MOD, the Foreign Office and the Friends. Remember? But seriously, I think you're going to have to bring the police up to speed, especially if you think you know the identity of these lads."

"I'm sure you're right," agreed Tim. The doorbell chimed. "My friends have arrived, Bob. I have to dash. I'll keep you informed of anything of interest. Our involvement may just end with us turning everything over to the police. Thanks for the info. Cheers."

Tim let the Campbells in. Megan couldn't wait to give him their news. "We've already narrowed it down. In fact, we think we know who they are."

"That's amazing," said Tim.

"Not really," said Megan. "To begin with there were fewer Kevins and Davids than we thought there would be. Seven Kevins and nine Davids. Now, when only two names were given at the same address, one male and one female, we've assumed these are most likely to be married couples and therefore non-starters."

"What else could they be?" asked Tim. "Oh, I see. You mean a widow or divorced woman and her son."

"Yes. They would be eligible, of course, so we haven't discounted couples, but to start with we put them on the back burner, while we looked for better candidates. That immediately brought the number down to four Kevins and five Daves."

"Plus any who have the middle name Kevin or Dave, but prefer it to their first name."

"I dare say there are some of those, but middle initials are not expanded in the register. I suppose we can go down that road later, if we have to."

"So was there any more likely whittling down you could do?" asked Tim, interested.

"Well, we did find one of the four Kevins and one of the five Davids were registered as living three doors from each other!" said Megan triumphantly.

"Bingo!" said Tim, then paused. "No, not quite bingo."

"Oh, very much bingo," said Doctor Campbell. "I slipped down to the Medical Centre, and had a quick word with Tom Martin. It took him no time to establish that the Kevin and Dave who are near-neighbours are both eighteen, and the others are all older by several years. So, I think definitely bingo!"

"Well we really have got something to take to the police now," said Tim. "In fact, I'll call them without further ado."

It came as no surprise to him to learn that "for the time being" any further information on the "incident" should be given to the community police, so Tim called them. A recorded message asked him to call a mobile number if the matter were urgent. A familiar voice answered.

"Community Police, WPC Armitage."

"Hello, Angela, it's Tim Sullivan." Tim had known Angela for years as a friend of his twin daughters.

"Mr Sullivan, how are you? I was sorry to hear about Father Mac. How is he?"

"He's pretty ill, but it could be a lot worse. He'll recover to some extent, given time. Anyway, I understand you've been asked to follow up on the break-in at the presbytery. I know Father Mac's sister was the one interviewed initially, but I've somehow got involved, along with Doctor Campbell and his wife, and Norah Walsh, his housekeeper. There are one or two aspects to the incident you won't be aware of. I probably know more about the whole background than anyone else. So I'm a sort of spokesman for all of us."

"All right, that'll suit me. I'm just doing a foot patrol at the moment. Kids sometimes need to talk, so I often make myself visible after school hours for about an hour to remind them I'm available. I'll be back in the station by four-thirty."

*****

At the police station, Tim went through recent events in detail, holding back only on the happenings in Canada, which, he privately conceded could have been unrelated.

"So you're saying these lads were not acting on their own initiative, but were hired by someone to look for something they thought might be in the presbytery?"

"Yes, that's what I'm saying. I think it was no coincidence that two complete strangers came sniffing around within an hour or two of Father Mac's departure, almost as if they were waiting for the building to become empty."

"I'll email HQ and see what they think."

"You can, of course, interview the two lads."

"As a Police Community Support Officer, I have no powers of arrest and I'm not authorised to interview suspects in a criminal case. Cheltenham will do that. But, if it's any consolation, I do know who they are."

"You know who they are?" exclaimed Tim, in astonishment.

"I'd already been told by Cheltenham that their names are Kevin and Dave. If you mention those names, especially to young people, they'll know exactly who you mean and ask you what they've been up to this time. I'm afraid there's a bit of hero-worship there by the young teenagers."

Tim produced a piece of paper on which he had written the names and addresses of the Kevin and Dave that Megan Campbell had found.

"Yes, that's them," said Angela. "I suppose you took a look in the electoral register. We use it all the time for one reason or another. Now, please keep this to yourself – I have word that both Dave and Kevin were away all night."

"You've been chatting to the kids round the cider press, haven't you?" said Tim with a grin. The cider press dated from the 1890s and had been donated to the town by someone who had found it in an outhouse on a property he'd bought. It was too big to house in the museum, and, after a bit of refurbishment, it had been placed on permanent display near the library. It had proved to be a magnet to youngsters.

"I get on OK with most of them, providing I can ignore a few chat-up lines from the older lads."

"Well, you are an attractive young lady."

"Don't *you* start, Mr Sullivan. Right, then, I'll convey the gist of our conversation to Divisional HQ and if they want to follow up personally, you'll be contacted. Was there anything else we need to cover? Oh, yes, do you know what was taken?"

"Some papers from his desk, probably bills and things, and some books."

"Were the books of any great value?"

"Norah Walsh can't really say what they were. Certainly they included some foreign language books. In fact, probably only foreign language books, in Greek, Russian, and possibly Arabic.

"I really can't see those being of value to anyone," said Angela.

"Nor can I," admitted Tim. "In which case probably nothing of value was taken at all. A small wad of money, about £30 I think, was not taken. It may have been missed, because they were interrupted."

"Sounds likely. Well, thank you very much for coming in, Mr Sullivan. Give my love to the twins when you see them. Oh, and when HQ briefed me they did say you or whoever can tidy things up in the study. They say they've seen all there is to see."

"Just one more thing," said Tim. "I'd like Father Mac's sister, the nun, to take a sneak look at Kevin and Dave. Do you know what their movements are?"

"Not really, though they are in The Plough most nights, especially Fridays and Saturdays, from about nine onwards. Or in the Red Lion, or the Royal Oak. Just ask the bar staff."

"Thanks."

As soon as Tim left, WPC Armitage composed an email.

*****

In the evening, Tim phoned Lucy and brought her up to date. He played down the break-in as nothing more than a piece of opportunism that went wrong when Sister Winifred heard them and chased them out. He mentioned their visit to Father Mac, and promised to let the priest know that Lucy was arranging a Mass for him in mama's parish. That was typical of Lucy. She was so thoughtful. It was one of the qualities that had attracted him to her in the first place, along with a sharp intellect, a combative personality and the best figure in university.

God, he missed her! They had had a very happy marriage, brought up their son and twin girls to be decent, hard-working citizens who, in their own turn, had carved out happy lives with good jobs and stable relationships. Work had now taken their son Charlie to Australia, but the twins, Sam and Mandy, were both nearby, and they saw a good deal of their grandchildren – cleverly organised at a boy and a girl each, the boys both eight and the girls both five. This was no surprise. They were identical twins, and had carried the intimacy of the womb into an almost frightening symbiosis in life. For example, Mandy had phoned to inform Sam that she, Sam, was pregnant because she, Mandy, was experiencing morning sickness, yet knew full well that she, Mandy, was not pregnant. They would meet and find that both had been shopping and, with no consultation, had bought identical outfits. It was spooky.

Later, in bed, sleep eluded Tim as he went back over the events of the last two days. There was no doubt that the break-in was the work of Kevin and Dave and, he was convinced, they were put up to it by the two foreigners. But what were they targeting? What was the prize they hoped to find in the study of a (let's face it) pretty impoverished holy man? And what of the "angel" Father Mac said he had seen, his face registering joy, despite the disfigurement of the stroke. Was this one of

50

those near-death experiences people spoke of, where you are supposed to be travelling down a tunnel with a brilliant light at the end, and family and friends who have gone before are encouraging you to join them? And at the last minute you are turned away to shuffle back into your mortal coil for a further spell on Earth. Tim had no idea whether that was how the system worked, but he certainly wasn't going to disbelieve the possibility. When exactly did Father see the angel? Was it, indeed, with the onset of the stroke, or was it later, in the ambulance? Or could it have been before the stroke?

He then went over the various things he had to do in the Parish to keep things ticking over until a new priest took charge. It could be months before a successor arrived. The Diocese would no doubt have to make absolutely certain Father Mac could not carry on. Tim had personally seen priests continue their ministry after serious illness, even operating from a wheelchair, such was the shortage of priests. Tim decided he would be the one to remain in close contact with the Dean. Someone had to, both to ensure that supply priests were welcomed, fed and watered, and to keep the Dean informed of Father Mac's progress. At least, thought Tim, it was not for him to worry about matters affecting the church premises, like getting the boiler serviced. That was the job of the Finance and Works Committee. Its Chairman was Mike McGuire, himself a builder, who knew every builder, plumber and electrical contractor for miles around, and could get the best value. Finally, sleep overtook Tim.

CHAPTER 7

By the week-end, a system to keep the Parish thriving, or at least functioning, in the absence of Father Mac had pretty well been agreed upon. It was for the Dean to arrange stand-in priests to say Mass at Bourton-under-Wychwood, looking first to the parishes, but sometimes requesting assistance from the monks at Prinknash, the Benedictine Abbey between Cheltenham and Stroud. The regulars provided an interesting change for the congregation, often delivering the most thought-provoking sermons. The monks welcomed the rare opportunity of outside duties, usually with a good lunch thrown in. That, as it turned out, was to be the solution for the first Sunday after Father Mac's departure.

For his part, Tim Sullivan set up a rota of special ministers for two Services of the Word per week. Six people were involved, including Tim himself. He also took it upon himself to get the locks replaced on Father Mac's desk. With the Dean's permission, he reviewed the contents, but could see nothing but bills (all paid), credit card transactions and, in fact, all the documentary paraphernalia that went with life in the 21st century.

One hurdle he had to overcome was access to Father Mac's computer. In Father's absence, someone (probably Tim himself) would have to grind out a Parish bulletin every week, and there was a ready-made template on the computer. It was not desperately important to use this template, as he could do it the hard way and compose something on his own computer – indeed he had already done so – but he also had an ulterior motive in gaining access to the computer: there might conceivably be something relating to the events leading up to the break-in, though he couldn't think what form that might take. As it happened, there was no problem. He discussed the matter with Sister Winifred and found that she actually knew the password. Tim was amazed, not so much that she knew the password, as the fact of a nun in her eighties being computer-literate.

"It should be no surprise, young man," she said. "We've got a hospice to run, and if you think of it, that's a pretty demanding business. About half the sisters can use our computer, including two who are even older than me. Now, I know Donald's password because he told me it in case of an emergency. No, I'm not going to tell you it without making sure we have Donald's permission. Though he's not talking properly yet, he'll understand what we want."

And so it proved. When they visited Father Mac in hospital five days after the stroke he was clearly delighted to see them.

"Wiffie," he said, his eyes lightening up. "Tim. Sore ay-je."

"Yes, Father, you saw an angel," smiled Tim.

Nurse Bingham appeared. "He's been a bit fretful today," she said. "He's making excellent progress, but he soon tires. He tried to hold his prayer book but it slipped from his grasp. I was able to prop it up for him on the pillow. The poor man's so frustrated."

"That'll be Divine Office," said Sister Winifred. "He normally says it every day. Donald, can you understand me?"

Father Mac gave his lopsided grin. "Ess," he said.

"Donald, Tim would like to use your computer for the Parish bulletin ..." she began.

But already the effect on Father Mac was startling. He smiled, moved his head about and said, "Ess, ess. Ess!"

"Well I'm blowed," said Tim. "There's no hesitation there, is there. He's positively urging me to use it. It's almost as if there's something there he wants me to see."

*****

The next day was Sunday, and Norah sprang a surprise on Tim. "Have dinner with us, please," she said. "There'll be Sister Winifred, and Father Daniel, too."

Father Daniel, from Prinknash Abbey, was an old friend of St Nicholas' Parish. He often officiated when Father Mac was away. He was always good value with his fund of stories about life among the Benedictines. Tim told him about Father Mac and the angel.

"Then he's a very lucky man," said Father Daniel. "There's no doubting they exist, and there may even be one assigned to every man, woman, and child on Earth. You seldom see them, but they're right there with you, quietly keeping an eye on you."

"The angel didn't prevent Father Mac having a stroke," said Tim.

"Then that would not have been in his job description," smiled Father Daniel. "But think how much worse things might have been if he hadn't been there."

After the meal, which was delicious, and Father Daniel's departure, Norah said, "Now don't touch a thing, you two. I'll soon clear up here."

Tim said, "Sister, could I have a look at Father Mac's computer now. It was too late for this week's bulletin, but I'd certainly like to use it in the future."

"Of course," said Sister Winifred. "I'll log you on to start with, just to make sure Donald hasn't changed the password."

"Log me on every time I need it," said Tim. "With you here, I don't really need to know it."

"There may be times when I'm not here, and you need to use it. I can't stay here forever. In fact, I really need to see the Dean sometime about Donald's long-term future."

They went into the study. "It's a good job they didn't take this," the nun said, pointing to the PC.

"They're not so much in demand as they were," said Tim. "A friend of mine who knows about these things told me laptops are what they're after – self-contained and comparatively light. And they sometimes contain data with a sale value."

"If you can get at it," said Sister Winifred.

"Oh, they can get into it, all right," said Tim. "If they can pinch it, they can access the data, or they know a man who can. By the way, we haven't mentioned the break-in to Father Mac. Should we do so, do you think?"

"Yes, but perhaps not immediately. There was little damage done. The main thing is he's lost a few of his books. He's got to know sometime. Anyway, let's boot this beast up."

She brought the screen to life and Tim turned away as she entered the password. Obligingly, after a pause, the computer advised that it was loading Father Mac's personal settings.

"Bingo!" said Tim. "Now, let's see what folders he's got. Well, look at that. Straight away, we find one labelled Parish Bulletins. And there's a blank for future use."

"Now, do you want to do anything else?" asked Sister Winfred.

"Well, I would quite like to browse a bit if I may," said Tim. "There might just be something we should know about, and Father Mac isn't likely to be able to tell us just yet."

"Carry on, then, as long as you like. I'll just see what Norah's up to. And by the way, you know what Donald calls me, don't you?"

"You mean Wiffie?" said Tim with a grin.

"Yes. Well, now you know the password."

54

"That's brilliant!" exclaimed Tim. "No-one could possibly guess it."

Sister Winifred left Tim on his own, and he began to explore the PC's contents.

*****

Many people have said there's nothing as boring as someone else's holiday photographs. After half an hour or so of browsing, Tim felt someone else's computer files ran a close second. He'd deliberately decided to begin by getting a general overview of the folders and files, but then turned his attention to the area where he felt he was most likely to find anything of interest: Father Mac's emails. These went back about two years. After a quick look at items held in various Parish, Deanery and Diocesan folders, Tim noticed a folder simply labelled "Ambrose" and found it contained a fairly hefty exchange between Father Mac and his friend, the priest in Canada.

He soon realised this had to be where anything relating to the present mystery would most likely reside. He also noted with interest that there was quite a cluster of messages to and from his brother Andrew. He'd take a look at those, too. He couldn't help feeling a little guilty at reading other people's mail, but on the other hand Father Mac had sanctioned this invasion of his privacy, so must have been happy in his changed circumstances to share with Tim whatever his correspondence revealed.

Tim began back at the beginning of the year, and found that was when Father Mac was already planning his holiday. This year it was to take place in May, a few weeks after Easter. Nearer the time, there were messages giving his flight details (Air Canada, arrive Ottawa 1600 local on Monday 16 May) and arrangements for "Andy" to collect him at MacDonald-Cartier International. Father Mac's plan to meet up with Father Ambrose on the first Sunday he was there came in the next email:

> My dear Ambrose,
>
> I look forward to seeing you in good time for 10am Mass on Sunday 22 May and to con-celebrating with you, if I am invited to do so. I would be happy, too, to give a homily. Try to reserve some time to visit Andy's campsite this time. He has fishing gear and a canoe,

Father Mac

> and there are other boats for hire nearby, or we can
> walk a nature trail together and experience the wild life!
> God bless you, dear brother, Donald.

Father Ambrose emailed his agreement with these arrangements. Correspondence became rather desultory for a month or two, then picked up in early May with an email from Father Ambrose:

> My dear Donald,
>
> Not long now to your visit. I may not be able to get
> away much, but still hope to fit in a day at Andy's
> campsite. Our Dean has heard you are coming and
> would like you to attend a supper party after our
> various Vigil Masses one Saturday. We're looking
> forward to seeing you. God bless you, dear brother,
> Ambrose.

Father Mac's response read:

> My dear Ambrose,
>
> I feel ready for my holiday. Lent is well behind us now,
> but it seems to leave me very tired these days (not like
> you youngsters in your sixties). Apart from the usual
> daily Mass in the morning, we also have an evening
> Mass three times a week during Lent to give our
> working parishioners the opportunity to attend. We also
> have Stations of the Cross followed by Rosary every
> day and various ecumenical meditation activities,
> which call for a great deal of preparation time. I'm sure
> you were similarly engaged. All this was, of course,
> simply the lead-up to Holy Week, the busiest week in
> the Church's calendar. Please don't think I'm
> complaining. I love Lent and adore the Holy Week
> liturgy, but I always feel physically and emotionally
> drained by the time Easter Sunday dawns. I am so
> completely overwhelmed by the love of God in
> sacrificing his only Son in redemption of our sins.
>
> I would be delighted to meet your Dean. I look forward
> to seeing you. God bless you, dear brother, Donald.

The days immediately preceding Father Mac's visit saw a flurry of brief, last-minute items on the weather and what to wear. There might even still be snow on the ground. Tim knew from his many conversations with Father Mac what would be in prospect for him. Ottawa is the second-coldest capital in the world (the coldest is Ulan Bator, of course) and routinely has ten to twelve feet of snow a year and temperatures down to minus thirty or lower. Snow can start before October is out, and hang around until early May. Some lakeside cottages stay open all year round as permanent homes, but most are second homes and close down for the winter. Preparations for re-opening them begin in about early April, even though the lakes might still be frozen. The bolt-together landing stages for the boats are still in storage for another week or so. Conversely, April might see a mild snap and preparation for the spring and summer could be accelerated.

Switching folders briefly, Tim saw that Father Mac's correspondence with his brother, Andy, reflected the travel arrangements, and the hope that they could spend a few days camping in Algonquin National Park, about a two-hour drive away. Golf around Ottawa should be possible: the last of the snow had now melted and groundsmen were busy on the courses. Andy was hoping his two daughters could come for a day with their husbands. Sue lived locally and Margaret lived near Prescott, down on the St Lawrence. The five children they had between them, Andy's grandchildren, were at various stages in their schooling, or, in the case of Sue's eldest, Andrea, at McGill University in Montreal.

So, thought Tim, what of the visit itself? The first hints of how it had gone were in an email from Father Mac to Father Ambrose on 1 June, the day after his return.

My dear Ambrose,

I'm back now and still getting over jet-lag. It was lovely to see you again and to meet your Dean and fellow clergy. They are certainly a jolly bunch. Now, where to begin on the other business? I'm in no doubt about what I saw. At least, I've brought some fragmentary evidence back with me. As you know, I tried the people on Col By but they claimed total ignorance.

How could they, when rescue teams actually arrived on the scene and we later found the area was cordoned off? It must have been something pretty hush-hush.

Father Mac

Did I tell you I contacted a military liaison chap in the High Commission? He at least took my name and address, but made no promises that anything would be released by the Canadians.

All countries had their own confidential information they didn't release to the general public. So, where do I go from here? I do happen to have, among my parishioners, at least one who clearly has the right background to advise me. I really did enjoy my break and despite a few unnerving experiences (not least on the road!) I'm feeling pretty refreshed, or at least I will be when the jet-lag goes. By the way, if anything else occurs to you on how to proceed or, indeed, whether or not to proceed, I'd be happy to be guided.

God bless you, dear brother, Donald.

The reply, sent later the same day, was in the inbox:

My dear Donald,

I must echo your own words, Donald. It was lovely to see you. I'm so glad your experiences here have not left you feeling too stressed. As you know, I wondered at the time if it was some military thing, perhaps something experimental that went wrong. Petawawa is not very far from the Algonquin, nor are Kingston or Trenton for that matter, and the people at Col By would certainly not acknowledge something like that.

I actually made a few discreet enquiries with the Ottawa Citizen, and they did say there was some rumour of a light aircraft in difficulties on the night in question, but had not been able to confirm this. So they've not pursued things. Where there is no info, there's no story, but, to be honest, there could be any number of air accidents simultaneously in such a vast area as Algonquin and nobody would be any the wiser. Anyway, I'll keep my ear to the ground, just in case. God bless you, dear brother, Ambrose.

Tim wondered what "Col By" could mean. He connected to the Internet and consulted his friend Google. The first thing the search engine said was "Do you mean Colby?" Did he mean Colby? Both Father Mac and Father Ambrose had inserted a space after "Col" and spelt "By" with a capital. Tim had no idea which was the more likely. Google assumed "Colby" was probably the subject of his query, and threw out several possibilities, including educational institutes in Maine, New Hampshire and Kansas. These had all spawned several websites.

Buried among all this was a single reference to a Lt. Col John By. Hmm. Worth a browse. Ha! This must be it, Tim thought with a frisson of excitement. John By was a British Officer in the Royal Engineers who, in 1825, was commissioned to plan and construct a canal linking the British naval base at Kingston on Lake Ontario with Ottawa, in order to bypass the stretch of the St Lawrence River that bordered the United States – a route that made British ships vulnerable to attack. This huge task, the Rideau Canal, was accomplished in only seven years and By became something of a national hero. In fact, the settlement that became Ottawa was first named Bytown in honour of him.

It took little imagination to deduce that his name lived on elsewhere and this was confirmed moments later when a street map of Ottawa showed Col By Drive right in the centre of the city. A bit more surfing revealed that, among other buildings, the Canadian Department of National Defence was located there. So that was clearly where Father Mac had tried to report what he had witnessed – whatever that was!

A day or so later, Father Mac wrote:

My dear Ambrose,

I've been examining those fragments I showed you, and I think I've made a little progress. The problem is I need someone to bounce ideas off. I'm sure I'll have to bring someone else into my confidence, and, as I mentioned earlier, there is one person I know I can trust, and who may have the right background. If he doesn't, then, as they say, he'll know a man who does. As a first step, I'm going to set all the facts down chronologically and with no embroidery. I'd like to do it all at one sitting while my memory is fresh, but with so many other things on my plate, I know that won't be

59

possible. It'll have to done bit by bit in the evenings.
God bless you, dear brother, Donald.

There was a brief lull in the correspondence, then the following Wednesday, 7 June, Father Mac delivered this bombshell:

My dear Ambrose,

Do you recall those two incidents on my way back from the campsite, both involving the same vehicle? Well, curiously, something very similar happened here yesterday. I was on my way back from a Diocesan meeting in Bristol. On the M5 Motorway a white van of the type favoured by tradesmen repeatedly overtook me and cut in sharply causing me to brake hard. He clipped me once and missed me by inches the other times. The first time was frightening enough, but after he'd had several goes at me I'd had enough and left the motorway early. The van (of course) had illegally filthy, unreadable number plates, and was completely anonymous, i.e., showing no company name anywhere.

I suppose I should have reported this to the police, but what could they do with no identifying info? My guardian angel was looking after me. It might even have been the one I saw in Algonquin! Yes, I do still firmly believe that what I saw was an angel, in spite of indications of some sort of military context.

I am still in the throes of recording everything in detail before my memory fades and have firmly decided who to pass this account to, though whether to involve him now, or leave it as a legacy after my death, together with the fragments, I'm not sure.

Perhaps you have a view. The fragments, of course, I keep well hidden where very few can find them. I'm sorry time did not allow you to have other than a cursory glance at them. I feel that sooner or later they really should be passed on to someone or some agency who might understand their true nature. I do hope you are well.

God bless you, dear brother. Donald.

Well, mused Tim, he didn't say anything to me about these incidents on the M5, nor, presumably to Sister Winifred, Doc Campbell or Norah, or they would surely have mentioned them. Nor did he bargain on a medical crisis a few days later that might put paid to his plans to pass on his detailed account of events in Canada. Or was his reference to leaving his account as a legacy a morbid premonition. Did he ever finish it? If so, where was it? And as for those mysterious "fragments," goodness only knew where they were likely to be. Perhaps his account would reveal their hiding place.

Father Ambrose had emailed back the same day:

My dear Donald,

Thank God you came safely out of that nightmare, and I'm sure one of God's angels was there looking after you. I do think you are wise to give someone else a full account of your adventures, and perhaps involve him in the study of whatever it was you came away with (if you had been here longer, I'd have been very interested to study them, though I am grateful for the brief look I had of them – they really are intriguing.) I saw Chantelle the other day. She says Andy might just as well not have retired. He's been working every day since you left.

God bless you, dear brother. Ambrose.

The only other email in the series came a few days later. Father Mac confirmed that he had finished setting down in detail his encounter with an angel. Tim was surprised to see his own name mentioned, but delighted to learn that he was the parishioner Father Mac had in mind to pass his account on to. That could well be why Father had seemed so keen for Tim to access his computer. Tim scanned the email exchange with Father Mac's brother, Andy. This was very much family-oriented, with updates on Andy's daughters, their husbands and their children. Father Mac had evidently shown the "fragments" to Andy, who had dismissed them as just so much litter left by hikers or campers.

The crucial thing now was to locate Father Mac's write-up. There was no obvious computer file. Perhaps Father Mac had buried it in his enormous files with diocesan and deanery correspondence. Or perhaps he had printed it (several copies?) then deleted the file. He'd ask Norah where it might possibly be if he had printed it. It would probably be in an envelope with Tim's name on it.

"Cup of tea?" It was Norah.

"I'd love one," said Tim. "My eyes are getting tired now, so I thought I'd take a break and have another browse tomorrow, say."

Tim joined Norah and Sister Winifred in the lounge. He told them about the incident on the M5. Both confirmed that Father Mac hadn't mentioned it to them.

"I'm not surprised the poor man had a stroke," said Norah. "It sounds like he was already a bit on edge after the accidents in Canada. This must have played on his mind even more."

"The other thing I got from the emails is the fact that Father Mac has apparently written a detailed account of his experiences in Canada – presumably his camping trip and the accidents. He also indicated it was intended for me. The problem is that, not knowing he was about to have a stroke and lose much of his speech, he didn't tell anyone where to find it. I suppose it could be lurking on his computer, but if it's been printed off, where do you think it could possibly be?"

"I can only think it would be somewhere in his study. In the desk or stuck between the pages of a book."

"What about his bedroom?" asked Sister Winifred. "I often keep things that are important to me in a bedside cabinet."

"But perhaps you don't have the same range of choice in your accommodation," argued Tim.

"No, I dare say you're right. Mind, that doesn't exclude Donald's bedroom. So it looks like a detailed scrutiny of the remaining papers in the desk and all those books. Plus the bedroom."

"The police did say we can tidy up the study," said Tim, "They don't need it as a crime scene any longer. Just as well, I've already had new locks fitted to the desk. Look, do you mind if I begin the search now, as I'm here?"

"I'm happy to help you with the search, Tim," said Norah. "But Sister, you're the one living here now, so it's really up to you. You may want a bit of peace and quiet now, and a chance to put your feet up."

"I'm not in the habit of putting my feet up," said Sister Winifred indignantly. "Of course we must at least make a start now. Look, Tim, why don't you and Norah take the study, and I'll search Donald's bedroom?"

"That's fine by me," said Tim. "There should also be a small package hidden away somewhere, too. In the emails there were references to some fragments Father Mac brought back with him. In fact, he said that he had begun examining them. Whether or not he's been keeping them all together – the package and the letter for me – is anyone's guess."

They set to, but after an hour or so decided to call a halt.

"I'm pretty sure there's nothing in the desk. It's all either financial or work-related: Diocesan, Deanery, and Parish," said Tim.

"I've looked inside every book he has," said Norah. "All I can say is that there are still a few books in other alphabets – you know, Greek and that Acrylic. Kevin and Dave didn't take them all." Tim had a quick look and confirmed the books as Russian and Greek, as well as one tome in Arabic, presumably the Koran, as a copy of the English version was next to it, despite Kevin and Dave's attentions.

Tim agreed, "I'd say they're mostly novels, probably the classics, and a few are clearly dictionaries. There are certainly no grammars. How did you get on, Sister?"

"Well, it didn't take long to confirm that there was no sign of the sort of thing we're looking for," said the nun. "But then I got a bit side-tracked. I found a photo album with snaps going back many years, including some with our parents and the three of us together, not long after Andy came along. I've got copies of some, but there were others I'd not seen for decades. I'm afraid I got a little weepy."

"I'm sorry," said Tim. "It's my fault for putting you in that position. Now, about tomorrow: I'd like to see Father to thank him for the write-up he's done and see if he can tell me where I can find it. But I don't want to take up someone else's place, like you, Norah, or Doc Campbell."

"Didn't they say two visitors per patient?" said Sister Winifred. "Surely we can visit in relays, providing there are no more than two at a time. You'd like to visit him, wouldn't you, Norah?"

"Yes, of course, and I'm sure Doctor Campbell would, too."

A phone call to the good doctor confirmed this.

"I'm hoping Doc Campbell will be able to get some sort of prognosis from someone. We need to think about Father's longer-term care," said Tim.

"I think I can get him into the hospice at least for a short time," said Sister Winifred. "We try to keep a couple of beds open for priests who are not terminally ill, but need some degree of nursing care until their longer-term future is sorted out. We can even organise visits by a physiotherapist."

"That would be brilliant," said Tim. "Now I'd better get back and call Lucy. Thank you, Norah, for lunch and thank you both for your search efforts."

*****

Back at home, Tim called Lucy.

"I was rather hoping you'd make the effort to come over and see us," said Lucy, with a slight edge to her voice.

"I know, love, I should have done. I was invited to lunch with Father Daniel and Sister Winifred, then we got sidetracked looking through Father Mac's papers and things. Look, it's not too late now. I can be with you in an hour and stay for a bit of supper if that's OK."

It was, and Tim was soon on his way. As he drove through the glorious Cotswold countryside, it struck him how blessed he was to live in such a wonderful part of the country – nay, of the world. The hills themselves with such delightful views from the limestone escarpment, the lush meadows grazed by innumerable sheep, the golden stone cottages in the villages, the quaint pubs, the churches and tiny chapels, some going back over a millennium to Saxon times, the wildlife – roe deer and the shy muntjaks, badgers and foxes everywhere.

He also mulled over what else was on the agenda for the next day. He could think offhand of at least three things: contact the Dean about Father Mac's long-term future; advise the police about the incident on the M5, which Father Mac had not reported but which, in light of other developments, might now assume some importance; and somehow get Sister a sight of Kevin and Dave. That would be better done before he saw the police again.

When he saw Lucy, he was immediately filled with remorse at neglecting her for the last few days. It's amazing, he thought, how much absence really does serve to make the heart grow fonder. Mama was in good spirits, too, and was clearly out of pain and on the mend.

"I think I'll soon be self-sufficient, Tim," she said. "Oh, and while you're here, I wonder if you could look at my talking books player. I seem to have done something to it. And there might be a blockage in one of the drains."

"All right, all right, mother," said Tim soothingly. "I'll take a look round the entire house while I'm here."

CHAPTER 8

The next day Tim took a car-load to Cheltenham General Hospital. Sister Winifred and Norah went in first, armed with a large get-well card signed by all the parishioners who were at morning Mass the previous day, as well a bunch of grapes and some chocolates. They found Nurse Bingham and checked that he could eat these.

"He is mildly affected in the facial muscles, but he can eat pretty normally," she said.

Meanwhile, Doctor Campbell disappeared to try to grab a few words with one of the consultants. He came back, smiling.

"We've got about five minutes in a quarter of an hour. I told them that's all we needed. Hello, isn't this Canon Whotsit?"

It was, indeed, Canon Potter, the Dean.

"Well," said Tim, "how fortuitous. We're going along shortly to see the consultant to get a prognosis on Father Mac. Why don't you join us?"

"That's one reason I'm here," said the canon, "and, of course, to see Father Mac. I feel a bit guilty at not getting here before today, but it really wasn't possible. Shall I go in now? He is in that ward there, isn't he?"

"Yes. They say they don't want more than two round a bed at the same time, but I'm sure Norah will be happy to pop out for a while."

"I can't stay long anyway. I just want to tell Father there are prayers and Masses galore being said for him. Now, is his sister with him? And Norah? I need to see them, too."

"Yes, and I'm pretty sure what you want to discuss with them. I think Sister Winifred was going to contact you anyway. Go right through the ward and round a bit of a corner. You won't recognise Sister. She's not in uniform, as she calls it. She says it frightens the patients. I think you'll find Father McNulty a bit frustrated at not being able to read Divine Office. He can read, but only in very small doses. He tires quickly."

A few moments later, Norah came out.

"The Dean said he only wanted a few minutes, and he'd like a word with me afterwards. You'll find Father in good spirits. I think it's dawned on him that there is life after a stroke. He's had a chocolate and he's propped up a little now."

Soon afterwards, the Dean came out, and Norah went back in. The three men walked down a few corridors and stopped outside a door. Doctor Campbell knocked.

"Come in, come in," said a voice. The owner of the voice was a tall, stooping man, with a small goatee. "Well, this looks like a deputation." Doctor Campbell made the introductions. James Bradbury was the consultant.

"You want a prognosis," said Bradbury. "I can't be very precise at this stage. Father McNulty's speech should mostly return, perhaps quickly, but he'll probably never lose that slight pull around his mouth. So the speech at first may be just a little slurred. As for the paralysis, again this is not very severe and I can see him walking pretty soon, with the assistance of one or two sticks. He shouldn't need a frame, except perhaps initially. Does that help?"

"Enormously," said Canon Potter. "It gives us the basis for longer-term planning."

"Well yes, but don't try to put precise dates on his progress. Yes, the damage is at least partially reversible, but the time-scale is anyone's guess. Certainly, you shouldn't bank on Father McNulty resuming work in the immediate future, though given time he may be capable of limited duties."

"I don't think a return to work is in anyone's mind," said the Canon. "It's more a question of where to accommodate him."

"I'm afraid I can't help you there. Wherever he is he won't be able to manage on his own. He'll also need access to physiotherapy. What I can say is that he should be able to leave here in the next week or so. There'll be nothing we can do here that can't be done outside."

They thanked Bradbury and as they returned to the stroke ward Canon Potter said, "I think we can see the way ahead, now. If Sister Winifred can look after Father for a period of weeks, perhaps months, at the hospice, then there's no reason I can see why he can't then stay on in the presbytery, not as Parish priest but as a guest of the Deanery. If and when the Bishop appoints a new Parish priest, we would expect him to live in the presbytery, and as far as Father McNulty's well-being is concerned, simply be there in case there's any problem overnight. This should be no great burden for the new priest. By way of compensation, he has the Cotswolds all round him instead of some crowded cluster of housing estates in Bristol, for instance. We can arrange for a carer to come once or twice a day."

"You said "if" the Bishop appoints a successor. Is that in doubt?" asked Tim.

"It could be," said the Dean. "You'll be aware of the shortage of priests. You may end up with a shared priest. And should Father McNulty be able to resume even limited duties, that would be a bonus over what might be. And you'd be surprised how many priests want to continue with some sort of pastoral involvement if they can after an illness. It can be excellent therapy."

Tim said, "Well, that clears the air a bit, Father. Thank you. So you'll keep arranging supply priests until we know a bit more. And, of course, Norah Walsh should continue as housekeeper or caretaker or whatever, and I've no doubt will be as happy to prepare meals for two priests as for one, as and when the need arises."

"Yes, indeed," said Canon Potter.

Back at the ward, Tim and Doctor Campbell went in while Norah and Sister Winifred left the ward. They lost no time in going over with the Canon the same ground he'd just covered with Tim and Campbell.

Father Mac was clearly delighted to see his great friend, Doc Campbell. His eyes lit up and the crooked grin he was able to muster stayed in place the whole time.

"I've seen the boss," said Campbell, "Mr Bradbury. He says you'll get your speech back but you may have to talk out the side of your mouth, like a gangster. So you'll soon be able to cuss me for beating you at chess."

Father Mac was dying to say something, but no words came about apart from, "You, you ..."

"That's it," said Campbell. "The more we provoke you, the more you'll want to answer back. Actually, Tim, I think I've won about twice in the last six months."

"Listen, Father," said Tim. "Thank you very much for writing an account of your trip to Canada. I read about it in your emails, but I can't find it. Did you print it?"

Father Mac looked puzzled, then tried to move his head.

"I think I can take that as 'no.' So, it's somewhere on your computer?" said Tim.

Father Mac gave his crooked smile. "Ess," he breathed, much calmer now.

"Can you tell me the name you gave the file?"

"At... At... At..." Father Mac strained, but gave up in frustration.

"That's OK, Father, now I know it's on the computer, I'll find it eventually."

They carried on chatting to Father Mac for a while, Doctor Campbell recalling some of the good times they had had, and expressing confidence that those days would return.

Finally, the doctor said, "I think we'd better let him rest now, Tim. Five visitors in the same afternoon would wear anyone out."

They said their farewells, then Norah and Sister went back briefly to do the same. Back at the presbytery, Tim said, "Don't bother changing, Sister, I'm picking you up at nine tonight."

"Oh?" she said, "Why's that?"

"We're going on a pub crawl," said Tim.

*****

The first thing Tim did on arriving home was phone Mike McGuire at his office. Mike was Chairman of the Finance and Works committee and still ran his own business. He was six feet five and seventeen stone of muscle and had played rugby lock forward to a high standard. Though now in his early sixties, he still had that aura of indestructibility about him that had intimidated opponents on the field.

Without being too specific on the phone, Tim filled Mike in on the general background to the robbery and explained what his plan for the evening was. "I want to find those two yobs and let Sister take a look at them. She might not be able to recognise them, of course, in which case we're no further forward. I don't expect any trouble, but I'd like you along as insurance. Are you on?"

"Sure I'm on," said Mike, "In fact, I know the lads. They did a bit of casual labouring for me in the summer. And that was the problem. They were too bloody casual. I had to drop them after a week. I was only doing someone a favour."

*****

Tim picked up Sister Winifred at nine and they ambled up the lane to the High Street, where Mike was waiting outside The Plough.

"I've got an idea, Tim," said Mike. "I'll go in because I know them. If they're not there I'll ask one or two of the drinkers if they know where they are. They'll assume I want them for a job."

68

Mike walked in and emerged a minute or so later. "They're in the Red Lion," he said, "playing in a darts match."

They walked round the corner to the Red Lion and entered the bar. Tim bought a couple of pints and a soft drink while Sister Winifred, with Mike towering over her, sat at a table that afforded a good view of the darts match in progress beyond the far end of the bar. Tim joined them.

" Well?" enquired Mike. "Any luck, Sister?"

"I think it's pretty obvious that the lad with the red hair is Kevin, though I must say it is only the red hair that I can identify, not the features – I didn't get a good look at them."

"But," said Tim, "you know that Kevin has red hair, we are told that he's here tonight playing darts, and there is only one lad with red hair here. Besides that, Mike actually recognises him. Right, Mike?"

"Oh, sure," agreed Mike. "Case proven."

"All right, then," said Sister Winifred. "I'm pretty sure which one is Dave. His beer mug is next to Kevin's and they chat to each other all the time."

"Right again," said Mike.

"But to be scrupulously fair to him, I wouldn't know him as the boy I saw in the presbytery. Kevin, yes, I will admit to recognising him. In fact, the more I watch him, the more convinced I am."

"I came prepared for this," said Tim. "I just want to see if we can provoke Dave into noticing you, Sister. Come with me. We'll get a bit closer and I'll pretend to be discussing him with you."

Tim and Sister Winifred moved closer to the darts match, and Tim stared at Dave, then pointed to him and appeared to write in a notebook. Dave was on the oche, needing a double top to win when he noticed an old bloke pointing at him and whispering something to an old woman, who looked vaguely familiar. This put Dave right off his stride. Two darts fell well outside the outer wire and one missed the board altogether. He strode over to them, furious.

"What the fuck are you up to, mate?" he seethed.

Tim made a clucking noise. "Dave, Dave, kindly moderate your language in front of a lady."

"You made me miss, you sod. And what's she doing here?"

"Seen her before, have you, Dave? About four in the morning? In the priest's house? Listen to me, Dave, and listen carefully. No, don't go away or I'll be forced to shout across to you. Then all your mates will hear."

"It's my turn," he said frantically. "They're waiting for me."

"No they're not, Dave. Unless I'm much mistaken, your opponent's just got the double sixteen he wanted. Now listen. You and Kev could be in serious trouble. You've robbed a priest and the police know it was you. And you were hired to do it by people from a foreign country. Oh, yes, we know all that. The thing is they were after something that could be important to our government. Now I personally don't know exactly who these people were, but somebody somewhere might know and you and Kev could then find yourselves being accused of helping enemies of the country. There's a nasty word for that, Dave. It's called treason, and it carries very severe penalties."

Tim called across to Mike. "Hey, Mike, what's the penalty for treason these days? Is it capital punishment?"

Mike appeared to ponder. "I think they only hang people in time of war. In peacetime I think it's just life, but I'm not sure."

"We never took nothing," Dave wailed. "Well, just a few books and a few papers."

"Just as a matter of interest, what did these foreigners want you to look for?"

"Books or papers in funny writing. There were no papers, but we thought we'd better give them a sample out of the desk to prove it. We gave them mainly books, and then only a dozen or so."

"Now look, tell the police what you've just told me. Go and see Angela Armitage tomorrow. She won't be able to deal with it without involving the HQ in Cheltenham, and they'll contact you. Tell Kev to do the same. Whatever you do, don't even think of disappearing. Now while you're here, you might like to apologise to this lady, who is the priest's sister. People like you frighten the lives out of little old ladies. Then go and join your mates."

"Sorry, missus," mumbled Dave, and rejoined the darts match. They saw him talking in a low voice to Kev.

"Little old lady?" said Sister Winifred indignantly.

"I was describing you as Dave might," said Tim defensively. "Anyway, let's get back and join Mike."

They filled Mike in on their chat with Dave, finished their drinks and left. Before they dispersed for the night, Tim said, "I'd like to play with Father's PC again tomorrow, if I may. I'll be conducting a Service of the Word at ten, so after that. Would you like to do the first reading, Sister?"

"I'd be delighted to," she said.

CHAPTER 9

Next morning at seven Mrs Dora Robinson of Mill Lane opened the back door and, as she always did at that time of day, called her cat. Tiger always came bounding in, hungry after a night on the tiles. Not so this morning. She called and called, then washed, dressed, and had her breakfast before trying again, just after eight. Perhaps she should get a cat-flap after all, though she had always been against them. She enjoyed romantic visions of a natural cat, a cat that didn't coddle itself indoors all the time, stirring only to poke through a cat-flap to do its jobs, in fact, a cat that was really a cat, and did a bit of hunting. He was a good hunter, often bringing home the remnants of small rodents as his gift to her. She wandered round the garden and into the Close, still calling. Eventually, she decided to report its loss to the Community Police.

When she got there, there were two lads waiting, that Dave, and what was the name of the other? Kevin? They were always in trouble. She knew Dave's mother vaguely – at least she knew who she was. She couldn't totally ignore them, so by way of a greeting she said in what she intended as a friendly voice, "I hope you two lads have been behaving yourselves." This did not elicit a friendly response.

"Piss off, Missus," said Dave.

"You bad, bad boy," said Dora. "I know your mother. I've a good mind to tell her."

Just then Angela Armitage arrived, unlocked her little office in the community centre, and beckoned Dora in. She was not long. As she left, Kevin and Dave heard Angela advising her.

"We can't actually spare the time to look for your cat, Mrs Robinson, so do as I suggest: knock on neighbours' doors, and put a lost notice with a description in the co-op, the post office and the newsagents."

As she left, Kevin and Dave walked in.

*****

Soon after this, Tim conducted the Tuesday Service of the Word, shared a coffee with Sister and Norah, then immersed himself in trying to identify the file he wanted on Father Mac's computer. He'd no idea what the file name was. All Father Mac had managed to get out was something that sounded like "At."

It finally occurred to him to search for a key word – one that was sure to be present in the file, but, he hoped, nowhere else. The obvious word was "angel." After only a few seconds the incidence count had reached five. Encouraging. However, after a minute the count was over fifty, so Tim knew this was not the most helpful word. He opened a few of the files cited and found a wealth of correspondence copied to the Parish of St Michael and All Angels, one of the other Parishes in the Deanery. He entered a space before and after the word "angel" in order to isolate it from compounds. Again, there were more entries than he had expected, some in files with what appeared to be Latin names. He tried a few at random and found several sermons and other notes based on scripture texts featuring an angel, including the Annunciation, when Our Lady was told by the Angel Gabriel the good news that she was to be the mother of Our Lord. Hmm. Time to try something else.

Tim decided to re-read the emails between Father Mac and Father Ambrose to see if any word there might meet the requirement of uniqueness or at least scarcity. He soon had a short list of words and names. The word "fragments" occurred several times, as did the place-names "Algonquin," "Petawawa," "Kingston," and "Trenton," and the name "Col By." He did a search on all of them. Three yielded only one file reference, and the same one at that. They were "Petawawa," "Trenton," and "Col By." The others had also occurred in that very same file, as well as in various notes Father Mac appeared to have taken from tourist brochures. He had now clearly isolated the file he wanted.

The file name was a bit of a handful: *"Itinera Alibi MMXI"*. Obviously Latin. *Alibi*? Didn't that have legal overtones to do with claiming to be somewhere else when an alleged crime was committed? On one of the shelves Tim found a Latin-English/ English-Latin dictionary and discovered that "alibi" simply meant "elsewhere." He soon worked out a reasonable translation for the file name: "Journeys Elsewhere, 2011" or perhaps, stretching the sense a bit, "Travels Abroad, 2011." With a stroke of inspiration, he also deduced that quite probably, "At" was Father Mac's attempt at telling him the file title was in Latin.

He opened the file and found it contained a substantial narrative, apparently begun before Father Mac had decided who to give it to. A quick flip through the file soon convinced Tim that there was no point in just picking at it here and now. This file needed careful study over a long period, with frequent recourse to the Internet and, perhaps, a number of reference books by his side. He'd already decided on the best course of action. He would copy the file to a CD and read it into his own computer. He'd brought a blank CD from home for the purpose. He'd make sure his PC had successfully read the file, then delete it from Father Mac's computer, just in case "the enemy" managed to get into the presbytery and access it.

Tim felt quite elated, then, on impulse, scanned the bookshelves. Just as he had hoped, over the years Father Mac had acquired a number of Canadian books and maps. He selected several maps and a comprehensive tourist guide to Ontario, then returned to Sister Winifred and Norah.

"I've found the file and copied it so that I can study it at my leisure," he said. "And I've borrowed a few maps. By the way, I won't be going to the hospital today. After this morning's Service, one or two people asked if they could visit Father, so I told them the rules. I'll make sure we include something in this week's bulletin."

"While you were on the computer, I had a phone call from that nice WPC, Angela," said Norah. "She'd tried you at home, and guessed you'd be here. She said there was no need to interrupt you, but could I pass on the message that she would like to see you. She'll be in all morning. Anyway, I'm popping round the shops now. Is there anything in particular you want, Sister?"

"Right, I'm on my way," said Tim.

*****

Dora Robinson had reached the shops and was getting a few things in the co-op, where she ran into her friend Liz Arnold. She told her all about Tiger, and reporting his loss to the police.

"And while I was there, those two tearaways, Kevin and Dave walked in. I wonder what they've been up to."

"Well, I did hear the Catholic pres-thing, you know where the Priest lives, Father Mac, I heard it was broken into in the early hours two or three days ago. There was a police car there about five-thirty. Fred Roberts saw it. He lives opposite."

73

Father Mac

While they chatted, a young man named Brian Jenkins, hidden from their view in the next aisle, took a notepad and biro out of his anorak, and hastily scribbled something.

*****

When Tim arrived at the Community Police office, Angela got straight to the point. "It may come as no surprise to you, Mr Sullivan," she said, "But Kevin and Dave were in here first thing this morning. In fact, they were waiting for me to arrive. They said they'd come to admit that they were the ones who broke into the presbytery last week, that they'd been paid to do so, but that all they'd taken were a few books worth nothing. Their main aim in coming in, though, was to make it absolutely clear to the police that they had no idea the men who paid them were foreigners. I'm not sure why they went off on that tack."

"I must admit, it was something I said to Dave," Tim said. "We contrived a way for Sister Winifred to take a look at them, and we saw them in the Red Lion last night. Sister Winifred has firmly identified Kevin, but could not identify Dave. I had a chat with Dave and persuaded him to own up. I'm afraid we ruined their darts match."

"We don't really encourage the public to do the police's job for them," said Angela. "Anyway, I've emailed Cheltenham, and they will arrange to see the lads. I think I'll be expected to bow out of things now, unless instructed otherwise, and we'd be happy if you did the same."

"Of course, Angela," agreed Tim. "Anyway there are far more pressing things for me to get on with now." (Like reading Father's Mac's file, and trying to locate the so-called "fragments," whatever they were.)

It wasn't until he was outside that Tim realised he'd had a mild rap across the knuckles. He hoped he hadn't alienated the police. He also hoped that with Father Mac's file he could somehow resolve a few things. It was quite clear from the emails that Father Mac would have requested him – and specifically him – to do so if his stroke hadn't largely robbed him of his speech. It was the least he could do for the kindly priest, enlisting the help of others if necessary.

What exactly was there to resolve? To begin with, what had Father Mac seen on his camping trip? And what were these "fragments" he had found? What was important enough to cause persons unknown, both here and in Canada, to make three attempts on his life – or were they intended as deliberate near-misses to frighten him and precipitate a stress-induced stroke? Could that sort of thing be arranged? And was the break-in organised by the same people? Were they after the "fragments"? And, if so, why?

We're making some progress now, he thought, with a small degree of satisfaction, if only by identifying the right questions to ask. He sensed there was a lot more to do. He made his way home.

*****

Brian Jenkins was a bright, energetic young man in his mid-twenties. He'd graduated in media studies, and thought he could walk into a job in radio, TV, or journalism. He and 10,000 others. He'd given up in despair and did any work that came along, labouring on a building site, helping a mate with his landscape gardening business, unskilled work demanding muscle, until he'd had a tip that the young lady who covered Bourton and the dozen or so villages in a six- or seven-mile radius for the Cheltenham-based *Cotswold Regent* was moving to another paper. He'd applied instantly, before the job was even advertised, spelling out his credentials and supplying some sample articles. Against the odds, he was taken on.

He had not let the Regent down. He could work from home, too, and sniff out stories by doing the rounds of shops, pubs and (surprisingly) churches, or at least the clergy. He also monitored police broadcasts. One day, he would stumble on something really big, get it accepted by the nationals, and then his career would really take off.

After hearing the two ladies gossiping, he knew what to do. He knew Norah Walsh by sight and saw her around the village most days. He might not see her today, but he was sure to do so one day soon. He strolled down Church Lane, reached St Nicholas Church, then strolled back towards the shops. And there was Norah on her way back to the presbytery. He smiled as he approached her.

"Good morning, Mrs Walsh," he said cheerily. "I wonder, could you tell me if anything valuable was taken from the presbytery? I've heard who was involved, but it would be a much more interesting story for readers of the Regent if I could put a little more flesh on the bones. You know, local thieves take advantage of Priest's illness and steal his prize so-and-so."

Norah was taken aback. "I'm sorry, young man, I thought everything was in the hands of the police, and only the police. Where did you hear that from?"

"Oh, it's the talk of the village. Everybody knows the bare outline of the incident. What they need now is a bit more information."

"I'm sorry, but you'll have ask the police," said Norah. "You'll get nothing from me."

"I quite understand, Mrs Walsh, I'm sorry if I intruded into areas that are perhaps sensitive. Good-day to you." He smartly turned round and carried on towards the shops, smiling. Methinks she doth protest too much, he thought, knowing he was on to a good thing. He had already learnt a few of the ground rules for a successful journalist. Like – pretend you know more than you do, and play people off against each other. Bit by bit, if there's a decent story, it will emerge.

Back at the presbytery, Norah immediately phoned Tim and reported her conversation with "that young man from the Cotswold Regent."

"Jenkins," said Tim. "I know his Dad. They used to live in Bourton, then they moved to Cheltenham. The last thing we need is the press sniffing around. We don't know what we're getting involved in, but it could have all sorts of security implications and even be something of national importance. Perhaps I should have a quiet word with him, as we did with Kevin and Dave. Anyway, don't you bother yourself about it, but thanks for telling me. I think you handled it very well."

CHAPTER 10

That evening, after phoning Lucy and promising to come over the next day, Tim fed the CD containing Father Mac's file into his own PC. He surrounded himself with pens, paper, and Father Mac's book and maps, then, with a feeling of nervous anticipation, he opened the file. Tim read:

My Dear Friend,

It will seem curious to you to learn that, as I write this letter, I am not completely sure of your identity, though I'm virtually certain who you are. It has come to you either because I am now dead, or because I have instructed it should come to you by reason of my infirmity.

In my judgement you will be the only person I feel I can trust these confidences to – the person with the right mix of intellect, discretion, and professional credentials to act upon them in the wisest possible way. Your options are simple, but your choice may be difficult: you either reveal these facts to what I will call for now "the appropriate authorities" or you may choose to keep them concealed. I myself tried to involve the Canadian "authorities" but to no avail. More of that later. There is also a package of items I would like you to study carefully. Those who have done work on the presbytery will be able to help you find it. Please do not open the package until you have read this letter, which will give a detailed account of how the items came into my possession.

As you will know, every year or two I take a holiday in Canada. My younger brother, Andy, lives there, near Ottawa. His wife, Chantelle, is francophone by birth, but of course, totally bilingual. Andy is largely bilingual, too. Though by training he is a mathematician, as a government employee of a certain grade he has to be reasonably proficient in both languages. Chantelle was an art teacher and both she and Andy have now retired. I watched their daughters grow up over the years, and, of course, they now have homes, children, and careers of their own. Andy and Chantelle are grandparents. How time flies. Another attraction of going to Ottawa is to see a brother priest, Father Ambrose. It was on one of my early trips to stay with Andy that I first met him. I simply went to Mass, got talking to him afterwards, found myself invited to lunch, and from those beginnings a close friendship developed. Father Ambrose has been over here (you may have met him) and we have both con-celebrated Mass in Bourton and Ottawa. All this is by way of general background.

Coming back to Andy, he and Chantelle are camping freaks. We always spend some of the time I'm with them camping somewhere or other. He is remarkably fit and loves walking the many trails in the area of whatever site we choose. A favourite destination is Algonquin Provincial Park. Imagine an area nearly half the size of Wales, thickly forested and punctuated with hundreds of lakes. It's the perfect place for peace and solitude. Once a centre for logging companies, attracted there in the early 19th Century by the maples and the huge red and white pines that grow there in profusion, Algonquin later gained the status of a provincial park and, as stretches of metalled road were laid down, gradually became a popular vacation haunt, though only the southern strip has really opened up. Here, the car-bound tourist has easy access to the many trails he can explore on foot, and to camping sites, canoeing centres and a few pricey motels. For the more adventurous, there are the longer back-packing trails, and a portage network leading deep into to the interior of the region, where moose, black bears and wolves hold sway. But enough of the tourist stuff!

I flew out on 16 May, a Monday, and, as planned, Andy and Chantelle met me off the plane at MacDonald-Cartier International. I had already arranged to see Father Ambrose the following Sunday, and it came as a surprise to learn that Andy had organised our camping trip for the day after my arrival. I should have told him of my plans. I was also a bit worried about the possible effects of jet-lag. There's only a five-hour time difference, but these days even that takes me a couple of days to get my body clock adjusted. Andy argued that I'd find camping really restful, and that I could creep away into my tent and snooze whenever I felt like it. I persuaded myself he was right, though past experience warned me that he'd soon have me in his canoe or walking a trail. Ah, well, as long as I was back by the Saturday, that would be fine. As it turned out, I was, indeed, able to get back by the Saturday, though a lot was to happen before then.

Chantelle excelled herself that evening with a wonderful welcoming dinner. The wine and the nightcap that followed were enough to ensure a deep night's sleep, and the next morning I felt rested and invigorated. I helped stow camping gear and provisions in one of Andy's two cars. Many families drove one car until the end of October, then garaged it, and drove the second car throughout the months of snow and ice. A big joke in Canada was the question, "What car do you drive in the winter" and the answer, "The wife's." Much to my surprise, Andy prepared the other car as well, explaining that he might just get called in to work (though he is officially retired, he seems to be in fairly regular demand as a "consultant"), and two cars gave a bit of flexibility. And by the way, I had brought my licence with me, hadn't I?

We set off about 10 o'clock, and I was pleased to find that I soon fell back into Canadian driving habits. I toddled along, mostly around 80 kph (mph had long disappeared). We had lunch at a roadhouse near Algonquin, then made for the campsite near Smoke Lake. Towards the opposite shore was Molly's Island, well known for its association with Tom Thomson and the Group of Seven, the Canadian post-Impressionists, who had occasionally camped there in their heyday, back in the 1920s. I was surprised to see we were the only ones at our site. "Who else but the retired have the time for weekday camping this early in the year?" said Andy, "and not many of them are stupid enough to do it. It'll fill up a bit by the week-end, but we'll be leaving then. Of course, there may be time for a few more days here before you go back."

Andy was right about my finding the camping restful. I was allowed not to be energetic, and I really enjoyed the break from the hurly-burly of modern life. I won't go into all the pleasures that camping in general brings, and camping in Algonquin in particular. Suffice it to say that I had a tent to myself, an inflatable mattress and a thickly padded sleeping bag. I was also pleased that the shower block that went with the site was in good working order. We cooked outside on a mini barbecue, and watched the chipmunks at play and the beavers building. Thank God there were no mosquitoes to speak of. They would be around in droves later. I even had a paddle in Andy's canoe. In the evening, it was idyllic to watch the sun set and hear the mournful call of the loons, then later, in bed, to hear the wolves howling in the far distance. Two days later, our camping trip was rudely interrupted. Andy received a call on the Thursday morning summoning him into work.

"Sorry, I have to go," he said. "I expect Chantelle will want to come with me." Chantelle nodded.

"There was no indication they would need me this week, but then suddenly I'm called in. It's quite unpredictable. It's – how shall I put it – largely driven by events. But," he continued, "that doesn't mean you have to go with us. In fact, I'd rather you didn't. I've no idea how long I'll be needed, but I don't expect much home time for a few days, so there won't be any of those little local outings. Look, you love it here, I know, and you always have done. You'll have your tent and we'll leave the barbecue with you and more than enough food. You can commune with nature just like Henry Thoreau."

I knew he was right. I'm ashamed to say that my first reaction to Andy's summons to Ottawa was one of feeling cheated out of two days of our short break. I almost breathed a sigh of relief. I could stay another two days and then drive back at leisure on the Saturday. I'd promised Ambrose a sermon at the Sunday morning sung Mass. I could now get on and put a few thoughts together, perhaps inspired by the beautiful surroundings.

Andy and Chantelle packed the large car with their tent and their bundles of clothes and sleeping gear. Andy strapped the canoe on the roof-rack, and by about 9:30 they were ready to go. Andy opened the road atlas and went over the homeward route with me. He left the atlas with me. I felt a small touch of guilt as I waved farewell to them. I would be having fun and they wouldn't.

We were at one end of a long, narrow lake. There were camping sites dotted about, and some distance away near the far end of the lake was a leisure centre, where canoes could be hired, camping gear bought or hired, and portage trips could be organised. I had my field glasses with me and could see little evidence of activity at the centre. I could see only one canoe on the lake, and its sole occupant seemed to be fishing rather than exploring the lake's little inlets. I sat there a long time just drinking in the scene. I then walked a short trail for an hour or so, leaving my campsite, confident that though it was unguarded, no-one would disturb anything. There was no worry that a bear might get at the food. It was all in a cooler in the car. That did not mean that Mr Bear would not come searching, but they were generally harmless, unless provoked. They fear man, but they do like his food.

After lunch, I indulged myself with a nap, and probably shook off the last remnants of jet-lag. This brief account of my time since Andy had left is pretty well representative of how I spent all that time. I was amazed at how quickly the time passed. I did manage to get down the bones of a sermon, something on the theme of "differences." I mentioned differences between my parish in Bourton, and Father Ambrose's parish in Ottawa, and between urban life and rural life, Algonquin being an extreme example. Most of all I touched on the differences between people around the world and that differences were there to be celebrated, not opposed. I hoped it all made sense.

Thursday quickly passed, as did Friday, and I remember admiring again the sunset, then watching the stars come out and seeing their pin-point reflections in the still, black waters of the lake. I had a nip of my favourite medicine, made in Scotland, then turned in. I immediately fell into the deep sleep that always comes after a day in the open air, and remained asleep for several hours.

Suddenly I was wide awake. It was a little after 4 am. What had first woken me was an intermittent flash of brilliant light penetrating the tent. One moment the interior of the tent was bathed in the brightness of sunlight, then the next moment it was plunged into darkness. I thought at first a particularly severe storm had struck, but soon realised no storm could cause such a dramatic strobe effect.

I crawled out of my tent, and as I did so the most unearthly noise rent the air – something between a hiss and a roar. Terrified, I looked up and saw a dark shape immediately overhead, careering over the nearest trees. Seconds later, there came the most tremendous rending sound. The Earth around me shook, I saw the tops of trees close by topple in a flurry of leaves, branches and flame, then there was silence – and darkness. The strobe light had gone.

I suddenly realised I was trembling violently, and it took me several minutes to regain some sort of composure. An air crash! What was it – a military aircraft? There were all sorts of military establishments in this part of Ontario – I knew of Petawawa, Trenton, and Kingston, and no doubt there were others. Or was it a civil airliner? Did the airlines come this way? Should I fight my way through the dense wood towards the scene of the crash with only a torch to guide me. Sunrise wasn't until about 5:30. What could an elderly priest do at a crash site anyway? Try and help injured passengers from the plane? Or simply seek out the dying and offer to administer the last rites? I had my viaticum (prayers for the dead and dying and a consecrated host or two) with me somewhere. A dozen or more thoughts crowded into my mind, and I just stood there, helpless, wondering what was for the best. I couldn't even summon help. When Andy and Chantelle were with me, both had mobile phones (or cell phones, as they called them), but when they left, preoccupied with Andy's summons to work, any thought of leaving one of the phones with me deserted us all. In any case, surely plenty of other people would be only too aware of the crash and would have plenty of phones between them. Sure enough, lights had come on in the Leisure Centre in the distance. Sooner or later, some official rescue body would be sure to show up and I could volunteer any help they thought I could give.

Meanwhile, perhaps I should at least try to get to the crash site, just in case there was something I could do. So I grabbed my torch, found my viaticum and set off into the forest. Finding the crash site did not prove too difficult, despite the dark. It was my nose that guided me at first. A strong, sweet smell of charred pine came drifting through the forest, and after about ten minutes or so I saw the first wisps of smoke. But even as I was beginning to make out a dark shape just ahead, there came a deep rumble. It got louder and louder and, as it reached a crescendo, there came a tremendous explosion and the whole forest seemed to erupt. Terrified, I dived for the cover of the undergrowth. Fiery debris cascaded all round, setting off blazing pockets in the branches of trees and in the undergrowth. There followed three or four other, smaller explosions, but equally frightening to me in the state I was in. All around me small fires were now burning, and glowing or charred lumps were still raining down. I realised the danger I was in and stumbled through the forest back towards my campsite.

I stayed there for what – half an hour? I'm not sure, but as the first grey, pre-dawn light appeared in the sky, I managed to convince myself there would be no more explosions. Tendrils of smoke snaked out from the forest here and there, but mercifully, there was no major fire in evidence. I was a little surprised no boat or canoe had appeared. I found my field glasses and conned the lake. There was some sign of people milling around by the leisure centre, but there was nothing on the lake. I decided to go back again to the crash scene, and set off. With the rapidly increasing daylight I could make out where I was going this time. Things seemed to have quietened down – there was no sign now of the isolated fires I had seen earlier, though a thin smoke haze hung around here and there.

Just as I was approaching the crash site, I caught a familiar, comforting sound in the distance. A helicopter – correction, several helicopters. There was no doubt this was the rescue party. Given the remoteness of the area, I suppose they'd done well to get their act together so soon. I could see them now, coming in low over the lake, the lead chopper hovering near the shore line, confirming the location of the crash site and gauging the best landing spot. This was one of the few parts on the lake that had anything like a beach in the vicinity and inside the next few minutes no fewer than five choppers, all a dull khaki in colour and with no markings, were disgorging men in dark coveralls.

I crouched behind a tree, wondering what to do next. Perhaps I should have approached the rescue team right away, but there was something about their demeanour, the cold efficiency with which they unloaded and checked bits of gear, then formed up in some well-drilled order, that made me hesitate. In any event, they would not get to the crash for fifteen minutes at the earliest, as the forest was particularly dense and they had equipment to bring through. So, instead, I carried on to the crash site and this time was able to get right to the scene of the disaster. As a result of the crash, a clearing had been carved out of the forest, and quite amazingly the craft had fetched up more or less at ground level, wedged between the amputated remains of several large pines. Equally incredibly, the craft seemed to have suffered little or no damage, despite the explosions I'd seen earlier. Perhaps, then, there could be survivors.

I walked slowly around the clearing, studying the scene, and as I did so it became increasingly evident that this was no ordinary air disaster. All I could see was fuselage. Where were wings, engines, tail plane? It slowly registered with me that this was no conventional craft, but something circular, maybe fifteen feet in diameter and about ten feet in height and a dull, silvery-grey in colour. A row of portholes flush with the side of the craft ran part way round low down. Above these portholes was what appeared to be an insignia – two crossed lines in green with a star in red above them. My inspection then revealed the same logo further round the craft on what was clearly its entrance. Again, constructed flush with the side, the door had nevertheless buckled and was now an inch or so ajar. Eddies of smoke trailed from the gap now and then.

As I watched, the door moved slightly, then a little more, and continued moving until it was fully open – or at least as open as it could be, given the slight damage to it. Gouts of smoke (or was some of it steam?) poured from the opening, but after a few moments I dimly discerned a flight of steps, or gangway, issuing from the craft. They touched the ground and a soft "clunk" from the top stair gave evidence that the steps had locked in place. How on Earth could those steps and the mechanism that operated them have come through the crash unscathed? But then, where was the damage to any part of the craft beyond the very slight buckling of the door? And what on Earth was the craft? Clearly, it was not a conventional aircraft. Was it some experimental vehicle, part of a research project that had gone wrong? Or was it a spacecraft from – from where? From – a foreign country? A space vehicle returning to Earth, experiencing technical problems and straying off course? Or was it from ... my mind raced. Dare I put it into words? From – an extraterrestrial source?

Unless some automatic mechanism had caused the steps to descend upon sensing the craft grounding, someone must have operated the mechanism. Therefore, there was someone inside who had survived the crash. One of how many? Surely not many in a relatively small craft. Should I climb up the steps and try to assist any survivors? The shouts from the rescue party were getting nearer, so perhaps I should leave it to them. But the decision was taken from me, for as I stared at the steps and the door they led from, a figure appeared in the doorway, emerging from a thick gout of smoke.

I could make out little at first, but then as he (or was it "she" or even "it" – I'll call him "he" at least for now) came lower down the steps, the smoke blew aside and a figure in startling white was revealed. He positively glowed and seemed to glide down. He wore no helmet, and if he came from a distant planet, he nevertheless seemed perfectly able to survive here, in the atmosphere of Earth. He was about five feet tall, slim and had regular features. His hair was black and his eyes rather larger than those of most people. He carried something in his hand. Surely this person, this man, could not have come from a far-off planet. Weren't they tiny, with large heads and enormous almond eyes and ears flush with the scalp? Was that not the stereotyped "alien" image adopted by all those who portrayed them in science fiction novels or in sensational books about so-called "close encounters" with "aliens." Well, nuts to them! This was my close encounter and it was with an "alien" who looked totally like a modern man from the planet Earth.

And why, I thought, shouldn't he? Surely people, wherever, were made in the same image and likeness as God, and there was no doubt what God looked like – He was like the Son He sent to Earth to redeem our sins. So if this stranger was from an extraterrestrial civilisation, why should he not look like people on Earth, albeit perhaps slightly "modified" by prevailing climate and other conditions on the alien planet?

For some inexplicable reason, I found myself overcome with a sense of joy. Perhaps it was the glow surrounding him. He was a stranger, but, somehow, already a friend. Unbidden, the words from St Paul's Letter to the Hebrews rushed into my mind: "Be not forgetful to entertain strangers, for thereby some have entertained angels, unawares." And that was precisely what this stranger, this alien, presented himself as – an angel, an identity I was to have irrefutably confirmed a little later.

He reached the bottom step, and we both instinctively moved towards each other. He held out whatever he was carrying, indicating, that I was to take it, In fact, it turned out to be a book – or what had once been a book, though, while still substantial, it was now reduced to clumps of pages. There was a good deal of charring, no doubt from the explosions inside the craft, and the fires they must have caused there. He was lucky to have survived. There were also, I then noticed, a few fragments that seemed to be unrelated to the book. I clutched the whole package, fearful of losing any part of it.

He looked at me with his large eyes, smiled and softly whispered something. I could not quite make out what he was saying, so I bent my ear towards his mouth.

"Molly's," he seemed to whisper, "Molly's" – or was it more like "Mollees"?

Was he introducing himself? Was it Molly's or Mollees? "Donald McNulty," I replied.

"Donald McNulty," he said. "Mollees."

Of course. He was referring to Molly's Island, though what its significance could be in the present circumstances I couldn't guess. As I deduced later, I was quite wrong, but these were my thoughts at the time. A sudden idea came to my mind. He had given me the charred remains of a book and a few more bits and pieces. I must return the compliment. All I had to offer was my sheet of Prayers for the Dying, so I handed it to him. The effect was remarkable. He became very animated and, looking round, spied a park notice. I forget what it was – possibly a request to comply with the park rules for the disposal of trash – and pointed to it, then to the sheet of prayers I'd given him. Why had he reacted in that way?

He gave me to understand I was to wait where I was. He quickly turned, went back up the gangway and into the vehicle, then a few moments later returned with another bundle of papers – I'd no idea at the time what they were – which he also thrust into my hand. They were warm, and, like the remnants of the book, had suffered from fire damage.

There was a shout from near at hand, then he bowed, turned abruptly and glided swiftly back to the door. There he paused and waved, then clearly indicated I should quickly leave the area. I saw him re-enter the craft and I moved as fast as I could back towards my tent, and away from the rescue party. The whole "close encounter" had taken no more than five minutes or so.

When I was well away from the crash site, there was another tremendous roar very like the earlier one, and flaming debris began raining down all around me. There was no doubt in my mind that my friend had gone back inside to destroy the control mechanism, perhaps losing his own life in the process, though if he were an angel, that, presumably, would not apply. It was probably standard procedure to ensure that, in the event of a crash, nothing remained intact that was of any use to a salvage party. I heard shouts from the rescuers, including no lack of expletives. I was well out of their way, and I sensed they had had no idea I had been at the crash-site.

I was still clutching the papers Molly/Mollees had given me, and, looking around, I found myself surrounded by charred fragments of one sort or another, mostly tiny, but here and there were what looked to be more parts of the book that I had first been given. Even at that stage, I had already made a distinction in my mind between the book and the other fragments the angelic man had first given me, and the other bundle he went back inside for. It was almost as if I had passed some sort of test and the second batch was the prize. If the rescue party found me and quizzed me on the whole incident, and on whether I had found anything from the craft, I would surrender the pages from the book, but I would not give up the other items, especially the second batch of papers. My friend had clearly felt them to be important, and if he felt that, then they must be. I would want to study them later.

I now had only one thought. I must pack up and return to Ottawa post-haste. I'd listen to news broadcasts and read the newspapers for any hint of what this was all about. I'd also let Andy and Ambrose know what had happened. There appeared to be no damage to Andy's car – there'd been so many explosions and debris raining down, it might well have been in the fall-out zone. The first thing I did was to conceal all the papers except the book first given me below the spare wheel in the boot, then I stowed the book under the passenger seat, having made quite sure, with a splash or two of bottled water, that none of these pages was still smouldering. I then struck camp, tucked the tent into its carrying-bag and loaded all my gear into the boot or on to the back seat. I was soon ready for the return trip. My only regret was that I had not made a photographic record of my recent experiences. Perhaps if the rescue party hadn't arrived so quickly, it might have occurred to me to do so.

I set off along the track that led from the camp-site and turned onto the narrow park road, an old logging track. After a few minutes, I emerged from the forest and encountered several police cars parked and the police themselves in the throes of setting in place road blocks prohibiting further progress towards the area I had just left. A few troops were there, too. One of the police officers waved me down. I was asked to get out of the car. He gave the camping gear a cursory glance and told me to carry on. I thought he might want to question me about what I'd seen but he seemed happy to let me go. I was the only vehicle coming from the crash site, though another that had evidently been approaching from the opposite direction had just been turned back. For some reason the driver stared at me, then sped off. A few miles further on, just before I left the provincial park, I had the shock of my life when the same car, a large red SUV, charged straight out of a side track. I swerved and almost lost control but somehow avoided being clipped, and righted the car. The SUV's actions now were curious: upon slamming on its brakes, the driver executed a perfect sliding 180° turn, then sped back up the track it had appeared from. This struck me as a manoeuvre that would not disgrace the repertoire of a stuntman. There was no merit in trying to pursue the car. I certainly would not catch it. The only thing I remembered seeing was a Blue Jays supporters' sticker in the rear window – the Toronto baseball team. I was shaken, but unharmed, and decided to put the incident out of my mind.

However, after I reached the major highway and was approaching Ottawa, an almost identical incident occurred. A large red SUV hurtled from a side road, this time right in front of me. Again I swerved and avoided a collision, while the SUV executed another pirouette and sped back the way I had come from. A medley of thoughts raced through my mind. The first was that someone was trying to kill me. It was the very same red SUV with the Blue Jays sticker, and its driver had made two attempts on my life. At the same time I almost admired the skill of the other driver. Not only had he managed to scare the life out of me, but had been careful to preserve his own health and safety and, perhaps, mine.

Had these been two "controlled" near-misses? If that were so, what were they intended to achieve beyond frightening me? I got the impression the driver of the SUV was well aware that some incident or other – some sort of air crash – had taken place, but had not succeeded in getting near the scene of the crash before being turned back, whereas I had witnessed the incident. For some reason he wanted to quiz me on it – something he could not do if he killed me. Or perhaps he suspected I had come by something from inside the craft. My problem with these conjectures was that I had no starting point. I did not know how much he knew to begin with, so I had nothing on which to superimpose the later happenings. It was all a mystery, and for now, I must just be glad I was still alive. I offered up thanks for my delivery to Almighty God, to Our Lady and to St Christopher.

I reached Andy's house safely, and was disappointed to find he was not there. "He said he'd definitely be home for dinner tonight," said Chantelle.

"How often is he called in?" I asked.

"Since he retired two years or so ago," she replied reflectively, "a dozen times or so, I suppose. When he is called in though, it tends to be for several days. Anyway, what have you been up to, Donald?"

I briefly outlined my adventures of the last couple of days, though confined the account to an air disaster in the general area of the campsite, mentioning nothing of my "close encounter" or the fragments I had brought back with me. I also played down my experiences on the drive back, not wishing to worry Chantelle with anything dramatic like someone was "targeting" me.

"You've really had quite a terrifying two days, haven't you? Poor Donald," said Chantelle sympathetically. "There's been nothing in the news of an air crash, but from what you said it only happened early this morning and in a pretty remote area."

"Perhaps I'll go and see Ambrose," I said. "I'm sure he'll be interested in what happened."

"I have a splendid idea," said Chantelle. "We were intending to invite Father Ambrose to dinner one day before you went back. Would you like to see if he's free this evening, about seven? You can discuss things with Andy and Ambrose at the same time, and I'm sure there are things you've not mentioned to me that will occur to you. Phone him up, then we can have a bit of lunch, and you can have a shower and a lie down. I'm sure you're ready for one."

It was certainly true that I'd not had a shower that morning. It was also true that I'd missed several hours of sleep, so I nodded gratefully to Chantelle. I then phoned Ambrose and was delighted to find that he was in and that he could get away immediately after the evening Vigil Mass. What a kind and inspired gesture on the part of Chantelle. I carefully stowed all the fragments in my case and gratefully subsided on to my bed.

*****

The dinner was delicious, and the company convivial. I recounted my adventures, this time in a little more detail, and everyone was astounded, though in Andy's case a little sceptical. I mentioned meeting the angel and showed them the fragments of the book he had first given me to gauge their opinion. I kept back the other fragments. I also described the two attempts to run me off the road.

On the crash, both Andy and Ambrose inclined to the idea of an experiment that had gone wrong, originating either in Canada or the US. Andy thought that my "angel," if he were not a figment of a fevered brow, was simply a surviving crew member (who perished in the later

91

explosion) though Ambrose said he would certainly not dismiss the possibly out of hand. "I say to Donald, 'Go with your instincts.' I can well understand experiences involving angels. In the course of a long priesthood I've met several people who claim to have seen and usually to have been helped by one."

Both of them felt that the road incidents could well have been coincidental – you only need one drunk on the road, and until he's stopped he will terrorise many drivers, some of them perhaps repeatedly. As to the book remnants, both agreed the key was to identify the language they were written in if that were possible, though Andy thought they may have been just litter from previous campers that happened to be lying around, and which had somehow got inside the spacecraft and ignited by the fire from the multiple explosions. The occupant was simply returning them to me for disposal. They agreed, however, that whatever had happened was a serious incident that might have a bearing on national security, and Andy suggested reporting what I had seen to the Department of National Defence on Colonel By Drive. They were certain to know about something that involved a search and rescue operation by the military, and might welcome eyewitness accounts of the crash.

"But don't mention anything about your angel or they'll start smelling your breath," he joked.

These then were the immediate thoughts of Ambrose and Andy. I must admit I was disappointed in Andy. For a man of his intellect he was, in my view, far too dismissive, cynical even, of the whole episode. His older brother was, perhaps, losing a few marbles. As I write this I have now had the benefit of a close study of the fragments and have set down my own detailed thoughts in a separate letter, concealed in the presbytery with the fragments. Let me move on.

The next day was Sunday and I again had the privilege of con-celebrating Mass with Ambrose. Andy had again gone into work (a retired government employee working on a Sunday! What on earth was going on?) Ambrose and I collected Chantelle and we ate out at a Fat Albert's. I've always been a pizza fan and I've never found one in England to compare with North American pizzas. Perhaps they skimp with the toppings in England. We then had a leisurely drive around the city, and caught up with Andy in the evening. He looked pretty tired and he soon had us all yawning. An early night was called for.

Next day, I did as Andy had suggested, and visited DND on Colonel By Drive. I explained to the uniformed commissionaire at reception that I wished to report an incident I had observed in the early hours of Saturday in Algonquin Provincial Park, and to offer my services as an eyewitness. After a number of phone calls, I was told that a Major Lebrun would see me. A dapper man in his mid-thirties soon appeared, requested some identification, and then organised a visitor pass for me. He took me up in a lift to the next floor and ushered me into an empty room.

"I see from your passport you are a priest, Father," he said with a smile. "So I think I can be confident that what you are going to tell me was not the result of some drunken orgy. We do get our share of those reports."

"Well, Major, I wouldn't necessarily always rule that out in the case of the Priesthood, though in this case you can."

"What exactly was it you saw, Father?"

I had planned to give a fairly full account of the crash, my meeting with the occupant of the space vehicle, the fragments I had been given and the arrival of the rescue party, but after only a few sentences he held up his hand.

"I know exactly what you're going to say. You saw several helicopters come in low over the lake, land, and discharge a number of men each?"

"Yes. To be precise, five helicopters, and four men from each – a total of twenty."

"I can explain this, though I must ask you not to pass it on. What you witnessed was a search and rescue exercise. A simulation of a real disaster. In these days of terrorist threats, we need to have a cadre of highly trained personnel who can respond rapidly to any terrorist incident, not least air disasters, and search for survivors. I don't know what vehicle was involved in this case, but

93

they have used balloons and radio-controlled drones to simulate an aircraft brought down. Explosive devices are placed on board and explosions follow a crash. Was that what you saw and heard?"

"Very much so, Major, but there was no question of this being a balloon, or even a drone. The vehicle was metal, certainly, but it was circular. There were no wings or tail-plane."

"Technology is very sophisticated these days, Father. Look, please accept what I say. We are not the only country engaged in this sort of training. It's fairly general."

"One thing I haven't told you. I have some documents that were on board the crashed vehicle. Or, rather, fragments. They must have been blown out by the explosions." In view of his negative attitude, I could not bring myself to mention that these had actually been brought from the craft and given to me by someone who was perhaps its sole occupant." On Andy's advice I intended to avoid use of the word "angel," but that was all academic now.

"They will have been there already. On the forest floor. Trippers of all nationalities leave trash all over the place, in spite of the notices to use the trash cans."

I could see further attempts at persuasion would be fruitless, so I thanked the Major, who accompanied me back to reception to hand in my pass, and left the building.

I didn't believe for one minute some of what the Major had said. I was in no doubt that specialist search and rescue teams existed, and that they exercised regularly, but this was not one such exercise. This was not a balloon or a drone. It was something originating far beyond Earth. It was interesting that he had said the fragments were there already, on the ground. Andy had said that, too. Were they singing from the same hymn sheet? It was even more interesting that he had mentioned that all nationalities were guilty of leaving trash around. I had not said the fragments were in a foreign language. I felt more and more that I had been given the standard PR release designed to cover up something the authorities did not wish to make public. The Americans have a phrase for it – "the bum's rush." That's what I'd been given.

I now felt instinctively that I should not tell Andy exactly how my interview with Major Lebrun had gone. I sensed there was a cover-up going on, and that Andy was somehow a part of it. Where exactly did he work, anyway, that he should apparently be in league with DND and part of the same conspiracy of misinformation?

I wandered around the centre of Ottawa, and found myself standing in front of the British High Commission on Elgin Street. On an impulse, I went in and asked if there were a military liaison officer available. I knew they had such a person. In fact, they had a whole staff – the British Defence Liaison Staff. I declined to explain what my visit was about, simply saying it was confidential. I expected to get turned away, but no. After a few minutes a fit-looking fellow in – I would guess – his early thirties came from the upper floor, and invited me into a small room. I pondered. What exactly was it I wanted to report? I didn't want to be seen to be criticising a close ally.

"How can I help you?" he asked pleasantly.

"I'm not sure whether you can, or indeed whether I'm right in even contacting you at all, but the fact is that I was camping in Algonquin last week and in the early hours of Saturday, I witnessed an air crash. It happened close by. Whatever it was, it wasn't a conventional aircraft. There were no wings or tail plane, and it appeared circular."

"And have you reported this to anyone else? The police, for instance?"

"Not the police, but I did report it to someone in DND. They tried to palm me off with some story about a rescue training exercise. Certainly rescue teams arrived by helicopter – five of them, in fact – but it was a real incident they were responding to, not some mock-up or simulation. My curiosity is getting the better of me. As I left the camping site, road blocks were being set up by the police. I wouldn't be surprised if a fully fledged cordon has been imposed by now."

"Look, there's not much I can do here and now to satisfy your curiosity, but leave me your name and a contact number, and I'll see if there's anything I can tell you. Of course, if this turns out to be something that DND for reasons of their own cannot discuss further, I might not be able to help. All countries have information that for one reason or other they regard as confidential and unless they wish to share it, there's nothing we can do." He produced paper and ball-point pen.

"I'm flying home at the end of the week," I said, writing my name and home address.

"Don't worry, if there's anything to tell you, you'll hear one way or the other," he said. He glanced at the piece of paper. "Enjoy the rest of your visit, Father."

"I will, and thank you."

Two days later, when Andy felt able to tear himself away from work, he suggested we go back to the campsite in Algonquin for another couple of days camping. We invited Ambrose along, but with much regret he said he'd have to cry off. Illness in the Deanery and a need to cover other parishes. I recognised that all-too-familiar scenario! So off we went without him. I warned Andy we were probably embarking on a fool's errand and as it turned out, we were. We got only as far as the entrance to Algonquin when we were turned back by a notice advising that the park was closed until further notice. What, the whole park? Yes, was the reply. Something to do with military manoeuvres. This confirmed in my own mind that something far more serious than a search and rescue "exercise" was underway, particularly when I saw a small convoy of those enormous vehicles we used to call "tank transporters" but which, in effect, carry any extra-wide load the army wants shifting. There were no prizes for guessing what they were for in this case.

Later that day, after our return, Andy said he needed to go into work for a couple of hours, while Chantelle had a few groceries to get. I pleaded tiredness, and they were happy for me to retire to my room. Once there, I took the opportunity to look at the fragments the visitor had put in my hand. I had so far looked in any detail only at the pages that all appeared to be related, and which I had shown to Andy and Father Ambrose. These appeared to be part of a reference book. I discovered something we had all missed before – that through the charring on the cover of the book and the first inside page I could faintly make out the same logo I had seen on the space-craft: two green crossed lines with a red star above them.

The other items consisted of a single sheet, some pieces that looked suspiciously like fragments of a map and (the item the occupant had gone back inside for) some pages from what appeared to be a medical publication. I carefully stowed in my case the single sheet and the map fragments, then began comparing the script on the pages from the two books. Yes, it was probably the same orthography, but so what? That's what I expected, wasn't it? After some ten or fifteen minutes, my plea of tiredness began justifying itself and I dozed off. I woke to hear Chantelle singing in the kitchen and realised I'd been asleep for over an hour.

*****

My visit to Ottawa was rapidly drawing to a close, but there was one further episode in this saga I should mention. On the Saturday I'd gone on my own to one of the large shopping malls to buy something as a parting gift for Andy and Chantelle, and after some thought I bought them a set of four limited edition prints. They loved local art, and were very fond of this particular artist's work – in fact I think Chantelle, a former art teacher herself, actually knew him. The prints depicted scenes of the Gatineau, a large expanse of forest and lakes across the river from Ottawa on the Quebec side. When I got back to the house, I tried to smuggle the prints into my room so that I could hide them in my luggage and spring the gift on them as a last-minute surprise. I suppose I was being rather stealthy. Anyway, Andy clearly did not hear my approach and as I entered my room I saw that the pages from what I was calling the reference book, which I had left on the dresser after a further look at them, were now spread out on my bed, and Andy was busy photographing them. I startled him.

"Sorry, Donald," he said with a rueful smile, like a little boy caught with his fingers in the jam pot. "I should have asked. I have a friend who loves curios of this sort, and I'm sure he'd like to examine the script to see if he's come across anything like it before. I'll let you know if he has anything positive to tell me. Do forgive me. I had this sudden thought, and decided to act on it before I forgot. I was planning to tell you."

What could I say? He was my brother, and also my host. Yes, it was discourteous of him to act as he had done, but no damage was done. Wasn't I prepared to hand over my bits and pieces to DND? They had expressed no interest in them, so any keen mind prepared to have a go at the fragments was surely welcome. And, as far as I knew, he had not seen the other fragments. They were concealed in the pocket of my suitcase under the bed. There was no point in making a scene. He and Chantelle had been kindness itself, so I did the sensible thing, and made light of it.

"That's OK, Andy," I said. "Perhaps I should have done the same thing. Photographed them, but I really don't think my digital camera could cope with high resolution pictures of rather charred bits of text."

"I can get you a copy," said Andy. "This is a special camera I borrowed."

"Fine," I said. "So would you like to eat out this lunchtime?"

"I think Chantelle has something prepared," he said. "We could go out this evening if you like."

"I meant to tell you, Ambrose has arranged a farewell do for me with the Deanery." Now it was my turn to feel guilty. I really should have told them, especially Chantelle, that I would be dining out, in case she was planning something elaborate for my last night. I suppose with a bit of guilt on both sides, whatever tension there had been had now diffused itself, and things were back to normal.

The thing I found very odd, though, was the fact that Andy had earlier dismissed the fragments as worthless trash left by trippers, yet its potential interest value had now apparently soared. Whether there really was a friend, or whether Andy was acting on behalf of the "authorities," I had no idea.

Later that day, with Ambrose and his colleagues from the Deanery, I had a wonderful evening. The Dean himself was a jovial man, who reminded me very much of Friar Tuck. When a group of clerics assembles for purely social reasons, they are no different from any other social gathering, as stories were exchanged of some professional mishap or other, or something a parishioner had said or done.

We got on to the subject of current practices in our act of worship. In fact, I told them how impressed I was at some of the innovations to the Mass, which, perhaps, had also been introduced in parts of the UK, but which I had not yet encountered there. In fact, I had been aware of these in Canada for several years now. The most interesting difference was the much more intimate involvement of the Ottawa congregation in the Mass. For example, after the homily, the celebrant would leave the lectern and walk up and down the aisles asking for people's views on what he had said.

A real knockabout debate would often develop. "What did you think, Joe?" Father would ask. "I don't agree one bit with the point you made about..." Joe would reply. This would go on for about ten minutes. The congregation loved it. When I had con-celebrated Mass that first Sunday, I had experienced at first hand this approach. Ambrose had warned me what to expect. In my case it went on for at least fifteen minutes. Ambrose said this was nothing to do with the wisdom of my words. They were just fascinated with my accent, many of them being of Scots ancestry themselves.

Another feature of Mass at Ambrose's church in Ottawa was the complete absence of hymn books. Words were instead projected onto large screens. Also, the bread for the Eucharist was not in the form of small circular wafers, but looked exactly like bread from the bakers. It came in loaves and the Priest broke it by hand. I'm sure it conformed in composition and preparation to the requirements for Holy Communion, but it was interesting to see what could be done.

I avoided talking about the incident in Algonquin, but did raise the question of angels, noting that I had met one, though without specifying where or when. The other priests to a man said they could well believe it, and one said he was deeply envious of me, and surely in this context envy could not be a sin. I'm not sure how the conversation came round to Andy and Chantelle, but at some stage someone asked where Andy worked. I had to admit I didn't know, but that it was in some Government Department. Ambrose surprised me by knowing more that I did. "Andy works for some bunch of initials on Heron Road," he said. "Do you mean the Tilley Building?" asked another priest. "Yes, I think you're right," said Ambrose. "That's the intelligence place," said the other priest. "I think they come under DND." Conversation drifted away then, but that little exchange spoke volumes to me.

Before I left him that evening, Ambrose drew me to one side and said, "I hope you don't mind, but I had a word with the *Ottawa Citizen*, asking them if they were aware of anything odd going on in Algonquin, because apparently the area had been cordoned off. They said there had been rumours of a small aircraft coming down, but as they could get no concrete information on this, as far as they were concerned, there was no story."

*****

And that more or less concluded my holiday. The next day I again con-celebrated Mass with Ambrose and, as Andy had managed at last to spend a day at home, we spent a few hours exploring some of the small lakes in the Gatineau. On the day of my departure my highlight was (you will not believe this) another visit to Fat Albert's (!) with Andy, Chantelle, and Ambrose, who'd managed to escape for an hour or so.

Later, I packed, carefully stowing the fragments from the air crash into the bottom of my suitcase, together with a CD containing a copy of the photographs Andy had taken of the book. I was so pleased to have it as a back-up. Andy drove me to the airport for the overnight flight. I thankfully slept for much of the journey. I should have felt refreshed by my holiday, but such a bewildering and, if I'm honest, at times frightening, chain of events had come my way that I felt I could do with a normal holiday to get over this one. And even when I was back home in my dear presbytery, among my dear parishioners, I was not to be released from the anxiety I continued to feel.

The day after my return, I was paid a visit by a young woman, seeking to buy books, and offering to examine the contents of my bookcases with a professional eye. Many people, she explained, were quite unaware that they might be sitting on rare books that had perhaps been handed down, and which were now quite valuable. I politely declined her offer. There was no reason to suspect this visit was all part of the same saga (someone aware I might have something of interest, or of value, in my possession and attempting to get hold of it). Perhaps I was simply becoming paranoid and ready to view with suspicion anything slightly out of routine. However, early the following week, I had more serious cause to be convinced that I was still being targeted by persons unknown.

I had attended a meeting in the diocesan offices in Bristol and was on my way back to Bourton on the M5, when I overtook a white van crawling along at about 40 mph in the inside lane. No sooner had I overtaken the van than it immediately accelerated, overtook me, then cut sharply in front of me, just touching my wing. It then resumed driving at an even slower rate, barely 30 mph in front of me. I hooted the van, then overtook it again. The van responded in the same way, tearing past me, cutting in, almost nudging me into the hard shoulder, then resuming its crawl. I was more than a little worried by now, but nevertheless overtook the van one more time. Exactly the same thing happened, so I pulled on to the shoulder and allowed the van to get some way ahead, then pulled back into the inside lane. Up ahead was the Stroud exit, so when I saw the van slowly pass the slip road, I took the exit, and came back via Painswick. I arrived home safely, and when I got out of the car, I found I was trembling.

I began this account as and when I could find the time, but that incident with the van lent urgency to the need to finish it. With some relief, I feel I can now close it. I will have to bring someone into my confidence fairly soon, or if these sort of incidents continue I might not survive to do so. As I have been writing this, it has served to confirm the identity of the parishioner I must give it to. I know few details of his former work, but I do know he alone of my parishioners has the right sort of credentials and, should the need arise, surely the right contacts, too.

As to the fragments, I have spent what time I could studying them and will consign them, together with the CD containing photographs of the book, to a "place of concealment" known (these days) only to the builders. Whatever thoughts I have on these fragments will be lodged there with them. I suggest the envelope containing them be opened after some study has been made of the fragments by yourself or your former colleagues. I have also made a suggestion so outrageous that I have arranged for it to be kept separate, but accessible. It will only be relevant if professional scrutiny of the "reference book" fragments in particular yields any conclusions as to their nature. Then I venture to suggest that my wild suggestion could be of immense use as corroboratory evidence. I suggest you hunt it down only if and when you reach any conclusions of your own. I have asked for it to be kept in cold storage indefinitely. Why do I play these silly games of hide and seek? Because I feel under threat and conclusions that might emerge would be explosive. Things simply must not fall into the wrong hands.

God bless you, the recipient of this testament. *Dominus vobiscum.*

Donald McNulty.

CHAPTER 11

Tim breathed a huge sigh. What an adventure! He could now quite believe that Father Mac's stroke had been precipitated by these recent events, particularly the events on the road, and perhaps even more particularly by the realisation that the trail of response had followed him back to the UK. Tim had to assume, then, that the driver of the SUV in Canada, the driver of the white van on the M5, the woman offering to evaluate Father Mac's library, and the two foreigners who had engaged the services of Dave and Kevin for the break-in at the presbytery were all employees of the same paymaster.

Someone, somewhere was orchestrating things – repeated attempts to gain access to information believed to be in the possession of an elderly priest, who had acquired it in Canada and had brought it back home with him. And who did we (the good guys) have pitted against the opposition? Tim had to concede that nobody but he and Father Mac were in full possession of the facts. But then, were there things neither he nor Father Mac could know? For instance, how had the people to whom Father Mac had divulged part or all of his adventures in Canada themselves reacted? Were they part of one or more chains of command that somehow coalesced at some senior point?

Tim was to learn later that Major Lebrun had reported his interview with Father Mac to a superior who liaised regularly with a senior officer at the Sir Leonard Tilley Building, to whom Andy reported and on whose authority he was summoned to the office as a consultant when needed. Tim was also to discover that the pleasant young man he'd spoken to at the British High Commission had spoken to his own boss, an air commodore serving as the Defence Advisor, who in turn had invited to his office a civilian first secretary, with no specific duties attributed to him in the Ottawa diplomatic listing. But all this lay in the future. Tim's immediate task now was to locate the fragments and to do that, he had to speak to Mike McGuire, as the one most likely to know the history of building and maintenance jobs in the presbytery. But not tonight. With a shock he realised it was nearly 11 pm. He had read Father Mac's testament slowly, painfully slowly – there was so much to absorb. Moreover, he found himself constantly referring to maps of one sort or another.

Father Mac

The more Tim thought about the priest's testimony, the more he was struck by another realisation. Father Mac was so badly shaken by the series of events that seemed targeted against him, that he probably rushed to get it down before his health cracked, and might well have finished the account on the very evening before his stroke. What prescience and what courage! A teasing end to the account, though. Why was he so coy about revealing his thoughts on the so-called fragments? What was there about these thoughts that, in his judgement, required a second opinion? And his final greeting "*Dominus vobiscum* – the Lord be with you" – in this day and age was positively quaint.

Tomorrow, Tim had planned to spend the day with Lucy and mama. He must certainly do so, but before he left he would leave his request with Mike to think about.

*****

Pigeons seemed to have taken over not only his own garden, but those of his neighbours. Wherever did they all come from? Only a few years ago, they had mainly blackbirds and starlings in the garden, with smaller numbers of robins, tits, greenfinches, and goldfinches. Green woodpeckers were frequent visitors, too, browsing on the ground for ants' nests, as were the slim and graceful collar doves. But plump wood pigeons, strutting importantly around the lawn, or sampling his vegetable patch, had now become the dominant species, and the most vociferous. Crows nesting in the Douglas firs in the nearby cemetery were pretty noisy, too, though they seldom invaded the garden.

Tim woke early, Father Mac's "testament" still buzzing around in his head. Then, against his will, he lay there listening to the pigeons, hoping he'd doze off for another hour. But no. He found himself listening more and more intently to them, as they carried on their non-stop conversations. One of them would repeat a phrase several times, then sign off with a single syllable. Another pigeon, more distant, would reply with the same phrase and also sign off with a single syllable. He couldn't help comparing their dialogue with a military exchange: "Ludo 2, who are you? Ludo 2, who are you? Ludo 2, who are you? Over." What nonsense filled his head. When he knew further sleep would elude him, he gave in, got up, and tottered into the bathroom.

*****

"I haven't a clue what you're talking about, Tim," said Mike McGuire scratching his head. "I don't know of any – what did Father Mac say? – "place of concealment" whatever that means. Well, I suppose it's pretty obvious what it means, but it sounds – I don't know – rather quaint and archaic. To be honest, I've never done any major work in the presbytery, nothing in the building line. And I don't get involved with stuff like re-wiring, which was the last major job done a few years back, and of course that didn't touch anything structural. Mainly lifting floorboards and replacing them."

"Father Mac was so confident the builders would know what he meant. I assumed that meant you and your Dad. What was the last structural work done, and when?"

"You're going back over twenty years now, not long after Father Mac started here, and, as it happened, Dad and I weren't involved. The firm was, but not us personally. That was Uncle Des. Mum's brother. He was never one of our partners, because he had his own business. We sub-contracted certain jobs out to him and he did the same for us. Uncle Des and his mates were very good with roofs. The presbytery had a leak in one corner of the roof."

"So what did your Uncle Des do to the roof?"

"I don't know in detail. I do seem to remember that he found something a bit odd: the main beam going across the top of the stonework didn't extend all the way to the far gable end. You can see it doesn't, if you look closely from right underneath. I expect he closed off the eaves more securely and replaced any damaged battens and slates. Whatever he did took care of the leak. Do you think this 'place of concealment' might be somewhere up in the roof, then?"

"I've no idea, but I do get the impression that it came to light when some building work or other was done. Father Mac seems to have discussed it with builders, though it now looks as if it was your Uncle Des who stumbled across it. Is he still in business?"

"No," said Mike, "I'm afraid he's in a nursing home and, well ..."

"Very poorly."

"Not physically. Dementia. It's very sad. I don't think it would serve any useful purpose to see him. Frank might be able to help. My cousin. He runs the business now."

"You know, I've met hardly any members of your family, apart from you and your parents, and the kids while they lived here."

"Well, Uncle Des didn't live here in Bourton. He and his family lived out by Stow, far enough away not to see much of them, except on

105

big family occasions, but near enough to get involved in a job here if we needed their help. His wife, Auntie Pat, still lives there. So does Frank and his partner."

"It so happens I'm going out that way today to see Lucy, who's looking after her mother. It wouldn't take much to swing by Frank's house if he'd be willing to see me."

"Oh, I don't think there's any problem there. I'll phone him. If he's not there, he'll have an answer phone with a message giving his mobile number. Hang on a bit."

While Mike went off to phone Frank, Tim considered his exchange with Mike. Nothing startling had come out of their discussion, but Tim felt better informed about the work that had been done to the presbytery. The germ of an idea was beginning to form in his mind.

"I got Trudy, his partner," said Mike, returning from the phone. "She said Frank will be back about six-thirty and will be delighted to meet a friend of mine. How's that for a welcome?"

"Just what I wanted to hear. Thanks for your help, Mike. You've given me something to chew over."

*****

Just as he was leaving, Tim had a phone call from Sister Winifred.

"Donald is being released tomorrow, and moving into my hospice. I've told the General not to waste an ambulance on the journey. I can take Donald there, as long as they're happy that he can travel without a couple of paramedics. I'd like to see him settled in. I told them that if an emergency occurred on the journey, I'm trained to handle it. Surprisingly, they agreed. I thought bureaucracy might defeat me."

"That's great news," said Tim. He thought for a few moments. "I would normally have made sure I visited him today, but I've promised Lucy I'd go over. In fact, you only just caught me. Were you planning on coming back here after your brother is in the hospice, or are you leaving the presbytery for good?"

"That would have been the best solution, but I have to come back because the boiler is being serviced in a couple of days, the one day Norah's away for the day on some family visit. Someone had to make the British workman his cups of tea. I'll go back to the hospice afterwards, taking with me anything else Donald finds he needs. There's a big difference between what he needs for a few days in a

106

hospital and what he needs for a much longer stay in a nursing home, especially as he gets more and more active, as I hope he will."

Tim pondered Sister's words. "Look, because I can't see him today, I'd like to go with you and him to the hospice tomorrow. They won't mind, will they? Then I can chat to him on the way. Better still, why not let me drive? I've a bit more room than a Mini, especially if one of us is an invalid."

"That's fine," said Sister. "To be honest, I'd not too keen on motorways these days, and it takes forever going through Cheltenham, Painswick, and Stroud. And you're right – it might be a bit of a challenge getting Donald into my Mini."

"One other thing. Can't I see to the men doing the boiler? Or Mike MacGuire? Or even Doctor Campbell? There are enough of us here. Or even just let them get on with it."

"No!" she said in a tone that brooked no argument. "I knew you'd say that, but you've all got your lives to get on with. Mike's still working, you've got Lucy away and you need to see her and her mother. I've no doubt the good doctor has plenty of other things to do. And I've told Donald I'd be here. I know that's what he wants. So let's have no more of this nonsense. In any case, I've got to come back here for the Mini."

*****

"Stroke Unit," said Nurse Lynne Bingham, "Father McNulty? You're a concerned parishioner? Yes, he's making good progress. No, he won't be here much longer. He's leaving tomorrow for a hospice. Yes, the Sisters of Perpetual Succour. No, he's not. They have a few beds for priests who are not terminal. Yes, Sister Winifred and Mr Sullivan will be taking him there tomorrow morning after rounds. They can give you further details. No, no, that's quite all right. Bye."

Lynne considered the phone call. It was exactly as she'd read in the papers. The large influx of Poles and other Eastern Europeans, many of them devout Catholics, was certainly being reflected in increased congregations throughout the country. In some Parishes there was now a Mass in Polish.

CHAPTER 12

Tim did not realise as he set off that before the day was out he would be much better informed on where to look for Father Mac's fragments – and he would learn this from a most unlikely source. The weather that day was what would generally be regarded as filthy, but to Tim it was glorious – just the sort of day he used to long for when enduring the searing heat of a foreign visit, or his posting to Washington: heavy drizzle, low scudding, slate-grey cloud, surface water, spray from other vehicles, lights on the whole journey. The day was so typically English, and he felt curiously proud of it! What other country could produce such gloriously foul weather in the height of its summer? The odd storm, yes, but an entire day of wet and total gloom? He also felt elated at the prospect of seeing his beloved Lucy. Over the last week or so he had let himself become preoccupied with the mysterious events surrounding Father Mac's visit to Canada, and had even forgotten the promised evening phone call to her on at least two occasions.

About an hour later, he arrived at mama's bungalow and was soon enjoying a warming coffee. Mama was clearly much better and, in fact, kept urging Lucy to go back with Tim.

"You know I can manage now, dear," she said. But Lucy was having none of it.

"The moment I'm out of your sight, you'll be trying to do some baking. I only left you for an hour yesterday and there was smoke in the kitchen from some culinary disaster."

"You know you like my cakes," said mama, "A bit of the mixture somehow got onto an oven shelf, but the cakes themselves were fine."

"That's as maybe," said Lucy sternly, "but it doesn't excuse the disobedience."

"Steady on, darling," said Tim, the peacemaker. "I think mama knows her limitations. Anyone can spill a bit of mixture."

Lucy opened her mouth to protest, but changed her face into a smile. "Anyway, Tim, what have you been up to? Still busy keeping the parish together?"

"No, my involvement has been pretty minimal. There's a whole bunch of us involved. Between us, we've been to see Father Mac every day. He's actually walking now with a frame. His speech is still a bit slurred, but it's returning. He's moving into Sister Winifred's hospice tomorrow. I said I'd drive down with him and Sister Winifred."

"I'm glad you've kept me posted on his progress. But, you've also mentioned one or two things over the phone I've not really understood. What happened after the break-in? And why did it happen in the first place? You never did tell me. I get the impression there's been a whole raft of things going on you've not really told me about. The odd hint here and there doesn't add up to a cohesive story."

"You're right, of course. Yes, there has been a lot going on. All right, I'll put you completely in the picture." He pointed discreetly at mama and raised an eyebrow. Lucy nodded.

Mama was not a gossip.

"I'm afraid you might find all this a bit boring, mama," he said.

"Nonsense. If there's some sort of mystery involved, I want to know about it," said the old lady. "I love mysteries."

So Tim recounted everything he knew. As he was telling Lucy and mama his story, he felt a tremendous sense of release. He had never so far had to present the whole saga to an audience largely ignorant of all the events contributing to it, and it became a wonderful and unexpected mind-clearing exercise. It served to consolidate in him the general feeling that, so far at least, he was on the right lines – that there was a plan in progress to find out what a simple parish priest had witnessed in Canada and to get from him, by fair means or foul, some unspecified fragments collected there and brought home with him to the UK. And that all might be revealed if only he could locate these fragments, which were clearly somewhere in the presbytery.

"A priest hole," said mama unexpectedly.

"Wh – what did you say?" said Tim in disbelief.

"A priest hole," she repeated. "This 'place of concealment' must be a priest hole."

"Yes," said Lucy. "We had a talk at U3A on old buildings, including some in the Cotswolds. That was very much about priest holes. I forget who the speaker was or where he came from. This was several years ago now. I know we keep records of speakers for a few years to avoid re-booking the same one, but whether we can go back what – four or five years, I've no idea. But I can find out."

"What did he say, this speaker? Can you remember? Did he mention the presbytery?" Tim was trying to contain his excitement.

"Yes," said Lucy, "I'm pretty sure he did. But I can't remember much of what he said, except that the presbytery was build by wealthy wool merchants who were Catholic."

"And, therefore, probably recusants who went in for priest holes," supplied mama helpfully.

"Do you know," said Tim, "I was actually thinking of priest holes, without really knowing much about them. Of course, you used to teach history, mama. I should have come to you before. What's this business about recusants? What were they?"

"Look, let me give you a potted history lesson. When the Pope refused to grant Henry VIII an annulment of his marriage to Catherine of Aragon so that he could marry Anne Boleyn, Henry set himself up as the head of the church in England. He got Parliament to pass an Act of Supremacy that said so. All those in public office or ministers of the church were required to take the Oath of Supremacy, agreeing to regard him as head. His successor was Mary Tudor, a Catholic, and she repealed the law. Then her successor, Elizabeth I, re-instated the Act, extending it to include MPs, academics, and eventually to all Catholics. Those who refused to take the oath were called recusants and could be hanged for treason if they were caught actually practising their faith. Despite this, some of the wealthier Catholics with large houses smuggled priests in to their homes to say mass. The homes were often searched and ingenious ways of protecting the priests were devised. These included hiding places called priest holes. There were also smaller hidey-holes for a priest's vestments and the things used on the altar – like the chalice, ciborium, and paten."

"I really knew all that," said Tim, "but it was tucked away somewhere at the back. Thank you, mama, for the reminder. "Places of concealment. Hmm. Do you know where they built them?"

"Oh, pretty well anywhere suitable. Between walls, in roofs, under floors, even in chimney-breasts. If an intensive search was mounted, perhaps over several days, a priest might starve to death. Some were even baked alive when troops lit a fire. Priests were willing suffer death rather than give themselves up. That would have led to the deaths of members of the family."

"Those were barbaric times," said Tim, "But equally barbaric when a Catholic monarch was in power."

"They were all as bad as each other," said Lucy with a shudder, "and things have not changed much. Some people are still persecuted for their beliefs."

Well," said Tim, "on that sobering thought, where shall we go for lunch? Mama, you choose."

*****

After a tasty pub lunch, Tim, Lucy, and mama spent over an hour in the supermarket in Stow, then insisted on a bit of window-shopping – that typically female pursuit that most men, Tim included, consider one of the most futile ways of spending time that had ever been devised. "If you don't want to buy anything, why bother looking at it?" he groaned. All he could get out of them was, "Men!"

The afternoon slipped by. Amid the gloom, it was practically dark by five o'clock – in June! Back at mama's, Tim found a few jobs to do, had a sandwich and some of mama's famous cakes, then got ready to leave for Frank's house.

"I'm sorry you're not coming back with me, love," said Tim gently.

"So am I," said Lucy, "but the others will take a turn soon. Anyway, I think even I can trust mama not to commit suicide after a couple more weeks. But I do wish she'd move in with us."

"I can hear you plotting," said mama.

"One more fall, mother, and you're moving in with us. Assuming you survive it," said Lucy darkly. "And that's final."

Tim and Lucy clung to each other. They'd been married now for nearly forty years, but still felt the same magic when they embraced. Tim kissed mama on the cheek, and left.

*****

Frank lived just outside Stow, off the Fosse Way. Tim had never properly met him, though when he appeared at the door Tim vaguely recognised him as someone he'd seen up a ladder at the presbytery. He would never have placed Frank in the same family as Mike Mcguire. Unlike Mike, he was small and wiry, with frizzy, sandy hair. His partner, Trudy, was dark and petite. Like so many these days, they were both victims of a failed marriage and had come together quite by chance. Frank and his father, Uncle Des, had been doing a job at the cottage hospital, Trudy was a nurse there, and on one occasion brought them a cup of tea. One glance at her was enough for Frank. The next day, when they broke for lunch, he went inside the building, apparently looking for the gents, but really looking for Trudy. He found her,

111

chatted to her, and extracted from her a promise to meet for a drink. Trudy was going through her divorce and was at a low ebb. The thought of a date with someone new restored confidence in her. Someone still thought her attractive enough to ask her out. And the rest, as they say, was history.

"So what was it you were interested in?" said Frank, after introductions and a bit of polite chat.

Tim explained as best he could. He wasn't really sure what he wanted to know. He had an idea there may have been, or perhaps still was, a priest hole in the roof of the presbytery in Bourton. If that were true, was there some mechanism involved to gain access?

"Let me stop you there," said Frank. "When you say 'priest hole' do you mean what I think you mean? A place where a person could lie in hiding? I have actually seen some of them, but this was years ago when we went on a school trip. I can't say if this fits the description of a priest hole or not, but we had quite a problem getting access to the part of the presbytery roof where there was rain damage. The bedroom ceilings were high and the only way into the roof space was though a trap door in what is now a walk-in wardrobe. It was narrow up there and I had to crawl on my hands and knees to the corner. But before I reached the end of the roof space, I had to get past the remnants of a stone wall. That was quite a squeeze. Good job I'm a bit of a short-arse."

"And what was that partial wall doing there?" asked Tim.

"Well," said Frank, "The only thing I could think of was that it was what was left of a false gable end. It had been mostly demolished, and beyond it the eaves were a little more spacious. I could at least work in a kneeling position. The interesting thing was that the main beam closing the roof off ended at the false gable."

"So how did they keep the rest of the eaves closed?" asked Tim with interest. "The bit beyond the false gable?"

"Well, perhaps they didn't. If this was a hiding place, they'd have wanted to allow plenty of ventilation. It would have been roasting up there on a hot day. So they either left the eaves open or closed them off with something lighter. They might have fixed some sort of soffit, to keep the worst of the weather out, and, in those days, to keep rats out. But all this was four hundred odd years ago. Goodness knows what changes have been made over the centuries. The only evidence we've got for your theory is the false gable."

"But wouldn't anyone searching for a hiding place be immediately suspicious of a main beam that only extended so far?" asked Tim.

"Not necessarily," said Frank. "Remember, the main beam was a complete tree trunk, and in competition with other purchasers, not least the navy, it was not always possible for a builder to get the length of beam he wanted. Many old houses I've seen relied on two smaller beams slotted together, or they simply closed off any surplus eaves with some other arrangement of timber. But that's a detail. I'd suggest the main give away is the extra gable end. And the fact that the far end of the eaves was roomier, because the floor dipped down."

"From what you've said, I'm pretty well convinced it's a priest hole," said Tim. "That's very helpful, Frank, it really is. Thanks a million."

"No problem," said Frank. "We must get together again sometime with cousin Mike."

"We certainly must," said Tim, "especially now that we know you live pretty close to Lucy's mother. Well, thanks again, Frank. I'm sorry to be so boring, Trudy."

"Well, at least stay and have a cup of tea or coffee," she said.

So Tim stayed with them for a while before heading back home in a fine drizzle, and across country roads flooded here and there. He was relieved to get home, and after phoning Lucy to assure her of his safe return, he collapsed into an armchair with a generous measure of Johnny Walker Black, and thought back to his conversation with Frank.

With some surprise, he found himself concluding that, priest hole in the roof or not, he simply could not see Father Mac crawling along under the eaves of the presbytery to deposit a packet on the far side of a mostly demolished gable. Even to get up there would have meant hoisting himself through a trap door. That was the sort of thing a slim, wiry man like Frank could do, but an elderly, rather portly man with a touch of arthritis – no. Tim would certainly investigate the roof in order to put Frank's information to the test but, he had to admit, Father Mac's "fragments" were likely to be lurking somewhere else in the presbytery.

CHAPTER 13

The next morning, Tim arrived early at the presbytery to have a look at the roof before setting off with Sister Winifred to collect Father Mac.

He soon found the bedroom that gave access to the side of the roof he was interested in. There, as Frank had said, was the trap door in the ceiling of a walk-in wardrobe. He noted with some relief that there was a cable coming down from the roof space to a light switch. He soon realised he'd need a set of steps, and found them in Father Mac's garage. He switched on the light, eased the trap door to one side, then with great difficulty he hoisted himself up into the roof space.

Although floor boards had been nailed at intervals above the insulation to assist anyone crawling, Tim's progress was slow and laboured. He found the remnants of the false gable end, but went no further. He could see perfectly well what lay beyond – a step down giving extra height for working (or hiding), and the evidence of Frank's workmanship in repairing the rain damage. Two things seemed clear to him: the end of the roof space could indeed have served as a priest hole; but equally clearly, there was no way Father Mac could have accessed it to dump his fragments.

"How are you getting on, Tim?" asked Sister Winifred from below. "And shall we have a coffee before we set off? We were told 10 a.m."

"Coffee would be grand," said Tim. "And I'll let you know how I've got on when I come down."

*****

"So, you say it probably used to be a priest hole, but Father Mac couldn't get to it." They were both sipping coffee at the kitchen table.

"That about sums it up," said Tim. "He might just conceivably have been able to get up the steps to open the trap door and then hurl his bits and pieces somewhere into the roof space, but how would he ever retrieve them? And in any case there was no package lying around anywhere. I crawled the entire length up to the false gable, and the space beyond was completely empty.

"So it's all been a bit of a let down. Perhaps we should have a word with St Anthony."

"Ah, yes, the patron saint of finding lost things," said Tim. "I'll try Father as well, on the journey."

"That would work out all right," said Sister Winifred. "In his physical condition, he'll need as much leg room as possible, and he'll get more of that in a front seat, where conversation is easier. Shall we go now? It's 9:30-ish."

*****

Father Mac was waiting for them, sitting on his bed. Nurse Bingham quickly materialised by their side.

"He's already graduated from a frame to a stick, but he may well need that for the rest of his time," she said with what Tim could only identify as pride at a job well done, or at having such a co-operative patient. "He's been no trouble. I think he wants to say a few farewells before he leaves."

Father Mac made his way painfully slowly across the ward, a stick in one hand, Sister Winifred on his other arm. He went to several beds and shook hands. Some of those he visited said a few words, and one of them made the sign of the cross. When they got back to his bed to collect his things, Sister Winifred produced from her bag a large box of chocolates, which she gave to Lynne.

"Oh, Sister, you are so kind," she said. "There's really no need for this."

"You deserve every calorie for putting up with him," she said with a broad smile.

"Well, they'll go into the nurses' goody box," said Lynne. "We always share everything."

She went and fetched a wheelchair. "It's policy for the less mobile to use a chair, even on discharge," she said. "By the way, a supply of his medication is in his bag, and a list of everything prescribed is there with it."

They soon got to the car, and managed to get Father Mac comfortable. Tim set off, heading for the M5.

He let the journey get under way a little, before broaching the topic he was burning to raise with the priest. He explained their conviction that there was a priest hole somewhere in the presbytery, and that Father Mac had used it as a place of concealment for the fragments he'd mentioned in his letter. Frank had pretty well confirmed that the

115

secret hiding place was in the roof. Tim himself had seen it and agreed, but had found nothing.

"It didn't surprise me," he said. "You're not the right shape to crawl around inside the roof, Father, and even before this present problem I doubt whether you could have hoisted yourself up there. It needs a slim, agile person. Someone a good bit younger, too."

Father Mac was grinning. "Ess, ess." he said.

"So then, where are these fragments?" It soon became clear that Father Mac was not making any sense with the fractured string of sounds that came out. Tim decided on another tack.

"Tell you what, Father," he said. "I'll ask you some questions, and you say 'Yes' or 'No.' Or, better still, because of the noise of the car and the traffic, perhaps you can raise your left hand for 'Yes' and your right hand for 'No.' Can we manage that?"

"Ess," said Father Mac, with a slight movement of his left hand.

"Right then," said Tim. He collected his thoughts. "Is the hiding place of the fragments in the roof, despite the fact that I failed to find them?"

"That's an awfully complicated question," observed Sister Winifred. "Why not just ask 'Are they in the roof?'"

Tim began to feel annoyed, but swallowed his anger. "Yes, you're right," he said. "Are the fragments in the roof?"

Father Mac struggled to say something, gave up and moved his right hand.

"No. Well, are they in your bedroom?"

Again the right hand moved.

"Are they upstairs at all?"

More right hand movement.

"So they're on the ground floor?"

This time, the left hand fluttered. Tim then went through the various rooms – the kitchen, the dining room, the sitting room, the study… The study. The left hand was again active.

"I should have known," said Tim.

"Give Donald a rest for a while," pleaded Sister. "Take it in easy stages. This interrogation is taking it out of him. You can see."

"I've got to think the next bit out anyway," said Tim.

They drove in silence for a while, then left the M5. Tim needed to concentrate now to get through Stonehouse to Stroud, then on towards Nailsworth.

116

"Let's carry on, Father, shall we?" asked Tim gently. "Now, we got to the study. The fragments are in the study, right?"

The left hand moved.

"Are they in your desk?" Right hand, but Father Mac looked rather puzzled. He tried to speak, but gave up.

"Are they in a book case?" Very unlikely, thought Tim, but I'd better get it out the way. He was right, but again Father Mac looked puzzled. The Priest's puzzlement was itself a puzzle to Tim, but he pressed on.

"Behind a wall?" Operated by some kind of mechanism, like a lever? No, again the right hand.

Where else was it mama had said? Ah, yes, under the floor.

"Under the floor?" Tim held his breath. Father Mac's left hand moved. Tim released his breath.

"So, you're telling me that the things you brought back from Canada are under the floor in your study?"

Again, movement by Father Mac's left hand, accompanied this time by a quiet but distinct, "Ess."

"We're nearly there," said Sister Winifred. "You'd better resume when he's settled in."

"I'm not sure that it's necessary," said Tim thoughtfully. "I mean, the study floor isn't such a huge area. It should be possible to find the precise spot pretty quickly. If not, I'll have to come and ask Father. I plan to visit him once or twice a week, anyway."

"Turn in through those gates just up there on the left," said the nun.

Tim entered the grounds of the hospice. A long gravel drive led to an imposing-looking stone building. Through the windows, as they approached, Tim could see two or three nuns moving about. Two ambulances were parked in the turning circle near the door, one from a nursing home, the other from the ubiquitous Great Western, who operated an NHS franchise over a wide area. Its rear doors were open and a metal ramp extended from them to the ground.

"Look, I'll go in and report our arrival," said Sister Winifred. "And organise a wheelchair for Donald. You two stay here. I won't be long."

She disappeared through the door, and within a very few seconds two men in yellow jackets came out of the hospice with a wheelchair.

"That was quick," said Tim, climbing out of the car to help Father Mac out.

The two paramedics or whatever they were almost lifted Father Mac into the chair and one of them began wheeling him to the door.

Suddenly he made a rapid change in direction and headed for the ambulance with its ramp extended.

"What do you think you're doing?" yelled Tim angrily. "Take him in the..." He got no further as a heavy blow to the head from the second man caused his knees to buckle. He was caught as he fell and dragged up the ramp behind the wheelchair. The two men closed the door, got into the vehicle and made off down the drive.

Sister Winifred came out of the hospice just in time to see an ambulance roaring down the drive, raising a shower of gravel. She saw Tim's car, now empty, and quickly came to the obvious conclusion. Kidnapped!

"Oh, sweet Mother of God," she cried, flying back into the building. She grabbed the phone at reception and keyed in 999.

*****

Leaving the hospice drive, the ambulance turned left and headed south on the A46 towards Bath, gathering speed.

"Not so bloody fast," growled the non-driver. "We don't want to get picked up after getting this far."

"Police always give ambulances quite a bit of leeway," said the driver.

"Only when the bloody siren's on," said the passenger.

They drove on in silence for about ten minutes, then slowed and turned left into a lane. After another mile or so, they pulled into a lay-by, where a large white van was waiting. The two men inside the van got out and opened the double door at the back, while the fake paramedics moved Father Mac down the ramp from the ambulance, then bodily lifted him, wheelchair and all, into the van. Tim was just coming to. The man who had struck him brandished a heavy spanner.

"Make any noise or try to run off, and you'll get this. And not just a light tap like I gave you last time. Now, get in the back of the van, and put your arms behind your back." Tim did as he was told. He felt his arms seized and bound at the wrists with strong nylon rope. A bench ran down one side of the van's interior, and he was forced on to it. His ankles were then also tightly bound.

The van pulled away, while the ambulance stayed where it was. After a while the van, having turned round by a field gate, came back down the lane, passed the ambulance and carried on to the A46. The

118

ambulance followed it a few minutes later, the driver lighting a cigarette.

*****

"Успешно," said the driver of the van.

"Да," replied the other, "Пока всё хорошо. So far so good, as they say here."

"Куда? Обратно?"

"Да, да, домой. И потом, будем искать. Священник нам скажет где искать."

"Если он может говорить Не забудьте, он очень болен."

Father Mac, ill though he was, was surprised at their plan: to go back "home" (wherever that was) then get inside an empty presbytery, relying on him to have told them where to look. They weren't even sure that he could talk, though. That was good news. Well, they'd find that he couldn't! He looked across at Tim, bound hand and foot. He still looked a bit dazed, but could see that Father Mac wanted to tell him something. The priest moved first his left hand, then his right, then his left again. Of course, Father Mac must have been able to understand the conversation. Russian, probably. He'd been an interpreter in his early days, hadn't he? Father must have wanted Tim to ask him questions. Perhaps this could be done discreetly if he could get the volume of his voice just right – loud enough for Father to hear, but without the two men hearing.

"Can you hear me?" whispered Tim.

The left hand fluttered.

"Do you know where they're heading?" asked Tim. Affirmative.

"Bath?" No. "Bristol?" No. Father Mac looked pleadingly at Tim, and tried to twist his neck round.

"What are you trying to tell me?" he whispered. "Wait a minute, do you mean they're not heading south, but in a different direction?" Ah, the left hand. West would mean the Forest of Dean or Wales, while east would mean what? Well, Cirencester, then Oxford, and eventually… London?

"West?" No. It must be London. "East?" Again, the right hand.

"No?" queried Tim, "Then where on Earth… Oh, we're going back to Bourton, and they're going to get in the presbytery, which they know is empty?" The left hand moved. Good God, mused Tim, what a bold move. But, come to think of it, the obvious one. Risky though, when Sister would have alerted the police by now... surely?

*****

Sister Winifred had had some difficulty convincing the police that two men, Father McNulty and Tim Sullivan, had been kidnapped in a hijacked ambulance.

"That would be a most surprising situation, Madam," said the police contact. "But, as you insist, I will alert the patrols. There has to be a first time for everything."

Moments later, a message went out, alerting police patrol cars to look out for ambulances engaged in "unusual behaviour."

Meanwhile, in the ambulance, the driver seemed at a loss. "Where to now?" he asked.

"Get rid of this fucking blood wagon," said the passenger.

"Where can we hide an ambulance?" said the driver petulantly.

"Where the fuck do you think?" said the passenger, "In a fucking hospital, that's where I got it from. Any hospital. They come from all over. I'm amazed how easy it was to borrow one."

*****

The police car, approaching Nailsworth from the north, noted the ambulance heading the other way.

"Well, that looks perfectly normal to me," said the constable driving. "Nothing unusual about their behaviour. We can't just stop every flipping ambulance. We might be putting a patient's life at risk."

They carried on. A few moments later the WPC in the passenger seat said thoughtfully, "Charlie, is it normal for the driver of an ambulance to have a fag in his mouth?"

"Oh, my God," said the constable. "Let's turn and chase the bastard. Report it."

They switched on flasher and siren, did a smart U-turn and raced back towards Stroud, the WPC speaking rapidly to control. As they entered Stroud, the occupants of an ambulance, hidden from view in a housing estate, watched them rush past.

"That was close," said the passenger. "Let's get to Stroud General via the back streets."

"Won't the police be there?" asked the driver, anxiously.

"Probably, but if we just drive in bold as brass, they won't suspect us. After all, if we was villains, we'd be avoiding them, wouldn't we?"

"I hope you're bleedin' right."

It was just as the passenger had predicted. They drove straight up to the reception area, got out and marched into the hospital. There were two other ambulances there and police were questioning two paramedics. It was also fortuitous that another ambulance arrived just in front of the hijackers. This threw the police into a quandary. They seemed uncertain in what order to deal with the vehicles. The two bogus paramedics went into a gents, divested themselves of their yellow jackets, threw them into an empty cubicle, and left the hospital through another exit, wearing jeans and sweaters.

Out on the street, the passenger said, "OK, I'll call Sid now. He should be circling around near here." Two minutes later, they were in a car and heading off to safety.

*****

Meanwhile, Sister Winifred was not idle. She phoned the presbytery. Norah was not there but she got her at home. The nun quickly explained what had happened, and asked for Doctor Campbell's number. Again she explained what had happened, leaving him to decide what to do. His first action was to contact Norah.

"In a wee while they'll be back at the presbytery," he said, "I'll tell the police. I know Sister Winifred has spoken to the local police where she is, but she won't have wasted precious time discussing with them all that's gone on at this end. Her priority will have been to alert them to a kidnap. I can try to persuade Cheltenham that it's all connected. We really need to keep the presbytery under permanent surveillance. Ideally, the police should do that, but they may not be convinced. Do you happen to know the incident number?"

"Sorry," said Norah. "I think only Sister Winifred and Tim knew it."

"Never mind," said the doctor, ringing off. He phoned the police.

*****

The constable in the incident room scratched his head.

"To be honest, Sarge, he sounded perfectly genuine, but that's how a fruit and nut case often does sound. I suppose we'd better humour

121

Father Mac

him. He may even be right. He claims to be the former Head of Practice at Bourton Medical Centre."

"A priest and another man kidnapped? By ambulance? Stroud reported something like that possibly underway. And there was a report from Great Western that one of their ambulances had gone missing from somewhere down that way, nearer Bristol. Yes, I like it. Something's going on. Of course, we don't know where they're heading. They could be lying low. I think we need a bit more info yet."

"He seems to think they're heading this way. In fact, he requested – no, he demanded – full-time surveillance of the presbytery in Bourton. Said it was broken into a couple of weeks ago by two yobs in the pay of foreign agents, who appeared to be after something valuable hidden there and that all this is connected. I mean, all that's missing is a beautiful female spy and a bit of seduction."

The constable was unaware that there was a bedroom scene, yet to come.

CHAPTER 14

The white van left the M5 at Tewkesbury, picked up the Stow road and eventually took a minor road through a number of picturesque Cotswold villages to Lower Stanford. The van stopped at a cottage far enough beyond the village to be effectively isolated from it. A dark BMW was parked outside.

The van reversed up a short concrete drive and into a garage. When about half the vehicle was inside, the driver switched off the ignition, and went round to the rear, undid the doors and pulled the ramp down. As soon as it touched the floor, Father Mac propelled the wheelchair towards him. It gathered speed on the ramp and caught the driver full on the chest, knocking him into a load of garden tools propped against the wall. He ended up in the midst of them, the wheelchair with Father Mac still inside landing heavily upon him. Big and strong though the driver was, he was clearly hurt. For his part, Father Mac began making an unearthly wailing noise. The passenger stormed round the side of the van.

"Дурак!" he screamed. "Ты ушибил старика! You've killed the old man."

Father Mac continued sobbing.

"Get up!" shouted the passenger. Father Mac shook his head.

"Don't be stupid," said Tim. "How can he get up? He could barely walk before. Now, he probably won't be able to walk at all. You've set his recovery back months, if not years."

He looked at Father Mac with concern and affection, and to his surprise he saw one eyelid move very slightly downward, then back up. This could, of course, have been no more than an involuntary movement.

"I'll set his recovery back permanently if he doesn't tell me what I need to know. Help me get him into the house. Try anything stupid and the old man will suffer."

The bonds round Tim's feet and wrists were removed and he and the passenger got Father Mac out of the wheelchair and half dragged, half carried him into the cottage, while the driver was left to extricate himself from the tools and wheelchair. He then limped painfully after them. Once in the cottage, however, his spirits recovered. Hovering in the kitchen was a young woman, probably in her mid-twenties. She had startlingly blue eyes, fair hair and a figure men would look at twice – women, too, probably, from envy. Altogether, a beauty.

"Мария, моя красавица," said the driver. "как поживаешь? How are you, my little pretty one?"

The girl ignored him and looked instead at the passenger, fear in her eyes. "I've made some soup and sandwiches, like you said, Stepan. And there's fresh fruit or yoghurt. You said the priest must eat straight away or he may collapse, because he's diabetic. I hope Feliks isn't in pain."

"Хорошо. И потом начнётся допрос," said the passenger.

Tim thought: Thank God they're going to feed us, even though it's only a snack. Father Mac will need to eat, as the girl said. They don't want a diabetic hypo on their hands if they're hoping to question him. Tim had once witnessed the distressing sight of Father Mac having a hypo. He'd gone too long without food, his blood sugar had dropped sharply and he'd had no emergency supply of sugar with him – normally a chocolate bar. Clever of the girl to tell us their names. Perhaps she will turn out to be an ally.

Father Mac thought: Thank God they're feeding us. I was beginning to feel a bit wobbly. I don't fancy this interrogation he said they've got planned for later. No doubt they want to find out where the fragments are. Good job I can barely speak. I'll make sure they think I can't speak at all. And there's that girl again. The one that was asking about my books. I knew she was working for them.

"That girl" thought: Poor old man. Look how ill he is, and his mouth twisted like that. I hope they won't hurt him, but I'm afraid they will. I wish I could escape and get help. I'm stuck with helping them, though. They said my parents would suffer considerable pain if I didn't." Her name was Mary, but they always Russified it to Maria.

Mary had been working as a receptionist in a prestigious hotel in Broadway. One of the guests had become friendly with her, wined and dined her a few times and impressed her immensely with his good looks and charming, urbane manner. His name was Stepan and his English was excellent. He said he was a businessman, with wide interests, one of which involved acquiring British antiques for the overseas market. They became lovers, then he asked her to become his secretary. For a couple of months all went well. It was only later when some of his activities were clearly more than a little dubious in their legality that she became concerned. Elderly people had been targeted,

124

and some had suffered physical violence. She told him she wanted no further part in his life. It was then that he had mentioned her parents. He knew exactly where they lived and told her how he could make things very unpleasant for them. Now, for this latest venture, she was keeping house for him, and desperate to rid herself of him. And as for that associate of his, Feliks… She shuddered. Built like a bouncer, he was essentially Stepan's minder and enforcer. He was always leering at her.

"Мария любимая, водка!" Feliks shouted at her. "Vodka, my love. I have some pain."

Stepan grabbed the phone and punched some numbers. "Миша," he said softly. "Слушай. У нас есть священник… в церковь, чтобы искать документы В случае моей неудачи, то… Tim Sullivan… Его адрес…"

Father Mac strained to hear what Stepan was saying, but could only make out the rough drift of it. He appeared to be speaking to another accomplice, Misha. He (Stepan) was going to the church to look for the "documents." If he was unsuccessful… Then Stepan ended with giving Misha Tim's name and address. So, there was another of them in the team, who might be needed as a back-up. It sounded as if Misha was somewhere in the area. Father Mac wondered how he could warn Tim.

At lunch, Tim helped Father Mac to eat, aware that the man they now knew as Stepan was nursing a gun in his lap. After lunch, things got serious. They left the girl washing the dishes and moved upstairs into a small bedroom, Stepan and Feliks manhandling Father Mac up the stairs. There they tied Tim to a chair and lifted Father Mac on to an old-fashioned iron bedstead. They then stretched him out, secured his hands and feet to the bed posts, and passed one length of rope across his waist and under the bed. A second length was passed under his chin and under the bed. He was totally immobilised. Stepan looked upon the scene with satisfaction. Feliks, who had gone back for his glass and the vodka bottle, poured another refill to follow the two or three he had had with lunch. More than half the bottle was now gone, but this did not seem to affect him.

Stepan leant over Father Mac and said, "As they say in the American movies: no more Mr Nice Guy. We know you were in Canada a few weeks ago, and that you witnessed some incident involving an unidentified craft that crashed and exploded. You recovered some documents from the craft and brought them back to England – to your home, in fact. We want those documents. We want them so badly we will cause you extreme pain if you do not tell us where they are. I had hoped to take you to your presbytery to point out their hiding place to me. But I accept that you cannot walk at all following that mishap in the garage, and I can't carry you into the presbytery. It would be noticed. I know you were the cause of that mayhem, and Feliks is longing for revenge. I know you can communicate to some extent. So you'd better summon up all your skill. If you don't answer me we will hurt you – badly. And perhaps we will hurt your friend here, Mr Sullivan, too. Now, old man, where are those documents?"

Father Mac appeared to try hard to speak, but only gibberish emerged. Stepan nodded to Feliks, who stepped up to the bed and smashed his forearm into Father Mac's face. Father Mac made a small whimpering sound, then spat out blood and a denture. A blow from the other forearm followed, this time a little higher. Father Mac's head snapped back and he began bleeding from the nose, which was probably broken.

"What the hell do you think you're doing?" screamed Tim. "Whatever ability he might have had to speak has now been totally destroyed. This is just wanton injury."

"It may seem crude, but it is actually very scientific. See. He has been hurt a bit, but has not lost consciousness. But perhaps you're right," said Stepan. "We'll speak to you instead. What do you know about the documents?"

Tim was in a dilemma. For the sake of Father Mac, he wanted to appear to be helpful, yet not give anything useful away. "You're right," he said. "I have heard that some sort of papers exist, but I've no idea where. We'd just got to the stage where we found out that centuries ago during the days of Catholic persecution, hiding places for Priests were built into some houses. We think the presbytery may have been one of those houses. That's as far as we've got."

"Fool!" roared Stepan, "That tells me nothing. Why are you giving me a history lesson when you've spoken to the man who knows. He must have told you."

"He can't say anything. He might as well be dumb."

"Can't speak, eh," said Stepan menacingly. "We'll see. Feliks, get Maria."

Feliks grinned, and left the room. He returned holding a frightened Mary round the waist.

"Do you like women, old man? A lot of priests do, don't they? Some get into trouble. Maria will show you the sort of things you've been missing. Maria, show the old man your titties."

The girl made no move.

"Do it now," Stepan said gently, "or someone will suffer. Let me see, who will it be this time? Ah, yes, Mr Sullivan. Maria, do as I tell you or Mr Sullivan will suffer. Move!" he roared.

Maria unbuttoned her cardigan. She had a white blouse on underneath. A tear escaped her eye as she began undoing it. She removed it.

"И бюстгальтер," said Feliks, breathing heavily. "Снимай бюстгальтер. Take off your bra."

Maria did as she was bid.

"Now lean over the old man's face," leered Stepan. "Let him enjoy himself."

Maria leant over Father Mac, weeping. Her breasts brushed his face. "Forgive me, Father," she sobbed. "Oh, forgive me, forgive me."

Father Mac was muttering something unintelligible, the blood dribbling freely from his mouth and nose. He carried on muttering, non-stop.

Stepan said in triumph, "You're speaking, old man, or very nearly so. What are you mumbling? Are you telling us where the papers are? You'd better speak more clearly, or it will get worse for Maria."

Tim knew perfectly well what Father Mac was mumbling. He even imagined he heard the word 'Mary' several times, but then he knew when to expect it. Father was praying to Jesus and to Our Lady.

"Может быть он предпочитает мальчиков," grinned Feliks.

No, thought Father Mac, I don't prefer little boys, though sadly many priests had brought shame on the Church with their actions. If people were into labels, then he was certainly heterosexual, but equally he was abstinent and had been since he was called. That poor child, being humiliated by that wicked man.

Stepan said, "I can't understand that nonsense you're mumbling, you stupid old man. Right. Maria, put your hands on your head. Now stand there perfectly still." Mary did as instructed.

Reaching down, Stepan took hold of the hem of Maria's skirt with both hands and lifted it up to her head.

"What gorgeous legs, eh Father? And what pretty little knickers. She is such a beautiful blonde, isn't she? But is she a blonde all over? That's why gentlemen prefer blondes. They love the challenge of

127

finding out. I'm lucky. I already know. But no-one else here knows. Feliks will have great enjoyment finding out. Feliks, remove them, please. Then you can have her."

Feliks licked his lips and moved towards the girl.

"Under the floor in the study," said a voice. Stepan looked at Tim. "I said under the floor in the study. I've not had time to look myself. I only found out today, but it should be easy to spot. Let the girl be."

Stepan said, "Put your skirt down, Maria. Move away, Feliks. Yes, I know you want her. You can have her when I'm gone. I must go now before the police get there before me. God help you, Mr Sullivan, and the old man if I don't find anything."

He tore out of the bedroom and went out through the garage, pausing only to pick up a tool kit. He jumped into the BMW and raced off.

*****

Doctor Campbell sighed with relief. He'd been trying unsuccessfully to get hold of Mike McGuire, who was working at a building site, converting a barn into a holiday cottage. At last he got him.

He quickly explained what had happened. "And God knows where Father Mac is now. He's got Tim with him, but at least Sister Winifred is safe. They'll be trying to get from Father the hiding place of those fragments. Trouble is, Father can't really talk intelligibly, and as far as I know Tim doesn't know precisely. These foreigners may hurt them both out of sheer frustration. Whether or not they find out, they're sure to come to the presbytery to look. I've reported all this to the police but I don't know if I convinced them to come here. I think our best course of action is for one or more of us to wait quietly in the presbytery while someone else tries to find out what the police are up to. I don't know how many parishioners to try to get involved in this. Anyway, you're the one with the keys, so I hope you can get here quickly."

"No problem," said Mike. "I'm on my way. Look, you wait near the presbytery in any case, and keep it under surveillance. Say, behind the car park wall. I'll be about ten minutes."

*****

Sister Winifred had found herself in a quandary for the first hour or so after the kidnapping. She was reduced to pacing up and down the corridors, thinking out every possible course of action. And there were several. She could just wait for things to happen, and be told later that all was well. But Sister Winifred was someone who wanted to make things happen herself. She was not a passive person. She was an active one. She could, of course, be both passive and active, if she spent the time in the little chapel in the convent. Prayer was a positive force that could make things happen, God willing. That was part of the problem. Was God really willing? Of course He was, she reasoned. But she must certainly not tell him exactly what she wanted to happen. His will should be done. Oh, but I hope it coincides with my will, she thought. Eventually, she paid a brief visit to the chapel, simply to ask for guidance.

Her prayer had been answered. Suddenly, the most extreme of the many possible courses of action became the only one that made sense. Whatever they'd done with Donald, they'd want him much nearer Bourton. He wouldn't be coming back here to the hospice until he'd been found. And Tim would be helpless without his car, when he was finally released. She could do nothing herself at the hospice that would contribute to a speedy and favourable outcome. So she must also get nearer the action. Ergo, she would drive Tim's car back to the presbytery. She had the keys, which Tim had left in the car when he and Father Mac had been kidnapped. She wasn't familiar with all the controls in his car, nor was she used to driving such a large car, but as long as she could move through the gears correctly and give stationary cars a wide berth when overtaking them, she should be OK.

She had found Sister Matron and told her the plan. Sister Matron had agreed, adding, "Our prayers will go with you." Sister Winifred climbed into the car, familiarised herself with the controls as best she could, and set off. She had soon realised it served little purpose to signal her intention to overtake a stationary car by turning the windscreen wipers on, but, having corrected that little error, it had been plain sailing, and as she now left the motorway at the Cheltenham exit, she wondered what awaited her at the presbytery. She only wished she'd thought of her plan earlier and told Doctor Campbell.

*****

Meanwhile, at the cottage in Lower Stanford, Feliks was weaving an uncertain passage through the bedrooms, looking for Mary, who had taken advantage of Stepan's departure to disappear into the bathroom and button up her blouse and cardigan.

"Приди сюда, пизда!" he roared. "Come here, you slut!"

When she sensed he was not nearby, she crept out of the bathroom, went into the small bedroom where Father Mac and Tim were still tied up, found Feliks's vodka bottle and took up station at the top of the stairs.

"Feliks, my big, strong man, come here. We must have a drink before anything else. See, I have your bottle here." The bottle was almost empty.

Feliks lurched after the voice, and found Mary. He grinned at her, drooling spittle out of the side of his mouth. As he reached for the bottle, Mary stepped back, swung the bottle, and caught Feliks a resounding blow behind the ear. As he teetered at the top of the stairs, she gave a push, and sent him headfirst down the stairs to land in a crumpled heap at the bottom.

Mary went down to the kitchen, stepping over Feliks on the way, grabbed a sharp knife, then went back up to the small bedroom. She quickly cut the ropes securing Tim and Father Mac.

"Nicely done!" said Tim gratefully. "By the way, where are we?"

"Just outside a small village called Lower Stanford. We must get away," she said. "I'll look for the keys to the van."

"Lower Stanford is only about four or five miles from Bourton. I must make a few phone calls, but first I'll try and get this nasty piece of goods into a chair and tie him up," said Tim. "I can barely move him. I'll need your help, Mary, before you look for the keys." The two of them finally got Feliks into a kitchen chair, and Tim bound him securely. While he was doing this, Mary searched Feliks's pockets.

No keys.

After several minutes, both Tim and Mary were sighing in frustration.

"I can't find them anywhere," said Mary. "Stepan must have both sets with him."

"Where is everyone?" said Tim, waving the phone around. "I can't get Doc Campbell or Mike McGuire. Mike's probably working. Norah's not at home. I know you don't know these people, but we need to inform someone that Stepan's on his way. In fact, he must be nearly there by now. Look, I've got an idea. When we first arrived we backed up into the garage, and after Feliks had opened the back of the van and let the ramp down the wheelchair knocked him over. I'm sure Stepan

130

then came storming round to the back of the van, too, helped get Father Mac on his feet, then carried straight on into the cottage. I'll bet the keys are in the ignition."

He went into the garage, skirting round the wheelchair, which lay on its side near the back of the vehicle. He climbed in at the driver's side and checked the ignition. The keys were not there. Another idea dawned. He got on his knees and groped around under the pedals. Success. The keys had fallen onto the floor and had somehow ended up under the clutch pedal.

"Now, it's just a small matter of getting Father Mac in," said Tim thoughtfully.

Between them they steered Father Mac down the stairs, though the kitchen, and into the garage.

His face was a mess, and he was not fully conscious. Tim soaked a clean towel under the tap and held it to Father Mac's face.

"I'm afraid that will have to do until we can get him proper medical treatment," said Tim.

"We'll never get him back into the wheelchair," said Mary. "And I can't see him sitting in the front. Why don't I sit in the back with him and hold him. There's a bench there. Perhaps I can keep that towel on him."

There seemed no better solution and, in fact, things worked out well. Just before they left, Tim had another look at Feliks. He was still out to the world. While in the house, on impulse Tim quickly put a call through to Bob. He simply told him a probable agent of a foreign power was even now breaking into the presbytery in Bourton to seek and steal documents that might contain information of great value to that foreign power. He hoped the police had things in hand, but he couldn't rely on it. This was the same story he'd told him about earlier, but things had moved on considerably. Oh, and one last thing: for God's sake, please, please, trust him. He rang off, and made for the van.

*****

The police had given up on any further updates. A car had finally left Cheltenham and was now heading out of the town towards the hill that led to Bourton. Sergeant Pierce and WPC Henderson were inside.

"Assuming this is not a wild goose chase, I don't really expect any trouble. Foreign agent, indeed. That's a laugh. Things like that don't happen in the Cotswolds, though that report of the kidnapping seems to have been confirmed. There's lots of loose ends here. Perhaps it's as well we're the only ones involved in trying to tie them all up."

*****

Stepan was entering Bourton on a warm, pleasant June afternoon. He'd have much preferred to break into the presbytery after dark, despite the need for a torch, because more people tended to be in their homes after dark. But things had not gone according to plan. Bright daylight might have some advantages. He should be able to move more quickly, and he would certainly need to do that. He had no doubts about his skill as a burglar, but would the hiding-place be totally obvious? Under the floor in the study. What was the floor like? Probably carpeted, in which case he'd have to rip it away to get at the floor. Presumably, if there were floorboards, the one that concealed a hiding place would stand out like a sore thumb. He smiled, proud of his knowledge of English idioms.

He parked a little way from the presbytery, and not glancing around walked straight up the drive to the door as if he had every right to do so. No-one appeared to have noticed him, or if they had they did not see fit to challenge him. So far, so good. He studied the lock, selected an implement from his tool kit and was inside in less than a minute – still, he believed, undetected.

*****

Stepan's progress had, in fact, not gone unnoticed. Doctor Campbell, behind the wall, had observed his arrival and entry into the building. Shortly after this, he heard the noise of a car approaching slowly – indeed more than one car. Was that Mike? The two cars followed each other into the church car park. The good doctor's cover was not quite blown. The car park was L-shaped and he slipped round the corner of the wall, as the first of the two cars entered. He sighed with relief when he saw it was a police vehicle. He sighed with even more relief when he saw the other car was Tim's, though to his amazement out stepped Sister Winifred. She marched straight over to the Police car, as the occupants were climbing out.

"Have you found him yet?" she demanded.

"Look, Madam, you're interrupting important police work. Please go away."

"The mode of address is Sister, young man, not Madam. Do you think I run a brothel? Where is my brother?"

"Please, Sister," said the sergeant wearily. "Kindly move on. We have reason to think a dangerous man may be inside, and he's unlikely to be your brother." A shadow of doubt passed over his face.

"Isn't he?"

WPC Henderson grabbed the sergeant's arm. "Sarge, this is the nun I interviewed about the robbery here. Her brother is the priest. Presumably the one reported kidnapped."

"Well done, young lady," said Sister Winifred. "I reported the whole incident, though not to you. To your colleagues in Stroud or Nailsworth. Now where is he?"

Just then, Doctor Campbell decided to show himself.

"He's inside the presbytery."

Sister Winifred said, "I must go to him." She made to move. The Sergeant grabbed her.

"Look, Sister, you stay around but don't get in our way. He may be armed."

"Donald? Armed? He's a man of God, for ... for ... God's sake!"

"Sergeant," said Doctor Campbell. "There's been some confusion. The man you're after, the foreign agent or whatever he is, is inside the presbytery. I've been keeping the building under surveillance until you turned up. Mike McGuire is on his way with the keys. Then you can arrest him. Not Mike, I mean the foreign agent."

Just then another car drew up in the road outside. Two men were inside. One of them got out.

"Where is he?" he asked gently.

"Why do you want to know?" asked Sergeant Pierce suspiciously. "Ah, you're in it with him, aren't you? Henderson, you'd better request reinforcements."

"I think you'll find we're on the same side," said the man, showing a badge. His colleague did likewise.

"We're waiting for Mike McGuire to arrive with the keys," said Doctor Campbell helpfully, "I wish he'd hurry up. There's quite a queue forming."

"Oh, I don't think keys are a problem," said one of the new arrivals. "My colleague and I can be in there in seconds, as our friend obviously did."

Another car turned into the car park. At last. Mike McGuire.

133

CHAPTER 15

Inside the presbytery, Stepan was busy tearing up the carpet in what was clearly Father Mac's study. He was vaguely aware of the odd car passing, but a quick glance outside told him he had not been detected. The view from one of the rooms which overlooked the church car park would have told him differently. The last of the carpet yielded to his tug. He surveyed the floor. Yes, that floor board definitely looked newer that the rest. He searched inside his tool kit.

*****

"Let's go in and get him," said Sergeant Pierce. "Sister, how many ways are there in and out?"

"Just the front and back doors. Unless he jumps through a window into the garden."

"Subject to any views these gentlemen may have," he said, indicating the two strangers, "I propose to enter through the back door and make the arrest. If he eludes me and attempts to escape, I want you – Mr McGuire, was it? – I want you by the back door. You're as big as the rest of us put together. Perhaps one of you gentlemen could be by the front door with WPC Henderson, and your colleague in the garden. When the target has been captured, I'll blow my whistle. You, sister, please stay away from the house."

"I only want to know where Donald is," she said fiercely.

She didn't have long to wait. As everyone else took up station, a dirty white van drew up. Tim said to Mary, "You stay inside with Father Mac, while I go and see what's happening. In case our friend Stepan appears, I'm going to lock you both inside." He climbed out of the van and approached the house, but before he reached the door, an elderly nun flung herself at him.

"Where is he? Where's Donald?" she implored.

"He's here with me. There's a girl looking after him. I've locked them in the van. One of the Russians drove here to break in and find the documents. What's happening here? There seem to be quite a few people around."

"They've gone in to arrest him. How is Donald?"

"Not too good, I'm afraid. They roughed him up a bit, on his face. He may have a broken nose. He passed out on the way here, but he's just about conscious now. I'll let you into the van, but I'll lock you in, too. And be kind to the girl. The Russians made her work for them, but she's very much on our side." Tim walked back to the van, unlocked it and let Sister Winifred in.

*****

One further pair of eyes had been witnessing the mass arrivals at the presbytery. Quite by chance, Brian Jenkins had decided to have another go at speaking to Norah, and not finding her at home, carried on to the presbytery just in case she was there. He arrived there just as Stepan came tearing out, only to run straight into the solid arms of Mike McGuire, who held him in a bear hug. Sergeant Pierce, hot on Stepan's heels, quickly put the cuffs on, then blew a whistle. Everyone re-assembled by the back door of the presbytery. Jenkins kept his distance, but remained within earshot.

"Well, well," said one of the strangers, "if it isn't our friend Stepan. How are all those ladies in your life? What a lucky fellow you, are. And where is that pet gorilla you keep company with?"

"He's dead drunk and tied up in a place called Forge Cottage near Lower Stanford. By the way, I'm Tim Sullivan. I drove Father McNulty and Sister Winifred down to the hospice just past Nailsworth this morning, and when sister went in to report our arrival, Father Mac and I were kidnapped and put into an ambulance, which then rendezvoused with a BMW with Stepan and Feliks inside. That's the car just up the road there."

"Yes, we're up to speed on all that," replied one of the men, "And, of course, we know all about you."

"Anyway," continued Tim, "they took us to Lower Stanford, tied us up and hurt Father Mac quite badly. Look, it's urgent that Father Mac gets to hospital. He's already blacked out once from his injuries. I've phoned for an ambulance. Sergeant, could you and your WPC take a quick look at him before he's whisked away. And you two gentlemen, too, if you wish. I assume you're Special Branch."

They nodded and Tim opened the back of the van, noticing that a little crowd had formed in the road. At the front stood Norah and Megan Campbell. Brian Jenkins was not among them. This was not the time to risk being recognised by Norah, so he had nipped into the drive next door, and taken up a position in the shrubbery where, as it happened, he could hear every word clearly. His pencil had flown over the paper. Thank God for shorthand. To think it was still one of many options on the syllabus!

Another spectator in the little crowd was also making notes – mental notes in his case. Misha could see now that he'd have a much more active role to play to guarantee a successful outcome to their mission.

Sergeant Pierce leant inside the ambulance. "Oh, my God," he said, "what have they done to him? Henderson, please give HQ a brief preliminary report. Tell them one of the foreign gentlemen is on his way. And ask them to get a car out to Lower Stanford for the other one. Forge Cottage."

"I have the keys," said Mary, quickly producing them.

"I should have explained," said Tim, "Mary was working for Stepan, under duress, as a housekeeper. They threatened to hurt her parents."

"Mr Sullivan, I'd like you to call in at HQ and make a statement. And you, Sister."

"I'm not doing a thing until I see Donald safely in hospital," said Sister Winifred with feeling.

"I understand, Sister, but come as soon as practicable. Now I'm going to get our friend here safely out of the way." He pushed Stepan into the rear seat of his car and climbed in after him. WPC Henderson stood by the car as she finished on the phone, then took the driver's seat and moved off.

"Thanks for coming so soon," said Tim to the two strangers, "All's well that ends well."

"Maybe, Mr Sullivan, but that begs the question – what was he after, and did he find it?"

That was a difficult one. Whatever happened, he didn't want to forfeit the chance of being the first to study Father Mac's fragments, after Father Mac himself, of course. Father Mac had asked him to do so. But at the same time, he had no wish to dissemble, especially after all the help Bob had been instrumental in laying on. He'd better steer a middle course, while sticking to the truth.

"To be honest, I don't know precisely what he was after. Father McNulty had come by some fragments of debris after some sort of air crash in Canada, where he was on holiday. For some reason, Stepan, or more likely the people who had hired him, thought that these bits and pieces were valuable, and also that Father had brought them back and hidden them in the presbytery. I've no idea what they were, and I've never seen them. All I can say is that if they are in the presbytery, Father McNulty is in no condition to lead us to them."

"Fair enough," said one, "But please let us know, through your contact, if you find them. Oh, yes, we do know you have a friend somewhere – not surprising given where you worked. That's why we're here, as you well know. It may be that someone will contact you, anyway. Here comes the ambulance. By the way, we'd like a quick word with the young lady, if only to see if a longer interview might be helpful. She probably knows our Russian friends as well as anyone."

Sister Winifred and Mary climbed out of the van and, as the paramedics transferred Father Mac to the ambulance, Tim led Mary over to the two Special Branch officers. She climbed into their car. Tim joined Norah and Megan and spoke to the small group of bystanders, most of them neighbours.

"Father Mac met with a bit of an accident while changing hospitals. He is leaving now for further treatment. Thank you all for your concern."

"Who was the man the police took away?" asked Fred Roberts.

"I think you'll have to ask the police that, and they may not wish to tell you. As you saw, he came out of the presbytery, so he's obviously been up to no good. Anyway, I think I'm wanted." Tim had seen one of the two Special Branch officers waving him over.

"Mary here has told us there was another accomplice, who did not live with the other two. He kept well apart, but visited them occasionally. She doesn't know his role in this business because they spoke among themselves in another language, presumably Russian. Sounds like a back-up of some sort or even the one directing the operation. So please keep your eyes and ears open. I hope you can take care of Mary for a while, until all this blows over. All right, Miss, you can go now. Thank you. You've been very helpful. We may need to see you again. I expect we'll be seeing you again, Mr. Sullivan."

I've no doubt you will," said Tim. "Thank you for joining in the party. Now I'd better sort one or two things out with Sister Winifred and the housekeeper." Tim walked over to them.

Tim said, "Here's what I think we should do. I'll drive Sister and me to Cheltenham General, then we'll call in to police HQ and make our statements, then come back here. Sister can sleep in the presbytery, and Mary can find a bed there, too. Norah, can you arrange this, please?

Then in the morning, Sister can go in her Mini to the hospital and back to see Father, and I'll see the boiler men and get them started. When we know how long Father will be in the General this time, we can make further plans. One day at a time, I think."

"I'll gladly put Mary up for as long as it takes," said Megan Campbell. Mary smiled at her gratefully.

"I couldn't face another day in that cottage, anyway," she said with a shudder. "I lived in fear of Feliks. The second night we were there, I woke and felt a hand under the bedclothes. I screamed, and Stepan came running. I put a chair behind the door after that. But he was always trying to grope me when he thought Stepan wasn't looking."

"You poor dear," said the motherly Megan. She and Doc Campbell, in fact, had no children of their own. Megan had been a nurse and their romance was straight out of Mills and Boon – pretty young nurse meets dashing young doctor, their eyes meet over a desperately ill patient in the early hours of the morning, desperately ill patient makes a full recovery thanks to their teamwork, their teamwork develops into romance and … well, you'll have to buy the book.

"I'll get Sister's room ready again," said Norah, "Then, when you both come back, I'll have a meal of some sort ready for you."

*****

Brian Jenkins, hidden in next door's shrubbery, could scarcely credit his good fortune. "Bloody hell!" he softly mouthed. "Bloody, bloody, bloody hell! There's a Pulitzer in this lot! That's really the only difference between local hacks and national journalists. Everyone can write, but what counts is pure unadulterated luck – being there when it happens! I'd better see if I can get a word with that gorgeous girl sometime, too. It sounds like she was right in the thick of it."

*****

Things worked out pretty much as Tim had suggested. He and Sister Winifred found they could at least accompany Father Mac into the A and E Unit, where they made sure he was identified as the patient the Stroke Unit had released the same morning, and that details of his medication were still on record. There was nothing more they could do. There would be no news until the morning.

At police HQ it seemed to take forever to make their statements. They limited their input to a factual account of the day's events, avoiding any speculation about what lay behind them. Sister Winifred had less to contribute, but her evidence was useful in corroborating Tim's account of the abduction.

They were told that the other partner in crime had been taken into custody at Lower Stanford. It was hinted that further statements might be needed if and when other police elements became involved in the investigation.

They were both glad to get back to the presbytery at around 7 pm, physically and emotionally drained, though at least happy that a disturbing chapter in their lives, and that of Father Mac, had apparently closed.

Norah quickly put together a tasty pasta dish, as they reminisced about the day's events.

"And here was I," said Tim, "assuming that returning to the presbytery this afternoon after escaping would somehow permit Father, despite his injuries, to point out the hiding place. I hadn't realised he had been hurt too much for that. At least our friend Stepan has pulled the carpet up in the study."

"And a fine mess he has made, too," said Norah. "I suppose you'll be wanting to inspect the floor."

"Yes, I would," said Tim, "after we've eaten. I've already had a quick look, and there were one or two places where the floorboard had been renewed. Those are the places that bear a much closer inspection."

*****

Tim gave the floor his undivided attention after the meal. Norah and Sister Winifred got down on their knees to help him. Every inch of floorboard was subjected to the closest scrutiny, especially areas showing signs of recent renewal.

"Apart from a bit of newness here and there, they all look absolutely identical," said Tim. "All nailed down, nothing loose. Perhaps Mike might see something where I haven't. But that'll have to wait till the morning. I'll get back home now. Have a good night's sleep, both of you."

Back at home, Tim wasted no time in phoning Lucy.

"I wondered where you'd got to," she said. "I tried loads of times to get you."

"Sorry, love, I've a bit tied up today (he smiled at his weak pun). I'll tell you about our little adventure sometime. Tomorrow I'm seeing the boiler men in, and Sister Winifred will be at Cheltenham General seeing Father Mac. There's been a bit of a delay in his going in to the hospice, but I could pop over in the evening.

"Good, then could you bring the address book over. There are several birthdays coming up. I've bought the cards but I need the book. I'll definitely be coming back next week sometime, but it will be too late by then. Oh, by the way, that man who talked to us about priest holes. Somebody Miller. He died earlier this year, about the end of March, I was told. There was an obituary in the *Telegraph*."

"Sorry to hear it. So that's one possible source no longer available. Anyway thanks for letting me know. Bye, love."

Though feeling pretty exhausted, Tim realised it was not even 9 pm yet, so he phoned Bob.

"I'm glad you phoned," said Bob, "and I'm glad we've got those two in custody. Basically, they're mercenaries. I can't tell you more over the phone, but we've come across them before. We've never managed to pin anything specific on them. Not any more. Abduction and torture are the least of it now."

Tim thanked Bob for all his help. "Thank God you were in when I phoned, and acted instantly. Excuse me yawning. I've had quite a day." He then collapsed into his favourite armchair with a tot of Black, and just about made it into bed before dropping into a deep, deep sleep.

CHAPTER 16

Boiler day! Tim woke, completely refreshed, hurried through his breakfast and made it to the presbytery just in time to see Sister Winifred emerging.

"I've phoned the hospital to make sure it's OK to visit Donald," she said. "He passed what they called 'a fairly comfortable night,' presumably under sedation, but they don't tell you that." She was actually humming as she got into her Mini-Cooper.

Minutes later, the boiler men arrived. They were from a local firm qualified, the writing on their van announced, for all sorts of national standards in gas fitting and servicing. There were two of them – one a young lad who was clearly under instruction. This was the first time this firm had serviced Father Mac's boiler. The older man outlined what they were planning to do, then caught Tim totally by surprise.

"I hope we're not going to find anything spooky here, like one of them priest holes or whatever," he said. "We'll just leave the job if we do. Only joking."

"What on aarth are you talking about?" asked Tim, barely able to contain his excitement.

"Well," said the gaffer, "a few years ago a mate of mine found something funny under the floorboards. That was when they did the rewiring. There was a sort of recess. Not big enough for a man, but big enough for a small child, say. People used to bury stillborns. There was a skeleton of a child found behind a wall in the Red Lion's cellar. So perhaps the thing here wasn't a priest hole."

"It might have been for priest's vestments," said Tim. "How interesting. How can I get hold of your friend?"

"Trevor Metcalfe? He's still in business. Lives in Abbey Fields. You'll find him in the book."

"I might have a word with him. I'm interested in things like that," said Tim as casually as he could. I must get hold of Mr Metcalfe as soon as I can, he thought, before he also snuffs it or becomes otherwise incapacitated.

He had a look in the phone book. Yes, there it was: T. Metcalfe, 25 Abbey Fields. He phoned, and got an answer phone, but at least the recorded message did include a mobile number. He tried the mobile, and was heartened to hear a cheery voice responding.

Tim introduced himself, and asked if he could interrupt his work for a few minutes with a question concerning the St Nicholas presbytery.

"We did a job there – what? Oh, five years or so ago. How's Father Mac?"

"Not too well, to be honest," said Tim. "Look would it be OK if I came over?"

"Yes, that's fine. We're at the building site opposite the Secondary School. Plot 5, on the right as you goes in."

Tim was round there in a few minutes. He soon found Plot 5, and waiting outside was a rosy-faced man in a battered pork pie hat. Tim recognised him as one of the many hundreds of people he knew very well around the village, but couldn't put a name to.

"The hole under the floorboard?" he said, scratching his head. "Yes, I remember it. It was in the study. Fairly big, in fact. What was odd was that when you got the floorboard up, an inch or two below was another piece of timber, flat like another section of flooring – a sort of false floorboard. That lifted and below was a sort of a box, in a lead frame and bedded into the top of the foundation. It may have been designed that way centuries ago, or altered later. The thing is you wouldn't really notice it with a casual glance. It's only when you take up the old cable and thread new cable through that you realise there's something funny. Father Mac already seemed to know about it."

"That's very odd," said Tim, "I've examined the entire floor of the study, but I've not found the floorboard. Some boards look a bit newer than others, but you'd expect that over the years."

"Look, I'll tell you what," said Metcalfe. "How about me coming round in my lunch break? I always goes out for a pasty and a pint. Say twelve? I always eats early, because I starts early."

"That would be very kind," said Tim. "Thanks very much. Twelve noon it is."

*****

When Tim got back to the presbytery, he made coffee for the boiler men and shortly after Sister Winifred returned. Without his having to ask, she announced, "I couldn't stay long. It was outside official visiting hours. Anyway, Donald's had fifteen stitches in and around his mouth, poor man, but the good news is that his over-all physical

142

condition is generally none the worse for his ordeal. He might have had another TIA, perhaps when we left that cottage. He was barely speaking at all. So he may be a little slower recovering his speech, but there's no further damage. They want him there for another couple of days then he can probably be released. Then it's off to the hospice with him. And I think we'll have an ambulance this time, without any bogus ambulance-men. Perhaps a couple of police outriders, too."

Tim made his way to the study and went over the floor again even more meticulously than previously. Again, nothing came to light. Yet Metcalfe had sounded so confident. Perhaps you really do have to lift several boards and study what lies below them. Just looking at them superficially would not do.

At last, it was time for Mr Metcalfe to turn up. And so he did. By now the servicing of the boiler was over and the men had departed for their next job. Norah appeared at the same time.

"I thought you had some family thing on," said Tim.

"Just a few hours baby-sitting at an awkward time. Anyway, I'm here now. I'll start getting some lunch. I know that man. Mr Metcalfe, isn't it?"

"Hello, Mrs Walsh."

Tim led the way to the study with Mr Metcalfe.

"No, not here. It was in the study," said Mr Metcalfe.

"This is the study," said Tim.

"No, that's the office, or the library, I forget which. Let's go to the study." He led Tim to where the boiler men had been working. "Here we are."

"B... but this is the utility room," said Tim.

"It may be that now, but at one time it was a study, certainly in the days of Father Mac's predecessor, that Monsignor man. Nice fellow, quiet. The room probably continued as a study for the first few years after Father Mac arrived, then he did what many others did. He joined the computer age, and found there was no room for a computer and all the per... what are they called? My kids'd know."

Peripherals," supplied Tim. "The printer, scanner or copier, and probably speakers."

"That's it, so they set them all up in a larger room. And having done that, he brought all the bits from the study into the computer room, like the bookcases and desk. Then had his new boiler installed in the old study and brought the washer and dryer in there to join it. Like I say, many people did that or something similar when they got a computer."

Tim called Norah. She came in wiping her hands. Sister Winifred followed her.

"Norah, you know the room where the boiler is. What do you call it?"

"I don't call it anything," she said, "Probably because I never use it. I don't like the old washing machine and tumble dryer. I'd much rather use my own. I put Father Mac's bits and pieces in with mine. Besides, it's much more economical than doing two lots of washing, each for one person, in two different machines." Good old Norah, always thrifty, always practical. "The washing machine and dryer used to be in the kitchen," she added.

"Well, what does Father Mac call the room?"

She pondered. "It's rarely if ever mentioned. Wait a minute. I think he calls it 'the old study.' It used to be a study, you know. I call the other room, the one with the computer in, the study. Where his desk and the computer are. But then so does Father Mac. Oh, dear Lord, I know what you're getting at. I'm so sorry. We should have been looking in there as well. It just didn't occur to me to mention it."

"Norah's right," said Sister Winifred. "I've heard Donald call the larger room the study."

Tim sighed. "That explains a lot." It could certainly explain why Norah hadn't thought to mention it earlier. It would have saved a close scrutiny of the wrong floorboards, but that was not her fault. They had been looking in the room everyone called the study, unaware there was another candidate.

"Look, Mr Metcalfe, could you point out the part of the floor where you remember finding this hole?"

"Yes, of course. I've already noticed it. It's partly covered by the washing machine. Look right there. Do you need a hand shifting it? No? OK, well then, I'll be off now."

"Many thanks, Mr Metcalfe. You have been a real help. Now, would you object to my joining you for a pasty and a pint, my treat. Or are there a group of you?"

"I wouldn't say a group. Depends who's working where, but there's usually two or three of us. Join us by all means."

*****

After an enjoyable lunch, Tim got to work. He slid a screwdriver down the side of the floorboard, gently levered it, and eased it off. Below was what appeared to be another floorboard. This was secured to whatever lay below, but it was screwed down, not nailed. With mounting excitement, he unscrewed the wood, and eased it up. It was as Metcalfe had said. Below was a box-like structure, resting in a cavity in the top of the foundation bricks. The box appeared to be empty, but as he groped around inside it, he realised it was much larger than it first seemed. He lay face down on the floor and extended his arm further. He touched something, but realised he had to stretch even further. He had no idea how extensive the cavity was. He could be in danger of pushing whatever it was beyond his reach. He made his fingers gently crawl over the top of the object. Finally, he came to the far end of the object.

He slowly breathed out. This was it now, he thought. All that remained was to get it out. He groped around for a hand hold, and succeeded in bunching some fabric together. Then he slowly withdrew whatever it was he was holding, clutching it as if it were the Holy Grail.

PART TWO

NUMBERS

CHAPTER 17

Tim Sullivan told Sister Winifred and Norah that he'd found Father Mac's fragments, earnestly entreating them not to breathe a word to anyone. He took the fragments home, stuck them at the back of the airing cupboard, then set off to see Lucy, bearing with him the address book. He was rather earlier than he'd said, but that was all to the good. He must curb his impatience to get at the fragments.

He gave Lucy and mama a summary of the previous day's events, but not mentioning Father Mac's injuries or his own bang on the head. They were appalled at the kidnapping.

"An ambulance, and in broad daylight!" said mama. "They must have been pretty desperate. They obviously thought the prize was worth it, finding out where Father Mac's hiding place was. Have you found it?"

"Yes, and I've recovered the package that was in there, though I've not yet had time to look at the contents. I'll have a preliminary look this evening."

"Do take care, love," said Lucy. "We don't want people breaking into our house. You might be better keeping them where you found them."

"I'm sure no-one outside our little group knows about the package, except the police, and they don't know I've found anything. Anyway, I've no idea what to expect, but I'd like to study the contents for a few days. I might then turn them in, when I've decided who to turn them in to."

Tim had some tea with them, stayed on a little longer then drove home.

*****

The big moment had arrived to examine the "bequest" from Father Mac. Tim retrieved it from his airing cupboard, and tentatively, with a caution almost approaching trepidation, conscious of the likely fragility of the package's contents (he was to learn later of their extreme robustness), he began the process of opening the package.

The package was in a hessian bag. This presented no problem. He simply pulled it out of the bag. It was in strong wrapping paper. As he prised aside the outer wrapping, easing the flaps from the Scotch tape securing them, he was aware that his hands were trembling uncontrollably. It took him the best part of five minutes to remove the brown wrapping. Inside was a second layer, this one of stout, opaque plastic, the flaps anchored by heavy-duty duct tape. With the help of his pocket knife he sliced open the overlapping edges and pulled them carefully apart. There were no more layers of wrapping.

He spread out the contents. On top was a sealed envelope, presumably containing the letter Father Mac had mentioned, with his analysis of the fragments Tim was about to study. Below that was the CD he had referred to, containing the copy of Andy's photographs of some of the fragments. Then there were four other items, all charred to varying degrees. He decided to give all four a quick once-over before immersing himself in a more detailed scrutiny of any one of them.

On top lay what appeared to be the map Father Mac had mentioned, or, more precisely, six or seven separate fragments of a map, folded and secured together by a paper clip. A cursory examination of the top fragment showed an uneven pattern of pastel shades and, in one corner, a bold outline delineating what must be some sort of boundary. He was surprised at how closely the fragment resembled, in its general presentation, the maps he was familiar with. But then how else would one represent the surface of a planet, assuming that's what it was. Features anywhere throughout the universe clearly varied in height and in many cases land presumably met water. Was this a navigational aid for their own homeland, or was it for use when arriving at Planet Earth? At this stage there was no obvious answer.

Tim's trembling had stopped. He carefully detached the map fragments from the pile and, as he did so, he noticed a number of other details. Here and there lines moved tortuously across the top fragment and one met the possible boundary line. Rivers? Dotted about were curious symbols or labels, some large, some smaller. What could this alien orthography signify? Physical features? Place names? He checked further speculation. This was meant to be an initial cursory examination.

Below the map fragments was a large, single piece of paper (was that the right word?) so badly charred that only a few faint symbols had survived. It was almost poster size when unfolded. There was nothing

150

to be gained at this stage from any closer study, and so, discarding it, Tim came to the third item.

Again, like the map fragments, this was a mini-package of several items, and here there appeared to be more to get one's teeth into. But not his teeth. There was not the slightest doubt that these fragments had formed part of an illustrated medical textbook – perhaps a reference book to consult in the event of on-board illness. This had also been Father Mac's assessment. This was the bundle of pages the space visitor had gone back inside for. As with the map, Tim confined his initial scrutiny to the top piece. He recognised the same orthography that appeared on the map – a bobbly, rounded script with a few straight lines set at various angles, and with intervals between groups of symbols, perhaps suggestive of text made up of discrete words or ideas. The page he was studying also contained an illustration – a representation of the human (or humanoid?) body, complete with the sort of internal detail he associated with this type of diagram – spaghetti with various shaped meat balls. Lines pointed to different parts of the anatomy and bobbly symbols explained what they were. A quick glance at some of the other pages revealed similar diagrams of the body, and in at least one case, a curious building, stepped and tapering, not unlike a ziggurat. Definitely something for Doc Campbell!

Tim came at last to the fourth and final item, which was much more substantial than the others. In fact, there were several items, all superficially identical and each of which formed a sizeable chunk of what must have been a pretty imposing tome. This was the book Andy had photographed. Fire had ravaged the binding and the edges of the pages and clearly whole sections had fallen away. But much had survived: several hundred pages altogether, at a rough guess. Again, the same bobbly script was in evidence – bubbles with intersecting straight lines. Bubble and squeak, he thought inconsequentially. Some strings of symbols were about twice the size of the majority. As he leafed through the pages, black flakes fell away. If he were to study these pages in any depth, extreme caution would be necessary in handling them. Andy's ministrations had not exactly helped matters.

From his initial examination, three salient features emerged: the book fragments were not illustrated; they were from a book set out in sections or chapters with headings; and at the top of each page were symbols, which appeared to follow in sequence, strongly suggesting a page-numbering system. Also (and a tinge of excitement gripped him), he was pretty sure the possible numerals included some he had already seen on the map fragments, and the pages of the medical text. What was this book? A novel? Did the occupants of the strange craft come from a culture that had brought forth creative literature? Was this the work of a galactic Dickens, Hardy, or J. K. Rowling? Or was this some dry work of reference, didactically organised by subject? Wait. There was another feature that had almost been obliterated by fire damage and that he had almost overlooked. Faintly on the cover and the first page was the same logo Father Mac said he had seen on the spacecraft. Two green crossed lines with a red star above.

He sighed, glanced at the clock and found to his amazement it was past midnight. Where had the evening gone? Time for a nightcap, then bed. Sipping his Black, he carefully collected the fragments to stow in his desk. He was certainly not going to cram them back in their plastic wrapping. As he transferred them one by one to the desk, he glanced again at the large, single sheet, which was quite badly charred in places. Yes, there were definitely symbols of some sort on it, but equally clearly these were not of the bubble and squeak variety present on the other items. He rummaged around in the bottom drawer of his desk and found a magnifying glass – that invaluable aid to all those over fifty who suddenly find they cannot read the telephone directory.

He studied the faint outlines of the symbols and was amazed to find they appeared to be in English – or, rather – Roman script. Surely that was a B and that was a C and those two were Os, or perhaps zeroes. In sum, the symbols seemed to add up to OC BOC, though there was the faintest possible suggestion of other symbols either side. Below those letters on a separate line (as it were) were two more letters BO. Curiouser and curiouser! He turned the sheet over and studied it under the magnifying glass. Yes, there was something here, too, equally faint, but certainly in the bubble and squeak alphabet. In fact, there were several dozen lines.

Of course, Tim could not sleep. His so-called cursory glance had quickly developed into an intellectual challenge and he was now going over again and again the tantalising half-clues that had presented themselves. Maddeningly, the clock on the parish church that night carried clearly on a soft breeze, telling each quarter-hour. Dawn arrived and with it faint, melodic bird-song, pigeon dialogue and the complaining of the crows, loud and raucous. Charlie, the milkman, clinked his way down the road, then moved on in his electric float. Five forty-five chimed. Still his thoughts were churning.

More chiming. He counted, eyes closed, expecting six – and heard eleven. Sleep had eventually captured him. Though it was not the best night he had ever had, with curtains drawn and a dull, lowering sky, he'd caught up at least a little on his beauty sleep, and he also felt far more refreshed than he had the right to feel. So with renewed vigour he leapt out of bed, showered, shaved, dressed, and quickly fixed a brunch. He thought about the next few days. Lucy would be here next week, a reunion he was looking forward to, but meantime, he would spend as much time as he needed to study Father Mac's fragments and decide what to do with them. He felt instinctively that sooner or later he'd have to discuss them with former colleagues at the funny farm.

Before he renewed his attack, he went to see Doctor Campbell with the medical fragments. The good doctor and his wife were at home and pleased to see him.

"How's the bang you had?" asked the doctor.

"Oh, pretty well mended now," said Tim.

"We're seeing Father Mac this afternoon," said Campbell. "We're picking Sister up as well. I think she phoned you this morning and got no reply. You must have been out."

"Or in the Land of Nod," admitted Tim, telling them of his recent activities. "I've got something for you, Doc. Guard it with your life."

"So you found those bits and pieces. Now, what's this you've got?" He glanced at the top page, then stared hard at it. Finally, he gave a low, drawn out whistle.

"Good God!" he exclaimed. The doctor was visibly shocked. "I'll see what I can make of this. I wonder if there are any clues about treatment of disease. Probably not, or if there are I won't be able to understand them unless these illustrations can tell me something. Still, at least I can identify the parts of the body indicated by the arrows, and equate the alien words to them, though what good that will do, I'm not sure."

"You'd be surprised," said Tim. "Put together with other material, it might help anyone trying to resolve the language. Anyway, I'll leave you now. Give my regards to Father Mac, and if you can do it discreetly, tell him I've found his package and we're looking at it."

Tim carried on into the village, bought a few odds and ends and parried one or two questions from those vaguely aware that something odd was going on, or had happened. All Tim admitted to was that there had been some delay in getting Father Mac into the hospice. Tim had no idea if the national or local press had got in on the act, and bought a

Regent to go alongside his *Telegraph*. On reaching home, he studied both papers and was reassured to find that there was nothing beyond a few lines in the Regent on the missing ambulance. Police were speculating that it was the work of a joy-rider. No arrest was imminent, and the ambulance had quickly been recovered.

A few household chores, a cup of coffee, and Tim was ready to resume his scrutiny of the fragments by two o'clock.

He retrieved his precious inheritance from the desk, armed himself with notebook, pencil and magnifying glass, sat down and pondered his approach. He quickly dismissed the single, charred sheet, the medical extracts were now with Doctor Campbell (Tim wouldn't understand them, even in English), so that left the "novel" (or more likely "reference book") and the maps. The novel offered no lack of material, but where was the starting point? He had read with awe of the scholars who had successfully deciphered the hieroglyphics and cuneiform scripts of ancient civilisations. They were no mere academics. They were a special breed who could harness pure intellect and linguistic flair to breadth of vision and imagination. But they did at least have a starting point – collateral. They knew from other sources something of the dynasties that had held sway at the time and of the general organisation of the largely agrarian societies. Arduous though their path was, and beset by hundreds of false guesses, it was perhaps inevitable that in searching for the names of royal personages of the past, they would at last find them, use them as an entry point for extrapolation, and slowly recover more and more of the ancient texts. But he – he had no collateral, and he wasn't exactly your brilliant scholar. Though his degree was in modern languages and he did have a feel for language, he would be the first to admit that it was more slog than pure shining intellect that had carried him through his finals. No, not slog. Why denigrate himself? Tenacity. That was a better word. He liked it. Well, he would need plenty of that now if he were to make anything of this little lot.

His thoughts turned to the map fragments. They at least offered him some sort of collateral. There was something of a common denominator here. He had encountered maps before. So, the map it was. It was the only possible starting point.

Easing the paper clip away, he carefully spread the fragments out on the desk. A few charred flakes broke off, but it seemed clear, as he handled the fragments, that away from the seared edges, they were quite robust. There were seven pieces in all, each, when unfolded, surprisingly larger than he had supposed the previous night. The basic "unit" of the cartography was a rectangle about one inch by an inch and a quarter, delineated by faint dotted lines. In the top left corner of each unit where that portion had survived was a small cluster of bubble and squeak symbols, presumably a grid label, though most of the units depicted lacked that vital label. Only one fragment included a complete grid unit (he couldn't strictly call them grid "squares"), all the others on that fragment consisting of parts of several contiguous units. This fragment was by far the most complete and was made up of parts of no fewer than nine grid units; there were also two fragments each of five partial units, one fragment each of four and three partial units, and two of two partial units.

Tim quickly realised that his desk top was quite inadequate to accommodate all these jigsaw-like pieces, so he moved his *locus operandi* to the large dining-room table. Laying out the seven pieces, he studied each in turn. Though he could not place the grid units in sequence from their labelling, he soon realised he could do so to some extent from the apparent boundary lines, which separated pink from yellow and which, for want of a better explanation, he was inclined to regard as coastline. So far, so good – perhaps. But which colour represented land and which sea?

Other clusters of symbols straddled the boundary lines. What were these? Certainly not more grid labels. Place names? He concentrated on the largest fragment, containing parts of nine grid units, and on the basis of the boundary lines, had no difficulty in matching a piece of three partial units that joined it to the right (or east?) Next, he confidently joined a fragment with five partial units to one with two, but this did not join up with the larger match. Then he was completely stuck. He was left with three fragments, of five, four and two partial units.

He stood back and surveyed his puny collage. Nothing leapt up at him and grabbed him by the balls, though that large bit did ring the faintest of bells. Surely he'd seen that outline somewhere before. But he knew equally that this feeling was predicated upon the hunch that he was examining a map of some portion of the Earth. He could be light years out – perhaps literally!

The three remaining fragments seemed to offer no hope. He studied them in minute detail in association with the assembled pieces. Tantalising fragments of boundary were there, but nothing substantial enough to be placed with confidence next to any of the pieces already assembled. Minutes led to hours and he suddenly felt hungry. Heavens – nearly seven o'clock! He felt drained as well as hungry, as he busied himself at the stove, lightly grilling a small piece of steak and churning some stir-fries in the wok. He popped a can of lager while the meal cooked. He treated himself to a glass or two of fruity Chilean red while he ate.

In matters of sex, alcohol is said to increase the desire, but diminish the capability. For the poet, it is said to sharpen the wit. The same was evidently true for those faced with a seemingly intractable intellectual problem, for no sooner did he cast his eyes once more on his partially assembled jigsaw, than he was drawn to the symbols in those grid units that contained them. There was no doubt that these were the sort of labels found in such grid squares on terrestrial maps, though it was unusual (and fortunate) that they had originally been present in every square and not only at intervals. Pulling his notebook over, he copied out in the order they appeared the symbols in the grid "units" he had already tentatively assembled. Each square had originally contained five tiny alphanumeric symbols. What were they? One alpha and four numeric, two alpha and three numeric, three alpha and two numeric or four alpha and one numeric?? The mind boggled. In the end he decided it really didn't matter. It was the sequence that counted. He soon saw that, in effect, he was dealing in many cases with a sequence affecting only three of the five symbols. The first, left-most symbol was common to all but one of the squares, and was therefore the symbol for a "major square." By contrast, the second symbol showed a wide range of variation – no fewer that ten different ones. He found that the third symbol was constant, the fourth nearly so, while with the last symbol there was again a wide selection, including the symbols occurring in the third and fourth positions.

With mounting excitement, he realised he had a very broad picture of the structure of the grid. There was no duplication of symbol between those occupying the first two positions on the one hand, and those occupying the last three. Therefore, the symbols in first and third positions were major labels followed immediately by their own kind. So, was it not likely that he was looking at two alphabetic symbols followed by three numeric or vice-versa?

He studied at length the three remaining fragments – a five-unit, a four-unit and a two-unit, but found he was short of information and however he tried could do no more than guess at their placement. Wherever he positioned them, there would be substantial gaps between them and the main body of the map. Oh, for some collateral to help him complete the jigsaw.

Collateral? You dumb oaf! It was right there in the desk. He opened a drawer and seized what he had dubbed the reference-book and carefully turned the pages. At the top of each was what he had already assumed was the page number. Yes, they were all there – all the grid square symbols he had guessed to be the numeric components. Moreover, he seemed to have assembled the map the right way up. The pages of the book all had a three-symbol label and without doubt all were numeric symbols. Ergo, while the map grids were labelled letter-letter-figure-figure-figure, the book pages were labelled figure-figure-figure. Hundreds, tens, and units. It had to be that. Turning the pages of the book, he noticed that, as expected, when a certain "unit" value was reached the "ten" value changed to another symbol on the next page. But wait a minute – this wasn't happening every ten pages. It was happening every twelve pages! He didn't know whether to laugh or cry at this discovery. It certainly helped him in slotting the remaining map fragments into tentative positions, allowing for what were now huge gaps, but of calculable size; and he was conscious that if he had thought earlier of the book he could have saved himself several hours of frustrating speculation, poring over the unplaced fragments.

What did this curious numeric system mean? Why did they use it? Why should units, tens, and hundreds be discarded in favour of what? units, dozens, and grosses? At the end of the day – and hell's bells, it was the end of the day, 1:30 am – he had made tremendous progress. The next stage was to consult Earth maps to see if he could pin down the region depicted on the visitor's map as indeed representing a portion of our Earth. He studied the over-all reconstruction of map fragments and gaps. The final pieces had included small additional portions of boundary, but with such large spaces separating them from those he had confidently reconstructed, it was difficult to visualise the continuum. Nevertheless, there was something about that boundary that struck a familiar chord, and the addition of the final fragments, vastly isolated though they were, somehow reinforced this impression. But, again was the pink the sea or the land? And the same for the yellow.

Wearily, but tingling with a sense of achievement, he collected up the bits and pieces, stored them again in his desk and went to bed, where he slept like a baby until something in his subconscious pushed itself forward with increasing urgency. He dreamed. He was back at the Oval with a crowd from work. Lucy was also there. She shared his love

157

of cricket. It was a marvellous day – hot and cloudless – and after a poor start, the English middle order were taking the – who was it? – yes, taking the Aussies apart for once. Yes, that was it, the Aussies. They came from down-under, didn't they, Australia? Yes, Australia. Yes, that was it, Australia!

He woke with a start. Feverishly, stark naked, he raced downstairs to the study, found his world atlas and, nearly tearing the pages, came to Australia. He reassembled the map on the dining-room table and did a comparison. The large, northernmost portion he'd assembled didn't fall into line very closely, but the other assembled pair of fragments could, with a bit of imagination, be made to fit the Sydney to Brisbane coastline. And wasn't that a part of the coastline on the west coast, north of Perth, and surely stuck out on their own way down south did not those two fragments suggest on the one hand, part of the Great Australian Bight, and on the other, an area west of Adelaide.

He pondered these possibilities for a while, but the more he studied the outlines, doubts appeared. The shapes were too approximate. Detailed comparison didn't stand up and there was that wretched pink/yellow land/sea conundrum. He went back to bed just as Charlie began clinking his way down the lane. The Milky Way, he thought sleepily.

CHAPTER 18

Tim again slept late, and only just got to Sunday Mass in time. Father Daniel again stood in. Tim announced that Father Mac's transfer to the hospice had been delayed, but would take place soon. He stopped behind and chatted to several of the parishioners, skirting round the events of a few days ago. Back at home, he again made do with a brunch. As he was finishing, the doorbell rang, and there stood Doctor Campbell. The mere sight of him brought home to Tim how much he'd neglected the people around him: the doctor, Sister Winifred, Norah, and of course, Father Mac, still in the General. He'd briefly seen Norah and Sister Winifred at Mass, but not to speak to in any detail. He'd even failed to phone Lucy last night. He really must make an effort to keep in touch with the here and now going on around him.

"Come in, Doc. Can I get you a coffee? It'll only be instant."

"No thanks, I'm not planning to stop. I just dropped by to let you know of a startling discovery I made from looking at the medical pages you lent me. You'll never guess."

"They've got two penises?" said Tim with a grin. "Or one of each. They're hermaphrodites."

"Curiously, you're on the right track."

"Sorry, I was being a bit daft. But I think I know. Our visitors from space had six fingers."

"How the hell did you know that? Have you got some more illustrations?"

"No. I was able to deduce it from reconstructing their numeric system. The pages in the novel or reference book I've got were numbered, as you might expect. I soon found that it took a sequence of twelve low units to cause a change in the next order of numerals. Anyone could have seen that. I then got to thinking why should that be. And I thought we're on a base of ten obviously, because we've got ten fingers, including the thumbs. Our numeric system must have evolved for precisely that reason. Ergo, theirs followed the same path, ergo six fingers per hand."

"Well reasoned, Tim. You must be spot on. I'm now toying with something else as well. I can't prove anything yet, but if my suspicions are right, we might think of adding a new approach to the treatment of disease."

"That's amazing. Anyway, for my part I've got to the stage of assembling the charred fragments of the map. I'm now going to try to identify the area in question by reference to an atlas."

"How do you know the area shown belongs here on Earth and not some other planet, including their own?"

"Good point. I'm very conscious of just that possibility. All I will be able to say is it looks like somewhere or other. There's no way I can prove it. By the way, how was Father Mac?"

"We saw him yesterday. He's still rather poorly from his ordeal three days ago. I think they'll keep him another day or two yet. Sister's going again this afternoon. Why not join her?"

"I think I will," said Tim.

"I'll get going, then," said Doctor Campbell.

When he had gone, Tim phoned Sister Winifred and offered to take her to the General in the afternoon, an offer that she gladly accepted. He then phoned Lucy, confessed to her that he had been totally immersed in the fragments, and was heartened to hear from her a warm endorsement of his neglect.

"Of course you must persist with studying all those bits," she said, "but be sensible and recognise honestly when you've reached the point when you can go no further. You must then consult others. Heaven knows, you were surrounded by enough brilliant people in your career." That was certainly as true then as it had been in the far-off days of Bletchley Park, where Churchill had once said something like, "In searching for brilliant minds, I asked you to leave no stone unturned but, by God, I did not expect you to take me quite so literally."

Several of the best minds had stayed on in the new peacetime organisation, when the emphasis had shifted away from Germany to other powers that posed a major threat, not least the Warsaw Pact alliance. The joke in the early 1950s was that the move of the department from London had caused the average IQ in Cheltenham to double overnight. Tim remembered those brilliant people with affection. They weren't all similar in appearance to Old Testament prophets, heavily bearded and sockless below sandals, but many of those who weren't displayed other eccentricities, of which talking to oneself was the least egregious. Sadly, the Bletchley generation had passed on, as had the Russian émigré aristocracy. His close colleagues

160

when he had first joined had included a princess and a countess. Yes, there were still brilliant minds around, but not so many characters.

*****

The visit to Father Mac in the afternoon was a sombre affair. The priest was clearly in some discomfort. He gamely tried to smile, but it was a painful process. Curiously, though, his speech was no worse – in fact, it was even a little improved. Sheer willpower, thought Tim.

Nurse Bingham said, "He's really been through the wars. I understand some thug hit him in the mouth. He also had a mini-stroke. We don't think it's anything deeper than that."

"I think if that's the case, he'd be just as well in the hospice," said Sister Winifred. "He'd get my undivided attention. Should I suggest that?"

"Leave it with me. I'll mention it. I think there's a lot of merit in what you say."

*****

Later that afternoon, Tim fished out the map fragments, assembled them on the dining-room table, and tried to recap on where he'd got to. What exactly had he achieved? He had confirmed that the apparent map was, indeed, a map, or rather remnants of a larger map, and probably intended as an aid to aerial navigation. It might be imprecisely drawn, though the fact of grid lines connoted some degree of confidence on the part of the cartographer. It might depict the visitors' homeland or some other planet, such as Earth. And, if the latter, the boundary lines, *faute de mieux*, might conceivably represent bits of Australia (a hypothesis with which, however, he was becoming increasingly disenchanted in the cold light of day). If the map did depict a part of Earth (Australia or not) then – something he had overlooked until now – the incidence of the possible rivers might afford a further clue, as might that of the bubble and squeak symbols dotted about, which he knew were probably place-names. Though he could not, of course, read them, their pattern of distribution could at least be compared with that of portions of Earth, such as Australia.

The only other thing he knew with any confidence was that he had reconstructed the visitors' numeric system and had established that they operated on a base of twelve – a deduction Doc Campbell had endorsed from the medical fragments. What did that do to pi, he idly wondered. Did it affect it? He was no mathematician. Sooner or later he would have to take others, better qualified, into his confidence. The immediate problem was: where did he go from here? Should he persist with the map, studying the possible rivers and place-names? Or should he launch into an examination of the other items in Father Mac's package? The prospect was daunting. Numerals were one thing. Language was quite another, especially with no collateral.

Tim sighed wearily. He knew he had no choice. Prove or disprove the Australia theory. Get it out of his system, one way or another. He doubted whether his own atlas was man enough for the job. He really needed a large scale series of maps. How about a reference library? Bourton library had got rid of its reference section to make way for more computer terminals. Cheltenham still had a decent one, but in the end he decided to try the Internet first. It was the work of no more than one frustrating hour to produce a firm thumbs down. Rivers stubbornly refused to be in the right place and the scantily populated bits of Australia were no match for the more generous population pattern shown on the visitors' map fragments, assuming the symbols there were place names. The coastal outline did not bear close comparison either. Well, at least he knew where he was. Back to square one – no, square two: he had accomplished something, part positive, part negative. So it was now down to the language itself, and that meant all kinds of complex possibilities.

At least one problem was absent. Students of ancient texts had often been confronted with a vast matrix with no idea whether to read upwards or downwards, and from left to right or vice versa. He knew from the layout of the book that his choice was limited to left to right or right to left and on the basis of the grid symbols of the map, probably the former. Another major problem with language was inflection. Did the visitors' verbs conjugate, and did nouns and adjectives decline, with agreement in case, number, and gender? Did the aliens even have nouns, verbs, and adjectives and all the rest?

Or was he dealing with an unstructured, agglutinative, language where ideas just got glued on to each other, like, for example, the Inuit tongues? Even more fundamental – did the visitors employ an alphabet in which each pure, discrete sound was represented by a single symbol, or did they link together single sounds into complex ones – in other words was their language based on a syllabary of consonants in alliance with vowel sounds? That clearly had to be the starting point, though where it would lead him, goodness only knew.

He had read somewhere in the works of the scholars who studied ancient scripts that, as a general rule, if the number of discrete symbols exceeded, say, 35 to 40, then you probably had a syllabary, rather than an alphabet, on your hands, or a hybrid – an alphabet peppered with some combined sounds. So that was clearly the first step. Study the book. Assemble a list of discrete symbols and count them. But how much longer could he allow himself before returning to his normal mode of life? Just the rest of today, he decided. He would not be able to compile his list of symbols in three or four hours, but he might be able to get started and decide whether to return to it later or enlist the help of others. He must then take a break and revert to domestic chores for a day or so. Lucy would be back any day now and would not want to come back to a pigsty. In fact, he'd go up to mama's again tomorrow to see her and Lucy. He could certainly use a break from trying to apply what intellect he still had to some pretty intractable problems.

Then one of those strange, unaccountable things happened that could be seen later as Fate intervening. The phone rang. It was the secretary of Bourton Bridge Club. Lucy and Tim had gone to the Club every Monday for years. They played as a partnership. When Lucy went away to attend to mama, Tim had mentioned that if anyone was short of a partner, he'd be glad to help out. That was before the drama surrounding Father Mac had entered his life. Now, he was being asked to step in tomorrow. Why not? He could still go to mama's in the morning and get back for the afternoon start. In a way, he welcomed the opportunity. He had become so involved with Father Mac's fragments that it was very tempting just to slog on with the work. But a bridge commitment would force him away from those tantalising fragments, and Tim would never back out of a promise made. So he agreed to stand in, not realising that in doing so, a door would open.

*****

Tim made an early start the next day and was at mama's before ten. The big news there was that Lucy was coming home in four days time. She'd just stay for the coming week, then mama would manage under her own steam, supplemented by a couple of hours a day, Monday to Friday, by a home help, and week-end visits from Lucy's sisters. Tim filled them in on the limited progress he had made on Father Mac's

163

fragments, and assured Lucy he would have a word with a few former colleagues.

"I know exactly who to talk to," he said. "Hugh Frobisher. He's just retired as Head of H Division, so he's only a bit younger than me. He and I used to lecture together on the customer courses. He even lives in Bourton now."

"I really think that's the wisest course," said Lucy. "I think I know his wife. She plays at Cheltenham."

Lucy was referring to bridge. She played far more than Tim. Cheltenham Bridge Club was one of the strongest in the country, boasting several internationals among its membership, but it catered for a wide range of abilities.

"That reminds me, I'm playing with Margaret this afternoon," said Tim. "I'm a bit scared."

"Oh, she's fine," said Lucy. "But I'm surprised she's back. She's been on holiday."

"Apparently she got back yesterday, only to find Shirley was ill." Shirley was her regular partner.

"You'll need to leave here by about 12:30," said Lucy. "We'll have lunch at twelve. Let's pop to the shop quickly and see what to have."

*****

After lunch Tim left them and went straight on to bridge. Margaret was waiting for him.

"Weak no-trump, transfers, weak twos, Gerber, Roman key-card. You happy?" she said.

"Yes, fine, plus unusual no-trump for minors," said Tim. "You don't do splinters, do you? Or is a jump to four clubs always Gerber?"

They quickly agreed on the major features of their bidding system, knowing full well that most of them would not be needed. Margaret excused herself and went to another table, where a group of four ladies were sitting. She began showing them her holiday photos. Tim busied himself, helping the director hand out the bidding boxes and the wallets with the cards in.

As he got to the table where Margaret was holding forth, he heard her saying, "Look, this was our itinerary. We flew to Istanbul and boarded the cruise ship, then we just slowly made our way round the entire Black Sea. There was loads of time ashore, and plenty to see." Tim handed out the boxes, glanced casually at the map Margaret was

164

showing, and felt his heart leap. Surely that map included his coastline, Father Mac's coastline, the little visitor's coastline. That bit in the northwest, leading towards the Crimea. It was certainly a possibility. He couldn't stop himself staring at the map, while five ladies were looking at him, askance.

"Have you been there, Tim?" asked Margaret.

"No, but I've often thought about a holiday there," he said lamely. I must change the subject quickly, he thought. "We did agree on Stayman, didn't we?"

Margaret looked at him curiously. "I would have thought that went without saying. It's one of the first things you learn," she said with mild reproach in her voice.

Oh, hell, I'm not exactly inspiring confidence in my partner. And throughout the afternoon, he found his mind straying to the map back in the house. Despite this, he and his partner did reasonably well, though he felt Margaret was carrying him to a large extent. He wasn't sorry when the session ended and he could get back.

No sooner had Tim got in the house than he dug out the fragments of the map, switched on the Internet and Googled his way to the coastline up in the northern part of the Black Sea. Hmm. Not precisely the same, but close enough for Government work (as the Americans would say). He breathed a sigh, reached for the local phone directory and found the names listed under "F."

*****

Hugh Frobisher was a large, shambling, teddy-bear of a man. He had a soaring intellect and with a first in Maths coupled with great personal charm had progressed rapidly up the ladder in H, the cryptanalysis division. There were a few others of similar intellect there, but in most cases they were best left on their own, working a specific problem. They were not exactly antisocial. They were more asocial, simply unaware of how to relate to others around them, or in some cases, totally unaware there were others around them. It was hopeless giving some of them staff to direct. Hugh stood out as the one person of his generation who was a born leader as well as a highly gifted mathematician. He was proud to bear the same first name as his illustrious predecessor, Hugh Alexander, the British chess champion who was one of the principal architects of Enigma, the wartime code-breaking computer at Bletchley Park (though, to be pedantic, "Hugh" was actually the great man's second name).

Frobisher, for all his intellect, was also a very physical man. He undertook walking holidays that to most others would be like major expeditions. He'd think nothing of covering thirty miles a day, often on his own, though he did sometimes find a companion or two who could keep up with him. He set himself a target for each day, with a specific inn as his destination. This would be booked in advance.

B and B for two. His wife was a sweet-natured woman who was perfectly content to drive to the target location with the luggage. There, she could sit and read in the car, or potter around the place, taking in the museum, the churches, and the shops.

"Hello, Tim," he said. "I've seen you in the distance a few times round the village, but never at close quarters. In fact, I've found there's quite a ghetto of us here. What can I do for you?"

Tim explained that he had something to show him that Hugh might find interesting. His experience before retirement might come in useful.

"Could you possibly pop round here? I don't want to disturb things." He gave Hugh directions.

"This really does sound intriguing," said Hugh. "Yes, of course. Give me about half an hour." There were sounds of chewing and swallowing.

"Oh dear, I've interrupted your meal," said Tim. "Sorry."

"No problem," said Hugh. "I look forward to seeing you. 'Bye."

*****

Tim began rehearsing in his mind what he was going to tell Hugh, but soon realised there was nothing he should refrain from disclosing. Father Mac knew there a strong likelihood Tim would want to consult former colleagues, so he wasn't breaching any confidences. And if he couldn't discuss things with someone like Hugh – one of the great minds of the day, and (like Tim himself) totally discreet as his job had demanded, who could he bare all to? The doorbell chimed. Tim opened the door to reveal a rather damp figure, removing bicycle clips. He remembered. Hugh always cycled everywhere under about five miles, and in all weathers.

"Come on in, Hugh. Can I get you anything? Tea, coffee, wine, beer, something stronger?"

"No, no. But thanks all the same. I must say, I'm thoroughly intrigued by all this. What on Earth have you come by that makes you want to show me it?"

"Well, there are three things, actually," said Tim. "There's part of a map, extracts from a book of some sort and a separate single sheet. There were fragments of a medical book, but I've lent them to a doctor friend. Come into the dining room. I've got the rest spread out there."

Tim led Hugh into the dining room and over to the table. Hugh looked at the display. Then looked harder, and picked up Tim's magnifying glass that lay on the table. At last, he gave a huge sigh, and turned to Tim.

"Tim, where the hell did you get this lot from? Not your parish priest, was it?"

Tim was dumbstruck. "How the bloody hell did you know that?"

"Look, let me admit straight away that I've seen similar collections over the last – what? – year, fifteen months. In fact, these things are the reason for my consultancy. We knew that, following the incident in Canada, another batch of documents had arrived, and had somehow got into the hands of a cleric from this area. Now, let's hear the story, and I know it will be colourful."

Tim recounted the whole saga, leaving out nothing. He briefly summarised Father Mac's adventures, then brought the priest's testimony up on the computer, so that Hugh could read the first-hand account for himself. Tim then told Hugh of Father Mac's stroke, the kidnapping of Father Mac and himself, and of their escape, and the capture of Stepan and Feliks.

"You're lucky to be alive," said Hugh. "That poor priest." He then studied the map and the book.

Two hours slipped by.

"Look, are you sure you wouldn't like something now?" inquired Tim.

"I feel I could do with a large gin, but I've got the bike. A small glass of wine will be OK if it's no trouble."

They both had a small glass of Chilean red.

"What have you deduced so far?" asked Hugh.

"Not a lot," said Tim. "I suppose my only real triumph has been to reconstruct their numbering system. It's on a base of twelve. Diagrams in the medical pages showing people with six fingers on each hand seemed to confirm this. I've also very tentatively identified the map fragments, but it might be best not to tell you where I think they relate

167

to, in case you study them in depth. A clear, unbiased mind might be more beneficial."

"You've done pretty well," said Hugh. "And we've not had any maps before, or medical bits." He took a gulp of wine.

"Can you tell me what this is all about?" said Tim.

"No, I'm afraid not," said Hugh. "What I will do is report what you've got and see whether they think you should come on board. If so, they'll want to give you the official briefing. And goodness knows what we do with your priest. I mean he's the one with the first-hand knowledge, not just of these bits and pieces, but of the whole incident itself. There may well be things M.O.D. want to ask him, though from what you say about his speech it may have to be a yes/no session."

"Don't forget he's written a few thoughts of his own about the various bits of paper he brought back. They may be helpful."

"I'd be inclined to doubt it, especially if he can't see beyond the presence of an angel. Any thoughts of his might be coloured by that conviction. But hang on to his comments. You never know."

"I'm afraid you're probably right," acknowledged Tim, "but won't the Canadians pass on everything they know? Surely this thing is so important it gets shared among intelligence allies."

"We're touching on aspects of this I can't possibly get into unless and until you get the official briefing. As I say, I'll recommend putting both you and the worthy Father Mac on the list. What's his name, did you say? There's no reference to it in his lengthy account. It isn't McNulty by any chance, is it?"

Tim nodded.

"Then if his brother works for CSE, I've met him at tripartite conferences. I've never collaborated closely with him myself, but he's highly thought of, I do know. Now I really must shut up about all this. I'm in grave danger of breaching security. Someone will contact you if it's decided to clear you. Oh, and by the way, they may want to take custody of these bits and pieces of yours. Not only to study them, but for safety. Although two people have been arrested trying to get hold of them, there may be others out there."

"That's fine by me," said Tim. "There is someone else in the gang. It will be a relief to be rid of the fragments. Technically, I suppose they belong to Father Mac, but I'm quite sure he'd be happy."

"Good, then that's settled," said Hugh with a grin. "I'm glad you asked me round and thanks for an interesting evening. I've no doubt we'll be seeing more of each other."

Hugh finished his wine, shook Tim's hand, put his cycle clips on and rode off into the drizzle.

*****

When Frobisher had gone, Tim mulled things over. He'd expected Hugh to be astonished by what he'd shown him, but this was not the case, though he did admit that medical pages and map fragments related to the other papers had not been seen before. It was clear that what Father Mac had stumbled across was something not only of national, but of international concern. This recent episode had originated in Canada, but it sounded as if there was good deal of collaboration on the subject, and presumably a sharing of whatever raw material turned up in the shape of documents, or even hardware. It also seemed it was an inter-agency problem, certainly in the UK and probably in the other collaborating countries. Tim felt his mind drifting away to more mundane affairs. He'd pretty well abandoned everybody for a few days. He had some catching up to do. It was a bit late in the day now, but tomorrow morning first thing, he'd touch all the bases (as his US colleagues would say. His three years in what they referred to as the "shoe factory" off the Baltimore/Washington Parkway still found echoes in his thought and speech).

CHAPTER 19

Before he could even reach for the phone the next day, the phone summoned him. It was Sister Winifred, excited.

"Donald's being discharged today. This afternoon, about two. He's made excellent progress. His mouth's still a bit sore, but there's no great damage. I've asked to go down in the ambulance with him. I'll make sure he's not kidnapped this time."

Tim reflected. "I'd like to see him before he goes," he said, "I won't bother them this morning. I can probably see him briefly when they wheel him out. Now, what about your car?"

"I can do without that for a while," said the nun. "It should be safe for a few days in the hospital car park. Or I could go by bus to Cheltenham and walk to the General."

"No, don't do that," said Tim. "Look, I'll tell you what. I'll drive you to the hospital today. That will suit me because, as I said, I'm hoping to see Father, then in a few days I'll come down to see how he's settled in. At the same time, someone else can drive your Mini down, and I'll bring them back. In fact, I know just the person. Leave me the keys."

"Oh, very well, then," said Sister Winifred. "Did you get anywhere with your look at his bits of paper or whatever they were?"

I'm certainly not going to discuss any progress I made on the phone, he thought.

"I'm afraid not," he said, and rapidly changed the subject. "Anyway, I'll pick you up at 1:30. I might see if Norah would like to come to see him off. Is she there with you?"

"No, but she will be round. I'll see what she says. If she'd like to come, there will be two of us waiting. I can't see her not coming."

Tim's next phone call was to Doctor Campbell.

"Hello, Doc," said Tim. "Sorry I've not been in touch. I got lost in those bits from Father Mac."

"As a matter of fact, so did I. The medical pages are absolutely fascinating. I can't understand a word, but the diagrams are suggesting some quite amazing things."

"Good. Now, I wondered if you'd like to wish Father Mac luck. He's leaving for the hospice at two. I'm taking Sister Winifred and perhaps Norah. I'm picking them up at 1:30. Sister is going with him in the ambulance."

"Thanks for telling me, Tim. Yes, I'd certainly like to see him."

"Is Mary still with you?"

"Yes. She's a sweet girl, but she's something of a displaced person. She contacted the hotel to try to get her job back, but there's no vacancy at the moment. The hotel was also her home. She had a room there. She's not keen to go back to her parents, so she's a bit lost. We've told her she can stay with us as long as she wants. She's earning her keep, too, doing shopping, cleaning, washing, even a bit of cooking. I'll be having a quiet word with Tom Martin at the Medical Centre to see if there's a vacancy coming up soon. They seem to have quite a turnover of receptionists. Mary's friendly and intelligent, and computer-literate. She'd do well there. By the way, she seems to have developed a friendship with a young man. I think he's a journalist, covers Bourton and the villages for the Cotswold Regent. They've been out for a drink a couple of times, and they had a pub lunch together yesterday."

Loud warning bells sounded in Tim's mind. "Thanks, Doc, for looking after Mary. I hope something turns up for her. Look, I'll be honest with you. I'm a little concerned about that journalist chap. He may well be getting fond of Mary. I mean, who wouldn't? She's an attractive girl with a pleasant manner. But his motive for cultivating her may well lie in his journalistic ambitions. I'm wondering if you could warn her. I don't know the full story, but I do know that for some reason this whole business is pretty sensitive A former colleague has told me at least that much."

"I'm sure Mary will be on her guard. She's a very intelligent girl," said Doctor Campbell, "I really wouldn't like to intrude into her private life."

Tim dug his heels in. "Please, Doc, I believe it's very important to get the message across to her. You needn't associate yourself with the warning. Tell her that I was asking her to be careful. I can come round and tell her myself, if you prefer. I spent several hours with her in that cottage. I know the sort of men that she was involved with. Like me, she knows them to be cruel and ruthless. I'm sure she will recognise that we have her own best interests at heart."

"All right then, Tim. I dare say you're right. Oh, by the way she told me she thought she saw the other man, the one who sometimes visited the two Russians. But she couldn't be sure. This was yesterday. She did try to phone you."

"I was out most of yesterday, seeing Lucy and mama in the morning, and playing bridge in the afternoon."

"Hmm," mused the Doctor, "And Mary herself was out last night. She's out again now, doing a bit of shopping. I can get her to phone you, if you like."

"No, don't worry her. But just pass on the warning. I'll mention this possible sighting to the police."

"OK, fine. Now, about Father Mac."

"As I said, I'm calling at the presbytery at 1:30 for Sister and Norah. Why not join us and make up a car-load."

"That would be very kind. I'll wander down to the presbytery, then you've only got one stop."

*****

At 1:30 the party left for Cheltenham. When they arrived, Sister Winifred said, "I'll go into A and E. They're expecting me. You wait here."

Tim left Norah and Doctor Campbell by the door and looked for a parking space. He was always amazed at the size of the parking area and the fact that it was always full. Where did they all come from? Mostly out-patients, he thought, or those driving them. Luckily, someone was just leaving, so he quickly grabbed the space, then got out and paid the parking fee. As he walked back to join the others, he saw a familiar face – inside a police car.

He waved.

WPC Henderson lowered the window. "Hello," she said. "Have you come to say farewell to Father McNulty?"

"We certainly have," replied Tim. "Sister Winifred's going with him in the ambulance. She's armed to the teeth in case there's another hijack attempt. No, not really. Are you following behind as an escort? Are there any others?" Tim imagined a vast cavalcade of vehicles and a few outriders racing down the M5, sirens blaring.

"Let's just say his progress will be discreetly monitored. He's a VIP now, for all sorts of reasons."

"Oh, I'm so pleased, constable. That really is reassuring. Did you get my message? About the accomplice possibly lurking around Bourton?"

172

"We certainly did, and passed it on."

"Well done. Anyway, I'd better see if Father Mac's emerged yet. 'Bye."

Minutes later, Father Mac appeared in a wheelchair pushed by an attendant, with Sister Winifred in close attendance. He was clearly delighted at the reception waiting for him. The ambulance staff stood nearby.

"Please give us a few minutes with the patient," said Tim. "We won't keep him long."

The ambulance staff nodded agreement, and Norah produced a large bag, which all of them had helped to fill with goodies. Tim had also included copies of recent parish newsletters. Father Mac seemed quite overwhelmed. He looked well, apart from some bruising on one of his cheeks.

"H'lo Nor, Tim 'n' Doc," he said. "You're ver kine."

"You can almost talk," said Tim with delight.

"An' you sh'd see me walk," he grinned, displaying as he did so a few livid areas inside his mouth.

"He's well on the mend," said Sister Winifred.

Tim said quietly, "I won't go into all the work we've put into your bits and pieces. I consulted a former colleague and he was extremely interested. I'll probably be asked to hand them over for further study and for safe-keeping. I said you would be happy with that."

"Yes," said the Priest. "An' don' forget. I saw ange. Read my conc…" he couldn't finish.

"Conclusions," said Tim. "Right, I'll let you know of any further progress. Doc has been looking at the medical bits and is very excited."

"I won't say anything yet," said Doctor Campbell. "But yes, I think they're important."

One of the ambulance men looked pointedly at his watch.

Tim said, "we must let you go now. Keep up the good work, Father. We'll be down from time to time to make sure you're behaving yourself. 'Bye Sister."

Sister Winifred climbed into the back and sat down. She waved, and the door closed. The ambulance moved off. As it did, Tim saw the police car follow after an interval, WPC Henderson talking on the radio.

The three of them climbed into Tim's car and set off home.

"I'm amazed at the progress Father has made," said Tim, "especially after the beating he took in that cottage."

"It might even be the reason," said Doc Campbell. "Trauma is like that. It can work both ways. It provides a shock to the system, usually with pretty nasty effects. But completely against the odds it can sometimes act as a force for good. Oh, by the way, Mary says thank you for your kind wishes and advice."

Norah wondered why Tim uttered a sigh of relief.

*****

When they got back to Bourton, Tim found two messages on his answer phone. One was from Lucy to say her sister could not get to mama's house until about nine in the evening on the Friday, so there was no need for Tim to leave Bourton much before eight. The second message simply gave a phone number that he vaguely recognised, together with an extension. It could only be his former employer. He got through to the switchboard, then keyed in the extension.

A quiet voice spoke. "GCHQ. Security."

"This is Tim Sullivan. You called."

"Yes. Thanks for getting back so soon. I'm sure you will know why I'm phoning. We would very much like to see you as soon as possible. Tomorrow afternoon if you can make it. A car will pick you up from home. And have an overnight bag ready. Don't worry, we'll feed you. Dress for comfort."

Tim considered. Yes, he could manage that. He had two clear days available before Friday when he'd be picking up Lucy. He would mention it to Lucy and she would certainly understand and approve. He'd let a few others know he would be away, without being more specific.

"I can get away tomorrow. What sort of time?"

"Four o'clock would be fine. Oh, and bring your passport with you, for identification. We understand you have certain materials relevant to this business. I personally don't know what these are, but you will. Could you please bring those and any other items you consider necessary. There'll be a few other people present, and after dinner they'd like you to brief them on certain events. Before that someone will give you a briefing. Do you have any questions?"

"Not that you would wish me to discuss over the phone."

"Good. Until tomorrow at four, then." The phone clicked.

So that was to be the format. Tim phoned Lucy and simply said he'd been asked to attend a meeting. She said she'd wondered when this would happen. He then phoned Doc Campbell and Norah. He'd give it another hour before phoning Sister Winifred, to give her time to arrive at the hospice. He decided to leave the answer phone on when he was away. Let people assume he was around, but out.

Then he got to pondering again about tomorrow. They wanted from him all the bits Father Mac had hidden. He supposed he'd better get the medical pages back from the doctor. And what about the CD Andy had given him, containing photo-copies of the "reference book"? They probably had no idea he had it. But the Canadians may have mentioned it, in which case they would expect him to surrender it along with everything else. But perhaps he could make a copy to use for a very limited period in case something came out of the meeting that he should discreetly follow up on, then delete it. With Misha lurking around, he would make a special hiding-place for it, and he knew just how.

The other thing that would be important was Father Mac's testament – that would form a good part of the briefing they wanted. He should probably copy it to CD and delete it from his hard drive. He decided to make a print of it as well, to refer to in his briefing. He should also delete the file from Father Mac's computer. And what about the emails? Yes. He'd also take them. They were the important lead-in to the whole business. He might just be asked about that. He would have to go to the presbytery to access and copy them. Hmm. There was quite a bit to do.

He set about printing Father Mac's testament, copied it to CD and deleted it from his system. He went to the presbytery and sorted out the various tasks he had to do there and had a quick look round. Norah had worked hard to get the place looking clean and tidy. There were still one or two things to do, not least replacing the carpet Stepan had hacked to bits. He skimmed through the mail Norah had been collecting and placing in the (new) study. Plenty of it, but nothing demanding a reply. He left, and called in at Doc Campbell.

"Sorry, Doc, but I'm going to have to take back the medical pages," said Tim. "I know you'll be sad to part company from them, but the Queen needs them, or at least some of her loyal subjects do."

"Look, Tim, I know it's not my concern, but I know instinctively that with a bit more work, we can elicit something of incredible benefit to mankind from them. I felt I was on the brink of it. Could you please let this be known. If it will help, I'll gladly write up my conjectures – they can't be more than that. What I want to avoid is these few pages getting shunted off to one side, when what you really need is a panel of experts to study them. As a former GP, that makes me by definition a generalist, and I could serve a useful function as a devil's advocate on such a panel. Toss that into your meeting as a talking point, if you could."

Tim could see how intensely the doctor felt about his tentative findings and how miserable he would feel to give up the pages. Perhaps Tim could find a way to get him reunited with them. Ask for them back? He felt the same about surrendering everything himself. Did the fact they planned to give him some sort of a briefing suggest a long-term role for him in the scheme of things? He had no idea. His two-way briefing visit may be all they wanted from him.

"OK, Doc, I'll feed your comments in," he agreed, "But I can't guarantee anything. This is all being handled very discreetly. I don't even know where the meeting is." That was true, but he was pretty sure it would be one of the Friends' safe houses. He'd been to a couple of them in the course of his career.

Back at home, Tim saw there was a message for him to phone Bob.

"I understand you're being invited to dine with a bunch of desperados tomorrow," said Bob. Tim could almost see the grin. "Well, this is just to reassure you that your house will be kept under surveillance. But that's mainly because we know it's under surveillance by the other side. They think the bits and pieces they want are either still in the presbytery, or have now reached you. As soon as the opportunity arises, they'll search your house. And that gives us an opportunity, too. To allow them to find something they want so that we can observe what happens to it. A little gift. We're not too worried about Misha himself, it's what he does with his gift."

Precise details followed on how Tim should prepare the "gift." How could he not comply after all the help Bob had given him?

Tim then phoned the hospice, and was delighted to hear they'd had an uneventful journey there and that Father Mac had settled in so well. After a meal he made a copy of the CD Andy had given Father Mac, labelled it and prepared the "gift" Bob wanted to be found. He then prepared a hiding place for the copy, together with the envelope containing Father Mac's own conclusions. He then put the emails he'd copied at the presbytery with the rest of the items, and put the whole lot carefully into a briefcase ready for the next day. The last few days had drained him both physically and mentally, to say nothing of emotionally. He was tempted to have one last look at the fragments, but resisted the urge. He would find nothing new with a tired mind, and they would soon be in the hands of people who could, or who at least had more intellectual fire-power than he. An early night was called for. The next day or two would bring their own demands.

CHAPTER 20

The next morning, Brian Jenkins surveyed his handiwork with satisfaction. True, it had taken the best part of five days to nurse his story into print. He'd spent some of the time corroborating one or two things by touring the area in which the story was set. He'd asked a few casual questions in Lower Stanford and taken a photograph of Forge Cottage. He's even had a chat with cleaning staff in a hospital canteen about a hi-jacked ambulance. These and other investigations helped to underpin his story. He had also had to convince his editor, who expressed some disquiet over its source. Information overheard could be information misheard. It was less to be trusted than documentary evidence, especially emails and personal websites. But his follow-on research was persuasive, and, in any case, the story had not been picked up by any other paper, so if there really was something in it, it was certainly a triumph to scoop the nationals with something that clearly had national (even international) implications. It was worth the risk to run with it. And there it was – his story. It even had his by-line. He now waited for the nationals to contact him and the editor. If the editor had any sense he would have alerted them by now.

The one disappointment had been the girl, Mary – at least until the Monday night. For the first three or four days he'd broached the topic of Father Mac's ordeal very gently, then a little more directly, but all he'd really learned was that the two people who had employed her as a secretary-cum-housekeeper in Forge Cottage had been foreigners who thought the priest had some information they needed, papers of some sort. What this information was, and how they came to think he had it, Mary could not say. She did at least mention that the poor old chap had got duffed up by the one that had stayed behind in the cottage, but then the thug got drunk and the priest, Tim Sullivan, and Mary herself had escaped. He knew most of that, anyway.

The worst thing was that he, Brian Jenkins, bachelor supreme, was actually falling for Mary in a way he'd never in his life fallen for any girl before. She was sweet and gentle. He'd wanted to include her name in the article, but she would have none of it. Whether or not it was true that mention of her name would place her in danger, as she had claimed, he had sacrificed a compelling journalistic detail (female involvement) on the altar of love (or at least a growing affection). But then suddenly, two nights ago, the night before he was ready to go to press, she happened to mention that she'd seen the third member of the gang. What third member? Suddenly, his article had sprouted an extra, tantalising, line. He also knew now how he must spend much of his time in the days ahead – just driving around, looking for a car acting suspiciously in the vicinity of the presbytery and Tim Sullivan's house.

*****

Tim always paid his daily visit to the shops in the late morning by which time the Cotswold Regent would have arrived. Today was no different.

"Hello, Mr Sullivan," said Caroline, "Bourton's getting to be famous. You even get a mention." She pointed to the headline on the front page.

PRIEST'S KIDNAP AND TORTURE LINKED TO SECRET DOCUMENTS: FOREIGN AGENTS IN CUSTODY

Tim silently groaned. This was most unwelcome.

"Where on Earth did they get this rubbish from?" he said.

"I expect someone put two and two together and made five or six. That will be Brian Jenkins. In fact, it says so."

"Well, I won't condemn him until I've read what he has to say."

"Despite that, have a nice day," said Caroline.

Tim went home, made a big mug of coffee and read the article. Photographs of Forge Cottage and St Nicholas presbytery accompanied it.

From Brian Jenkins

It has been revealed that Father Donald McNulty, parish priest of St Nicholas Church in Bourton, was the victim of a daring kidnap by foreign agents seeking unspecified documents thought to contain secret or sensitive information. These documents came into Father McNulty's possession on a recent visit to Canada and he is believed to have brought them back as souvenirs, unaware of their sensitivity. How he came to acquire them is not known.

> Following a stroke some two weeks ago and treatment in Cheltenham General Hospital, Father McNulty was driven to a hospice near Nailsworth for rest and recuperation, where he was kidnapped together with a parishioner, Mr Timothy Sullivan, and transferred to a stolen ambulance, originally believed to have been taken for joy-riding by youths. Mr Sullivan is a former member of GCHQ, the spy base. The kidnappers, thought to be agents from Eastern Europe, later transferred their hostages to another vehicle and took them to Forge Cottage, Lower Stanford, where Father McNulty was assaulted under questioning. One of the assailants then proceeded to the presbytery of St Nicholas Church, where he was apprehended following a tip off. The other agent was arrested in Lower Stanford. It is not known whether the agents have links to a terrorist organisation. A third associate is thought to be at large.
>
> Father McNulty is now recovering in Cheltenham General Hospital.

Well, thought Tim, it could have been much worse. The reference to a terrorist organisation was almost mandatory these days in the context of unexplained criminal activity, so that could be a useful red herring. And there was nothing about Father Mac's transfer to the hospice again. There was no evidence either that Mary had revealed anything of value, except perhaps the reference to the "third associate," but Mary herself, thankfully, wasn't mentioned. This was restrained and – dare he say it? – responsible journalism. The real problem was what might happen if the national press picked up the story. They clung on like terriers if they sensed there was more to be elicited with the help of a cheque book. He'd better have a quick word with the security people who would be picking him up later in the day.

He phoned security and explained what had happened.

"I can only think the reporter, Jenkins, was near the presbytery when the arrest was made. There was a bit of a crowd there. I know that was nearly a week ago, but he'd need a bit of time to go sniffing round places like Lower Stanford. And he knew enough to make the connection with the hi-jacking of the ambulance. By the way, the office gets a brief mention because I used to work there. I don't think any harm's done. Yet. It's a question of whether the nationals pick it up."

"Thanks for the tip. I'll feed it into the system. On the nationals, we'll cross that bridge when we come to it. They may want to have a D-Notice ready. I'm not surprised the *Regent* managed to mention us. They always do if they can find the remotest reason to."

That was certainly true. The movement of GCHQ from Eastcote to Cheltenham in the early 1950s had proved a godsend to the Regent. They found it impossible to ignore the fact that, sitting right on their doorstep was this wonderful milch-cow, ready to offer the basis for another headline, usually beginning with the words "Spy Base ..." (Spy Base Man Found Dead, Spy Base Faces Staff Cuts, etc., etc.).

*****

Tim decided to rest up after lunch. He didn't know how tiring the next day or so would prove, so he put the alarm on for 3:30 pm and lay down on top of the bed. In what seemed minutes, he was roused by the alarm, changed, packed his overnight bag, and put it by the front door with his briefcase. Dress for comfort, the man had said. Jeans would not quite do, so he wore cream coloured corduroys with a turtle neck. He assumed he would be indoors the whole time, but he took his trench coat (his flasher mac, as Lucy called it) and an umbrella, just in case.

Precisely on time, the car pulled up outside his house. Tim grabbed his bag, his briefcase, his mac, and umbrella, locked the door behind him, and went over to the car.

On his dining room table lay a CD.

*****

Mikhajl Petrovich Kuznetsov, known to his friends as Misha, had gone to ground after his colleagues' arrest. He would dearly have liked to spend a part of every day maintaining a sporadic watch over both the presbytery and Tim's house. He was not certain that whatever documents the old priest had hidden away were still in his presbytery, but suspected they might by now have been moved to Mr Sullivan's house. Sullivan could, of course, have handed them over to the intelligence people. Misha was well aware the Security Service knew of his existence and could probably put a face to him, but he was certain that they did not know where he lived. He was "of no fixed address" as they said over here and he had to keep it that way. He was obliged to move around, spending no more than a couple of days in the same hotel

181

or Travelodge, and changing his hire-car every couple of days. The best he could do in Bourton was drive past both the presbytery and Tim's house as frequently as he dared, without loitering more than a few minutes. Sooner or later Sullivan would leave the house for long enough for Misha to risk having a look round. Nearly a week after Stepan's arrest, his luck was in.

Misha had stopped some distance past Tim's house, pretending to consult a map while observing the house in the rear-view mirror. He had to be careful, as there was a man nearby, obviously a resident, using a foot-pump on his tyres and an old chap in the distance walking his dog. A car drew up outside Tim's house and a minute or so later, the Sullivan man came out clutching a briefcase and small bag, and clambered into the rear of the car. Misha took stock. The bad news was that Sullivan had a briefcase, probably containing the documents. That was ominous. The good news was that Sullivan was being taken somewhere in an official car, and would, therefore, be away for an hour or so at the very least – perhaps even overnight, given that it was already 4 pm. But what good would that be, if there was nothing to find? He considered a careful collision with the official car, but knew that was a non-starter. A second car would be tailing Sullivan's car and emergency procedures would immediately take over, resulting in his arrest. All he could do was have a look round in the house, later on, when the road had settled down to its evening routine. You never knew.

*****

Tim found he was the only passenger. They took the scenic route via Stow and joined the A40 at Burford. Near Oxford, they left the A40 and took a succession of minor roads for about forty minutes. Finally, they stopped by a pair of large wrought-iron gates. The driver spoke briefly into a mobile phone, and an unseen mechanism caused the gates to open. They turned into a gravel drive, which wound around for some distance until they stopped outside a large house. It was an old, rambling residence that might well have served as a farmhouse in its time. It was hidden from the road.

A tall, slim man probably like Tim in his early sixties, his face wreathed in smiles, came out to greet them. He was dressed in a blazer and flannels, and reminded Tim of the secretary of a golf or country club.

"Tim Sullivan, how do you do? Are we glad to see you! Together with your bits and pieces, I hope. We heard you had found them." They entered the old house. "My name's Charles Fenton, and I'll be your host. Now, first things first. Let's get you settled in, then we'll brief you on what this is all about, though I dare say you'll have formed some opinions on it. We'll have a spot of supper, then – a serve-yourself do. Informal. A few others will have joined us by then. You'll know some of them. After that, we'll listen to your own information, and that will include the account by Father McNulty of his adventures in Canada. I assume you've brought that with you?"

"Yes. And I've copied it to a CD, which I've also brought."

"Good. The most helpful thing will be for us simply to let you talk without interruption. A sort of mini-presentation. I know you've done plenty of those in your time. So take us through every aspect of your own involvement in this business, including the good Father's story, then we'll give delegates their own copy of his evidence. We'll print those from the CD."

"What about the various fragments Father McNulty brought back?"

"Don't worry about those for the moment. Most people are staying overnight for further discussions tomorrow. This was to have been one of our regular progress meetings, but the agenda has been adjusted to include this latest episode. We can pick up on the fragments after we've heard from you. We'll put them in a safe, for now. Bring them down with you. Anyway, let's find you a room." He beckoned. A thick-set man, probably in his early forties and dressed in a smart suit, materialised by his side.

"Mr Marshall will show you to your room. Let's see. It's five-forty now. I'll see you here at six."

Marshall knew better than to separate an intelligence officer from his briefcase, so Tim carried it himself, up one flight of thickly carpeted stairs, then along a corridor. His room was at the end.

There was no lock. The room was basic, but comfortable – bed, wardrobe, small chest, bathroom en suite with toilet and shower. A few pictures. No TV. It looked out on to a rear garden, well tended. In the far distance, houses could be seen dotted about, enough to suggest a small village or hamlet. It was deathly quiet everywhere. Tim freshened up and, taking the briefcase with him, went back down to the hall, where he found Fenton waiting for him, holding a box-file.

"Ah, Tim," he beamed, "let's go to one of the briefing rooms." Tim followed him and they went into a small room decked out like an office, with a computer work-station, a filing cabinet, a small table, and a couple of easy chairs. A tray with tea and biscuits awaited them.

"Right, sit yourself down. What I would like you to do is simply to read a briefing sheet. There are several versions of the briefing designed to meet a variety of needs, some of a general nature for senior management, like the Prime Minister, some a little more detailed for most purposes. We're giving you the standard working-level briefing."

Fenton rummaged in the box file and produced a sheet of paper headed Top Secret ELK ONE.

"ELK stands for "Extremely Limited Knowledge." You're joining a very exclusive club. There's an ELK TWO, as well. I'll explain that later. Anyway, just go ahead and read."

Tim settled back in the easy chair and read the briefing paper.

TOP SECRET ELK ONE

For many years now, our planet has been visited by vehicles originating in other civilisations. Evidence from recent visits strongly suggests that some, at least, of these vehicles form a common grouping, presumably all originating from the same source. This series has been designated Group A.

So far (here the present day's date had been inserted) sixteen such visits are known to have been made, all but six of them to Russia. The others have been two each to the United States and Canada, and one each to Australia and the United Kingdom. Three vehicles have crashed, one each in Russia, the United States, and Canada. The possibility that visits have also been made by Group A vehicles to other countries, while considered unlikely, cannot be totally discounted.

The countries named above are in possession of documents, in the form of books, jettisoned by vehicles in Group A while briefly alighting. These books are in an alien orthography and appear to be identical. They also appear to be intended as gifts, presumably for the governments of the countries visited. In the case of crashed vehicles, fragments of the same book have been recovered.

It is of the utmost importance to the security of the United Kingdom and of the world in general to establish the content and nature of the books. It is not known at this stage whether the contents, if they could be read, might reveal details of propulsion or weapons systems, but this must be considered a possibility. Any power capable of exploiting the content of the documents could gain military ascendancy over all others. For this reason, it is vital that the materials in question do not fall into the hands of countries hostile to the United Kingdom and its allies. It is possible that some of these countries may already have some documents, but it is essential that additional such material does not reach them. It is known that a number of agents in the pay of an unknown authority are routinely mobilised in an attempt to reach the site of an alien visit before the intended recipient.

The United Kingdom has entered into an information-sharing agreement with the other countries that have received visits from these vehicles and have received or recovered copies of the books. At present, as noted above, the countries (known as Primary Users) are: The United States, Canada, Australia, Russia, and the United Kingdom. These countries, all of whom have established working groups to study the books, are pledged to keep each other informed of any progress made in reading them.

A number of other countries have received a limited briefing on these matters, but are not party to the sharing of materials or results unless agreed by all Primary Users. Australia is responsible for briefing New Zealand, while the United Kingdom briefs France and Germany. Countries hostile to the United Kingdom and its allies are not party to any agreement.

Within the United Kingdom, the following responsibilities have been assigned and are conducted in collaboration with counterpart organisations of the Primary Users:

a. **The Ministry of Defence (Defence Intelligence):** study of intelligence relevant to the propulsion systems and weapon systems of visiting space vehicles.

b. **Government Communications Headquarters**: study of documents recovered from space vehicles with a view to resolving their content. Also, monitoring communications of potentially hostile countries to try to establish whether they are in possession of similar documents.

c. **Secret Service (MI5):** in collaboration with appropriate police authorities, surveillance of persons thought to be involved in efforts to acquire illegally documents forming the basis of such studies, or to gain access to results from such studies.

d. **Secret Intelligence Service (MI6):** development of contacts with persons in a position to know of the acquisition by potentially hostile countries of any such documents.

Any queries on activities covered in this briefing note should be addressed to the relevant ELK ONE Control Officer.

*****

Tim sighed. "This mostly confirms my guesses on the whole business," he said, "Though I hadn't realised everything was so well organised and involved such close collaboration with those nations you mentioned. The US, Canada, Australia, and New Zealand I can understand. This is no different to UKUSA, the Sigint alliance. Germany and France are prominent as NATO members, but Russia is a bit of a surprise as an intelligence partner – though, as you said, they have had the most contacts."

"Yes," agreed Fenton. He paused. "Actually, they approached us for help. I think they were worried the landings posed a threat. And who can blame them? They knew the United States and Canada had had similar visits, decided they needed a few allies, so who better to turn to? They have also been impressed by the effectiveness of our Sigint agencies. By the way, that last bit, about the relevant ELK ONE Controlling Officer. Although I'm the one briefing you, your Control will obviously be in Cheltenham. Very few 'outsiders' receive this briefing; by 'outsider' I mean someone not a current working member of the agencies mentioned. One is Hugh Frobisher, then there's a retired chap from MI5 and an eminent scientist who might have something to contribute on the technical side. You'll meet him later. I think it's possible your priest will also need a briefing. I understand he

186

was right at the heart of that business in Canada. Oh, and by the way, there is also a special briefing for what we call "inadvertent disclosure." It is very possible that one or two friends of yours will have to sign that one. You were not to know that by involving them you were exposing them to what you now know is highly sensitive information. That briefing doesn't give any detail. It just alerts them not to go blabbing about the bits they do know."

Tim was well aware of that procedure, aimed mainly at situations where classified papers somehow got handled out of channels. A sleepy post-room clerk at, say, an embassy, might absentmindedly open envelopes plastered all over with codewords or caveats he was not familiar with. It could scare the daylights out of him when he found he was required to sign an acknowledgement to that effect, and saw the penalties he could incur were he to shoot his mouth off.

"Now," continued Fenton, "I'll just explain ELK TWO. Whereas ELK ONE is concerned with documentary evidence retrieved from the visits, ELK TWO is concerned with hardware, and particularly the technical capabilities of the vehicles. Surprisingly, for what must be an incredibly advanced civilisation, three vehicles have crashed, in each case leaving no more than a shell. As far as we know a self-destruct device has always been triggered, so the ELK TWO committee exists just in case something useful might be recovered, and to theorise on the technology. The scientist and a member of the Defence Intelligence Staff are the only ones on both committees to look out for cross-pollination opportunities. OK? Any other questions, save for later. There'll be time for discussion after your presentation later this evening. We'll be eating at seven. I'm afraid we don't run to a bar before dinner. There'll be wine, of course, with the meal, and after business an informal bar is laid on for nightcaps. Now have you brought those bits and pieces with you?"

Tim opened his briefcase and gave Fenton Father Mac's precious fragments, which he had brought in the original hessian bag.

"Thanks. I can hear others arriving. I'll introduce you to them. Follow me when I've locked these away." He placed the bag in a stout wall safe with a combination lock.

Tim followed Fenton into a large reception room, where he found six people standing or sitting and chatting animatedly. One of them was Frobisher. He was speaking to two others. Tim hadn't met them but instantly recognised them for what they obviously were – SIS types, wearing the standard SIS uniform for informal gatherings – cords, open-necked plaid shirt, cravat, and woolly pully slung over the shoulders with sleeves knotted in front. Yachtsmen frequently affected a similar dress-code among their peer group. The other group consisted of Nick Watson, the current head of H Division, and two M.O.D. representatives he recognised from past working groups. Even as Frobisher started making the introductions, another gaggle of new arrivals entered the room. They included two women, one a scholarly looking type with glasses and a grey bun, the other younger, a petite brunette in a smart trouser suit.

Fenton called for quiet, then said, "Dinner will be served in ten minutes. Most of you will know where the dining-room is. This chap here is Tim Sullivan. I know you've all heard of him. He's hi-jacked our agenda this evening, I'm pleased to say. Don't bombard him with questions now. Wait for his briefing after supper."

"May I just ask one question?" said the school-ma'am. "How is that brave priest of yours? We've been told the barest bones and I know you'll cover it in detail. I just wanted to pre-empt on that one point. All right, Charles?"

Fenton nodded.

"You probably heard he was roughed up a bit," said Tim. "That was on top of the stroke he'd recently had. I'm glad to say he's now recovering pretty well. Thank you for your concern."

The school-ma'am nodded. "Good," she said. "Good."

"Tim, why not just circulate and we'll all introduce ourselves," said Fenton, "Then we'll move into the dining-room."

Tim went first to the grey-haired lady, who introduced herself as Debbie Faulkner. He was interested to learn that she was from the Cabinet Office, a member of the Assessments Staff of the Joint Intelligence Committee. She chaired the working group. He could not remember all the names thrown at him as he did the rounds but it was enough for now, he thought, to remember which organisations were represented. Predictably, these were the intelligence collection agencies, GCHQ, SIS, and SS, together with the Foreign Office, and Defence Intelligence from M.O.D. Also, of course, the JIC through the group's chairman. The other woman worked for Nick Watson, in H, presumably as his team leader in the attack on the documents that came their way. She was introduced as Kathy Webb. A tall, lanky man with a scattering of white stubble was also in the group. He introduced himself as Alan Lewis, the senior scientific advisor.

In the intelligence community, two agencies, GCHQ and the Secret Intelligence Service, MI6, are responsible for foreign intelligence, that is, intelligence about foreign countries, in particular political and military intelligence, though increasingly, terrorism and criminal activity involving narcotics, illegal arms shipments, and money laundering In the case of MI6, information comes largely from cultivating human contacts (Humint), while in the case of GCHQ it is derived from the intercept of communications (Comint), or of electronic emissions from, for example, foreign radars (Elint). The two are known collectively as signals intelligence (Sigint). Both GCHQ and MI6 are Departments of the Foreign Office.

The Security Service, MI5, by contrast, is responsible for threats to the "home base." It seeks to identify people and situations likely to threaten the democratic and peaceful conduct of life in the United Kingdom, and is ultimately administered by the Home Office. Another very active player, though not a collection agency, is the Ministry of Defence. There is a good deal of liaison among all these departments. The use of secret intelligence resources is an expensive business and customer departments are encouraged to ensure a requirement cannot be met by overt sources before requesting use of covert resources. The requirements process is an annual exercise thrashed out under the supervision of the Joint Intelligence Committee and fine-tuned on a day-to-day basis in response to world events.

There were fifteen delegates altogether in the safe house, all friendly and clearly looking forward to Tim's presentation. He'd done a little preparation, more in terms of the structure of his talk, than its content. As a general drift to the dining-room began, a familiar voice called "Sorry I'm a bit late Debbie. I got caught up in an operational thing."

"Bob!" cried Tim, "I knew you were somehow involved in things after your retirement, but I'd no idea you were part of this working group. You are, aren't you?"

"I certainly am, Tim," he beamed. "I think I told you, I'm what's called a consultant. I've just been lining up a few ducks."

"I know we've spoken a few times, but I hadn't realised you were so closely involved."

"I was on the point of phoning you that first time you phoned me. I'd heard of your priest, Father Mac, and knew what he was supposed to be sitting on. I'm so sorry he had to suffer. You, too."

"Oh, my whack on the head was nothing. Anyway, let's eat."

CHAPTER 21

The meal was excellent. There was a large assortment of vegetables and a choice of meat, carved by a chef in full regalia. Turkey or beef. Or both. Mr Marshall reappeared in the guise of sommelier. Uncertain who knew exactly what, Tim seated himself with Frobisher and Bob. He confined his conversation to reminiscing, and finding out about former colleagues. Dessert and coffee came and went. The time flew by, until finally, at half past eight, Charles Fenton said, "Right, we'll meet in the large lounge in fifteen minutes. Come with me, Tim, and I'll get your notes. We'll keep the bits and pieces where they are until tomorrow, unless for any reason the Chairman rules in favour of a quick glimpse tonight."

When they went into the lounge, Tim saw things had been set up for the "fireside chat" style of presentation, not the classroom style with lectern and hard chairs. Sofas and easy chairs were the order of the day. Tim was pointed to a chair near the large, open fireplace, next to the Chairman, and his audience arranged themselves in two semi-circles facing them.

"Right, Tim, it's all yours," said Debbie Faulkner. "I think we'll let you go straight through unless someone has a vitally important request for clarification. By the same token if you have a pressing question to ask of us, please go ahead."

Tim looked round at the expectant faces. "About a month ago, my life as a retired intelligence officer was proceeding along its placid, uneventful way. Then all hell broke loose, when my parish priest had a stroke. First, let me say a few words about him. I think a brief pen-picture is called for. His name is Father Donald McNulty, he's the parish priest of St Nicholas Catholic Church in Bourton-under-Wychwood in the Cotswolds, and he's affectionately known as Father Mac. Everyone calls him that – fellow clergy, including the Bishop, his parishioners and everyone in Bourton. He's in his late seventies and has an older sister in her early eighties. She's a nun called Sister Winifred. She's also a qualified nurse and, not surprisingly, she lives and works in a convent, which also incorporates a hospice. A few beds are available, too, for the care of priests who are discharged from hospital after a serious illness. Father Mac also has a younger brother, Andrew, who married a Canadian girl and lives in Ottawa. It's only in the last few days that I've discovered he was a cryppie in CSE, the Canadian counterpart organisation to GCHQ. I believe Hugh and Nick Watson know him. Every year or two Father Mac flies out to Canada to stay with Andy. These visits usually include a period of camping. Proper camping, under canvas. Inevitably, over the years Father Mac has developed friendships with the local clergy in Ottawa and with one priest in particular. That's probably enough to set the scene, Madame Chairman. Do you have any queries at this point?"

"Just one thing. I believe I heard Father Mac is an accomplished linguist and among other languages speaks Russian. Not that this is relevant other than to highlight the general direction of his academic interests and achievements outside of the Church."

"Yes, that's right. Before his vocation and ordination, he did National Service, as most young men did. In his case he was one those few men trained to interpreter level in Russian. He did this at Cambridge. Some interpreters were trained in London. Many later reached eminence in their career fields. Some of them joined GCHQ."

"We recruited some, too," said an SIS man, whose name Tim could not recall. Name tags would have been useful.

"As it happens, Madame Chairman," continued Tim, "Father Mac's knowledge of Russian is particularly relevant. It meant he could understand what was going on when our adversaries discussed things with each other. Anyway, as I was saying, he had a stroke. In the event, it was not too serious as strokes go, but it did reduce sensation down his right side, and largely robbed him of his speech, although that does seem to be coming back pretty well now. His sister came to stay in the presbytery, so that she could have a base for visiting him, and perhaps to look after him when he was discharged. One other thing that's relevant is that a group of us, myself, his sister, his housekeeper, and his close friend, a retired GP, discussed his general state of health leading up to the stroke, and we concluded that ever since coming back from Canada a week or so earlier he had been very subdued – not at all his normal, ebullient self. His sister, the nun, said perhaps he was suffering from stress, following two road accidents, or near misses he'd had while he was in Canada. These incidents came as news to the rest of us.

"Now, the same morning Father Mac was taken off to hospital two strangers, both men, appeared on the scene asking about his illness and what would happen in his absence. They were foreigners, in fact Russians named Stepan and Feliks, as we discovered later. All this seemed very suspicious, particularly when it was followed by a break-in at the presbytery. This happened the same night, which was also the first night Sister Winifred was in the presbytery. In fact, she interrupted the intruders, and following a bit of detective work by ourselves and the police it was soon established that two local lads, both eighteen, were involved. It later transpired they had been paid by the two strangers to gain entry and to search for and deliver any documents they found that were in what they described as "funny writing." Father Mac, as we just said, speaks a number of languages and enjoys reading books in these languages. Our two likely lads grabbed a few armfuls of books in Greek, Cyrillic, and Arabic and fled. I don't think their paymasters would have been too pleased.

"On visiting Father Mac in hospital, I found that he was desperate to tell me something. After a few visits I could just about make out two things: one was that he had seen an angel, or so he claimed. It made me wonder if this explained his quiet, contemplative mood of late." Tim paused here, waiting for laughter from his audience, but there was none. "The other thing I was able to deduce was that there was some document, probably on his computer, that he was anxious for me to see. After a few false starts, I eventually located the file. I found it after browsing through a large number of emails between Father Mac and the priest in Ottawa. I won't go into these emails in any detail. Suffice it to say that the ones before his visit related to plans for the visit, and those after his return mainly alluded to some event near his campsite, apparently an air crash of some sort, and measures taken to hush the whole thing up. The full story is in the file itself, the one Father Mac was so anxious for me to see. As I said, I succeeded in finding it and I've been asked to read to you in full the contents of that file as the basis for discussion. Tomorrow, copies will be available to those who need one. Copies are also available of the emails I've just described. They add little to the account by Father Mac of his adventures in Canada, but they do mention a number of related events that occurred after his return to the UK. Is it your wish, Madame Chairman, that I now simply read Father Mac's ... er ... testimony?"

"Yes, Tim, I think so. All that preamble was very interesting, and, I'm sure, quite necessary. We now have a useful context in which to hear the detailed account. So please go ahead. I know it's lengthy, but it will be extremely helpful to the work of this group."

It took Tim the next forty minutes or so to read Father Mac's story. He took it slowly to allow those who wished to, to take notes. As he read, Tim noticed that some parts of the testimony elicited a frisson of recognition in his audience. Some were particularly excited when he got to Father Mac's description of the logo on the crashed spacecraft. His abortive attempts to discuss the incident he'd witnessed to the Canadian DND brought a few grins, and there were nods of approval at the Priest's interview at the British High Commission. Father Mac's account of the incidents after his return brought sympathetic shakes of the head. Tim finished reading the priest's testimony, and turned to Debbie Faulkner.

"That's the end of Father Mac's account," he said. "As you can see, attempts to involve him in a road accident that were begun in Canada followed him home. The small group of us in Bourton who have been following things closely are convinced that they are all related, as was the break-in at the presbytery the night after his stroke. The road incidents in Canada seem designed to disable the vehicle Father Mac was driving without damaging any fragments from the crash he might have had with him, or perhaps to seize Father Mac and remove him from the scene before anyone else, especially the police, showed up. They were aiming at a controlled crash."

"I think we would share that view, Tim, especially in light of subsequent events," said Debbie Faulkner. "Their paymaster clearly thought, as we do, that the books left for us on these visits may somewhere contain a description of their propulsion system and he wants them intact. Thank you for reading Father Mac's account. I'm sure we all found it fascinating, and I for one, am so pleased he had the foresight to make this record. Now, why not round it all off by reminding us of the most recent chapter of events."

"Right. Immediately after I had located the document I've just read to you, I was determined to find the fragments Father Mac said he had hidden in the presbytery. I'm sure you don't want to know of the various enquiries I made with builders and others about nooks and crannies they might have discovered during past work on the building. Oh, by the way, I mustn't overlook the brilliant intervention by my dear mother-in-law. She really started the whole chain of events that led to their discovery by reminding me that what is now the presbytery of St Nicholas Church was built in the sixteenth century by wealthy wool merchants who were also Catholics. To continue practising their faith meant constructing one or more priest holes. And that's where the fragments turned up. In a carefully crafted hidey-hole under the floor. Meantime, Father Mac was considered well enough to be discharged

193

from hospital, and his sister, the nun, found a bed for him in her hospice. I believe you know what happened then."

"Not all of us, Tim," said Ms Faulkner.

"Well, with the hospital's permission, and with some vague idea of sparing their resources, I volunteered to drive Father Mac, together with Sister Winifred, down to the hospice south of Nailsworth. In view of Sister Winifred's medical training, this was agreed. When we arrived at the hospice, bogus paramedics grabbed Father Mac and me and bundled us into an ambulance they'd borrowed. A few minutes later we were transferred to a van containing the same two gentlemen who were sniffing around the day Father Mac was first taken ill, and we ended up in a small village near Bourton, where they'd rented a cottage. We were tied up, and Father Mac was interrogated, then beaten up when he refused to disclose where the fragments were. To prevent further suffering I told them the fragments were in the presbytery under a floor board. I hadn't at that stage found them myself, but one of two villains, the one called Stepan, raced off to the presbytery to look for them. The other, Feliks, the thug who'd hurt Father Mac, got drunk and, with the help of the girl they employed as housekeeper/secretary, who pushed him down the stairs, we got free and pursued Stepan. All sorts of other people turned up, and as you know, Stepan and Feliks were taken into custody. We are most grateful to those who were involved in the arrest. We do, however, have two loose ends."

"Only two?" quipped someone.

"Only two I'm aware of," said Tim, "though there are loads of things I don't know that I'm hoping you'll allow me to ask about shortly. The two loose ends are firstly that there is a third man."

"There's always a third man," said another voice amid general laughter.

"The third man this time is called Misha. He's the one I'm concerned might try to get inside the presbytery or my own home. We know the fragments are with us here. I brought them with me. But Misha doesn't know where they are. So this might be an opportunity to nab him. The second loose end is that the local press have got some whiff of the story. There was a short item earlier about the stolen ambulance, but this takes the story much further. We think the reporter was among a small crowd of bystanders outside the presbytery when our friend Stepan was arrested. I've brought the cutting with me." Tim read them the clipping. "I don't think too much harm has been done. There is no conjecture about the content of the so-called documents or their precise provenance. I suppose it depends on whether the nationals pick it up and try to expand on it, especially some of the tabloids."

"Yes," sighed Ms Faulkner, "the press are always a potential threat to security. You can't beat investigative journalism for bringing scandalous behaviour in high places to the notice of the general public, but at the same time you can't beat them for undermining national security. If they think they sniff anything at all sensitive or delicate they often drive a coach and horses through it and do untold damage. They seem to think it is the nature of intelligence agencies to act irresponsibly. I can understand your concern, Tim, but I wonder if this is anything to worry about. It might not look like a story worth pursuing when no more information is forthcoming. The press get hold of so many stories purporting to deal with terrorist activities or planned activities, some genuine, many based on unfounded speculation. The local press may be doing us a favour in this case. This story may well die, as do so many others. Now," she continued, looking round at everyone, "I suggest we deal with the questions Tim said he'd like answers to. Are we all agreed?"

There was a general rumble of assent around the room.

"Good. OK, Tim, go ahead."

"Well, to begin with," said Tim slowly, "if there is a general exchange of data, why did the Russians use agents firstly in Canada, then in the UK to try to steal material salvaged from a crash in Canada that they already had?"

"They didn't," replied an MI5 man sitting next to Bob. "These three beauties, Stepan, Feliks, and Misha are Russian, but no longer agents. We do know of them. We've encountered them elsewhere. They seem to form a unit."

"So they're not working for the Russian government?"

"No way," said Bob's colleague. "They were originally members of the KGB, then the FSB, but after further changes in intelligence, they found themselves out of a job. But they and others had marketable skills. Those people couldn't do much on their own, so they became part of a larger group, who had been around for several years. You can compare them to a group to mercenaries, though their stock in trade is not killing soldiers in some African or Asian country, but contracting to pinch specific information, or simply nicking for the highest bidder anything they themselves consider to be sensitive. In the early days, just after the collapse of the Soviet Union, redundant or retired nuclear scientists were much in demand. Or rather, their specialised knowledge was. The group later expanded and diversified. Now pretty well anything goes. Military and industrial espionage, arranging financial mayhem, you name it. They have also been known to do the odd job for one or other of the major crime syndicates. And bumping off, to order."

"Including fellow-members of their own group as punishment for a botched job," interposed Bob.

"That's right. Misha is just a local organiser, and overall he's way down the pecking order. He takes a back seat most of the time. Stepan does most of the practical work. He's even been employed as a gigolo to get near to someone important through the missus or the daughter. So has Misha occasionally. Feliks is just muscle. Members of the group also recruit locals on an ad-hoc basis. We've no idea who the group's paymaster is for this present job. Several Asian countries, particularly in the Middle East and Far East, spring to mind. Even one or two in Africa, but they may be no more than intermediaries. It's one of the things we'd dearly love to find out. Probably no more than two or three people at the very top of the group know."

"Misha's group is not the only one recruited to hunt documents from these vehicles, is it?" asked Tim.

"No, it's not. There are several independent outfits like this one, but this is probably the largest, with foot-soldiers in many countries, some resident, some deployed for a specific job. We don't know how many have been mobilised for this particular operation – perhaps all of them, or at least several hundred – and that would cost the sort of amount that suggests government funding by some country or other, rather than a private employer. But to be honest, it's probably all a bit of a lost cause. The opposition don't know any more than we do where the next vehicle is going to come down. All they can do is deploy a token group in possible target regions, based on whatever knowledge they have of previous landings. It shows how desperate they are. We, on the other hand, have the combined manpower of the police and armed forces in several countries to call upon. As soon as a vehicle arrives, people from the nearest police station or military post are ordered to the scene to secure the area. Anyone found involved in document retrieval gets a very thorough interrogation. If they are clearly innocent souvenir hunters who just happened to be there, they get the "unauthorised disclosure" briefing – the one that says "Shut up, or watch out!" I'm not aware of any transgressions."

"I see," said Tim, nodding. "Another question is why did the Canadian Department of Defence not want the fragments from the crash that Father Mac offered them?"

"Two reasons," said Ms Faulkner. "First, accepting your priest's kind offer would have shown an interest they did not wish to disclose. And second, more importantly, they would have been tipped off by Andy that any documents offered by Father Mac would be those normally jettisoned by these vehicles. But he couldn't be sure. And he had no guarantee that if Father Mac took them home he would pass them to the right people in the U.K. However, as Father Mac was actually staying under his roof, Andy was confident he could photograph the fragments secretly, only to be caught red-handed by Father Mac. He then tipped us off about all this. We, for our part, clearly couldn't march up to Father Mac and demand this material, but we were pretty sure that in due course it would occur to him to share his secret with others, particularly as he was convinced, according to the Canadians, that an angel was involved. As it was, he must have spent a week or so studying the various bits and pieces. Then wisely he decided to set down an account of the events he was caught up in, in case he were to get wiped out on the M5 or fall ill, which did, indeed, happen. Fortunately for us all, Tim, it was you that Father Mac chose to confide in."

"However," Tim said thoughtfully, "Andrew did not copy all of the fragments. Only the book. The others, including those that the space visitor went back in for afterwards, were in Father Mac's suitcase. When you see them tomorrow I'm sure you'll be intrigued. I think they could turn out to be some of the most valuable bits you'll have seen."

"And that gives rise to a new problem." The speaker was Professor Lewis, the scientific advisor. "Do we send copies of these other fragments to all members of the Primary Group? I understand some of them are extracts from a medical book."

"Well, on the face of it, yes, that's what they are." said Tim. "Those are in fact the ones our visitor went back for. You'll see them tomorrow."

"It's true we've had nothing like this before, Alan," said Debbie Faulkner thoughtfully. "We'll have to consider whether these other fragments should be part of the exchange. My off-the-cuff feeling is 'Yes, why not?' We can discuss this tomorrow."

"But surely," said Tim, "you wouldn't expect a complete sharing of information. I mean, if I were at the helm in, say Russia or the United

197

States, and something never encountered before fell into my lap, I'd feel pretty disinclined to copy the whole lot umpteen times and send the copies to all the other signatories before thoroughly studying them here."

"But sharing documentary evidence from the Group A vehicles is exactly what we are pledged to do, though naturally we can't be sure we get absolutely everything. And it's just possible that vehicles in that group have visited countries outside those who are party to the agreement, including countries hostile to the UK. SIS and GCHQ in their respective ways have been trying to determine this."

"So, if the ultimate prize is knowledge of propulsion and weapons systems, do we know if these hostile countries are ahead of us in the game?"

"I doubt it, but it's not the job of this working group to get involved in things like that. Look, Tim, we need to make a distinction between the supply of documentary material for shared analysis, and technical studies on propulsion systems or weapons. Every country has its own effort on things like that. We certainly do, and it brings together some of the most brilliant scientific minds in the country. We don't want to get involved with arcane technical studies here, in our little Working Party – we are not competent to do so – but there are other working parties, with their own handling rules and caveats and restricted access, which are doing just that. These other working groups have existed for many years, certainly before we came into existence a year or so ago. The ELK TWO party is a recent offshoot of a well-established group, and was set up specifically to work with the ELK ONE party on the recent space visits."

"And some people are common to both the ELK ONE and ELK TWO groups to promote cross-pollination, as someone put it?"

"That's correct. As I said, we're very much concerned with documentary evidence and its analysis, and safeguarding these things. When we began to accumulate materials from a specific grouping of vehicles, identifiable both by their logo and their pattern of behaviour, we realised we might one day unearth something of value to the scientific community. So we have Professor Lewis and an M.O.D. liaison officer on this present working party. Nothing of sufficient moment has come our way yet. Indeed, we believe that if a vehicle crashes, and at least three have done so, a self-destruct mechanism is activated. So, the key is to get into the language. We've accumulated plenty of material over recent months. So far all of it are copies of the self-same textbook or whatever it is. But this recent haul sounds more promising."

"Speaking of crashing," said Tim, "if they're such an advanced civilisation and can travel across the galaxy over many light years, how come they've crashed – what – three times now?"

"Let me answer that," said Professor Lewis. "The short answer is we don't know. I'm quite sure the first two vehicles are being examined for clues, as will the third be tested. If anything relevant to the ELK ONE party emerges, they will be told. What I can say is that in our view these are one-man vehicles assembled in a mother ship parked somewhere in the solar system, perhaps between Saturn and Jupiter. Quite a bit of theoretical work would have gone into the design of something that could not actually be tested in the specific alien environment it was intended for. Frankly, these crashes do not surprise the engineers I've spoken to. Clearly, a certain amount of tweaking aboard the mother ship has been possible, or the track record might have been worse."

"Thank you, Professor, that's jolly interesting," said Tim. "Now, one final question if I may. Did the man I spoke to in the High Commission pass on the information I gave him?"

Ms Faulkner nodded. "He certainly did, or at least he got it into the right channels. The Canadians had in fact reported the crash to us already, so Father Mac's eyewitness account actually did no more than corroborate the report, but it did persuade us of the need to interview Father Mac at some point. The account we've just heard goes a long way towards satisfying that requirement."

"Ah," said Tim, nodding slowly. "Thank you for all that. It's making a lot more sense now. I've been struck by the fact that you all seem to be accepting quite calmly that these are space vehicles from another civilisation. We're in the realm of Unidentified Flying Objects, or flying saucers as they were first known in the 1940s, aren't we? People professing a belief in them were usually ridiculed, certainly in those days."

"Yes, Tim, we are in that realm. Many people pooh-poohed the idea, and that suited successive governments around the world, who publicly followed a policy of denial, fearful of mass hysteria. They all remember the Orson Welles radio production of 'War of the Worlds' in the United States and the panic it caused. HM Government has, in fact, accepted the existence of these spacecraft for decades now. Long before the particular series of visits that gave rise to the creation of this Working Party, the evidence has been irrefutable. There have been debates on these vehicles in closed sessions of the UN Security Council."

"Really? And do we know where this particular group of vehicles originates?"

"No, but we do know they are benign, and seem anxious to pass some information or other on to us. They always give us prior warning of a visit so that we look out for the book or books they leave. They send a radio signal. In fact, it's just a loud blast with a very wide bandwidth, so that we won't miss it. There's no modulation. It's just incoherent noise. We hear one blast about 36 hours before their arrival and second one about 6 hours before."

Tim digested this point. Hence Andy's summons back to Ottawa not in the least aware that this time (ironically) he'd be better actually staying where he was.

"Of course," continued Debbie Faulkner, "if we can hear the warning blast, so can the opposition. But this is technical stuff. Perhaps you would add a few words, Alan."

"By all means," said Professor Lewis. "We can initially detect them approaching the Earth when they've reached this side of the sun, but we cannot track them in the final stages of their approach until they are virtually at their destination. You can be sure a number of cars will be circling likely areas and a helicopter or two on standby. Then it becomes a race to get there before the bad guys. As you've heard, we've always succeeded, though in the case of the recent crash, it was touch and go. Father Mac was just ahead of them."

"One final point," said Tim. "Have there been any surviving crew members? I'm particularly interested in the spaceman Father McNulty saw. What will happen to him if he has survived?"

"I'm afraid we're getting way outside the remit of our working group. All I can say is that provision has been made for that eventuality."

"If Father McNulty's friend has survived, I'd suggest that Doctor Campbell try to elicit something from him about the medical pages. The good doctor believes he is on the brink of some startling discovery in the field of treatment."

"I can pass that on," promised Ms Faulkner. She smiled. "You are pretty relentless, Tim."

"And, please let Father Mac meet him. He's convinced he met an angel."

At this point, Bob excused himself from the meeting. "Phone call, Madame Chairman. This may be important."

"I think we'll suspend things till Bob gets back," said the Chairman. There was a mumble of assent, and a flurry of conversation among those present broke out. Within a couple of minutes Bob was back.

"The bad news, Madame Chairman, is that Tim's house was entered by friend Misha about an hour ago," he said. "The good news is that he's being tailed."

"It can hardly be bad news if there was nothing there worth taking," said Miss Faulkner, pointedly.

"That is so, isn't it?"

"If you don't mind, Madame Chairman, I think we're in danger of impinging on operational matters. A particular scenario is playing itself out and it's too early to say exactly how things will end. May I respectfully request that we don't go down this road? There may be something to say tomorrow."

The Chairman sighed. "Oh, very well then," she said, a little testily. "Let's move on. Now, following Tim's excellent presentation, is there anything we need to get into tonight? Personally, I think we'll be better armed tomorrow, when we've seen the fragments given to Father McNulty." She looked round. "Right, I wish you all goodnight. Charles?"

"Breakfast from 7:30 tomorrow. Business begins at 9 o'clock. Mr Marshall will be serving drinks in the small lounge," said Fenton. The meeting dispersed. Bob button-holed Debbie Faulkner and beckoned Tim over.

"I'm sorry to have sprung that on you, Debbie," he said. "The fact is I primed Tim to leave some bait around – a CD labelled 'Fragments from Canada' or something like that. In reality it contains something quite different. Misha seems to have taken the bait, which is good because we need to see who his paymaster is. At least the local one."

Ms. Faulkner nodded. "I assumed it was something like that. And what do you expect to happen?"

"There are several possible outcomes. It depends very much on whether he decides to look at the CD himself. If he does, he'll realise he's been tricked and the last thing he'll want to do is contact his paymaster or his intermediary, if there is one. If he doesn't look at it, then he'll want to get rid of it asap. Again, there are several ways to do this: personal contact, dead-letter, posting it, or even by email. We can deal with all those, though email is pretty unlikely."

"What if he does none of those things, suggesting he's examined the CD? "

"We're not sure. He might try something bolder."

"Hmm. We'll cross that bridge etc. etc." she said sceptically, though on the whole the Chairman seemed reasonably mollified. "Now presumably you're not interested in recovering this spurious CD. You just want to see who it's delivered to. You've had the other two rogues in custody for a few days and I know they've been questioned. Didn't they know who their paymaster is? Surely they'd heard something."

"Apparently not. But they're small fry. Totally expendable."

"OK, thanks, Bob. Thanks for all this. I look forward to tomorrow, Tim." Tim mumbled a "goodnight" still feeling a little guilty at not coming clean on making that extra copy that he'd hidden away for Doc Campbell.

When Debbie left them, Tim and Bob wandered into the small lounge. About a dozen men were standing around or waiting in a line to be served by Mr Marshall. Both women had retired.

"The first drink's on the house," said Bob. "After that, a trust system takes over. Pour your own and sign a bar chit. Settle up before you leave. Typical officers' mess routine."

Tim knew the dangers of getting drawn into a bout of heavy drinking with another busy day looming. He'd been involved in situations like this before, where the philosophy of "it seemed a good idea at the time" ruled. Getting back to his room an hour later, slightly squiffy, he realised he'd got off lightly. He'd left Bob and about six others down there. Before turning in, he rehearsed in his mind what he would say the next day.

CHAPTER 22

While Tim and the rest of them were busy with Tim's briefing, dramatic events were unfolding in Bourton and its vicinity, as was evident from Bob's phone call.

Misha had waited patiently in a lay-by outside Bourton until he considered all the breadwinners in Tim's road would be safely home, had fed themselves, and were settling down to watching TV or engaging in other evening activities. He parked some way up the lane, confident that his new hire car, rented only that morning, would not be tied to him. He was relieved to see the road empty. He left the car and made his way to Tim's home, which, like all those in the road, was a large detached house with a wide frontage, standing in nearly half an acre of grounds.

Misha had only to pass two other houses before reaching Tim's. He unlocked the front door, peered round it, located the control box, aimed a small torch-like device at it, and quickly deactivated the alarm (the wonders of modern science!). He moved silently around the ground floor and when he reached the dining room could scarcely believe his eyes. There on the table was a CD actually labelled "Fragments from Canada." Obviously a trick. But was it? Sullivan had probably had to organise prints and CDs for his meeting or briefing or whatever it was. It was so easy to make a simple mistake. Misha knew he could not waste time debating the issue, so quickly decided to take it.

He quietly let himself out, and strolled unobserved up the lane to his car, where he punched numbers into his mobile and issued instructions before moving off. Somewhere in Cheltenham, two people got ready to act.

As Misha emerged from the lane, another car already on the main road, carrying two police officers, Norm Hobbs and Steve Bentley, fell in behind him at a discreet distance and followed him up the hill towards Cheltenham, the passenger, Steve, speaking on a mobile phone as they did so. Another man, who had earlier been seen by Misha stamping on a foot-pump, emerged from the lane and brought up the rear. It had paid him to keep Tim's house under frequent observation. Misha knew full well he was being tailed by the police, but was quite content. He was unaware that the car behind the police was not simply another road-user, but a journalist from the Cotswold Regent. Norm and Steve, though, sensed that the car behind them was not a casual road-user, but some idiot tailing them. They did not, however, deduce that Brian Jenkins's real aim was to tail Misha. "Get the number of that smart-arse, and phone it in," growled Hobbs.

The sun was very low as the procession reached the top of the hill, auguring a gorgeous sunset over the Malverns. They moved down the other side of the hill, then crossed over to the Evesham Road and carried on to Cheltenham racecourse roundabout, where they turned left towards the Park and Ride, then right shortly after into Albert Road. A few moments later, the cortege turned into Pittville Park, where Misha stopped and parked, while Hobbs and Bentley halted some twenty yards behind him. Jenkins overtook both cars and stopped about thirty yards in front of Misha. The park opened out to their right. Misha sat for a while, glancing at his watch, then, evidently satisfied, got out. The others also disembarked.

Created in 1825, Pittville Park is a large, beautifully maintained public park and leisure facility. A network of paths winds its way throughout the park and an abundance or railings with small gates built into them are still in place, a relic of the past: whatever restrictions may have been placed on access in the early days have long gone. At this time of year, the park is popular at almost any time of day or night. At about 9 pm, when the three cars drew up, there were still many people strolling about, singly, as courting couples, as families, or as dog-walkers. There were also the usual joggers, some in small clusters, some preferring to run alone.

Jenkins watched as Misha entered the park through the large, wrought-iron gates of the major entrance and set off briskly down the path, with Norm and Steve not far behind. His own position, well to the left of the others, conferred two advantages on Jenkins. First, he was not very obviously tailing anyone, and second, by trotting along in parallel well to the side, he could view things from a different angle. Though evening was well advanced, the daylight was still pretty good, only a few days past midsummer. After about fifty yards, Misha's path forked. To the right lay access to the children's play area across a bridge, where the lake narrowed. To the left, after a few yards another path appeared that wound sharply to the right and down a steep slope to the Evesham Road subway, a damp, brick-built tunnel, brightly lit to display the mural executed on a Council initiative, and later embellished by graffiti from a legion of spray painters. Misha chose the subway. This placed him out of sight of Norm and Steve for about ten seconds, while they broke into a trot to catch up.

Misha got bogged down a bit by a group of people, including a few joggers, exiting the subway as he was entering, but then hurried through and upon emerging, stopped and chatted to a young man, while the two tails slowed, then loitered. There was a certain amount of gesturing, then Misha resumed his brisk pace and about fifteen or twenty yards further on, he stopped an elderly lady with a dog and again engaged her in conversation before hastening on.

The two tails briefly conferred. "You get the bloke and the old dear," said Steve, "and I'll keep tabs on our friend." The other nodded. But from his different angle, Jenkins had seen something they hadn't. Among the crowd of people emerging from the underpass as he was entering was a jogger – a young woman – whom Misha had had to sidestep to avoid. In that brief hesitation, something was transferred to the woman, who in turn transferred it to her track-pants pocket. All this took place in the blink of an eye, but Jenkins was certain he'd seen it. So, unlike the others, he turned round and followed the progress of the jogger. As he suspected she would, she made for the line of parked cars near the main gate, where she unlocked a Clio, moved something from her track-pants pocket into the glove compartment, consulted her watch, grabbed a towel, rubbed her face with it, then climbed in and drove off.

Jenkins was in two minds: should he follow the jogger or simply take her car number and rejoin the action in the park as his journalistic instincts prompted. If she was going only a short distance, though, perhaps he could enjoy the best of both worlds, Oh, come on man, make your mind up, the Clio's already moving. He quickly leapt into his car and caught it up at Pittville Circus roundabout. The girl carried on to Hewlett Road, then on to Prior's Road with Jenkins some fifty yards behind. She waited for the light, then turned into the car park of the new Sainsbury's.

The jogger parked, retrieved something from her glove compartment, then strolled over towards the entrance to the store. Jenkins climbed out of his car, ready to follow her inside, but instead of going in, she placed her hand briefly in the rubbish receptacle then hurried back to her car. Again doubt entered Jenkins's mind. Follow her, retrieve the package himself, or wait to see who retrieved the package? He had the Clio's registration number, and the police would have no problem finding her, unless there was a level of sophistication at work, involving false registration plates, which he thought extremely unlikely. These bit players were surely no more than that, weren't they – outsiders recruited to do Misha a favour or earn a few quid, then to be discarded? So, one choice disappeared. Another quickly followed.

As soon as the Clio began moving, a boy on a mountain bike raced into the car park, skidded to a halt by the rubbish bin, dipped his arm deeply into it and came up with what was clearly the package left there by the girl. A few late-night shoppers glanced curiously at him, but no-one challenged him. The general public usually ignore odd conduct, regarding it either as a bit of eccentricity to be smiled at indulgently, or as something vaguely threatening to be studiously ignored. Jenkins started the car with plans to follow the lad, but, of course, it proved completely impossible. The lad had every possible advantage, jinking away at speed, mounting pavements, cutting up side streets, ignoring traffic lights. Confident he was not being pursued, he executed a couple of celebratory wheelies, sped up the side of his house and propped his bike against the shed in his back garden.

*****

Lennie Gill said "Well?"

Colin Gill said nothing. He handed the package to his dad.

"Anyone see you?"

"I think some bloke was waiting to see who collected it, but you can't chase a bike in a car. Too many rules of the road."

"You sure he didn't see you come in here?"

"Yeah, Dad. Stop worrying."

"OK. Now you forget the whole thing, right? If you breathe a word of this to anyone, including your Mum, I'll belt you so hard you'll be sore for a month."

Colin Gill gulped. "I know, Dad. So I won't tell anyone." He'd had a lifetime of being belted by his Dad, sometimes even when the old sod was sober. Well, Colin was getting bigger every month and could take care of himself pretty well among his peer group. One day, he'd try out the old man for size. Give it another year or so.

Lennie looked at him steadily for what seemed an age. Then, apparently satisfied, pulled out a wallet, found a £10 note and handed it to his son.

"Here you are," he said, "and don't fucking spend it on strong cider. Oh, I know what you and your mates get up to, and you're not even sixteen yet." Lennie didn't really care. £10 for Colin out of £500 paid up-front was pretty good value!

Colin pocketed the tenner. The mean old sod had probably landed several hundred for this job.

*****

Over in Pittville Park, Norm Hobbs, interviewing the young man, met with no lack of willingness to cooperate. "Police?" said the man. "That man is wanted for questioning? No, he stopped me to ask the way to the racecourse. I thought what a frightfully stupid question at nine o'clock at night in the middle of the flat season. I told him, of course. No, he didn't pass a package to me. Yes, I'd be glad to give you my name and phone number." The elderly lady was less than cooperative, and all the while her scruffy little Yorkie worried Norm's trouser leg.

"Police? If it's about my dog licence, you don't need them now. Didn't anyone tell you, and you a policeman. That man who talked to me? No, of course I don't know him. I thought you were going to say he was the Pittville Park flasher. There is one, you know. Probably more than one. No he didn't give me a package. Certainly not. And don't you dare search me! He asked the way to the Pump Room. I told him to turn round and go back the way he came. But the silly man didn't. Now, are you sure you don't want to interview my dog?"

Meanwhile, Misha had surged ahead. He had ignored the first track past the subway which led off to the left to a small gate that provided access to the Evesham Road and carried on to the second turn. Here there was a signpost marked "Town Centre ½ Mile" leading to a more substantial exit. Misha turned up the track and quickly dodged into the conifers lining the footpath. But by now Steve was hot on his heels. Right, my friend, he thought, got you. Steve felt a sudden, sharp pain in the ankle, and saw with surprise a dark, wet patch developing where the pain was. Misha turned and made his escape through the exit into a residential area.

"Bastard's shot me," groaned Steve in surprise. "You miserable sod!" His colleague abandoned the elderly lady and raced up.

"Keep away!" gasped Steve.

"He's gone now," said Norm, flipping his mobile open. "We need to get you into A and E asap."

"Must report in, too."

"Look, you get back to the parking area," said Steve through teeth clenched in pain. "The ambulance will need directions. And our friend will need to come back for his car. Wait near there. This is bloody painful, but it's not life-threatening."

Returning to collect his car was the last thing on Misha's mind. Hire cars, at least those hired by the criminal fraternity, were made to be abandoned. He was quite happy to take a train to anywhere and simply hire another.

Norm saw the elderly lady he'd just interviewed and asked her to stay with the police officer who had been shot.

"I used to be a matron, when they still had them," she said. "Of course I'll stay with him. I'll see if I can make him comfortable." Not such a hostile old biddy after all.

After the ambulance had arrived and he had directed it to the scene of the shooting, Norm kept Misha's car under discreet surveillance, but after about ten minutes was convinced Misha was not planning to reclaim it. They could have tailed Misha to the park, arrested him immediately and recovered the package. But no. Their orders were strictly not to arrest him, but establish who he passed the package to. They wanted to identify the next layer up in this particular criminal hierarchy. Instead, the evening had been a total disaster! He then became aware of a young man staring in his direction. He looked vaguely familiar. The young man approached.

"Excuse me, officer, if you want Misha, I'm pretty sure he's gone. But if you want whatever it was he nicked from Tim Sullivan's house in Bourton-under-Wychwood, I can tell you where it is. Or at least, where it was."

"I'm sorry, sir, who are you? And what's all this about something stolen?" A bell rang in his mind. "You followed us here didn't you?"

"I was really following Misha, but let's not get into that please. I'm sure time is of the essence. I know all about this business you're concerned with. I work for the Cotswold Regent and I've been following things. Misha slipped something to a jogger near that tunnel thing. I saw it him do it. I followed her and saw her put something into her glove compartment. It was a small square package. I then followed her car. I can give you her car make and registration. It's a blue Renault Clio." He gave the registration number.

"Would you mind holding on a minute, sir." Norm punched a series of numbers on his mobile. He repeated the registration over the phone. "I'm hanging on. This is urgent. Right, go ahead. Chloe Martin, age 21.

Yes. What was the road? New Barn Close, Prestbury? Near the racecourse. Got you. Many thanks. Cheers."

"There's more," said Jenkins. "The young lady carried on to the new Sainsbury's on Priors Road and dumped the package in a litter bin near the entrance. It was very quickly picked up by a teenage lad. I tried to follow, but you can't really follow a bike in a car."

"That's very helpful, sir," said the policeman. "Sainsbury's, eh?" What an irony, thought Norm, the one built on the former GCHQ site. "Now, may I have your name, address, and phone number. Mobile, too, in case you're out. Please stay in your house as much as possible until further notice, or at least in the immediate vicinity. And keep your mobile switched on when you're out. We may need to contact you any time of day or night. I'm very grateful to you, and I don't often say that to journalists."

"If you're very grateful, how about fixing me up with an interview with your boss."

"You never know, sir."

"By the way. That ambulance that just arrived and drove off into the park. It wasn't by any chance for your colleague. I know there were two of you. The Regent will find out sooner or later, so you might as well confirm it now."

"I think not. Now, name, address and phone, please." He scribbled the information, then got in the car, slammed the door and took off. Should Jenkins follow him? After only a moment's reflection, he decided that to do so would cancel out whatever goodwill he'd forged with him. Besides, he'd seen the ambulance had stopped only a hundred yards or so away, lights flashing. Perhaps there was something else to be gleaned there.

*****

"Mr Martin?"

"Yes."

"Police, sir." Norm showed his badge. "I'd like to speak to Chloe."

"She's not here. She's out jogging. What's this all about? We're watching the telly. Is she in any trouble?"

"I'm afraid I can't talk about it. Look, I do need to see her urgently. Would you mind if I wait for her?"

"What's up, love?" Mrs Martin suddenly materialised behind her husband. She had an ample figure and a concerned look.

209

"Chloe's not in any trouble, Mrs Martin. It's – er – a bit like 'Crimewatch.' Chloe may be a useful witness."

"Oh." Mrs Martin nodded vigorously. "I'm sure our Chloe would want to help if she could. She sometimes goes for a drink with friends after jogging. Or sees her boyfriend."

"Oh, that was weeks ago, Mother. We've not seen him lately. Didn't he say he was going back to Poland?"

"He was a Polish plumber," explained Mrs Martin, "Nice looking man, but too old for Chloe."

"If you've no objection, I'll wait for her in the road. Please don't warn her I'm waiting here. It sometimes frightens people if they know the police want to see them. We do need her evidence. It's most important."

"We can't stop you waiting in the road. But come in if you want. How about a nice cup of tea?"

"That would be very kind, Mrs Martin." The last thing Norm wanted right then was a "nice cup of tea," but an invitation into a potential witness's household was not to be sneezed at.

Chloe arrived after about a further ten minutes. She breezed happily into the house, humming.

"Guess who I've just seen," she said. "Mum, what's up?"

"There's a very nice policeman to see you, dear."

"Oh, that's – er – nice." She smiled, a little nervously. Hmm, thought Norm, both Stepan and Misha could certainly pick them and both clearly preferred blondes. Chloe had bouncy, shoulder length hair, and a bouncy bosom to go with it.

"Sorry to bother you, Miss Martin, but I'd like to ask you a few questions. I don't mind if we do this privately, or whether your parents are present."

"Oh, let's go into the dining room," she said. "Mum and Dad would rather watch telly."

"No, dear, we're very happy to be with you. There's nothing worth watching at the moment, anyway." Mrs Martin went into the lounge and decisively turned the television off. She went off to make the tea, while the others found seats in the room.

"Now, you were asking your Mum to guess who you'd seen this evening. I think I can guess. It was your friend Misha, wasn't it?"

"Yes," she said, obviously surprised. "Is he involved with the police?"

"I'm afraid he is."

"It's those stupid antiques, isn't it?" said Chloe, mournfully. "I knew there was a bit of sharp practice going on. Still, I don't suppose plumbing pays all that much."

"Plumbers do pretty well," said Dad, "Not the same as dentists and bankers, but they do very nicely, thank you."

"Not if you have to send most of it back to help support two disabled parents," said Chloe with feeling.

Norm quickly intervened in what threatened to become a heated economic argument. "Did Misha give you something to deliver to someone else? Let me put that a different way. We know that Misha gave you something to deliver. It's vitally important that you tell me who you gave it to."

"I can tell you what it was, too," she said. The officer held his breath. "It was a CD. You've no idea what a cut-throat business antiques is. There were two or three of them involved together. He was really the brains, but couldn't always get to auctions or those estate sales. One of the others went. Misha would go through the catalogues and list all the items he was interested in and his price ceiling. He'd put it all on a CD and give it to one of the others."

"And that happened this evening in Pittville Park. He was seen passing the CD to you. Why was he being so secretive?"

"He said he was often under surveillance by the opposition, whoever they are. He said this was a really important auction, the one coming up. He thought there were some items that were greatly undervalued. He really was a specialist. I'm surprised he even did plumbing."

"A fall-back job," said Dad, who knew most things. "To make sure the income was ticking over. And these auctions only come up at intervals. Self-employed, he could make his own hours to some extent."

"This must have called for pin-point accuracy," said Hobbs, "For you to be coming out of the underpass just as he was going in."

"Easy, really. He phoned me and told me to carry out a plan we'd rehearsed before. It only took me ten or twelve minutes to get to the Evesham Road by the little gate into Pittville Park. I waited there till I saw him arrive across the park and get out of his car. When he started off down the path, I went through the little gate, and came through the tunnel from the far side."

"Hmm. Very clever. So, did you deliver the CD to one of his colleagues?"

211

"You mean like Stepan? I've no idea. He just told me to leave it somewhere for someone else."

"And where did you leave it?"

"Funny place, really. He asked me to drop it in the litter bin outside the new Sainsbury's. The one in Prior's Road."

"Miss Martin, you've been extremely helpful."

"I hope you catch the rotten swine," she said. "I thought we were an item, until I found he was seeing a couple of others. I don't know why I let him use me. No, I suppose I do really. He's such a sweet talker. If he walked in the room now and said a couple of words and gave me that special smile of his, I'd fall over myself to do what he said, even though I hate him. He's – he's just like that," She dissolved in sobs.

Time for Norm to get out of the way. He took the Martins' phone number and Chloe's mobile number and left, with further thanks to Chloe and her parents. One thing was clear. Whoever was engaged to collect the CD, it was not Stepan or Feliks, both of whom, unknown to Chloe, were safely under lock and key. Some teenage boy, that journalist had said, probably acting for his Dad or some other older bloke. Just one more cut-out, casually recruited for the right price.

On his way to Sainsbury's he phoned in and was told his colleague, Steve, was undergoing emergency surgery. Extra cars had been sent to patrol the area around the park, but there had been no sign of Misha.

*****

Brian Jenkins hurried down the park road and through the underpass towards the scene of the accident, if that's what it was. He had to leap for safety as two police cars, sirens wailing, raced up behind him. I'm a bit too late, he thought. They'll keep the public away.

A sergeant, two PCs and a WPC climbed out of the cars, and the sergeant quickly took charge. He addressed the small gaggle of gawkers. "All right, all right, there's nothing to see. If anyone witnessed what happened here, give your name, address, and phone number to one of the constables and a brief statement of what you saw. You may have to give a more detailed one later. The rest of you, please move on."

Three people, besides Jenkins, remained behind. He was counting on being the one not spoken to initially, so that he could try to catch what the others had to say. One of the witnesses was an elderly lady with a Yorkie. Jenkins cocked an ear.

"I didn't actually hear the shots fired," she said. (Jenkins craned forward. Shots?) "But I stayed with Mr Bentley until the ambulance arrived. I could see his ankle had been badly fractured, if not smashed to bits. I'm a former hospital matron, but I could do nothing for him, except to try to comfort him. His colleague called the ambulance, then had to try to find the villain they were pursuing." (Shades of "Murder, She Wrote" thought Jenkins.) "That man was right near the incident." She pointed to a bald-headed man, being interviewed by the WPC. Jenkins shifted his position.

"There were at least five shots," he was saying. "I mean there were five that I heard. There may have been others. The bloke with the gun wore jeans and a black T-shirt. He was quite slim and had black hair. He buggered off through the trees to that exit up there. I didn't hang about then, but I came back in case you wanted witnesses. Has he been caught?"

"I can't say, sir. Thank you for that. Now, let me have your name and address."

Jenkins heard nothing of what the other witness, a young man, said, as he was asked to give his own statement.

"I saw the gunman passing something to a young lady. A jogger. I've already told this to the injured man's colleague, together with the car registration number of the young lady. He then dashed off, presumably to interview her." (No need to mention the trail leading to Sainsbury's, he thought.) "I did not see this incident here, but I came forward to put you in the broader picture in case it helped. I've given my name and address to Mr Bentley's colleague, but you can have it, too, if you wish."

The PC scribbled away. "That's most helpful, sir," he said, privately thinking, "what a condescending bastard, but right on the button." He wondered, too, why did Jenkins say "the gunman" when he hadn't even seen the incident? Obviously he'd tuned in to the others.

"May I ask you, sir, what your occupation is?"

"Of course. I'm a journalist with the Cotswold Regent. I wrote the article about the kidnapping of the priest. This is all tied in."

"I saw the article, sir. May I ask you please not to report this incident until there is an official police release. You may jeopardise future investigations."

"I'll certainly bring your advice to the attention of my editor."

"And we'll certainly do the same. Goodnight, Mr – er – Jenkins, wasn't it?"

Father Mac

Jenkins made his way back to his car. He could certainly make sure the story did not feature in the *Regent* but he couldn't give a similar guarantee for any other newspaper, including the nationals.

CHAPTER 23

Breakfast in the safe house was a buffet of cereals, croissants, and hot food, with fruit juices, tea, and coffee. Tim felt fresh and rested. Bob arrived a few minutes later, looking equally chipper.

"What time did you turn in?" asked Tim.

"Oh, not late. Just after one. There was bit of gossip to catch up on," said Bob with a grin, "and a few drinks."

"I'll bet there was," said Tim. "Anyway, our host wants me to meet him in about ten minutes to collect my bits and pieces."

"Ah, yes, the famous fragments," said Bob. "I'll be interested to see them."

Tim left him a few minutes later, retrieved the fragments, and followed Charles Fenton into yesterday's briefing room, the bigger of the two lounges, which now had a large table in the centre. The chairs had been pushed back to make room for it. As nine o'clock neared, delegates drifted into the room. Two or three had already left the safe house to return to their offices. Debbie Faulkner strode purposefully over to the table.

"Good morning. Find a chair, or stand if you please. This is not going to be another presentation. In fact, there's a slight change of plan. There are a number of fragments that Tim will shortly display on the table here and talk us through them, with additional observations from Nick or Hugh, as necessary. What we are not going to do is attempt any analysis on the hoof. Detailed study of most, if not all, of these fragments belongs with GCHQ. Would you like to say anything at this point, Nick or Hugh?"

"No," said Nick Watson with a smile, "not at this stage. Kathy Webb or Hugh or I might chip in later on. For those of you who don't know, Kathy is our main analyst on the book. I'm sure she's dying to get her teeth into the other fragments." Kathy smiled and coloured slightly.

Debbie nodded to Tim.

"We have four different types of fragments or sets of fragments to discuss," he began. "Of the four, one set consists of pages from the book we're all familiar with." Tim spread some of the pages across the table. "I have been referring to these as the textbook or reference book, because that's what it seems to be. It is clearly organised into chapters.

But then you already know that from the more complete copy or copies you have. I assume it's the same book. You can just make out the logo on the cover and first page."

Kathy intervened at this stage. "I've not studied these pages yet, but yes, you're right, they should duplicate others we already have," she said. "In fact, every time we have had a visit which has led to the recovery of documents, they have always been of this type and in most cases the country visited, usually Russia, has collected one or more complete copies of the book, whatever it is. The logo is clearly visible on most of them. The other countries have always sent photocopies of a few sample pages. All countries in the exchange have at least one complete copy."

Tim studied her. She was probably in her late thirties, attractive in an understated way, with little or no make-up, well-dressed without being downright elegant, and confident in her delivery. He assumed she was married or in some other sort of partnership. By way of contrast, Debbie Faulkner was ten or more years older and dressed rather untidily – not quite like an unmade bed, but with various bits and pieces of extra and unnecessary clothing hanging from her, a scarf round the neck, a stole over the shoulders, something hanging from her bun.

"Have you made any progress with reading the text?" she asked.

"We've no entry point," said Frobisher. "We have at least recovered their numbering system – in fact, we got that far several months ago – so we know we have everything in the correct sequence. One day, this may help. I think we'd better move on, Madame Chairman." Ms. Faulkner nodded.

Tim selected his next exhibit. "As you will see, this set of fragments is clearly from a map." Tim spread them randomly across the table. People bent over to inspect them. There was some ooh-ing and aah-ing.

"Have we identified the area depicted?" asked a M.O.D. delegate after a while.

"I've fooled about with these bits for a few hours," admitted Tim, "and I've come to a very tentative conclusion, which I'm reluctant to reveal as I had to make a number of assumptions. Besides, I don't want to put a preconceived idea into the minds of anyone who does a detailed analysis. There are several problems. Firstly, we don't know whether this is a map of somewhere on Earth, or somewhere else. Secondly, we don't know the scale. We could be trying to reconstruct something on a scale of ten thousand to one or a hundred to one.

Thirdly, although it seems reasonable to assume that the two colours used, pink and yellow, represent land and water, we don't know which of the two is which."

"But, apart from that..." said Bob mischievously, to general laughter.

"There are two more features to draw your attention to," continued Tim. "Note the faint grid lines and the symbols in the top left of the grid squares where that portion is present on a fragment. These are clearly grid references. As Hugh mentioned, we have recovered our visitors' numerical system and can say firmly that the last three symbols of the grid are numerals, and the first two symbols are not. So we assume they are letters. I expect Kathy can quickly confirm that. The other thing is the symbols mainly straddling the boundary lines. These contain no numerals and could well be place names."

"Could we have our own copy of these bits?" asked one of the M.O.D. reps. "We all agree GCHQ needs them to help with language recovery, but we'd like to have a go at identifying the area shown."

"I'm sure that won't be a problem," said Ms Faulkner. "Subject to the usual custody provisions. Charles, can you organise that, please?" Fenton nodded.

The working group continued looking at the map fragments for some time until the Chairman indicated they should move on. Tim collected up the fragments and handed them to Fenton.

"Now," continued Tim, "Here's something equally intriguing." He spread out several pages from the medical book. "These are the pages our visitor went back in for. Is there a doctor in the house?"

There were gasps of astonishment from those around the table.

"There are about thirty pages in all. I won't show them all. These ones are pretty representative."

"What interesting illustrations," said Ms. Faulkner, "and there's one here showing a building made of some sort of shiny stuff. And what an odd shape. Like one of those ancient pyramid things – a ziggurat, I think they were called. What on Earth purpose could it serve?"

"How about a hospital," a voice called out. "That's what you'd expect in a book like this."

"And what's this here?" she asked, pointing to an illustration on another page.

"Looks a bit like that double helix diagram of the DNA structure," said Bob.

"Very plausible," said the Chairman. "What are your comments on these pages, Tim?"

"My own view is that it's a reference book for use in cases of on-board sickness. I would have thought such a manual is a must. As we've already mentioned, we've recovered their numbering system. Simply by analysing the page number symbols in the big textbook, we know they count on a base of twelve. The illustrations here would seem to corroborate that. The anatomical drawings depict six fingers to each hand."

There were gasps from Tim's audience.

"Perhaps there's something in that DNA diagram that ties in," said Bob.

"No knobs and sticks," said Professor Lewis decisively.

"I'm sorry, Alan?" said Debbie Faulkner.

"There are no knobs and sticks," repeated the professor. "The classic representation of the DNA structure consists of knobs and sticks. This one doesn't. I'll certainly concede that does not disqualify the diagram, but it is showing absolutely no information on the double helix. Just some connection at the base where it disappears into something or other. There are a few more pages that seem to be related, and quite a bit of text here and there, though no great, long narrative. Perhaps it's not intended to be explicit for the purpose of this particular book. Perhaps it really is a book meant for laymen."

"That was only a guess on my part," said Tim. "And to be honest, I'm not competent to draw any medical conclusions. But I did turn the pages over to Father Mac's close friend, the retired GP I mentioned, Doctor Campbell. He feels instinctively that some of them may reveal new approaches to the treatment of various illnesses. I think he may be right. It does seem to me that your assessment of the visitors is correct – that they are benign, and eager to help us in some way. Father Mac's contact really wanted him to have these pages." Tim looked around and saw several heads nodding in agreement.

"I'd just like to throw in another thought here," added Tim. "Doctor Campbell feels strongly that a team of medical people from different disciplines should form a small working group and study the pages. This material should, of course, remain with the GCHQ team as part of their overall study of the language, and it's just possible that some sort of two-way feed could develop. Doctor Campbell has volunteered to be a member of any such group."

Ms. Faulkner smiled. "That's very kind of him," she said. "Alan, do you have a view on this?"

"I'm not really in favour of creating yet one more working group," said Lewis. "Sorry to put a damper on the idea. I would like to talk to this doctor friend of Father Mac, though, before discounting the idea. He seems to have formed some useful ideas. We could perhaps talk with one or two specialists."

"Oh, and by the way," said Tim, "we mustn't forget Father Mac has left us his own conclusions. I haven't brought them with me. In fact, I've not even read them yet. If Kathy's team are holding all the other material, she ought perhaps to add his letter to the pile, to be opened at her discretion."

"That's fine," said the Chairman. "Now, Tim, is that the lot? Wasn't there something else from this latest event?"

"Well, yes," agreed Tim. "But only just this single sheet of barely legible writing." He held up the poster size sheet, then placed it on the table. "Interestingly, although there is the usual alien script on the other side, the side I'm displaying contains a few Roman letters. All I can make out is a B and a couple of Os and Cs. Look, you can see for yourself." They crowded round the display.

"Forensics could enhance that," suggested a man Tim recognised as one of Bob's former colleagues.

"Could your expert visit us with his stuff?" asked Kathy, "or do we need to come to you?"

"Oh, some of our stuff has to be portable for crime scene work," said the man.

"Then we'd welcome the help," she smiled.

"I'm probably teaching granny to suck eggs," said Tim, "But it's just possible that normal forensic materials could ruin the paper used. I'm calling it 'paper' for want of any other label. We don't know what it's made from."

"Point taken," said Bob's colleague, "but we have analysed samples from the reference book for general fact-finding and they were compatible with normal processes."

"Any more for any more?" asked Ms. Faulkner "Yes, Tim?"

"I think you said that the only documents anyone had up to now were extracts from the reference book?" The Chairman nodded. "Harking back to last night, have we decided yet whether or not we are going to share all these new inputs, the ones we've been looking at this morning?"

219

"I'm sure this will be debated at a higher level," said Ms. Faulkner, "I myself see no reason not to. It would seem to me against the spirit of our agreement to hold something back, though of course we've no evidence this has not already happened."

"When this is debated," said Professor Lewis, "in case I'm not involved, my own view at the moment is that we could photocopy the map fragments and the single sheet, though I'd prefer to hold back on the medical pages for the moment until we've looked at them in more detail. It would be much more helpful if we could supply some informed comment with them. We'll earn even more brownie points that way. Perhaps we can release the pages in what we may find to be related clusters."

"What a good point, Alan, not that we're in the market for brownie points. I'll certainly feed that in if you're not around. Anyone else? No? Well then, if there is nothing else to say, we'll retire to the other lounge for a farewell coffee, while Charles and Nick arrange transit and custody of all these fragments. Our very warm thanks to you, Tim. I certainly feel we'll make progress with these new inputs."

"If only we could find an entry point!" sighed Hugh, joining the general move into the small lounge, where coffee awaited.

Bob made his way quickly to the Chairman, beckoning Tim to join him. "I'm sorry to say, there was a bit of a drama involving friend Misha yesterday evening. Apparently, he was followed to a park in Cheltenham, where he slipped the CD from Tim's house to an intermediary who to all intents and purposes was simply one of the many joggers they get there. Our officers pursuing Misha didn't notice this and continued pursuing him, but he shot one of them in the ankle. Misha, of course, then disappeared. Priority had to be given to the injured man, so the pursuit had to be abandoned. The officer underwent emergency surgery. His ankle bone was shattered, so longer term reconstructive surgery will be necessary. The other officer was tipped off by someone who had seen the CD passed across. He was a local journalist who happened to be there, and he very astutely took the jogger's car licence. This enabled the uninjured officer to go to the jogger's home, interview her, and learn where she had delivered the CD. A litter bin, would you believe. Outside the new Sainsbury's, Tim."

"God, what a cheek," said Tim. "Right where some of the most sensitive work in the field of intelligence used to take place."

"The journalist, who had followed the jogger, hung around in the Sainsbury car park to see who retrieved the CD. It was a teenage boy on a bike, presumably working for an adult. He quickly nipped in and out of the car park and was impossible to follow by car. The good news, of course, is that the CD was only a dummy. The bad news is that we're no further forward in finding the overall paymaster for their little operation here and in Canada."

"Never mind. There may be other opportunities," said Debbie Faulkner. "And I'm so sorry about your officer. Do give him our best wishes for a full recovery. I'm sure something more official will be arranged. Thank you for their work, anyway."

"By the way, Bob, was this journalist our friend Brian Jenkins?" asked Tim.

"Sorry, I forgot to ask," he admitted. "I'll let you know later."

*****

After coffee, Tim thanked Charles Fenton and Debbie Faulkner and said farewell to Bob and the others. Bob promised to keep him posted on Misha.

Tim found he was driving home with Hugh.

"You're one of us now," said Hugh. "You've had the official briefing, so there's no need to be coy about where we hold our meetings. When you came here yesterday, you had an escort about half a mile behind all the time. That was to protect your bits and pieces. You've left them behind now with old Fenton. They'll be sent on to us. We keep all documents, including sample pages copied and sent from other countries in the agreement. The first pages we received were from the Russians. Later we had our own visit from these aliens and were left a few copies of our own."

"Our own visit," mused Tim. "I remember from the briefing note that we'd had one, but no-one mentioned it. Where did it take place?"

"It's not considered relevant to the work of ELK ONE. It's curious, really. We know that about half the Russian visits have been to the Crimea. We also know that the latest visit ended in a crash in Canada. But we don't know where the one and only UK visit terminated. Security, I suppose. Need-to-know. As far as I know, it was just a standard event. The vehicle came down, jettisoned a couple of books, then disappeared in a puff of smoke. The whole incident took no more than a few minutes. I understand it was in a very remote area, and it never made the press, even the local press. My own guess is Wales or the Lake District."

"I'm glad to hear you mention the Crimea for the Russian visits," said Tim. "I didn't mention my thoughts on those map fragments to the assembled company, but perhaps I can tell you: that's the region I thought the map covered. Parts of the Black Sea. By the way, I noticed Ms. Faulkner didn't set a date for the next meeting."

"How could she?" said Hugh. "We're largely driven by events, such as the next visit by our space friends. Mind you, if there were to be a significant breakthrough in our study of the language, it might be worth calling one. Similarly, if there were some shattering security problem, we may need to meet to discuss our response. Now," he continued in a businesslike tone, "We need to put things in hand to bring you back into the fold. Leave that to me. I'll also discuss with Nick the question of Doctor Campbell."

Now that Tim knew all the fragments would be kept with Nick's people, he felt more than ever how brainless it had been of him to make an extra copy of the reference book. He and Hugh continued to review where things stood, and what needed to be done. They agreed that, subject to Nick Watson's concurrence, they should all meet – Hugh, Nick, Tim, and Kathy Webb and her team – and have a brain-storming session or two as soon as Tim got his pass.

Conversation moved on to the personalities at the meeting.

"Kathy Webb seems a bright young woman," said Tim.

"Oh, she's a sweetie," enthused Frobisher. "She began her career as a maths teacher at the Ladies' College, then was blatantly recruited by some unscrupulous chap in GCHQ. Seems this chap's wife was also a teacher at the college, and invited her to a meal, where she met this chap and learned how much more there could be to a job in mathematics than simultaneous equations and Pythagoras." He grinned.

"You?" he asked.

"Guilty," he said. "She came in on the fast track and has never looked back, except in her personal life. She had a partner for several years until he left her for someone he met on the perfume counter at Boots. He was getting something for his mother, would you believe? Anyway, when the ELK business burst upon us, Nick had no hesitation in taking her off her normal job to start the effort on analysing the language. She's actually doing both jobs at the moment. She's done some very useful preparatory work on the structure of the language, but I think we're at a dead end now. She'll think of some new approach, perhaps inspired by these new fragments. She may then get involved with it full-time."

"What about Ms. Faulkner?"

"Army. Rose to major in the I-Corps. Got a posting to M.O.D. Met and married a civilian there. Left the army. In fact, left everything to have a family. Two girls, I believe. When they were old enough, she went back to M.O.D. as a civvy. Did brilliantly. Got a secondment to the assessments staff, and here she is, God bless here. She's got a sharp mind and is good with people. Also, her army discipline has never left her. I think she controls our working party admirably, even funny old Professor Lewis."

"I barely met him. Is he difficult?"

"Oh, no, nothing like that. It's just that he can be so single-minded. He seems to abandon everything else if he's got some pet idea he's nursing. I find him stimulating. If he's not nursing some obsession or other, he can really open up a subject, you know. Go down avenues nobody has thought to explore."

They continued in a like vein over a pub lunch, and arrived back in Bourton in mid-afternoon. Hugh dropped Tim off.

"I hope we'll get you sorted next week some time. If there's anything urgent before then, we'll get you in as a visitor."

Tim was glad to get home. As he entered the house, he was not surprised to find that the alarm had failed to activate. He knew Misha must have neutralised it. The CD he'd left as bait had, of course, also disappeared. He made a coffee and sat down to think out his next move. Perhaps he should let everyone know he was back, then think about destroying or wiping the extra CD he'd made. He'd also better give the house an all-over clean before he picked Lucy up tomorrow. With Lucy in his thoughts, his first call was to her.

"I'm looking forward to seeing you tomorrow, love," he said.

"Meeting go well?"

"Very well. I hadn't realised it, but it turned out to be the Tim Sullivan show. Or rather, the Father Mac show with me acting as his spokesman."

"Just like old times, giving presentations on intelligence."

"Well, not quite. Oh, by the way, they may want me to sign on as a consultant, so that I can have further discussions with them in the office."

"So, you won't get under my feet so much."

"They didn't actually give that as the reason. How's mama?"

"Pretty well back to normal."

223

Father Mac

After a bit more chit-chat, they swore undying love and hung up. Doctor Campbell was next.

"Tim, look, let me come round. There are a few things I want to mention."

But not over the phone, thought Tim. Actually, that would suit Tim, too.

"That's fine. I'm just phoning around to say I'm home. I'll fit in a couple more calls while you're on your way. Give me about fifteen minutes."

Tim phoned Sister Winifred next. She surprised him by putting him through to Father Mac, who was in the day room. Tim had serious reservations about speaking to the elderly priest, assuming he'd be completely incoherent over the phone, but to his amazement Father Mac, despite a slight residual slur, was almost entirely intelligible.

"You sound terrific," said Tim. "Now, there's something important to tell you. I can't go into details, because it's all rather sensitive, but I've been away, giving various people a briefing based on the account you left me of your recent adventures on holiday. They, in turn, put me into the wider picture. They've asked me to join their study party, and if you're up to it, they may want you to join in a few sessions."

"I'd be 'lighted to," said Father Mac. "It might sa' them lots of work if they let me do this soon."

"I'm sure you're right, Father. I'll pass that on. Anyway, how are you, and how are they treating you?"

"Wiffie very cruel. Make me pract... practise talk and walk. Get very tire."

"I'm sure it's all for your own good. By the way, I'm fetching Lucy tomorrow. Mama can manage pretty well now. I'll come and see you in a few days after I've been back to the office. Now I'll have a quick word with Norah, then Doc Campbell is coming over. Have you any message for him?"

"Tell him come down here and play chess. Wan' see if I can still beat him."

"OK, Father," said Tim. "I'll let you go now. See you soon. 'Bye."

Tim was very encouraged at the progress the old chap had made. He phoned Norah.

"Now, I know what you're worried about," she said, "weekday services." It was true that he was concerned that they carry on, then suddenly realised he'd missed a turn. "Well, they've decided to take you off the rota. We know you've been busy."

224

"Actually, Norah, I suppose I am relieved. I've been not so much busy as preoccupied."

While he was still talking to her, the door bell went. It was Doc Campbell. Tim rang off.

"I've got some good news for you," said Tim. "Father Mac is doing well and wants you to go to see him, and have a game of chess. And on the other business they'd like to hear your views. There's a scientist attached to the group. He'd like to pick your brains, then perhaps take you with him for discussions with a specialist or two."

Campbell beamed. "That's great, Tim. I think I can understand broadly what those pages amount to, but I'll probably have a hard time convincing others. I'd love to have another good look at them. Anyway," he turned serious, "I'm still worried about Mary and that fellow Jenkins she's seeing. She says that all week he's been on the lookout for Misha. He's convinced Misha's still after something either in the presbytery or in your house. She's frightened Jenkins is getting himself involved in something dangerous. She's obviously very fond of him."

"He is getting involved in something dangerous," said Tim. "I heard about Misha's activities while I was away. Did you know he broke into my house yesterday and took a CD. Fortunately, it's only a spoof one."

"No, I didn't know that," said Campbell. "This morning Jenkins told her that Misha shot a policeman last night and they were trying to hush the whole thing up. And Misha's still at large. Jenkins was somewhere near there when it happened. This was in Pittville Park."

"I heard that a journalist had tipped off the police about who Misha's contact was in the park, but my friend, Bob, didn't know his name. So that completes the picture."

"Mary said Jenkins was a bit shaken up about the whole thing. The shooting was so cold-blooded. The only redeeming thing is that Misha seems to have used the gun to hinder, and not to kill. He could have aimed for the head or the heart."

"That's true, I suppose," pondered Tim. "My next worry is if he'll write something for the Regent."

"Mary said he's been asked to wait for the official police release."

"Well, let's hope he does. Oh, by the way, Doc, I wanted to ask Mary if she'd like to see Father Mac."

"I'm sure she would. As a matter of fact, I was thinking of driving down myself with Megan and Mary."

225

"Why not ask Mary if she could drive Sister Winifred's Mini Cooper down there. Sister must have missed having it. You could then bring Mary back."

"A splendid idea," said Campbell. He left, with Tim thinking about his next move.

After Doc Campbell left, Tim decided to erase the copy he'd made of Andy's CD while it was fresh in his mind, so he went to his cache and sifted through the various items. Yes, there it was. That's odd, he thought. Hadn't he left the label blank? The one he was looking at was labelled "Fragments from Canada". Evidently he'd labelled both CDs, including the spoof one, the same. Unless .... Feverishly, he inserted the CD into the drive. He knew the real CD contained a brief introduction by Andy so he put the speakers on, too. Where was Andy's voice? It failed to appear. Instead, a sweet soprano voice serenaded him. "The hills are alive with the sound of music."

Tim uttered a mild expletive, then sat down with his head in his hands.

"What a bloody idiot I am," Tim said to himself at last, "It was probably the result of all that running around I did, printing various stuff, copying CDs, deleting CDs, hiding CDs. This is the one Bob asked me to leave as bait for Misha. I labelled the genuine one. Now friend Misha's got it."

That had to be what happened. The only other explanation was that Misha had somehow found Tim's hiding-place and switched the bait for the genuine one, but Tim soon dismissed that as highly unlikely. No. He'd better own up straight away, though the horse had bolted via a litter bin outside Sainsbury's. Tim reached for the phone. He got Bob and explained what had happened. Bob went silent for a while.

"It's as much my fault as yours, Tim. It was my hare-brained idea. Anyway, it may not be as bad as you imagine. What was on the CD? Bits of the big book. Nothing else. We've already had quite a few dumps of the big book, and it's possible that some countries outside our agreement have had a visit, though, assuming they have, we don't know whether they were also given copies of the book. Anyway, look on the bright side. It's not as if those extra bits you showed us were on the CD, and those might be the key to unlocking the big book."

"God, I hope you're right," said Tim doubtfully. "I'm desperate to find an escape clause. Are you going to let Debbie Faulkner know?"

"My own boss first," said Bob. "Then I'll follow his advice. Don't worry, Tim. It's unfortunate, but not the end of the world."

"I suppose I'd better let my people know, too," said Tim glumly. "Anyway, thanks for the reassurance, Bob. We'll be in touch." He rang off.

Tim phoned Hugh Frobisher and confessed to him what had happened. Like Bob, he was rather philosophical about the whole thing.

"It's probably true that a few countries outside our agreement have got at least some parts of the reference book," he said. "The main difference is that we have the entire book several times over, between us. The other difference is that we're mounting a unified attack on the book with members of an alliance, while other countries are probably beavering away on their own."

"Are you planning to go in tomorrow, Hugh?"

"Yes," he said, "I want to get the business of getting Doctor Campbell on board started. He'll need to be PV'd of course, and that will be the delay."

"Of course," groaned Tim. Positive Vetting could take several months, at least. "Isn't there a fast track?"

"There certainly is for government ministers and other VIPs. A change of government brings a flurry of security activity, getting new people on to various lists, and debriefing outgoing ministers. I'll see what we can do."

CHAPTER 24

Friday dawned, warm and clear. Lucy was coming home. Tim whistled as he hoovered and dusted. He paused for a coffee, then checked on the food in the pantry, the fridge, and the freezer. He decided just to get the basics – milk, bread, and potatoes. Lucy would prefer to get the bulk of the shopping herself. She'd actually enjoy doing it – this was a mind-set he just couldn't understand. He'd avoid changing the sheets as well, even though they were probably ready to walk down to the machine themselves. He wasn't exactly sure which were the clean ones for their bed. There were so many. They had five bedrooms, four of which had beds in them. The fifth contained the detritus from three bereavements and a broken marriage – their son's. After coffee, he walked into town, bought the paper and, of course, some welcome-home flowers. Back home, he mowed the lawns, front and back, then finally cleaned the car and checked the oil, water and tyre pressures. He was exhausted, so he heated an instant dinner then collapsed in an armchair.

*****

Seven miles away, Brian Jenkins was in trouble. He was summoned to the presence – the editor.

"Look, Brian, I just don't know where you are half the time. And you haven't submitted copy for a couple of days. We've cut you plenty of slack to follow up this kidnapping thing but you don't seem to be getting anywhere."

"Sorry, Boss, things have moved along a bit, but we're waiting on the go-ahead from the police. There's to be an official release, but I don't know when."

"An official release to us and all the others. Fat lot of good that'll do us."

"I can use the release as the basis for my story and add to it. I'm sure no-one else has the complete story."

"Well tell me what this story is and let me be the judge."

"A policeman was shot in Pittville Park two nights ago."

"And you were there, of course."

"Yes."

"And why did you happen to be there at that precise time?"

"I followed the gunman there. Well, to be more accurate, I followed the police who were tailing the gunman."

"You followed the police who were tailing the gunman?"

"Yes, I saw the gunman slip the CD containing the sensitive information to an accomplice. She ..."

"She? A ravishing blonde, no doubt."

"How did you know that, Boss? Look, I've been helpful to the police. They've acknowledged this, but they've sworn me to silence until they put the release out. They were supposed to be contacting you."

"I'll contact them. Do you know any names?"

"The gunman is called Misha."

"I meant the names of the police. How do you know the gunman was called Misha?"

"It's a long story, Boss."

"And none of it's getting into print. I thought your earlier story about the kidnapped priest would have sparked the interest of the nationals. If only we could add all this new stuff to it. I've half a mind to. How about drafting something?"

I'm sorry, Boss. I don't wish to be obstructive, but anything I say now would be half-baked. Just a few sensational sentences that don't hang together. We can glue them together, but only by venturing too far into the realm of speculation."

"Put something on paper for me, Brian, and we'll sit on it for a bit."

*****

Lennie Gill went to the corner newsagents and bought a small padded envelope. Back at home, he took from his wallet a bit of paper with an address written on it, copied the address on to the envelope and put the CD inside. It was one of those anonymous addresses, a post box number somewhere in Southeast London. It could be anywhere. Ah, well, that was not his concern.

He'd phoned in sick. A touch of Friday-itis, they would assume, he thought with a grin. Well, sod them. Now, where should he go to post it? At least 20 miles away, he was told. Preferably 30. Swindon? Or up the M5 to Worcester? He settled on Stratford-on-Avon, via Broadway, a pretty run.

Father Mac

In fact, he could make a day of it. The missus would be out all day, working. He'd have a pub lunch, then spend a bit of time (and a bit of money) in a bookie's. He smiled at the prospect.

*****

That same afternoon, while Lennie was enjoying himself at the bookie's and thinking wistfully of the redheaded barmaid he'd chatted up, his son, Colin, sauntered home, let himself in and, as usual, changed into his jeans, got himself a snack and went to turn on the telly. As he did so, he noticed a slip of paper on the sideboard. An address. The Charity Council, PO Box 7093 London SE. This must be the address his Dad had sent that CD off to. The Charity Council? Yeah, I bet. Pull the other one. Someone he was secretly up to no good with. I know what. Suppose I nick this. See if he misses it. Yeah, why not? That'll teach the old git. When he starts moaning, Mum'll tell him it's his own fault. If he will leave stuff lying around, she's as likely as not to chuck it away to keep the place tidy. Colin picked up the bit of paper and stuck it behind his bus pass in the holder. It might even come in useful.

*****

At last the time had come for Tim to drive over to mama's to collect Lucy. Her sister, Ann, was there when he arrived. He stayed for the compulsory cup of coffee and round-up of family news, then he and Lucy headed back home.

"Why does she always think she's doing us a huge favour when she spends a few days with your mother?" he asked.

"It's just her way. Ignore it," said Lucy. "Now listen, I've got an idea. Unless anyone else has a prior claim, I'd like to have Father Danny over for Sunday roast. If I hadn't been with mama for the last few weeks, we'd have cooked for him at least once by now. I expect Norah is bearing the brunt."

"She is, but she doesn't think of it in those terms. She tries to fend off all the others."

"Talking of others, I'd like us to have a few others at dinner, too, including Norah and the Campbells. Who else?"

"I think that's quite enough for now."

"How about that girl staying with the Campbells?"

230

"Mary? You'd like her, but I expect she'll be planning something with that Jenkins lad. The reporter. We can but try. There'll be plenty of shopping to get. There's not much in the house."

"I expected to spend tomorrow shopping, cleaning the house, and washing."

"It's a bit late to contact everyone tonight, so I'll do it first thing in the morning. Except Father Danny, of course. He's quite content to do what he's told."

*****

Early the next morning, Hugh Frobisher phoned. "Ah, Tim, I tried to get you yesterday. Just to say that I've cleared the way," he said enthusiastically. "You've only been retired a couple of years, so your PV is recent enough, and OSA never dies until you do." It was true: the Official Secrets Act was a lifetime commitment. "And you're already on the special list. So can I pick you up on Monday about eight? By the way, we're at Oakley. M Block. They didn't demolish quite everything." M Block was a large green building on the old Oakley site that had survived the demolition when GCHQ's splendid new building, the "Doughnut," was opened at Benhall, across town.

"No, you can still see the Jolly Green Giant up on the hill. OK, eight o'clock on Monday's fine."

"We may not have your new bits. They'll probably still be in transit, but we can let you see what we've been up to on the stuff we already have."

"Fine," said Tim. "I'll see you Monday then. Oh, is it all day? If not, can you get me back?"

"It's not all day. We'll only be there a couple of hours on your first visit. Later, when we have all the bits, we may want you for longer. Anyway, we can talk about all that on Monday. Oh and by the way, Doctor Campbell will be no problem. I won't go into the fine print, but basically because this stuff we're dealing with and want him to be involved with is not Sigint, other rules apply. See you Monday."

Hugh rang off.

"Well, they don't muck about," said Tim. He was glad they'd be working at Oakley, and in particular in M Block, a large, futuristic building that dwarfed all the others around it. That was where his last job had been before the move to Benhall.

231

Saturday morning flew by in a flurry of shopping and other domestic activities. Against his better judgment, Tim went with Lucy to the supermarket, and actually enjoyed the experience. He knew why. His beloved Lucy was with him again, bringing a bit of discipline back into his life and – well, just being there. In several respects, the cupboard was no longer bare. He felt he was embarking on a new chapter in his life. He'd spent pretty well all the time Lucy was away in an intellectual haze, groping to understand things never before encountered. Now, he'd pretty well passed the buck on. Others were sharing the burden. For him, there was nothing more to do – until the call came.

Norah and the Campbells were free for lunch the next day and, as predicted, Mary was spending the day with Brian Jenkins. Tim felt Norah was secretly relieved to take a break from feeding Father Danny. She was a wonderful cook, though probably not the most stimulating company for him.

Tim and Lucy went to the vigil Mass in Broadway that evening. There was no way Lucy could cook a Sunday roast for six and somehow fit in Mass the same morning.

*****

Tim collected Father Danny from St Nicholas the next day and got home just as the Campbells and Norah were arriving.

Father Danny enjoyed his outings away from the disciplines of the Abbey and considered the prospect of a good old Sunday roast with friendly parishioners well worth the gauntlet he would have to run to earn it. He knew exactly what was coming – all the issues these good people did not like to air with their own priest. They would see the monk as a devout, scholarly man with little knowledge of them or their day-to-day lives. This distanced him from them. The first issue they raised was, predictably, the compulsory celibacy of priests, Norah's pet obsession, followed by the ordination of women, both hardy annuals. Then Lucy intervened.

"Is the Yorkshire Pudding all right, Father? Good. What does seem to me such a pity," she continued, "is that, as an activity to be proscribed, artificial birth control seems to command equal status to the two other major social issues exercising the Church: abortion and euthanasia. They're surely quite different from birth control. Abortion and euthanasia are about denying or curtailing life. Some would go so

232

far as to say they are thwarting God's timetable for calling a soul to heaven. With birth control, on the other hand, there is neither a body nor a soul. It is simply preventing, or postponing, the creation of a new life that God would have invested with a soul."

"Gosh, dear, that's a bit deep," said Tim.

Lucy gave a deep sigh. "I'm so sorry, Father, that we're bombarding you with all these knotty issues. We've no right to, but the problem is, once we express unease in one area, it all comes tumbling out. These are the issues exercising ordinary Catholics today. The Church can be so right in not budging an inch on what most Catholics would regard as the really important issues of doctrine like abortion and euthanasia, but so wrong in other areas where imposed disciplines are concerned. Surely in the matter of disciplines, the Church should move with the times. If it doesn't, it stagnates, and is in danger of dying. Radical thinking is not necessarily wrong, but the Church fears it. It shouldn't. It should rejoice in it."

Tim looked at Lucy at once shocked and proud. I married this loving, intelligent, exasperating, charming, belligerent, feminine woman, he thought.

But Father Danny said, "You're absolutely right. And, of course, Jesus was the greatest radical the world has known. What a legacy he left us. He built on the Mosaic law the fundamental disciplines most people would agree with for any ordered society, with his teachings. Look at the Sermon on the Mount for starters. Wow! Did that throw the cat among the pigeons! And yes, the Yorkshire pudding is fine, as is the rest of the dinner. It's delicious."

Lucy laughed. "You came for dinner and pudding, and you get a nine-course meal!"

"You want to try being married to her, Father," said Tim with a grin.

"I'm sure you're the richer for it," he said. "Bring all these points up on your next retreat. Those that conduct them are far more qualified to discuss them than I am. That's where you'll get a good dialogue going. Now, how's Father McNulty?" Tim sensed he was glad to change the subject.

"None of us has seen him since he went back into the hospice – what, five days ago now," said Tim. "I've spoken to him on the phone and I'm amazed at how well his speech seems to be returning."

"Is he still talking about seeing an angel?"

233

"So far as I know, yes, he is." Tim was anxious to ask Father Danny about what Father Mac might really have seen, but knew he had to be careful after his recent briefing. Perhaps there would be an occasion when the others were not there. Yes, of course: when he drove him back to the church to collect his car.

As it happened, the Campbells were expecting a visit from Megan's sister and her husband, and left about 2:30, after coffee. Norah soon followed them, after unsuccessfully trying to help with the dishes.

"There's nothing to do," insisted Lucy, stacking the dishwasher.

"More coffee, Father?" asked Tim.

"No, no," Father Danny shook his head emphatically. "Thank you both very much, especially you, Lucy."

Tim then ferried Father Danny back to his car at St Nicholas.

"There is just one more thing I wanted to ask you," said Tim, on the way there. "Your mention of Father Mac's angel got me thinking. What is the Church's position on extraterrestrial life forms? I'm not talking about microbes or minute organisms. I mean persons, people, humanoids, or whatever you want to call them."

Father Danny laughed. "I'm certainly no expert on that sort of thing either," he said, "though I do happen to know that, perhaps surprisingly, our conservative old Church keeps a pretty open mind on the subject. In fact, they take it quite seriously. The man you really need to see is Brother Simeon. He's young, still in his twenties, I believe. He trained as a physicist before he joined the community, and he's also a keen astronomer. He actually has a telescope – a pretty powerful one, I understand."

"And he's allowed to use it?" asked Tim in surprise.

"Oh, yes. Father Abbot also takes an interest. Why don't you come over and meet Simeon, say between Vespers and Compline. About 7 pm any day."

"I'll make it Tuesday, then," said Tim. "Thank you very much. Could you please warn him?" He left Father Danny in the church car park and returned home.

Tim found it difficult to settle for the rest of the day. But things did seem to be moving along now, at least at the intellectual level, with the first of what he hoped would be many sessions back in the office coming up tomorrow, and the promised chat with Brother Simeon the day after.

CHAPTER 25

The next day Hugh Frobisher found Tim waiting outside for him. Lucy came to see them off and a few minutes later they joined the line of traffic heading over the hill to Cheltenham. Bourton was largely a dormitory town now. It was a pretty slow drive, but about twenty minutes later Tim was entering the only part of the formerly vast Oakley site left untouched by the builders. Here, amid a small cluster of low huts one large, green, highly ornate building dominated the scene. M Block. At the security gate he found he was expected. He produced his passport and was allocated a visitor's pass. They entered the building, went up in a lift, and Hugh led the way to a small room where Kathy Webb was already waiting. A table was stacked with various documents, including several weighty computer prints. Tim and Kathy exchanged greetings.

"You'll be a visitor for the time being," said Hugh. "We don't really know how necessary it will be to get you permanent status. In your case, your most important contribution is likely to be on the map and the medical pages. They are new sources. In my case, I've been involved in several things simply for continuity. The trouble with retirement is that in certain fields of intelligence it doesn't always come at a convenient time. A wealth of experience can suddenly go down the drain, never to be replaced, so I was asked to soldier on as a consultant until the department felt able to let me go. Actually, I'm being slowly phased out now. This is the only project I'm still involved in."

"Before we get started," said Tim, "tell me why GCHQ was given responsibility for studying these texts we have. It's certainly not cryptanalysis or even Sigint, come to that."

"No, but who else could you give it to?" said Hugh, "We've certainly got the people with the right aptitudes."

"But so have some of the universities," argued Tim, "I know of one or two projects that have been farmed out to specialist places in academia. Propagation studies, technical stuff like that. The Americans do the same."

"It's really a question of the right mix of credentials," replied Hugh. "Here we can call on people with aptitude for languages, aptitude for cryptanalysis, mathematical skills, and, of course, massive computer power in case it's needed."

"OK, OK, you've convinced me," laughed Tim. "But the Sigint Charter says 'at least one end foreign.' Does this stuff satisfy that?"

"I can't think of anything more foreign than extraterrestrial," grinned Hugh. "Everyone happily accepted the JIC ruling, without the slightest territorial whinge. Anyway, let's get started, shall we? I'll hand you over to Kathy."

"Firstly, Nick Watson sends his apologies. He's at the Doughnut this morning. Now, as you know, our starting point is some sort of reference book," she began, "although even that is an assumption. We first came by what turned out to be pieces from the book about sixteen months ago. These were from the Russians, seeking our help."

"Oh, yes," said Tim, "Charles Fenton mentioned that at my ELK briefing."

"Well, since then there have been fifteen more incidents, some of which have led to an entire book being found, or even, in some cases, several copies. On three occasions, including the recent Canada visit, the vehicle crashed, in all others it briefly alighted and jettisoned the book or books – almost as a calling card. But none of that is our concern. The sum total of all these incidents is that we now have several copies of the same book. The other countries we collaborate with have also sent us sample pages from their books. Detailed comparison of the alien texts indicates they are identical to our own copies. So we all have the full version. Just over 2,000 pages."

"Really?" said Tim, impressed. "And I believe Hugh told Debbie you've got nowhere with reading the text?"

"Nowhere at all," said Kathy. "What we desperately need is some sort of Rosetta Stone. That's why we're hoping the other bits Father Mac was given might provide some sort of collateral to get us started. We know nothing of the people responsible for the book – their society, their culture, their history, the nature and location of their home planet. So there's nothing we can look for."

"We do know one thing," said Tim, "and that's their physiology. According to Father Mac, they look like us and can live in a similar atmosphere. OK, so they've got twelve fingers, but that's just a minor trait of evolution. Human beings apparently have evolutionary aberrations, or so the experts say. They argue that we were probably not intended to have the entry points to the digestive and respiratory systems so close together. I'm not altogether convinced. I'm quite sure

236

the Almighty could have corrected this if He thought it was a major concern."

"Anyway," said Kathy, "let me talk about what little we – that's to say Hugh and I – have managed to do. The first step was to reconstruct some sort of alphabet. That meant compiling a list of all the letters or elements. That was not too difficult, because every letter in a word appeared separately. There was no joining together, so no scope for ambiguity. We identified 42 discrete elements altogether. This was pretty time-consuming, but an essential first step before computer power could be applied."

"I looked at Father Mac's pages for about four or five hours, and I came up with 37," said Tim, feeling pleased that he had been so near the mark. "At least, you could pretty well confirm you didn't have a syllabary on your hands. I mean, pairing most of the consonants with every vowel would have taken you well over the 100 mark, probably around 150 elements."

Kathy continued, "Yes, though of course that doesn't mean there aren't the odd syllables represented by a single element. Some languages have a single letter for 'ch' and 'sh' for example. So, after satisfying ourselves we had the complete alphabet, we then assigned an arbitrary digital label to each letter, and to the separator between words, and scanned in all 2,000 pages of the book, creating a file of them. They don't seem to have punctuation as we understand it, just separators – spaces, in fact, the same as we use. We then ran a program to convert all the text images in the file into their digital values. This is what this computer print here is."

Kathy pointed to a very thick print. "That is just a small part of a 2,000-plus page book in digitised form complete with separators between the words. "Our next stage was to look at the words themselves. Here, a 'word' was a group of letters varying in length from a single letter to about twenty letters, preceded and followed by a word separator. We tasked the computer with reading the entire book in its digitised form and compiling a file of words occurring. Every time a new word was encountered it was added to the file. That print there is the file. There are nearly 8,000 entries. A third file contains an incidence count of all 8,000 words. Oh, and by the way, the total word count is 1,372,000."

"That's amazing," said Tim. "Just one thing, did you reconstruct any alphabeticity?"

"No," smiled Kathy, "and for the moment it doesn't really matter. It's sufficient to list all 8,000 words in groups all beginning with the same letter."

"When the map fragments arrive, you will at least be able to put two or three letters in their correct sequence by looking at the progression of the grid-square labelling," said Tim. "Though that's only a drop in the ocean."

"Anyway, we've now organised things so that we can interrogate these files in any number of ways. We can, for instance, ask the computer to display the most commonly occurring word." She moved to a computer terminal.

"We have to treat this as an open-ended study, which could escalate in any number of directions, so we've got everything on one of the mainframes. This is just a terminal into it." She pressed a few keys, and the screen showed an alien word, together with its digitised counterpart and the incidence count, in this case 58,322.

"That must be Bubble and Squeak for 'the' if they have definite articles," said Tim. "Though, of course, you don't have to look beyond Latin to find a language that doesn't."

"The same with Russian," said Kathy, "and there must be many more. Probably more that don't have a definite article than do."

"I suppose it could be the equivalent of "and." Most languages must have conjunctions."

"You can do no end of conjecturing," said Hugh. "And why not? One day we may find the magic piece of collateral that will give us a start. Did I hear you call the language 'Bubble and Squeak'?"

Tim nodded. "Yes," he laughed, "what do you call it?"

"Nothing very imaginative," said Kathy. "We just call it Alienspeak."

"Oh, I like that better," said Tim. "I think I'll call it that, too."

"We couldn't use 'Lincos' because it's already in use," said Hugh.

"Lincos," said Tim, "What's that?"

"Oh, I don't really want to go down that path," said Hugh. "Basically, it's the abbreviation of 'lingua cosmica.' which, of course, is Latin for 'cosmic language.' It was designed nearly fifty years ago by a German mathematics professor and was intended to be understood by any intelligent life forms elsewhere in the universe. At least one powerful transmitter is blasting it out – somewhere in the Crimea, I think. The flip side to that is that our friendly visitors are sending us signals, warning us of their approach. They mentioned that at our recent meeting, if you remember. Something like a dozen times now, a short burst of energy has been detected about 36 hours before their arrival and another burst about six hours before arrival, but try as we might to predict where they will land or briefly touch down we can't track them continually in the final stages."

They spent the next hour or so looking at the computer prints, and interrogating the files.

"I think we'll call it a day now and let Kathy get back to one of her other jobs," said Hugh. "We'll reconvene when your other bits get here. They may even be here today."

They thanked Kathy, and Tim handed in his pass. At Tim's request, they stopped briefly at Sainsbury's at the bottom of the hill. Tim always got nostalgic when they went there.

"It still feels strange," he said. "I'm sure I can identify the exact spot where I used to wait nervously for a promotion interview. It's right over there by the pasta sauces. Sorry to drag you in here, Hugh. I only want the paper."

"That's fine," said Hugh, "I can get the missus some flowers. She'll wonder for days what mischief I've been up to. Chance would be a fine thing. No, seriously, our wives have had to put up with a lot. At first, I used to envy other men their ability to pour their heart out to their wives after some disaster at work, or even some huge triumph. Our lips are forever sealed."

"Yes, some of our friends can't understand how we can put up with it, day after day for thirty or forty years. I think wives are marvellous putting up with it themselves, this compartmented life we lead. They sense when we've had a disappointment, and are sympathetic though don't know exactly why. Anyway, thanks for giving me such an informative introduction to this project. I can see you've done everything you can to prepare the ground for the magic day, when it comes."

Tim selected his paper and as he was leaving the news display, he noticed the headline on the front page of the Regent. Policeman Shot in Pittville Park – Foreign Agent Sought.

"Here we go," said Tim. He picked up a copy. "I'll read this aloud as we go home so that you can hear it. Funny, though, it doesn't credit young Jenkins with the story. Perhaps it's just a press release."

As they drove up Bouncers Lane into Prestbury, Tim read the article:

POLICEMAN SHOT IN PITTVILLE PARK
Foreign Agent Makes Off with Secrets. Spy Base Denies Knowledge

From our Crime Editor

Police sources have confirmed that one of their officers was shot and seriously wounded last Wednesday, 25th June, when he and a colleague pursued a man thought to be in possession of sensitive documents. The shooting took place in Pittville Park at about 9:15 pm and is believed to be linked to the incident on 19th June when Father Donald McNulty, Parish Priest of St Nicholas Roman Catholic Church in Bourton-under-Wychwood, was kidnapped in a hijacked ambulance. The priest is known to have acquired some secret documents on a recent holiday to Canada, not realising their sensitivity, and to have brought them home with him as souvenirs. The content and the source of the documents remain a mystery.

Two accomplices of the gunman, who were responsible for the kidnapping, were taken into custody after one of them broke into the priest's house, searching unsuccessfully for the secret documents. The gunman allegedly stole the same documents from the house of a parishioner to whom Father McNulty evidently passed them on. The gunman, said to be of Eastern European extraction, is still at large. He is known, in turn, to have passed the documents on to another accomplice.

The injured man is Det Con Stephen Bentley. He is in a stable condition, but will need further surgery. Police are anxious to interview any eyewitnesses.

A GCHQ spokesman has denied knowledge of the documents. He said "We have no knowledge of these documents or what they might contain."

There were photographs of the policemen, St Nicholas presbytery, and, despite the denial, of GCHQ.

"There's more there than a police release," said Hugh.

"I agree" said Tim. "I think someone at the Regent took the basic release and added a bit of embroidery of his own. And somehow, I don't think it was friend Jenkins. Trust the Regent. They can't resist making mention of the office, even when there's nothing to say."

Hugh said, "Look, we'll have to warn Debbie. I'll do that. I can email it to her or she can get it straight off the website." He dropped Tim off, and Tim went into the house.

"Oh, Tim dear, Doctor Campbell called asking if you'd seen today's Regent. I told him no."

"I'll phone and tell him yes," said Tim, thrusting the paper into Lucy's hand.

Campbell confirmed what Tim suspected. "This article was not written by Brian," he said emphatically. "In fact, he's very angry about the whole thing. He wanted to stick to the police release, which was about two lines, but someone went in over his head and embellished it. Between you and me, I think he's getting a bit disaffected with his job. I've not actually seen Brian. All this comes from Mary."

"How is Mary?"

"Oh, fine. She's working part-time in the library now. And still helps Megan around the house. She's a good little gardener, too. I hope she'll be able to stay a bit longer She's certainly under no pressure to leave."

After ringing off, Tim looked at Lucy. "Well," he said, "That was a very interesting morning."

"Ruined by the Regent," she said.

"Well, yes, I suppose so," said Tim, forcing a grin. "Anyway, do you need any help?"

"Do I need any help?" she mused, "We – ell, let's see. You can give the shower a good clean-out, the grouting's getting all yellow again, mow the lawns, water the greenhouse plants and the hydrangeas out the front, and clean the car. But those are just your jobs. If you want to help me, you can hoover upstairs and make the bed. It's clean sheets, by the way. Then..."

"OK, OK," said Tim. "How about I just lay the table? I can see dinner's nearly ready."

"I'll settle for that," said Lucy. "As long as you come shopping with me this afternoon. We need some new curtains for the small back bedroom."

There was no answer to that.

*****

Tim and Lucy were not the only ones shopping that Monday afternoon. Brian Jenkins and Mary decided to go into Cheltenham for a few odds and ends. Mary needed a new pair of casual shoes and Brian needed various computer supplies and a few groceries. But their greatest need was simply to be together. Having Mary in his life compensated for the hassle he was going through at work. More than compensated. Just being with Mary, and studying that little frown that crept over her forehead as one pair of shoes after another were considered and rejected was reward enough. Finally, they had what they wanted apart from the groceries, and as it was on their way, they called in at the new Sainsbury's. As they waited at the lights to turn in there, a school bus drew up nearby and a dozen or so teenagers spilled out. At first, Brian didn't give them more than a glance, but he suddenly sat bolt upright and pointed to a well-built lad, a blazer slung over one shoulder, shirt-tails hanging out, and school tie partly undone and drooping down. He carried a bag of books.

"It's him," he breathed to Mary, "It's that kid. The one who picked up the CD or whatever it was. Look, I must find out where he lives. Oh, the filter arrow's on, I've got to turn now. Don't lose sight of him." He made the turn and stopped on the approach road to the Sainsbury's car park. "Just keep an eye on him. See which way he goes. I'll turn round and pick you up, then we'll slowly tail him." He dropped Mary off, turned into the car park, followed the arrows round and came back out.

Mary climbed in the car and pointed. "He went up there, towards the football ground. See him?"

"Yes, he's in my sights. I can't crawl, so I'll have to let him get ahead a bit, then do a spurt."

Despite the odd toot from other road users, he managed to tail the lad without his being aware, and soon had his address, near the Robins' ground.

"Tell you what," said Brian. "How about we get this to the police right away?"

*****

At police headquarters Brian spoke to the desk sergeant, a rather bored-looking fellow, whose demeanour suggested he'd had a long day. Brian came straight to the point. "I have some important information for the officer I spoke to when Stephen Bentley was shot in Pittville Park. My name is Brian Jenkins."

The sergeant immediately perked up. "Do you have any information on the perpetrator, sir?" he asked. Why did the police use these pompous words? thought Brian.

"You mean Misha?" said Brian. "No. Sorry. But the information I do have might help trace the sensitive information he stole. Tell him that the lad who collected the package from the bin outside Sainbury's lives at this address." He handed over the piece of paper he'd written the address on.

"I'm not quite sure I understand all this, sir," said the Sergeant, looking baffled.

"It's a bit complicated," said Brian. "And it would take a long time to explain. Please accept my word that this is very important, so please get this into the right hands as soon as possible. There must be someone around who is following up the shooting and the whole business behind it."

"I'll make enquiries, sir," said the Sergeant. "Now can you give me your name again, and your phone number."

"Do you think he will pass it on?" asked Mary, when Brian was back in the car.

"I'm quite sure he will," said Brian. "I think I got someone who wasn't close to the case, that's all."

Sure enough, as they drove off, the sergeant picked up the phone, spoke briefly, started an entry in the log, and pressed a few keys on a computer terminal. He then completed the entry with the names of the occupants of the address in question appearing on the computer screen. He pressed a few more keys, entered a password and sat back. Interesting. Mr Gill had a record. Not extensive, just a couple of GBHs and receiving stolen goods, but Hobbsie would be interested.

*****

Detective Constable Norman Hobbs was quite sure the CD was already in the hands of its intended recipient, so there was no longer a need for haste, but there might still be value in knowing who that recipient was. He was sticking his neck out a bit, acting on a tip, but he had faith in the source, Brian Jenkins, so was happy to take the risk. He had been impressed by the journalist's initiative in Pittville Park, though he was none too happy with the story in the Regent after the press release. So, friend Gill had a modest record. He was a dishonest bastard with a short temper. Certainly the right credentials to be recruited by the likes of Misha.

Hobbs wanted to be sure the Gill household were all at home when he called, so he waited until early evening. He had WPC Henderson with him when he parked outside the Gills' semi and rang the bell. Mrs Gill answered.

"Good evening, Madam. Mrs Gill?"

"Ye-es," she said uncertainly.

"May I have a word with your son?"

"Oh dear, he's not in trouble, is he?"

"What's going on?" Lennie came to the door, moved his wife out of the way, none too gently, and took up a confrontational stance.

"It's Colin," said Mrs Gill. "This policeman wants to talk to him."

"Oh he does, does he? What about?"

"You can be present while I ask him a couple of questions, Mr Gill. In fact, you should be present."

There was a sound of a door slamming somewhere in the house.

"Sounds like you're too late, mate," smirked Lennie.

*****

Colin raced out the back door, and ran down the side of the house and into the road. Before WPC Henderson could get out of the car, he was past her. She quickly followed and drew level with him, lowering the window. As she was about to ask him to stop, he spoke to her.

"Pull up round the corner," he said in barely more than a whisper, continuing to run, his eyes straight ahead.

WPC Henderson did as she was bid. Colin ran past the car, dropping a scrap of paper through the open window. It landed in her lap. She drew level with him again.

"Look, you've got what you want now. He left it lying around. Now bugger off. I'm going to get a bloody good belting anyway."

He crossed the road and disappeared down an alley.

Hobbs then came round the corner.

"He's given me the address. It was already written out." She handed the paper to Hobbs. "Poor lad," she sighed. "He's going home to a belting."

"We'll see about that," said Hobbs, grimly. "Head back to the house and wait there. I'll walk." He wanted a few minutes to devise his strategy for protecting Colin from his brute of a father.

In the house Lennie said, "Well, that's got rid of them. Wait till that little bugger comes in. I'll bet he called the cops. He'll get the biggest belting he's had in his life." He looked out the window. "They're here again. Well, they can bloody well stay out. I'm not having them in here. If they ring, don't answer."

Norman Hobbs strode up to the front door and rang. There was no reply. He rang again, then again. He hammered on the door. He signalled to WPC Henderson, who spoke into her radio phone.

"Mr Gill," shouted Hobbs, "you must open your door. There are more of us on the way here, and we'll force an entry."

He waited several minutes, then signalled the WPC again. Suddenly the air was rent by the wail of their siren. Within seconds, faces appeared at windows and people appeared on doorsteps. Lennie's door abruptly opened.

"Shut that bloody racket off," he yelled. "Look, now you've got all the neighbours gawking. What are you trying to do? All right, all right. What do you want? The little bugger's gone. You drove him off. I hope you're satisfied."

"We'll shut the siren off when I'm in your house and being spoken to politely."

"Oh, come in," said Lennie in a resigned way. "But I'm not admitting anything." As soon as they entered the house, the siren stopped. Mrs Gill had made herself scarce.

"Now listen carefully," said Hobbs when they were sitting down again. "We know you sent a package to a London address. We have officers in London who can find out things like that from their end. We suspect you got Colin to collect the package for you. But we don't know for sure. What we do know is that you were the one that got rid of it. Now, who got you involved in all this? It's important we find out, because the information in the packet is top secret."

Lennie was fidgeting uncomfortably. "Some bloke I met in the pub."

"Local chap, was he?"

"No, I'd never seen him before. I think he was foreign. Dark bloke."

"How did he come to approach you?"

"He seemed to know I'd been inside. But that was years ago. I've gone straight since then. There was nothing criminal in what this bloke wanted. He just asked me to do him a favour. Post a package for him. He said it was financial advice to investors. Tips on the market, you know?" Yes, I know, thought Hobbs. It was all too plausible.

245

"The problem is, that was not what the package contained. Something much more important than that. The other problem is that the help you gave was to a foreign power. That can attract a very heavy sentence, and it's no defence to say you didn't know. OK. You have at last been co-operative, but I'll have to report this. I can't say what the outcome will be. Oh, and one more thing. Colin is in no way to blame. All he did was collect something for his dad. He sounds like a good, helpful son. I'll be keeping my ear to the ground. If I hear the slightest whisper that you've taken it out on him, I'll be back. And I'll not be in uniform. I'll be off duty. It'll be man to man. I can be a real bastard out of uniform. You wouldn't like to meet me. Now, I'd better call off those other men with the forced entry gear. And by the way, have you seen this?" Hobbs produced the article on the front page of the Regent.

"See what it says, do you? Policeman shot in Pittville Park. Foreign Agent Makes Off with Secrets." He's fighting for his life, that policeman. And you know what? He's my mate, probably my best mate. So remember, I'm a very angry police officer."

Hobbs left, climbed into the car and gave a last blast on the siren before WPC Henderson drove off.

"He's got the message," he said. "Look, isn't that the boy? Standing on the corner there. Slow down."

He wound the window down. "Thanks, Colin. Your dad won't hurt you."

"If he does, I'll kill him."

"I didn't hear that," said Hobbs. "Look, try and get to know your dad better, and keep him out of mischief. He wants to go straight. His problem is he can't recognise mischief when he sees it."

Colin stared after them as they drove off.

CHAPTER 26

Next morning Tim and Lucy went to the Service of the Word, bought a few bits and pieces in Bourton then, back at home, Tim began thinking of the questions he hoped to put to Brother Simeon later in the day. His thoughts were interrupted by a phone call from Hugh Frobisher.

"Your fragments have arrived. Would another session tomorrow be convenient?" he said.

Tim looked at Lucy. "OK for me to go in tomorrow, love? It's Hugh." Lucy nodded.

"Yes, that's fine," he said. "Same arrangements? I'm happy to drive this time, if you like."

"OK. It'll start a bit later. We'll be joined by Professor Lewis. You know – the chap you met the other day. He'll be coming up from London. Can you pick me up about 10:30?"

"OK. No problem."

*****

Tim left at 6:15 pm for his visit to the Abbey.

Prinknash Abbey (pronounced Prinnish) occupies a large estate between Cheltenham and Stroud, near Painswick, and first came into the hands of the Benedictines over 900 years ago. After the dissolution of the monasteries it passed into private hands and served at one time as a hunting lodge for Henry VIII, guaranteeing a minimum of 40 deer for the chase. It remained in use as a residence of the nobility until 1928, when the owner gifted the estate to the Benedictines of Caldey Island, off Tenby in South Wales. A new monastery at Prinknash completed in 1972 was occupied by the monks for some 36 years, while the old residence, known now as St Peter's Grange, served as a conference and retreat centre. The community, now somewhat depleted in numbers, have moved back to the Grange. On the drive there, Tim recalled the many retreats he had spent in the Abbey.

Appropriately, as they climbed from their cars, birdsong seemed to be everywhere. A few rabbits could be seen at the far end of the lawn. Father Danny was waiting outside the Grange to greet him.

"Come on in, Tim," he smiled. "Father Abbot sends his apologies, but he's rather busy at the moment. We'll go to the lounge. Brother Simeon should be there."

They walked down the flagstone corridors to the main hall and turned into a comfortably furnished lounge. Tim suddenly recognised the room. The last time he'd been there was to make a confession on a retreat several years ago. During retreats for twenty or thirty people, several rooms were pressed into service for confessions, not the forbidding "black box" variety, but chatty occasions with priest and penitent in full view of each other and sitting in armchairs. A monk in an off-white habit stood waiting for him. He was rather on the small side and had carrot-coloured hair, and a face generously decorated with freckles. A huge grin with slightly buck teeth dominated his features. He shyly held out his hand, as Father Danny made the introductions.

"We're very lucky Brother Simeon joined us," he said. "He is a man of many talents. He takes care of all our IT needs, and is our general scientific consultant."

"To be honest," said Brother Simeon, "the IT needs are pretty modest. My 10-year-old nephew can run rings round me. When he visits, he brings his play-station with him. Just to show me, you understand. I don't think Father Abbot would approve of me actually playing with it." The grin expanded. "Anyway, Tim, what can I do for you?"

Father Danny interrupted "May I leave you two? I also have a few commitments." He left Tim and Brother Simeon to get acquainted.

"First, thank you for seeing me," said Tim. "What can you do for me, you asked. Well, for one thing, I'm interested in the Church's stance on life elsewhere in the universe. I mean developed life forms. Not bacteria or microbes."

"What got you so interested in this?" asked Brother Simeon.

Tim had to be careful here not to bring the intelligence angle in, and the official interest the incident in Canada had elicited.

"My parish priest, Father Donald McNulty, may have seen a – a space visitor," he said. "He actually claims that what he saw was an angel. This was on a recent visit to Canada. He was camping in a remote area. I just wondered if it could have been something other than an angel, in view of the circumstances. There seems to have been some sort of air crash, and Father Mac told me they cordoned off the area."

248

"You're assuming the thing that crashed was from some alien civilisation?" The grin had been replaced by a look of concern on Brother Simeon's freckled face.

"Well, yes, crazy as it might sound."

"It might not be so crazy," said the monk.

"Does the Church believe in extraterrestrial life, then?" asked Tim.

"Let me put it this way," said Brother Simeon. "The Church does not exclude the possibility of its existence. Indeed, for many centuries theologians have debated this possibility, together with its implications. Some argue that it is not only feasible, but both logical and likely. If angels exist, and the Church accepts that they do, then they were created as a higher order by God, who made all things, including us. Is it not very likely, then, that God also made other life forms elsewhere in the universe, some less evolved than man so far, but some much further ahead in their evolution – a form of life that in a sense bridges the evolutionary gap between man and angels. I mean, the universe is God's gift to his creatures. He made our Earth in our solar system in our galaxy, the Milky Way. But our sun is just one of at least 200 billion stars in the Milky Way – think of it, 200 billion! Are we saying there is not one of the other 199,999,999,999 suns that has a planetary system that includes a planet capable of supporting life? And our own galaxy is but one of at least 10 billion."

"Put that way, it sounds extremely plausible. But how on Earth could they get here?" Tim asked, voicing the obvious question. He was quickly brought back on track.

"That's a totally different consideration," said the monk. "Let's stay for the moment with the question of the existence of these beings. You can play the numbers game and the theory of probability, you can argue on theological grounds, or you can apply a purely philosophical approach. In all cases you must come to the same conclusion. There is extraterrestrial life that includes forms of life which have evolved beyond the stage of man. OK, that may still only be at the theoretical level, but when you add to it the vast body of observation and contact, yes – contact, this conclusion becomes virtually irresistible. It has been suggested within the Church that the advanced evolution of some of these beings has involved the soul more than the body. Their bodies, if anything, have shrunk and perhaps discarded some of mankind's present physical traits, while the soul, together with all the goodness and positive qualities enshrined within it, has grown closer to God. If this is true, then Father Mac might have seen either an angel or one of

249

these more spiritually advanced beings." He took a deep breath, and grinned. "By the way," he added, "There is a science called astro-biology. It was lurking in the shadows at one time, but it's now perfectly respectable. That is a measure of how confidence has grown among the scientific community on this whole subject."

"Why do you say Father Mac might have seen either an angel or a spiritually advanced being?" asked Tim, puzzled.

"Because if a crew member survived, that's who he met. But if they all perished, he (lucky man) would have seen an angel. No, don't protest. Think about it. Do you think a catastrophe such as this – a journey of perhaps several decades ending in a crash – would not have brought forth an angel to complete the contact that was evidently planned? Remember, angels are purely spiritual and can instantaneously be wherever they want to be, or wherever God wants them to be, and if they have good reason to appear in visible form, they can do so."

Tim quickly dismissed the temptation to admit that the plan did not involve merely establishing contact, but handing over some documents. That was very much the essence of his briefing in the safe house. He changed the subject.

"I understand from Father Danny that you have a telescope," he said. "Do you use it regularly?"

"Yes, it's one indulgence I'm permitted. It is in tune with the Vatican's great interest in astronomy. You probably know they have their own observatory – two in fact, one near Rome and a much more advanced one in Arizona."

"No, I'd no idea," he admitted. He pondered this. "So do the Vatican tell you what to do? Is there a sort of network of telescopes all reporting to the Vatican?"

Brother Simeon chuckled. "What a brilliant idea," he said. "I can just see the Holy Father sitting there with bated breath and saying, 'Any news from that Brother Simeon in Prinknash?' No, Tim, nothing like that. I've no idea if other religious houses have telescopes. I dare say the odd one or two might. We only came by ours as part of a legacy. We do get a few legacies most years, and we're most grateful for them. They usually involve a sum of money, but in this case we were offered the entire contents of the house. Our benefactor was the father of a member of our community. Most of the items we sold or gave to others, but Father Abbot decided to keep the telescope. Astronomy has been described as a means of gaining a closer appreciation of the personality of the Creator. But, to answer your question, no, there's certainly no systematic tasking levied on us from some central authority in Rome." Not a bit like Sigint, thought Tim.

"So what do these Vatican observatories actually do?" asked Tim, by now fascinated.

"To be honest, I don't really know, at least not in any detail. I imagine they're just looking deep into space for any event that appears anomalous."

"Such as the arrival of alien space vehicles?"

"I would imagine so. Let's not be coy, about this. The Vatican is highly interested in space. They got egg on their face over Galileo. You no doubt know that he espoused the theory first put forward by Copernicus that the centre of the universe, or at least our part of it, is the sun and not the Earth. Galileo was able to confirm Copernicus's theory by personal observations with an instrument he invented and called a telescope. However, in 1633 Galileo was tried as a heretic and forced to recant. He was sentenced to lifetime house arrest. Since that howler, the Church has been striving to shake off a reputation of being hostile to science. The Vatican opened its first observatory in the late 18th Century in Rome. They by then realised the value of cosmic observation, not least in helping to construct, then fine-tune, the Gregorian calendar."

"I knew a little bit of this," said Tim, "Do carry on, this is fascinating."

"Well, the original observatory was moved several times because of things like pollution and modern street lighting. Some time in the 1930s, it was moved to the Papal Palace at Castel Gondolfo. It's now in a former convent nearby, but this was largely due to restructuring in the palace to make more room for the papal reception of diplomats."

"Now, what about the other observatory? In Arizona, did you say?"

"Yes, on Mount Graham. It was opened in 1993 and is manned by the Jesuits, I believe. Don't ask me what exactly they do. They call themselves the Vatican Observatory Research Group."

"But among other tasks, they could be searching for alien life?"

"I suppose so, but obviously I can't confirm that. As I said earlier, perhaps they're just looking for anything that constitutes an anomaly, whatever form this takes. All I can really say on the question of extraterrestrial life, is that the Church are deeply interested in the subject. The implications are quite staggering. If these beings exist, are they created in God's image? If so, do we regard them as another group of souls we should evangelise? It brings a whole new dimension to mission work."

"I think on that note, I'd better let you go," said Tim with a broad smile. "It's been totally stimulating, and you've left me with plenty to mull over. Anyway, how did you come to be here?"

They carried on chatting on a more personal level for a while. After graduating, Brother Simeon had decided to take a gap year before settling into a career. He'd always had a yearning to help the disadvantaged in some way or other, and enlisted for Voluntary Service Overseas, where he got involved in sanitation work in a particularly poor African country. He found himself working with engineers from several countries, and as a committed Christian he was also enlisted to help a mission in providing basic schooling to children of different ages. Some as young as 10 had served as soldiers in a civil war, and needed counselling and basic rehabilitation – in other words, all the love in the world. From this developed a sense of vocation, but he had no clear idea how to channel it. He had to return home after a year for family reasons, and suddenly knew what to do. He was pointed to becoming a Benedictine. He had no idea why, but just knew it was what God was asking him to do.

Finally, Tim dragged himself away, thanking the monk and shaking his hand vigorously.

"I'd like to make a small donation to the Abbey," he said, "May I leave it with you?"

"That's very kind, I'll pass it on to Father Abbot."

"Say goodbye to Father Danny for me, and I'm sorry if I've disrupted life at the Abbey."

"Of course you haven't," said the monk with a huge grin. "I've enjoyed our little chat. You must come here again."

Now that, thought Tim as he left St Peter's Grange, is exactly the sort of chap we need on our working party. I wonder if they'd have him. Anyway, Father Abbot wouldn't release him.

When he got home, he gave Lucy a kiss. "What an interesting evening," he said.

"You may find tomorrow equally interesting," she said. "Hugh phoned to say he's arranged for Doc Campbell to join the group tomorrow. He said they won't get involved in the naughty bits, but just have an intellectual discussion. He's spoken to Doc, and you're picking them both up."

"That's terrific," said Tim. He felt something was happening now. There was movement.

*****

Tim slept fitfully, his mind still stimulated by his chat with Brother Simeon. The odds he had quoted in favour of extraterrestrial life were staggering, and these, he knew, were reinforced by goodness knows how many reports by sane and sober men and women of vehicle sightings and even of meetings with their occupants. The case for alien life was overwhelming. And with that as a starting point, all sorts of other things became possible. Some scholars considered life forms included beings much more spiritually advanced than those on Earth. How did they get to that stage without God's help? Did they have the advantage of escaping the taint of original sin? And if extraterrestrial life became irrevocably proven, this would surely strengthen, not weaken, the Church. The Church never compromises, yet survives. It always adapts. It has cast aside heresies, some real, some imagined. It got some things wrong, like Copernicus and Galileo, but corrected itself; it even assimilated Darwin. God always provided a supply of right-thinking men to do the fine-tuning needed in any age. Tim must have fallen asleep some time in the early hours, because he failed to hear Charlie clinking his way up and down the road.

CHAPTER 27

Tim was glad he was not picking up the others until 10:30 and grabbed the chance of a minor lie-in.

"We'll eat this evening," said Lucy, as the time drew near. "So you can be as long as you like. Better take a banana and a few digestives, though, to be on the safe side. We haven't got any chocolate bars."

After being warned he was on the margins of type 2 diabetes, and having felt decidedly faint a few times when he had been unexpectedly delayed, Tim always carried a mini-snack on those occasions that could be open-ended, to give his sugar-level a quick jolt. Father Mac was similarly afflicted.

"Good thinking," he said. "I'll take something."

He set off, picked up Hugh and Doc Campbell, and they were soon heading over the hill. On the way, Hugh said, "As I mentioned, we've got Alan Lewis coming this morning. Professor Alan Lewis. You met him the other day, Tim. He's a general scientific consultant to the government. He gets roped in on any occasion where an unbiased scientific opinion is required. Sometimes those closest to a subject can't see the wood for the trees. And if he can't help, he always knows a man who can. As you know, he's on both our working party and the scientific one. Debbie Faulkner decided after the meeting that our thoughts on the new material might benefit from his opinion."

"Does he have medical knowledge?" asked Doc Campbell.

"He's bound to," said Hugh. "He's not had your specialist training, but I'm sure he has some knowledge on the fringes, as he does with so many subjects."

"Bit of a polymath," said Tim.

"I don't think he'd claim that," said Hugh, "They tend to be equally expert in several subjects, but not too many. Alan has less expert knowledge but over an amazingly wide range of subjects."

"I didn't really meet him the other day, but I'm beginning to hate him already," said Tim with a grin.

When they arrived, Kathy Webb already had the professor in tow, signing him in. Doc Campbell and Tim were also issued with visitor passes, and they all went up in the lift, making the introductions as they went. Nick Watson was there in Kathy's office, waiting.

"Good morning, gentlemen," he smiled, "and Kathy of course, but we've already met today. I'm so glad you could join us, Alan, and you Doctor Campbell. We have a veritable brains trust here today. Now, let's have a coffee to start with, shall we? Or tea, of course. Nothing elegant. Just mugs and instant. We don't run to a canteen here. There are so few of us this side of town." Soon they were all nursing mugs of hot coffee.

"Oh, by the way," said Kathy, "I may have to duck out before we finish. I've got that forensics chap coming to play about with that single sheet."

"Good. More possible progress," beamed Hugh. "Now, Alan, you heard Father McNulty's evidence."

Lewis nodded. "Very interesting and very perceptive," he said.

"And you've also had another chance to look at the map fragments. You saw M.O.D.'s photocopy, I understand. You can have another look at the originals now, Alan. Play with them, too."

Kathy produced the map fragments from a metal box. The box had a combination lock, but had already been opened. She placed them on a large table.

Lewis studied them, then started moving them about. Inside about two minutes, after a bit of trial and error he had placed them in position to his satisfaction.

"I must admit I haven't spent long on sorting these bits out," he said. "But this layout does, at least, suggest a particular region of the world to me? Does it ring any bells with anyone else?"

Tim studied the reconstruction. He was impressed, but could see it didn't quite accord with his memory of his own version.

"Would you mind if I repositioned a couple of pieces?" he asked tentatively.

Lewis smiled and said, "Of course not." Tim reversed the position of two fragments. "Why did you do that?"

"Because in those positions they fit the sequence of the grid co-ordinates."

"Ah, do you know, I tried to solve that, but there wasn't quite enough to go on."

"Of course, you didn't have the crib," said Hugh. "The thing we call the reference book is numbered, so, as I think you know, we recovered their numerical system."

"Yes, of course," said Lewis. "Because the map makes perfect sense now. It's part of the Black Sea."

"Bingo!" said Tim. "I'm so pleased we're in full agreement."

"To be honest, even with some bits in the wrong place, I had a hunch that was the bit portrayed. It's where our visitors seem to want to go. And there's a powerful transmitter in the Crimea they probably home in on, too. The only problem is …"

"We don't know the scale," supplied Tim.

"Absolutely right," said Lewis. "I thought at first the map must show somewhere in Canada because that's where the vehicle came down, and in fact if you assume a large enough scale there are several possible configurations of lakes that might just fit. But I like the Black Sea much better. If you're miles up this must be the sort of scale you'd want."

"Of course, they might have had other maps in other scales," said Tim, "but perhaps this is the most likely scale our friend thought Father Mac would recognise. I wonder if he knew he was in Canada when he came to grief. He at least seemed to know he was in an English-speaking, or at least a non-Russian speaking area."

"I'm sure he wouldn't know he was in Canada," replied Lewis. "They probably know nothing about the geo-political divisions of the planet Earth."

"Assuming, of course, it is Earth," said Tim mischievously.

""Oh, I'm certain it is," said the professor. "Now is there anything else we need to do with these fragments? Do they contribute in any way to the problem of reading the language?"

"We've not thought much about that yet," said Nick. "Kathy and Hugh have been concentrating on getting the parameters of the alphabet finalised. Except, according to Tim, the first two elements of the grid references are letters, right Tim?"

"Yes, so as you follow the references across you can at least place two letters in sequence."

"OK," said Nick, "So we can agree that we have a tentative identity of the map. Should we move on?"

They continued gazing at the map fragments for a while longer, but after a bit more desultory chat, agreed to move on.

Kathy went to the cupboard and found the medical pages.

"I'm not sure how you want to play this," said Nick. "Page by page? There are too many to display all at one time."

Tim did a swift calculation. "Looking at the number of the first page we have, it would be just over page 100 in new money," he said. "So we pick up the book somewhere in the middle."

"I find this book really exciting," said Professor Lewis. "I thought so when I first saw it the other day. Yes, let's do it page by page, slowly." They studied the first page, which depicted a frontal view of what was clearly a male. The organs were displayed in a variety of colours, and lines from some of them led to groups of symbols.

"That group of letters must be Alienspeak for heart," said Kathy.

"Notice the configuration of the hands," said Nick.

"Six fingers on each," said the Professor. "So they calculate on a base of twelve. Much more sensible in some ways. Decimal is so restrictive. Binary is only useful in black and white, yes/no contexts. Computery, of course, and jolly useful it is, but you can't organise your life around it. Mind if we turn over?"

Kathy carefully turned to the next page. It looked very like the first page, except the heart had a different colour this time.

"It also has a different name," said Hugh, "Look." He flipped between the two pages.

"Except on the first page the symbols are not letters," said Tim. "They're numbers; 25, I think."

"Are any more of them numbers?" asked the Professor.

Tim scrutinised the two pages. "Yes, there are several on both pages. Let's move on and see if there are more."

"Why do they refer to the organs as numbers on some pages and presumably names on others?" asked Nick Watson, intrigued. "Do they refer to them in that way in their normal medical currency? I say Dr. Alien, I think we're going to have to operate on this patient's number 17. Or remove his 22. It's diseased." There were a few chuckles.

All this while, Doctor Campbell was getting more and more agitated. Hugh noticed this.

"I'm sorry, Doctor Campbell, we've not really brought you in yet. After all, you're the only one who has really studied these pages."

"Yes," said the Scot testily, "for three days, almost non-stop. If you carry on turning the pages, you'll find the same pattern of labelling. I suspected some of the labels were numbers, because the symbols seemed identical to some at the top of the pages. No, I didn't think the organs themselves were numbered, I thought the numbers referred to the method of treatment. I also think that whichever organ is depicted in red on a page, is the organ of primary concern. On some pages more than one organ is numbered, the red one, and one or more others. I believe these others are secondary to the main organ of concern, but need some sort of ancillary treatment to guarantee success. "

Father Mac

There was a stunned silence, then Hugh broke into applause and the others joined in.

"But he's no good at chess," said Tim with a grin. There was an explosion of laughter.

"Carry on, doctor, please," said Professor Lewis.

"I said that on some pages more than one organ is numbered, but in some cases an organ is indicated by two numbers, one in black and one in green." Doc Campbell flipped through the pages and pointed to examples.

"And how do you explain that?" asked the professor.

"I've no idea," admitted Campbell, "unless, say, the green numbers are shorthand for the actual medication that is required." There was no applause this time. They continued turning the pages. About half way through, the book took on a different theme.

"What on Earth are these supposed to depict?" said Nick, pointing to a whole series of illustrations over about a dozen pages, showing a body partly clad in a sort of armour. Sometimes the armour covered just one limb, an arm or a leg, or just part of a limb, and sometimes part of the torso. In a few cases multiple parts of the body were covered. In three cases the entire body was cocooned, with only the head peeping out. In several instances the body, regardless of how much or how little was covered, was suspended above ground level by a gantry device. In every illustration the covered part was labelled with one of the numbers used in the earlier ones.

"I think there are four different labels," said Campbell.

"In fact, numbers?" said Lewis. "This is getting very interesting. What are the numbers?"

"Tim?" asked Nick Watson, "you're the expert here. I think we made a crib somewhere, but you know them off the top of your head by now I should think."

"Let's see," said Tim, doing a rapid piece of translation of the alien symbols. "We have 11, 25, 67, and one of the extra numbers between 39 and 40."

"Hmm," said Lewis, clearly disappointed. "I was hoping these might be atomic numbers, one of the Universal constants. But those numbers don't make any sense. Sodium, manganese? And a couple of others."

"Atomic numbers?" said Tim. "Please remind me. I'm only a simple arts graduate."

"They're assigned on the number of protons in the nucleus of an atom," said the Professor, rummaging in his pockets. "As I said, they are one of many universal constants. Ah, here we are." He produced a dog-eared diary. "Any scientist worth his sodium chloride knows these off by heart, or at least most of them. Let's see now. Hmm, perhaps this other one makes more sense – holmium. Used for lasers in keyhole surgery."

"I think," intervened Kathy Webb, somewhat diffidently, "That though Tim converted the alien symbols, we didn't do the next step – convert these numbers into our own equivalents."

"Oh, my God, yes, you're right," said Tim, colouring a little. "What an idiot. So that means we have 13, um, 29. 47 and…"

"79," supplied the professor triumphantly. "A perfect quartet."

Just then the phone rang. Kathy answered. It was security.

"Excuse me gentlemen," she said. "Our forensics friend has arrived. I've got to escort him and stay with him while he does his stuff. I've set a room aside for him. I understand it won't take long. You may even still be here when I get back. I do hope so." She retrieved the single sheet of paper from the box, placed it carefully in a folder and left them.

"You mentioned a perfect quartet," prompted Nick.

"Yes," said Lewis. "These are the four metals that have most interested man since time immemorial. They were among the first to be discovered, all of them in prehistoric times, they were played around with by the alchemists and they still command a great deal of interest. Gold and silver, though precious metals, have other properties of value to science, as do copper and aluminium."

"Ah, so that's what they are," said Nick Watson.

"And I know at least two of them have a role to play in medicine," said Doctor Campbell. "Not my forte as a humble GP." He looked at the professor. "Conducting agents?"

"I would imagine so," agreed Lewis.

"Then why do some illustrations depict more than one of the four metals in use at the same time to encase different areas of the same body?" pondered Tim.

"I'm not sure," said Lewis slowly. "One thing I think might be possible is that where a body appears to be suspended, it's relying on the natural electro-magnetic field of the planet, whereas in the other cases a locally generated source may be involved."

"You mean plug it into the mains?" said Tim.

"Well, yes, I suppose, or whatever passes for that in their world. Look, I think we may have to refer this problem to a specialist group. I don't think it's a good idea, on security grounds, to hawk this book around. What I would suggest is that we reproduce the drawings without the alien text, and translate what we do know into plain English. In other words, produce a totally sanitised version. I wonder if Doctor Campbell would like to be in charge of the work. I can tee up the specialist contacts. Of course, it might mean the occasional day trip."

"I could always take Megan with me," said Campbell with a broad grin. "Yes, I'd like that."

"You may be making a false assumption," said the Professor. "I think the experts we need to involve are in the provinces, in the major hospitals there, and perhaps the odd research establishment. I must think of a venue to bring them together. Certainly not London."

"Well, to be honest, that makes it even more attractive," said Campbell.

"At our last meeting," said Nick Watson, "it was suggested we set up a separate medical working group. I suppose what you're suggesting would serve the same purpose."

"Better, I think," said Professor Lewis. "In this way, sanitising the bits we use, I think we'll get a higher level of expertise because we'll be opening it up to the best people. Of course, I can't promise the idea will get off the ground. But," he smiled, "I've got a pretty good track record. One thing I hope we'll all agree and that is that the priority will always be to resolve the language as soon as possible and search for clues on propulsion systems or even weapons systems. The medical questions are interesting and important in their own way, but not related. I'd be inclined to regard them as a gift from well-wishers. So it's correct to shunt them off into a siding."

"Surely, they won't have weapons," said Tim. "I get the impression these are peaceful missions designed to help Mankind. As you said, the medical bits point that way. A gift."

"True," said Lewis, "but they may have the means of self-defence, if needed."

"But we on Earth can't possibly threaten beings so far ahead of us."

"No. But remember, vehicles that form this group are not the only ones with a calling card. Those outside the group are the ones that might pose a threat to our benign visitors."

Everyone nodded sagely. "Star Wars," said Tim uneasily.

"There are one or two other things depicted in the medical pages," said the professor, carefully turning them over. He pointed to the strange edifice, the stepped pyramid. "I really can't explain this. Except to agree with the suggestion someone made of a hospital. It comes immediately after all those illustrations of limbs and torsos covered in metal, so that sounds like a good bet. It also seems to be covered in metal. What a complex arrangement – you could have a patient cocooned in a metal tunnel inside a building covered in the same or a different metal." He chuckled. "Alternatively, I suppose it could be a boring old block of alien flats."

"What comes next?" asked Doc Campbell.

"Here's that DNA diagram," said Professor Lewis," for want of a better description."

"Where are the knobs and sticks?" asked Campbell.

"That's exactly what I said the other day," said Lewis. "There are a few more pages immediately following, but they don't seem to explain things. They may be enlargements of some part of it. There are also several chunks of alien script, including some numbers."

"All interspersed with the letters, "said Tim slowly. "I wonder what all that signifies."

"I'd really like to study these pages a bit more," said Lewis. "Do you think you could get them copied for me, Nick? Just the DNA bits. I don't think there's any urgency to photocopy these medical pages for all the other countries just yet though. We agreed to forward copies when we thought we had something to say about them. In fact, I'm not sure there's any particular urgency to copy anything. Debbie was going to discuss it in the JIC."

"I don't see why you shouldn't have a copy of a few pages," agreed Nick. "But will you mention it to Debbie please, just to cover our arses." He grinned. "I can say that now that Kathy's out of the room."

The phone rang. Nick answered. "Good. Good. Fine, let me check with the others." He turned to them. "Kathy says he'll be about another ten minutes. Then she has to escort him to the gate. Can you all hang on? It's only just after twelve now." There were nods all round. "We'll hang on then, Kathy. With bated breath. Fine. Thanks."

"Some slight enhancement," reported Nick. "But the paper and ink, or dye, or whatever, was simply not as responsive to treatment as the home-grown product. And there's nothing anyone can do."

"Well, some progress is better than none," said Tim philosophically. They carried on their discussion, going over the day's findings and

261

agreeing that good progress had been made, Hugh as ever bemoaning the lack of an entry point to the reference book or whatever it was.

"I really think we should read the notes Father Mac left us," said Tim. "Or, better still, get the dear old fellow along here in person. Here we are struggling, and we haven't even looked to see if he has any worthwhile ideas. We're being a bit arrogant, in my view."

"I'm inclined to share that view," said Nick. "As you may have guessed, we've been postponing getting him involved because he was too ill to be consulted, and in any case, we thought we could solve everything ourselves. We know now that the problem we're faced with doesn't respond to traditional cryptanalytic techniques. We can take things only so far. We've prepared the alien text for future exploitation by identifying all the discrete elements, assigning an arbitrary binary equivalent to each of them and digitising the texts. Great. But we need a trigger. The priest might just have the trigger. It will have to be some extra information. Something he has that we don't. Ah, here comes Kathy."

Kathy opened her folder. "Here's the original sheet with both sides cleaned up a bit, and here are two photographs of the two sides just after treatment. He said the photos are in case the original sheet he's been working on deteriorates in quality after time as a result of the treatment. On the other hand, it could conceivably improve." She laid the two versions on the table.

Tim thought back to his initial scrutiny of the sheet of paper as everyone looked first at the side with the Roman letters. He remembered he'd seen a B, two Os, and two Cs in the sequence OC BOC.

Now, some distance to the left he could faintly make out a P then another C a short distance to its right. And that was it, except that the treatment had served to confirm the earlier identities. The sum total of all this was now P C OC BOC. The others also studied the sheet, but reached no conclusion. The reverse side was much clearer, which was just as well, as it was crowded with Alienspeak. There seemed to be (Tim counted) nineteen items of information, all of varying lengths, each separated from the next by a small gap. There was a slightly wider gap about half way down. Heads were shaking in unison.

"Well, despite a little progress, there's still a long way to go," sighed Nick.

"That's right," said Tim, "Here we are with four separate documents and we can't get beyond tentatively identifying a map as part of the Black Sea, and some medical pages as portraying some advanced methods of treatment involving metals. We've decided that is worth a special study in its own right with Doc Campbell taking the lead. OK, that's progress – a slight entrée into the mindset of our space visitors. We know them, or at least this particular group, to be benign. And over the months they've left behind them large portions of a reference book of some sort, also clearly for our benefit. I'm sure they've become aware we're not clever enough to read it, so I think these extra bits they gave Father McNulty are intended between them to provide a starting point, though, as we've said, the medical pages may simply be a gift to help us improve treatment for various conditions. Look, Father Mac has almost given his life trying to protect the secrets these documents contain, on several occasions, too. As we were saying just now, I really think the least we can do is consult the notes he has left. I still have them, but they remain unopened, because we have been asked not to consult them until we have spent some time studying the fragments. Well, surely that time has arrived. Kathy has spent much of her time doing just that. Ploughing our own furrow is fine for a time, while we learn to fight our own battles. But I for one am ready to admit defeat. Let me at least consult Father Mac, and find out the sort of thing he knows that we don't."

"Surely, he'll just say he saw an angel," said Hugh. "Anything else will be garbled, because of his condition."

"I don't think so," said Tim, "Don't forget, he studied the fragments, wrote his account, and composed his notes all before he fell ill. His stroke doesn't change that. I think we're all trying to shelter him from getting further involved in something that's already impaired his health, possibly for good. These are worthy motives, as long as we can exploit the new material. We can, but only up to a point, so his comments might help. His speech is recovering fast, by the way. Let me at least broach the problem with him."

"I would agree with that," said Nick.

All right," said Hugh, looking round. He saw Kathy and the professor also nodding.

"But didn't he say that there were some other comments somewhere separate?" Lewis pointed out. "Do we consult all of them? What was it he said about the second lot?"

"That they contained a theory so outrageous that we were not to bother with those other comments unless and until we discover the nature of the 'reference book.' I can't think why he should say that. I would think any port in a storm, etc. But we'll do as he says and just take a peek at the first lot. I'll go and see him. I'm about due a visit. I want to get Sister Winifred's car back to her, too." He looked at Doc Campbell. "Mary will drive it down and I'll bring her back."

"Well, I think that about wraps it up for today then," smiled Nick. "Thank you all for coming. If there's any progress to report by anyone, especially you Tim in light of your visit to Father McNulty, we'll reconvene as soon as we're all available."

There were farewells all round. Kathy was taking the professor for a pub lunch, while Nick had to get back to the Doughnut. Tim, Hugh and Doc Campbell set off for Bourton.

"Wait till I tell Megan about my new job," beamed Campbell. "She'll enjoy coming along for the ride."

"Yes, well, it won't happen just yet," said Hugh, "In our enthusiasm, we've jumped the gun a bit. There may be the odd bit of admin. Some sort of contract of employment, for starters. So if you tell Megan anything, mention it as something that might happen some time in the future."

CHAPTER 28

Misha had gone to ground. After shooting the policeman and escaping from Pittville Park, he had sauntered back to the town centre, confident that any police car cruising around would not pick him out in the fading light. By the following day, he had rented a room in a shabby little apartment in Bristol, paying for a month in advance. He had prepared his own meals and barely went out. It was four days later that he had had the phone call, the first on his new mobile.

"Thank you for your email," said the voice. "I have forwarded it." Good, he thought, the CD was on its way, presumably by diplomatic bag. I can go home.

The voice continued, "Our contact here had visitors. They invited him round to their place for a party. It went on for so long he had to stay overnight. You have not chosen your friends wisely. You might want to see one of them about this." The phone clicked.

He had no difficulty in understanding the thinly disguised message. Though the paymaster was pleased to get the CD, he was not impressed with Misha's performance. Their PO box in London had been compromised and the contact there – someone from North Africa he'd never met – was taken in for questioning and detained. It was suggested that Misha should effect retribution. So, back to Cheltenham, then, with any luck, a flight home.

Now, here he was, back in his old stamping ground again, late on a Wednesday afternoon. He would need to kill a few hours, because that Gill oaf was probably at work. He was tempted to look up the delicious Chloe again, certain she'd be amenable to half an hour of bliss. Just for old times' sake, you understand. But that would be sheer arrogance, bordering on recklessness. He had also been tempted not to adopt a disguise. Let Gill see the friendly foreign gentleman he'd met in the pub. But he needed to move swiftly afterwards.

So here he was in his favourite short, tidy beard, a dusting of grey in the hair and wrap-around shades. What a handsome fellow – even more so than in his natural state. Perhaps he'd change permanently. Grow the real thing. What did it matter if the Gill family called in the police and described the new-look Misha? He couldn't see that happening. They'd be frightened out of their wits. Besides, their priority would be to get an ambulance to the house. The ambulance crew might call in the police, but he'd be well on his way to the airport by then in his latest hire car, which, by the way, he'd thoughtfully smirched with mud here and there, partly obliterating the number plates. Not totally, of course – that might have led to his being stopped by an alert police patrol.

He cruised around the town, then drove to Pittville Park, where he stopped for a while, recalling events there a week ago. He wondered how that policeman was now. Interfering fool. He'd got what he deserved. In a chase, it was good policy to maim. Misha knew that from past experience. It always concentrated the minds of others on getting treatment for the victim, while he escaped. An obviously fatal shooting would be left for later attention, while the chase continued, barely interrupted. Traffic around the park picked up noticeably around five. What passed for the rush hour in Cheltenham was underway. He waited while it peaked, then, just after six, eased off. He didn't want to get bogged down in traffic.

He slowly nosed into Gill's road and went past his house. Yes, the family car was in the drive. He turned and came back, stopping just before the house. He checked the inside pocket of his linen jacket, then climbed out and walked unhurriedly to the front door. He rang the bell. Colin answered.

"Mr Gill, please," said Misha pleasantly.

"Dad," yelled Colin. "There's a man to see you."

"Tell him if he's selling anything, to bugger off," came a voice from somewhere inside. Misha smiled and shook his head.

"He's not, Dad," shouted Colin.

"Oh, all right," grumbled Lennie. "I'm in the middle of me tea. We all are." He appeared, wiping crumbs from his mouth. "Oh, don't I know you? Colin, go back to your tea. Yeah, you were in the pub. You got another job for me?"

"No, no, Mr Gill, there's a small extra payment for the first job. A sort of bonus." He reached inside his jacket, took out the gun and shot Lennie through the ankle. Colin and his mother peered anxiously round the dining room door.

"If you report this to the police, we will be back," smiled Misha. He turned on his heel and reached his car, climbed in and drove off.

"Oh, look," said Mrs Gill. "Your dad's bleeding all over the hall carpet. I don't know how I'll get it off."

266

"Dad!" wailed Colin, as realisation had dawned in him of the reason behind the shooting. It was his dad's punishment for Colin's act of betrayal. "Oh, Dad!" The boy flung himself onto the floor beside his father, sobbing uncontrollably. After a short while he said, "We must get the ambulance. I'll do it."

"What about the police?" said his mother. "You can't just go around shooting honest people."

Or even dishonest ones, thought Colin. More composed now, he picked up the phone and pressed 999.

"Ambulance, please," said Colin, in answer to the enquiry. "There's been a bad accident here." He gave the address. "It's sort of a domestic accident. He's losing a lot of blood." He replaced the phone. "And we're not calling the police, Mum," he added, "Didn't you hear him? They'd be back."

*****

An hour later, Lennie was being treated in Cheltenham General, and the police were ringing the Gills' doorbell, following a tip-off from a paramedic. Detective Constable Hobbs saw a pale face peering round the curtains. He gestured to the face.

"Oh, let them in, Colin," said Mrs. Gill, "or they'll switch on that howling thing. And flash them lights. They know we're in. They can get a battering ram to us if we don't. I saw that once on telly. Only it was drugs. Or was it terrorists?" She went off into a dream, trying to recall a distant TV programme.

Colin knew his mother was right, and reluctantly opened the door.

"They said if you came here, they'd be back for us," said Colin.

"They always say that, son. It's part of the script," said Hobbs. "Look, let me come in a minute. I'm very sorry Mr Gill was shot. You already know from my last visit that he carried out an illegal act for the man who shot him. And for some reason, he's come back to injure your husband, Mrs Gill."

"It's my fault," said Colin, "I gave you the address, and they've come back to punish Dad." He began sobbing quietly.

"Oh, you bad boy," said Mrs Gill.

"Quite the opposite," said Hobbs. "He's a brave boy. For all he knew he might have been the one they shot. Anyway, I suspect this is

267

all water under the bridge now. Our friend with the gun has probably gone for good, and no-one will be back here."

"So you won't be able to catch him?" she said,

"It's probably not worth the effort," said Hobbs.

"Anyway," sniffed Colin, "he's got a small black beard and sunglasses. Dad recognised him, though, but he was up close."

"Yes, well, that makes it a little more difficult. There's little doubt he's already well on his way to his homeland, wherever that is these days. Now, I understand your husband was shot in the ankle. So was my colleague. It seems to be this criminal's trademark. I'm afraid your husband will be unable to walk for a while yet, Mrs Gill. There's no question of working."

"He won't mind that, as long as he can hobble to the pub," she said. Then a thought occurred. "Can he get compensation?" she asked.

"You can enquire if you like, but I don't think so. He brought this on himself. Your best bet is having the right clause in his life insurance policy. Assuming he is insured."

"Ooh, I don't know," said the loving wife. "I know we're covered for contents of the house, but I don't suppose that counts – though in a way he is part of the contents..." she added hopefully.

Well, you can always enquire," said Hobbs. "Now I'd better be going. I'm sorry for this very sad turn of events. Thank you for your help. I hope Mr Gill makes a good recovery. Good evening."

Hobbs wasted no time making a brief report over the car radio, though suspecting Misha was well away, heading for some airport he was sure was not Heathrow.

*****

While Misha was exacting retribution on Lennie Gill, Tim had been busy arranging a visit to Father Mac and Sister Winifred in the hospice for the next day. This was not quite as straightforward as he'd imagined. The first thing to clear up was the insurance. This turned out to be no problem, as the car belonged to the convent and could be driven by anyone nominated by Sister Matron and it was a simple task to phone and get oral permission. His plan had been for Mary to drive the Mini Cooper down there and come back with him and Lucy. Then Doc Campbell said he thought someone should travel down with Mary. Anyway, he and Megan would like to see Father, too, so they would go with Mary, as long as Tim could get five in his car for the return journey. Tim had agreed. Then Brian had offered to go with Mary, too. In the end Doc Campbell and Megan had decided that was a much better idea, because then he and Megan could go a day or so later. This would give Father Mac the enjoyment of two separate days with visitors. They could take Norah, too.

The only slight problem, to Tim's mind, was that with Brian there, he could not speak so freely with Father Mac. And the fact that Brian was a journalist, with a journalist's instincts for enquiry, made it potentially even more risky. In the event, Brian must have sensed this and said he'd like to meet Father, but would then withdraw from the scene and wait outside. Tim's estimation of Brian rose sharply. It rose even more when Brian popped round to the church's tiny car park and checked the oil, water and tyre pressures of Sister's Mini.

All that was yesterday. Now here he was, poised to set off for the hospice. They decided to go via the M5 and come back in Tim's car via Painswick. There was no need to travel in convoy, because Brian knew his way around North Gloucestershire as well as most.

Tim had had a preconceived idea that, despite the progress Father Mac was obviously making, they'd nevertheless all be crowding round a bed, slightly embarrassed at seeing someone with all the accoutrements of a patient, perhaps wired up with monitoring lines. Nothing had quite prepared them for what they did see. There he was, dressed, and sitting alone in the day room with a stick nearby and surrounded with the day's papers and back numbers of the "Tablet." Sister Winifred materialised from nowhere.

"Now, who's this young man?" she said sternly. "Don't I know you?"

"I was at the presbytery when the police arrested that man. That's when you saw me. My name is Brian Jenkins. I work for the Cotswold Regent."

"Are you a friend, or an enemy?" the nun persisted.

He grinned. "Very much a friend, Sister, not given to journalistic flights of fancy."

"He's lovely, Sister," said Mary. "You can trust him with anything."

"Including a girl's affections, no doubt." Her stern look dissolved and she beamed all round. "Well, what do you think of this old fellow? Donald, show them your party tricks."

"Trick number one," he said, picking up a copy of the "Tablet." He then proceeded to read from it flawlessly. He earned a round of applause.

"Trick number two." He pushed himself up from the chair, grabbed the stick and set off a little uncertainly around the room. Sister Winifred walked alongside in case he stumbled.

"That's absolutely incredible," said Tim, a sentiment echoed by the others.

"'Tis the power of prayer," said Sister. "I see it here all the time. I've seen patients diagnosed as terminally ill almost literally take up their beds and walk. Some have had a miraculous remission lasting several years. Others have had a happy release from a cruelly painful condition that threatened to linger for some time."

"Doc Campbell would be interested in that," said Tim.

"Sister, I'll leave Father alone with his friends," said Brian. "I know they have things to discuss that don't concern me. I just wanted to meet Father. I'd heard so much about you, Father, and I know what you've been through. I wrote about some of this in the Regent. Anyway, I feel privileged to meet such a brave man."

"That's very kind of you, my son," said Father Mac, "and I'm so pleased you're looking after Mary. She's a very brave girl. She's a real treasure."

"Oh, go on with you, Father," said Mary blushing. "Anyway, I'll wait outside with Brian." She bent over and surprised Father with a kiss on the cheek. "Oh, and by the way, Sister, if ever you want to sell your Mini, I'd be interested in buying it. It really goes like a dream."

"You should have seen her on the M5," quipped Jenkins, "overtaking all those police cars."

"Oh, you," said Mary, punching his arm. "Come on, out we go."

"Perhaps I should leave, too," said Lucy.

"No, I don't think we'll get into the sort of detail that would make that necessary, love," said Tim,

"Besides, I don't want to deprive Father of your delightful presence."

"Hear, hear!" said Father Mac with his crooked grin.

Tim gave Father a brief run down on what he had been up to, and the recent involvement of Doc Campbell. He expressed the team's satisfaction at the progress so far made, but also the frustration everyone felt at not getting further ahead.

"The key to so much of all this is getting into the language," he said with a sigh. "I've tried to persuade them that we should open the letter you left me with your own thoughts. But they won't do this lightly. I think they're worried about opening a can of worms and having to involve you closely, to the detriment of your health. I wonder if there's not a bit of arrogance there, too, this certainty that they'll succeed, because they should be good at this sort of thing. Our organisation and its wartime predecessor have had incredible successes in the field of code-breaking. Sometimes this has been the result of sheer brilliance, but occasionally some hint of a context has turned up, some piece of what we call collateral. That's certainly not the case with this problem. And this isn't exactly code-breaking. What do you think?"

"I'd be happy to get them started," said Father Mac. "Perhaps you know that in any case it was my intention from the start to make the authorities, whoever they were, work things out for themselves and to help them only if it were really necessary. I thought if they could resolve things, they would be well-equipped for anything they might encounter from this source in the future."

"You mean your notes really do give tips on how to progress?"

Father Mac considered. "Yes, I suppose you could say that. Remember, I was concerned that my life was under threat, so I quickly dashed off the account of my visit to Canada and of the events that followed after my return. The thoughts I had on the fragments I acquired were recorded no less hastily, and might not be very helpful to others until they had made their own study of them. But you seem to have reached that stage now."

"I'm sure we have and we'd certainly be glad of anything that can move us forward."

"Good. Now, as you'll recall, there are two separate notes. One you'll have, the other is kept apart. Read the first, but don't bother with the second unless you make any progress in identifying the contents of big book. The second note may then be seen to be totally irrelevant."

"So you know something we don't?"

"No. It's just that quite by chance I have a particular mix of – what shall I say? – credentials to make a few – deductions that might not occur to you. Call me your collateral. I should add, though, that these deductions, not based on the large book, are so way-out as to be laughable – if they weren't so plausible."

"Now I'm really intrigued. Would you mind, then, if I told the team that after talking to you, you would recommend that we open your first note?"

"No. And, look, I'll gladly speak to your team, if they would like."

"You're sure you'll be up to it?"

"Yes, though perhaps you could let them digest my thoughts a little first. Look, Tim, please, don't get it into your heads that I'm ill. I've been extremely lucky. Yes, what I had was technically a stroke, but it really was a mild one. I'm almost unscathed. I've already spoken to the Bishop and the Dean – in fact, the Dean paid me a visit – and I've told him that, given perhaps as little as a week or two, I could probably resume my duties again, at least in a limited way. He said if that were so, it might be possible to find a deacon to carry some of the burden. In fact, ours isn't the only parish with problems, so an extra deacon to work across the Deanery might be the solution. Anyway, what have you been up to, Lucy?"

"Oh, the usual. Keeping the happy home together and making sure Tim washes behind his ears. The normal sort of things."

The conversation drifted into domestic matters, so Tim went to see if Mary and Brian would like to come back in to say good-bye till the next visit. Mary came, gave Father Mac a hug and a kiss on the cheek, and they all made their farewells.

"Now, don't forget, Tim, Dominus vobiscum," said Father Mac.

"Et cum spiritu tuo," replied Tim, with a grin. Strange, Father lapsing into Latin from the Mass. "Dominus vobiscum, the Lord be with you," so Tim had felt obliged to provide the response, "and with thy spirit."

When they got outside, Lucy said, "What was all that about? That Latin?"

"I've no idea," said Tim. "I know Father Mac makes no secret of his love for the Latin Mass. Perhaps he was just emphasising his keenness to get back in the saddle. Anyway, forget all that. Now, shall we have a meal at the Royal William? Brian? Mary? Our treat."

Before they left, they found Sister Winifred and made their farewells.

"We're delighted at Father's progress," said Tim. "Doc Campbell and Megan will be down to see him soon."

"Tell the good doctor that Donald keeps talking about another game of chess. We do have a board here, as it happens. Perhaps Megan would like to have a look round the convent and the hospice while she's here. She used to be a nurse."

"Sounds a good idea. You could even conjure up a bit of nostalgia for her by giving her a bedpan or two to empty."

CHAPTER 29

The Royal William lies just past Painswick, in Cranham. Prinknash Abbey is only a little further along towards Cheltenham. The pub offers an all-day menu, so they decided to make this their main meal of the day. When they had ordered and were relaxing with a drink, Brian said, "I know you're a little concerned about my journalistic instincts. Please don't worry. I'm having a bit of a battle with my editor at the moment. He keeps wanting to put two and two together and making about nineteen."

"I know that last story wasn't your work," said Tim.

"I know it will only get worse," said Brian. "Just before we left this morning, one of the subs phoned me about another shooting. A tip off from his mate in the ambulance service. The police will release something, but haven't done so yet."

"And you have reason to think it's connected with all the previous business?"

"Judging by the address, it sounds like Colin's dad. You know, the lad at the litter bin."

Tim gave a whistle. "Bloody hell! Sorry, ladies. I can see what a story that would make. Especially with a bit of embroidery."

"Look," said Brian, "I know quite a lot of what this is about, but not enough to make a cast-iron story. And the reason I don't know enough is because the system is working as it should. The bits I don't know are the bits I'm not allowed to know. Here's what I do know. It started with Father Mac finding something on his holiday in Canada that for some reason appealed to him, so he brought it back home with him. He may even have been given it. I think the 'something' was in the form of documents. They looked interesting, perhaps they appealed to him as a priest, or perhaps as the brilliant linguist he's also reputed to be, some Inuit tongue or other. In fact, though Father Mac did not realise it, those documents were in some way sensitive in intelligence terms. Somewhere along the line they got copied to a CD. A foreign power enlisted the service of a freelance group of operators both in Canada and in the UK to nab these documents, which Father had hidden – people with the right credentials: an intelligence background as well as combat training. They in turn recruited one or two others, locally. I get the impression the ambulance job was only one of several attacks on the good priest. Now, here's what I don't know. The nature and content of the documents, precisely where they came from, why they are sensitive, and if they are in some meaningless form that will involve deploying techniques found only at GCHQ to resolve them. Because it's my job to be nosey, I've found myself at close quarters to some of the action. And I've probably deduced more than the average person. What I have not deduced, I must not be allowed to deduce, as an outsider. And so far, as I said, the system's working."

Tim looked at Brian with new respect. "Officially, I can't comment on all that, but I will say how much I admire your intellect and integrity. I can't see much future for you in journalism."

"Exactly," said Brian. "All my sympathies are with the police and the intelligence services, probably because I've had a few glimpses of them at work. I never thought I'd hold those views quite so ardently, as a journalist. The received wisdom in my trade is to treat them with suspicion, and if you can find something to justify that suspicion, shout it from the rooftops."

"Now you know why I like him," said Mary. "I got at close quarters, as well. We have a few things in common."

Their meal was served, so there was comparative silence for a while. On the way back to Bourton, the talk was mainly by and about Mary. She was really enjoying her part-time job at the library. One morning a week, children from the primary school came in to choose a book, and to hear a story read to them. Mary got roped in for that, and found she could not only establish a rapport with the children, but hold their attention throughout the story. She also got involved with a toddlers' group that met to sing nursery rhymes with their mothers.

Lucy was particularly interested. "Why don't you go in for teaching?" she asked.

"Funny you should say that. I'm enquiring at the moment about training to be a classroom assistant. I left school after 'O' Levels, really because Mum and Dad needed more money coming in, so I don't think I'm qualified enough for teacher training. But I got a good job in a travel agency, then got lured into work as a hotel receptionist. It seemed glamorous, but it was pretty hard work really."

"You're still very young," said Lucy. "You've got your whole life before you. You could go back to school and become better qualified if that's required as a starting point. You may even find a course that will give you 'A' Levels and teacher training. You may be able to combine this with a part-time job to keep at least some money coming in. There's more pick and mix around now. If you've got the aptitude for teaching, keep looking."

"That's what I tell her," said Brian. "Anyway, I'm a few years older than Mary, but I've got a feeling I'll be looking around for a new challenge, too."

When they arrive back in Bourton, Tim wasted no time in phoning Bob.

"Yes, we knew about the shooting," he said. "It was certainly our friend. Same modus operandi, same weapon by the sound of it. We think he's gone for good now. Scarpered overseas. We've asked the police to sit on it."

"And we don't know his destination?"

"No. We thought he might opt for one of the smaller airports. We suspected Bristol, so we put a watch on. He's pretty well disguised, too. Anyway, no luck."

"He may not have gone yet," said Tim hopefully.

"No chance," said Bob firmly. "The longer he delayed, the more chance for us to try to winkle him out. No, he's gone."

*****

Bob was right. Misha, in fact, had chosen Birmingham, near enough for convenience – only an hour or so away. Not huge like some airports, but large enough to offer a fairly wide menu of destinations, at least for the first stage of his journey. He had now completed that first stage, and here he was in one of his favourite airports, Schipol. He was tempted to break his journey and visit some of the girls he knew in downtown Amsterdam, but found there was space on a flight leaving within two hours, so he grabbed it. The "authorities" would have no idea where he was heading. It was probably one of the last places they'd think of. His flight was even now being called. He showed his boarding pass, went through the gate and strolled casually towards his plane. The air hostess who welcomed him aboard was very pretty. They always were on KLM.

*****

Tim's next phone call was to Hugh. He found him in.

"You'll always find me in in the afternoons," said a sleepy-

275

sounding Hugh. "I always need a nap of sorts – sometimes half an hour, more often over an hour. It's my pills."

"I just wanted to say I saw Father Mac this morning and he's not only happy for me to open the magic envelope, but is even prepared to come and join us in the office. Are you happy for me to go ahead?"

"Oh, yes, by all means," said Hugh, "That was certainly the consensus at our last session."

"Fine," said Tim, "I just wanted to give you a chance to stop me if you had any reason to. Perhaps something London had said."

"No, they just let us get on with it, relying on us to keep them informed of anything exciting."

"That's what I thought. Right, then. I'll be in touch."

Tim rang off, then went to his hiding place. It took only a minute or so to extricate the envelope. He tidied up the hidey-hole, then sat down and opened the envelope, full of nervous excitement. A single sheet of paper was inside, with just a few lines on it. Tim read:

Dear Friend,

If you're reading this, you will have successfully retrieved the fragments I carefully hid, and you, or more likely, a group of you, will have studied them and made a number of deductions. You will probably have ground to a halt. I was luckier. My singular credentials have led me to a possible understanding of the single sheet of paper, but it remains very much a long shot without corroboration, and that can only come from the other fragments, particularly the "reference book." If there is a breakthrough there, then we're left with a potentially explosive situation. My thoughts on how to proceed with the "reference book" are given below. My wild theory on the nature of the single sheet is recorded separately. If I were simply to hand it over on a plate, others might well be less equipped to progress further, hampered by a preconception of what to look for – an approach highly dangerous if I'm barking up the wrong tree. If and when you wish to view my thoughts on the single sheet, I gave that to a certain second-row forward for safe keeping. You must ask that person for it.

By the way, if this note you are now reading falls into the wrong hands, it would not be the end of the world. If they both do, that would be unfortunate, but perhaps no more than that. Perversely, it might even be a benefit!

Now, as to the other fragments: it was quite clear to me how I should proceed, but I had so little time to apply my thinking to the materials I was given by the angel. I had been threatened, indeed nearly killed, on several occasions and I could feel my health suffering from the stress of what had already happened and what might come in the future. My speculation of the single sheet's significance was also a distinct burden. Below, I am suggesting how you might proceed without the benefit of the single sheet. It is how I would have proceeded even if I had not hit upon a possible interpretation of that sheet.

It is essential in my view that "the authorities" themselves solve the problems presented by the alien writings. This will give them the strongest foundation for future study. So, here is a possible first step. It's pretty elementary and I suspect it will have occurred to "the authorities." Comments on the single sheet are in the enclosed envelope. If you are well on your way already, then you may as well open the envelope straight away, since it might well provide corroborative evidence of your own findings. But until you reach that stage, I suggest you leave it sealed.

Dominus vobiscum, Donald McNulty

First step:

You will know that the map fragments cover part of the Black Sea, including much of the Crimea. You will see, too, that groups of alien symbols are scattered about, mostly straddling the coastline. You will have deduced these are probably place names. Indeed, what else could they be? But which particular place-names are they and what do they **sound** like? Are they sounds made up by the visitors? Just some noises consistent within their own alphabet, but essentially arbitrary? They could have done this. In English, many foreign place-names are either an approximation of the native version or bear no relation. Köln becomes Cologne, but Deutschland becomes

Germany (or, in French, Allemande, in Spanish Allemania etc.).

I've made an assumption – a bold one perhaps, but we have to start somewhere. I've assumed that the alien symbols representing place-names on the map are actually pronounced by the visitors **as the natives do.** If this is so, the 35 or 40 "letters" in their alphabet can be given a phonetic equivalent, or at least those of them that are present on the map (though beware of possible syllables). These can then be drawn up into a list for use when examining the text in other documents. I suggest the most logical starting point would be the "words" in **larger** letters both in the "reference book" and in the separate medical pages. I suspect that **something** meaningful will emerge, especially from the "reference book," where there is much more text to play with. Don't ask me by what means our visitors came by the knowledge of how the native population pronounce the place-names (persistent monitoring over a long period, or even some physical interaction?) I have no idea, but with a civilisation so evidently vastly in advance of us in every field, we must surely credit them with this ability.

That was where the guidance ended. Tim found himself a bit disappointed. It wasn't exactly Earth-shattering, was it? Just a bit of common-sense. Worth pointing out, he supposed, but he felt sure Kathy Webb would have made the same assumption and had perhaps progressed further. Father Mac had also reached a possible understanding of the single sheet, and it had served as a better starting point than Kathy had at her disposal, but he was confident that it was possible to progress without it.

Unfortunately, Tim himself didn't have anything useful with which to put Father Mac's suggestion to the test. All he had was a map of the Crimea, stuffed with place names, but, of course, he didn't have the alien map with all its symbols. What he did have was list the letters of the Roman alphabet, study the place names as they appeared on his map in Roman letters and tick every letter on his list when he found it. They were all there except c, h, j, q, w, and x. There were good reasons for the omissions. Even a non-linguist could deduce why. Take the letter c, for example. There was no room for it in the transliterated

Russian place-names. The hard "c" in English was always going to be a "k," while the soft c had no application with "s" serving the same purpose.

What he needed, of course, was a map of the Crimea with place-names in Cyrillic. Was Father's "first step" worth a visit to Nick and Kathy? Yes, of course, if only to reassure them he'd got Father Mac's notes, and that there was perhaps something more informative from him to come. He sat for some time re-reading what Father Mac had written and pondering what actually was to come. Which direction had he branched out in? The extra sheet would tell him. The one in the hands of a second-row forward.

That could only be Mike McGuire. Father Mac was not taking any chances, putting another slim layer of security in place to prevent things possibly falling into the wrong hands. Outsiders might know something about Tim himself, as a major player, but would probably not know much about the history of a fringe player, like Mike. Father Mac's thoughts must be worth protecting. How did he describe them in his narrative? Worthless or explosive? Well, he was probably justified in his protective approach, anticipating all he might have to go through if faced with really determined opponents. How sensible and prescient to keep the crucial letter apart from the fragments, yet easily accessible to the right person.

Just as he noticed it was gone eleven, Lucy came in, gave him a kiss and said, "I don't know about you, but I'm going to bed!" Tim locked up and followed her.

CHAPTER 30

While Bourton slept, and before Charlie had begun clinking his way around the town, Misha was arriving at his destination. This was one of his favourite cities, vibrant and attractive in so many ways.

Multicultural, too, though due more than with most cities in the Western world to an infusion of Asian blood. Here you would be likely to live with a Macgregor on one side and a Chang on the other; or a Williams on one side and an Ng on the other. He'd been told to lie low here since his last job. One major operation a year was enough to keep him in luxury. He'd been waiting for his next summons.

It was a balmy evening, warm but with a gentle breeze. He headed for the hire cars, filled out the paperwork, then went to the payphones and reserved a room in the Holiday Inn in downtown Vancouver, not far from the attractive waterfront. As he was talking, a young man wearing a baseball cap, jeans, T-shirt, and sun-glasses opened the door, stopped, looked foolish and said, "Oh, gee man, I'm sorry. I wasn't looking properly. Sorry to intrude." He left and peered along the row of phones, found an empty kiosk, and went in. Misha studied him. Any unexpected incident immediately put him on his guard. If he was being tailed, there was sure to be an accomplice and a sign might pass between them. There was no obvious sign, but the fact of looking for and entering an empty kiosk may itself have been the sign. Perhaps Misha's beard had generated the need for a closer look – to make sure.

If they were interested in him, who were they, anyway? Friend or foe? He had been told that a contract had been agreed with an unspecified paymaster. A letter had been passed to him in the street to this effect. This was nearly a year ago. He was told to burn the letter after reading. He was to remain on standby until he received further orders or was told to stand down. He knew his organisation commanded a large workforce deployed around the world, many with similar orders to his own. It was clear to Misha that his superiors were lining up their ducks ready for an expected event, or series of events, but had no idea where or when these would occur. It must be incredibly important for them to spent millions of dollars just to keep a huge work-force idle.

There had been no role for him for many months. Then suddenly a few weeks ago he was placed on instant standby and a week or so later was sent to England, with orders to retrieve certain items. He had quickly summoned two others from Europe to join him. The old firm was reunited. Now, after an adventurous time in England, he was back home. He had failed to obtain the documents the old priest was supposed to have, but surely everything they wanted was on the CD. True, he had lost two colleagues and a contact in London had been compromised, but these were all replaceable. So, all in all, he was reasonably pleased with a successful operation and had every reason to suppose that another lucrative payday beckoned.

Misha found his hire car in the company's parking lot, checked out the controls and drove off. Should he drive straight to the motel or randomly drive around a while? A circuit of Stanley Park would be very pleasant. On the other hand, that might give any adversaries more time to organise something or summon a few reserves. Did they know his destination? Had the young man heard something of his conversation? He thought. All his instincts told him to go straight to the motel. He could generally deal better with possible adversaries while he was not driving. He'd had enough high-speed chases or attempts at ramming in his career, including some he'd initiated himself. At the motel there might be the option of valet parking, so he could avoid a confrontation in the underground car-park, often the venue for an attack.

On the journey, he could see he was being blatantly followed. Halfway there, another car picked up the tail and the first car disappeared. It was so blatant he could almost believe he was being followed as a courtesy. At the motel, he drew up outside behind an attractive young woman who was just getting out of her car, showing a large length of shapely leg, and handing her key to an Asian boy who looked about twelve. Good. There was valet parking.

He retrieved his bag from the car, handed his car key to another young Asian boy, then went in to register. The attractive young lady who was by now at the desk saw him, smiled, said, "Why, it's you again, how wonderful," and flung her arms round him. Before the instincts instilled into him with years of training as an agent could kick in, other instincts more basic and earthy leapt the queue and made him smile back and surrender to the hug. Who would not? Who would not think their luck was in? Misha immediately felt a scratch on his neck and knew instantly he had about one minute to live. The girl, anticipating he might scream out "I've been poisoned by this woman" began screaming and continued until he lost consciousness. The desk clerks raced round to see what was happening. Other guests stood around, looking concerned, but showing no wish to get involved.

The young woman had by now recovered her composure. "We were just greeting each other, then he fainted."

One of the desk staff, clearly with some basic first aid training, felt for a pulse, then a heart beat and pronounced, "Sorry to say this, Miss, but I think the worst has happened. An ambulance will be here soon. Sam is calling the emergency service." He pointed to another desk clerk. "I hope he was not a friend or relation. You seemed to know each other. Sorry, am I being intrusive?"

Yes, you little shit, you are, thought the pretty lady. "No," she said, "I know him quite well. We were at the same trade convention a few weeks ago, and I just happened to recognise him. Excuse me, this is very distressing. I must have a quick word with a friend outside."

She went out to a waiting car, climbed in and quickly made off into the wilds of British Columbia. Using a brand-new cell phone, she reported a successful mission, sending a text to Misha's Canadian controller wishing him a happy birthday, darling. The phone ended up in the Turner River.

Misha was duly collected by the ambulance and taken to hospital, where he was consigned to the morgue. The police were first interested in the contents of his pockets. None of these provided a lead to the man's identity. Forensics then became involved, tentatively concluded that death was caused by the ingestion or assimilation by the body of a poison, or of a cocktail of several poisons, but that much more detailed analysis was required. It took several days to confirm the preliminary findings. The police were not happy with the identity of the toxic agents. They had been associated mainly with political assassinations. Hotel staff were closely questioned about the young woman. Her disappearance seemed to confirm her involvement in the death. She had only just registered in the name of Natalie Dubois. She was never traced.

Eventually someone decided to alert Interpol.

Several months later, a retired intelligence officer in the UK, who now acted as an occasional consultant, would tell a colleague, "I think we can close the file on Misha. Looks like his superiors did away with him. Why? I mean, he delivered the goods. True, he did compromise one of their contacts and lost two of his operatives. Harsh punishment. But these are ruthless people."

"By the way," his colleague would reply, "what was the consensus on Misha? Quite a few said he was part of some government apparatus, not the Russians, but some Middle Eastern or Far Eastern outfit. Others said he was freelance."

"Oh, definitely freelance, though not as an individual. He belonged to one of those maverick groups that sprang up after the collapse of communism, composed of people made redundant under the new order, but who have highly marketable skills. Initially the demand was in the nuclear field, but later the emphasis shifted to financial aces, IT wizards, terrorism experts, and so on. We believe Misha's group was among the larger ones with people scattered around the world. Misha was a low-level controller. In army terms a junior NCO. We think there were several hundred members of this group scattered around the world, who in turn enlist the help of others for one-off errands. As we now know, they have their own terminator branch. The question is: when will they disband their whole effort on this project? Come to think of it, when will we?"

"Perhaps Stepan and Feliks will sing now there's no reason not to."

"Oh, they're pretty small fry. They won't know who's who, beyond Misha. That's the problem. We know something about the general structure and composition of groups like this. The real question is: who hired this lot for this job?"

He would never find out.

*****

At about the time the forensic pathologist had completed her preliminary examination of Misha's body, and concluded that a much more searching examination was called for, perhaps with a small team, some 5,000 miles to the east Brian Jenkins was entering his editor's office.

"Ah, Brian, have you seen that police release I left for you?"

"Yes, Boss, I've tarted it up and pushed it through."

"You knew the victim, didn't you?"

"Yes. He's the father of the boy who recovered the CD for him."

"So this is all connected with that priest story, the ambulance, foreign agents, all that stuff?"

"It may well be. I see the nature of the injury was not disclosed. I would bet a fiver it was a bullet in the ankle by the same foreign agent. Same modus operandi. Punishment motive."

"What a terrific story. Put it all together."

"No, Boss. I think we could be putting public safety at risk."

"Oh, get out of my hair, you idiot. You can't see a story when it sits up and bites you."

"Yes, I can. You know I can. I've given you most of it. I can even conjecture a bit more. I could write a story that would make your hair stand on end, what's left of it. Better than Clancy or Ludlum. But it would be totally irresponsible to publish it. "

By now, the Boss was seething. "Oh, you... you! You'll never make a journalist. I'll write it up. I want you to go to Diddington. A tractor caught fire, but a 12-year-old boy was driving it. Find out what the insurance implications are and any possible criminal charges."

"Look, Boss, you're an urban creature and you don't know the ways of the country. I don't know a farm in the area where boys aren't driving a tractor by 12. Some even earlier. It's one of those things the police are aware of and if they've got any sense, turn a blind eye to. It's always been the case. At least since the war. It's a skill that could be needed. Look, I've got a better story. There was a local WI meeting where someone filled the sugar bowl with salt. Ruined the whole evening. How about that?"

"Oh, get back to your office. I'll call you later."

"No. When I leave your office, I'm going to keep on walking. You refuse to accept my advice, which is based on my first-hand knowledge of events and contacts with the police and the intelligence people. You can take my job and stick it where the sun doesn't shine. I'm well aware of my contractual obligations, but as far as I'm concerned, you've driven a coach and horses through them." Brian strode out, slightly amazed at his audacity.

"Brian," called the Boss. Brian kept on walking. He had no particular reason to make any fond farewells. Those he was closest to were out on assignment. He did shake a few hands and kissed two of the girls on their cheek. Then he was off. As it was Friday, he could see if Mary would like a week-end away somewhere.

CHAPTER 31

Tim decided he must get things rolling on Father Mac's "First Step." He got hold of Hugh, only to be told that Nick and Kathy were in the main building, across town. "Their basic work must go on, and there's plenty of that. They can't just stare at bits of paper and hope something will emerge. It won't, without some sort of crib. I'll see if we can grab them on Monday for an hour or so."

Tim had to be content with that, and spent the day in a dissatisfied gloom, doing nothing productive and getting under Lucy's feet.

"You're in one of your sulks, aren't you? I remember you having them before you retired, just because things weren't going your way. You're like a little boy."

"Sorry, love," said Tim, ashamed. "You're right. It's just that it will be three days at the earliest before we can all get together again."

"Well, there's plenty to do in the garden. And you still haven't looked at the grouting in the shower."

Tim shuddered at the thought of reviving the yellowing grouting, and wandered into the garden. He did actually enjoy gardening, but only certain aspects of it: digging, growing vegetables, and lighting and tending bonfires. He didn't really mind weeding – at least there was a pleasure worth earning at the final results. He left anything to do with flowers to Lucy. He had too often failed to distinguish between flowers and weeds.

The day dragged on, but he did perk up a bit in the evening when a call from Hugh confirmed that they would go in on the Monday, about mid-morning. He re-read Father Mac's guidance, and wondered how far Nick and Kathy had got. He treated himself to an early night.

*****

The next day, Lucy's sister brought Mama over for lunch and gossip, then in the afternoon the three ladies went shopping in Cheltenham. Mama was able to get about pretty well with a stick. While they were out, Tim had an unexpected visit from Doc Campbell. He looked like a cat with two tails.

"Professor Lewis has already organised a meeting for me. Next Tuesday. Nick or Kathy got those pages photocopied with no text. Sanitising, they called it. I thought they meant they'd sprayed them with Dettol. Lewis doesn't hang around, does he? Just as well. Kathy said he's got some sort of obsession with the DNA bits. Anyway, Lewis and Kathy between them have given me guidance on introducing the diagrams."

"That's great, Doc," said Tim. "I know how keen you are to move on this. Anyway, I've now had a look at Father Mac's notes. The ones we hadn't looked at before. I'm popping in on Monday to pass them on to Nick and Kathy." Tim realised he mustn't overplay his hand here. "It's only a few ideas about trying to get into the alien script."

"That sounds pretty important," said Campbell.

"Not really," said Tim. "It might suggest what the language sounds like, but it won't translate it for us."

The rest of the day passed pleasantly enough – a spot more weeding, a bit of sport on TV and family gossip with the ladies. Mama was still in her usual feisty mood, and as competitive as ever when they dealt a few hands of bridge.

*****

The following evening Tim, conscious of the meeting arranged for the next day, dug out Father Mac's "First Step" again, and tried to conceive what a second step might be like. The key was in somehow applying the sounds of the Alienspeak letters, as derived from the equivalent Cyrillic version of the place-names, to something in the "reference book." But what? Kathy would know, clever girl. He had a high regard for her intellect. Hugh might well be able to develop any findings a bit further. Nick, too, was no slouch, though nowadays, as Head of Division, he was more of an administrator than a cryppie. So he should at least know if and when to bring the beard and sandals (no socks) brigade in, not that there were many thus attired these days. The next thing he knew was Lucy shaking him, and telling him it was bedtime.

*****

When Tim and Hugh arrived in Kathy's office the next morning, she had already re-assembled the fragments of the map, and had laid out the various computer prints. Most of the medical pages were also there, but

286

the DNA diagram and the few pages following it had been abstracted by Professor Lewis and set aside in a separate envelope. He had said that whatever else was eventually copied, these pages should not be. He was given permission by Debbie to borrow them as and when needed. He had the standard government-issue steel furniture in his office and the standard OHMS briefcase with a wrist chain and padlock. The only way one of the bad guys could get possession of it was by knocking the prof to the ground, locating the key and releasing the chain, but that would cause a scene and Lewis might get some assistance from a few public-spirited souls. Or, the more popular method, a bolt-cutter applied to the chain or, as was not unknown, to the wrist itself.

Kathy seemed to be in incredibly high spirits. She was humming away and clearly ready to get started. Nick Watson, in his own office down the corridor, noted their arrival and joined them.

"Kathy can hardly contain her excitement," said Nick. "She's come up with a few ideas, but had to set this work aside on Friday. So she came in over the week-end. Now I gather from Hugh you've found the guidance Father Mac left?"

"After a bit of a treasure hunt," said Tim.

"Well, why not take us through it, then? Let Kathy pick things up from there."

Tim retrieved Father Mac's note, which he'd reduced to a meaningless shorthand. The others looked at him expectantly.

"Father Mac's first assumption accords with our own: that we've identified the map as part of the Black Sea, including much of the Crimea, and that the groups of alien words straddling the coastline are place-names."

"So far, so good," smiled Kathy.

"He then discusses the pronunciation of these place-names and he reasons that our visitors have not assigned some arbitrary sounds to them, but that the alien symbols represent place-names as they are actually pronounced by the native population. He does concede that he has no idea how the visitors might have come to know how the natives pronounce the names. Perhaps long-term monitoring of the radio environment, or even what he calls some 'physical interaction' though I'm not sure what that means."

"I'm not sure Father Mac knows either," said Kathy. "I thought long and hard about the pronunciation," she went on, "And I had to conclude that without any other possible evidence to steer me one way

287

or the other, it was the only way forward. As it turns out, we were both right."

"Really?" said Tim. "Then you've done particularly well. Father Mac reached his conclusion after some sort of reassurance from the single sheet of paper, which he claims to have solved."

Kathy pondered. "All that might do is confirm that the content of the 'reference book' and that of the single sheet are intrinsically related. I don't think the single sheet contains what we would call a crib. I think if you can somehow get from the place-names a sense of how the alien letters sound, you could apply this knowledge to the text of the 'reference book' with, in Father Mac's case, a good idea of the sort of thing to look for based on the single sheet – chemistry, engineering, biology, I don't know. In our case, we have no such idea. By the way" – here Tim noticed a slight quaver in her voice – "I don't think any of those subjects are relevant. They were just examples. So, did he draw up an alien alphabet with the phonetic equivalent of each letter?"

"He didn't get that far, though he did identify that as the next step. As we now know, he was living under threat, and had to carry on his parish duties with that fact hanging over him."

"The poor man," said Kathy.

"The final piece of advice he gives," said Tim, "is to concentrate on the words in larger letters in the "reference book." He says something meaningful may emerge."

"And I have a feeling that, based on that single sheet, he has some idea what. In fact, for the record if you like, I'd already decided those large-lettered words would be the first lot to attack and have begun doing so" – again that tremor in her voice. "I've already completed the other steps. Here is my phonetic list for nearly all the symbols in their alphabet, based on the place-names. I think the sounds are pretty pure, as I used a map in Cyrillic."

"I think I once saw one in Father Mac's bookshelves, unless Kevin and Dave nicked it."

"Who are Kevin and Dave?" asked Nick.

"Two local villains who were involved earlier on," said Tim. "Anyway Kathy, you were saying…?"

"Yes, the map." She pointed to the place-name Евпатория. "This is pronounced 'Yevpatoriya.' The first two letters of the transliteration represent the way the letter 'Е' is pronounced in Cyrillic. Similarly, the last two letters 'ya' represent the single letter 'я' in Cyrillic. So we immediately have Alienspeak equivalents for the sounds ye, v, p, a, t, o, r, i, ya. We don't need many Cyrillic place-names to get most of the forty sounds in the Alienspeak alphabet. Take Симферополь next. This is pronounced 'Simferopol.' So we can now add s, m, f, and l."

"What about that little letter there?" enquired Tim, pointing to the final symbol ь. "It's years since I did the basic Russian course here – the one designed just to help you recognise the alphabet and a few phrases likely to be used by a radio operator. Isn't that what they call a soft sign?"

"That's right," said Kathy, "It's not a letter. At least not a voiced one. It just makes the 'l' sound liquid, as if you want to add an 'ee' sound after it, but just stop yourself in time. The letter 'l' can also be hard, but I'm not going to differentiate in my table of equivalents. Now, let's move south to the north Turkish coast. Here's a place-name Зонгулдак. In English, this is 'Zonguldak.' So we can now add z, n, g, u, d, and k. We now have nineteen sound equivalents of the forty alien letters. I won't take up your time with any more of the place-names. In fact, it took me the best part of two days, poring over large-scale maps of the area and with many more place-names on them, to recover most of the alien sounds. This was over the week-end. I'd found time on Friday to go to the map room, and relieve them of five or six maps. I'm not surprised Father Mac had to abandon his efforts."

"So what was the total return from your week-end's efforts?" asked Tim eagerly.

"Of the forty alien letters, I have equated 35 to Cyrillic sound equivalents."

"So have you tried applying your conversion table to the actual text of our so-called 'reference book' or, more specifically, the words in larger print?"

"I certainly have," said Kathy.

"And ...?"

"Obviously, I targeted initially the words occurring the most frequently."

"Computer count," supplied Nick helpfully.

"One word stood out as by far the most popular. There were well over 3,000 occurrences of it. There were also over 1,000 occurrences of the same word with an extra letter or two, but I didn't know whether these were quite unrelated words in their own right, or ..."

Tim instantly recognised a likely possibility. "Inflections?" he breathed.

"That's what I thought," said Kathy. "Case endings. In which case" – she smiled at the unintended pun – "there are over 4,000 occurrences."

"Did the sound produced by the word convey anything meaningful?" asked Hugh.

"No, and nor did most of the other frequently occurring words. But there were a few that did suggest something familiar, or, perhaps, someone familiar. One word in particular – the one in second place with a thousand or so occurrences – a few hundred more if you include words very similar, where an extra letter has been added."

"More inflection," said Tim unnecessarily. "And what did the word sound like?"

Here," said Kathy in a trembling voice, "You can see for yourself." She opened the "reference book" and pointed to a word in Alienspeak. "You can see it even occurs several times in this same small piece of text. The first letter equates in sound to the Cyrillic 'и' or 'ee' in English, as in the word 'meet'. The second is pronounced like the 'e' in the word 'bet' . Then we have a ... we have a ..." her voice trailed away. Then they saw her shoulders shake, and she dissolved into uncontrollable sobs. Hugh and Nick helped her into a chair.

"Quick, get her some water," said Hugh. Nick hurried off.

"Do we need the nurse?" asked Tim with concern.

"I don't think so," said Nick returning with a cup of water. Kathy seemed to be composing herself.

"I ... I'm sorry," she said. "I know what's coming. The next letter would be the Cyrillic 'с' or English 's.' We then have the Cyrillic 'у' or English 'oo' sound, then a final 's.' In Cyrillic 'Иесус' and in English ..." Kathy began sobbing again, and sat down, clutching a handkerchief.

"In English ' Ee – e – s – oo – s.' Jesus?" breathed Tim incredulously. "They were... they were Christians?!"

PART III
REVELATION

CHAPTER 32

No-one spoke for fully a minute as the enormity of the discovery slowly sank in. The implications were profound, and tumbled into the mind, one quickly following another.

"Are – are we sure?" ventured Hugh at last.

Kathy, again more composed, said, "There's no doubt. Look, the word is sometimes accompanied by another one in large print – another proper noun." She found another page. "Here, and here," she said. She pointed to her equivalents table. "The first letter is the Cyrillic 'X' followed by 'p' 'и', 'с', 'т', 'o' and 'с.' Христос. In English, Khristos. Christ. Jesus Christ." She began sobbing again, then smiled through her tears.

"I don't know what to feel," she said. "For some reason I feel incredibly happy. It's as if things are now much clearer. I've never had a strong faith, in the sense that I don't go to Church much, only, you know, only for weddings and funerals. This business is bound to affect me. It may even change my life. But at the same time, I also feel sad. Something seems to tell me this discovery will spell trouble, too."

"I don't think there's much doubt about that," said Nick, "If it becomes widely known."

"I think that's the nub of the whole thing." said Tim gravely. "But one thing that immediately occurs to me," he added with a chuckle. "It seems very probable that our friend Misha has delivered a Christian bible to a paymaster who may be anything but. They were expecting data on propulsion or weapons systems. Instead … he broke off. "Hey!" he cried excitedly, "As you know, I'm no Russian linguist . But isn't that second word a bit like some of the letters on Father Mac's single sheet? The pattern they occur in? If you look at it as Cyrillic, not English. Do you have it handy, Kathy?"

"I think you're right," she said. "I've not had time to follow up on that." She went to her cupboard and fished inside a security box. "Here it is." She laid it out flat on the table. "Yes, she said, "it's much more meaningful in Cyrillic. We already have P C OC BOC. You can fit a Cyrillic X right at the beginning, and И and T in the gaps and you get 'ХРИСТОС' which means Christ. But what the other bit means I've no idea."

"I'm quite sure Father Mac does. I bet he solved it instantly, and all along knew he was dealing with documents from a Christian civilisation light years away. It was the short cut he referred to. His special mix of credentials – Priest and Russian linguist. And you know what?" He could not keep the excitement out of his voice. "I'll bet this was the 'outrageous theory' he outlined in the note he left us separately. We don't need it now." He smiled. "I'll have to go and tell a particular second-row forward you've not met."

Nick shook his head. "What a burden to carry round with him. I know the identity of the 'reference book' was not confirmed, but the potential was clearly there. I think it was this realisation that caused the stress in him, and the subsequent stroke, rather than the possible attempts on his life. Or at the very least it aggravated the situation."

"He may even know what all that crowded writing on the reverse side could be," said Hugh.

"Speaking of which," said Tim slowly, "if we now know we have a Christian Bible on our hands in the shape of our 'reference book' and we can recognise the words for 'Jesus' and 'Christ,' can we not look at the pattern of the occurrences of these words in their bible and identify what passage of our own Bible a passage from theirs equates to?"

"I was just thinking along the same lines," said Hugh. "But all you'll get, at least initially, is a paragraph by paragraph equation, or, at best, a sentence by sentence match up. The meaning of individual words may not be possible, especially as we know nothing about their grammar and syntax."

"I don't think anything immediate would fall into our laps," said Nick, "But surely over time, similar phrases will be recognised in several places with slightly different contexts surrounding them, and by looking for this sort of thing throughout the Bible, individual words will eventually emerge." They all looked at each other.

"That," finally said Tim, "sounds like a task for about a dozen or so clever people for a year or so."

"So certainly not a job for GCHQ," said Nick, "We just couldn't spare the manpower."

"I don't know," said Kathy. "I think the first step is to examine whether any of this apparently formidable task would lend itself to a computer application. At least we know the bits with Jesus Christ in are from the New Testament. Perhaps after some manual analysis, some sort of programme will occur. The whole Bible is at least already

294

digitised word by word. I wouldn't mind fiddling with this problem for a while." She looked at Nick. "Boss. Please."

Nick smiled. "I'm quite sure using one of our brightest stars in this way is a minor consideration compared to the huge can of worms we're about to open up. We'll have to get Debbie down here a.s.a.p. and I wouldn't be surprised if her Boss, the Chairman of the JIC, didn't get personally involved in all this."

"In my experience," said Hugh, himself a recent incumbent of Nick's post, "Director-level involvement is inevitable. There are so many facets to this. It's not just an academic exercise. There'll be political fall-out. It's ready made for factional conflict. Do we reveal to the wide world what we've discovered, or don't we? I can already see compelling arguments both sides of the fence!"

"Let's back up a minute," said Tim. "We really do need to be sure of our facts before we involve lots of very senior people. Do you think they will swallow our basic findings. 'Christian?' they'll say, 'It's not possible. These space visitors come from a civilisation that originated centuries before us – probably millennia – but Christianity is only 2,000 years old."

"Is it?" said Nick. "You mean Christianity as we know it. Is there an earlier form of Christianity? An earlier civilisation on a distant planet to whom Christ appeared? What do you think, Tim? You're a regular church-goer."

"That I may be," said Tim. "But I'm no theologian."

"Another alternative is that our space visitors, though way ahead of us in physical evolution, were simply exposed to Christianity much later in their evolution," suggested Kathy.

"Good point," said Nick, "but the thing is, we don't know. We can throw this whole thing around and get nowhere. We simply don't know. Two things seem clear to me. Firstly, as I said, we need to get Debbie down here as soon as possible. She's the one to convince in the first instance, because only she can trigger action at the very highest level, and goodness even knows what that would entail. I mean, this thing is dynamite! I can see Chairman, JIC, presiding over a meeting with CDS sitting alongside the Archbishop of Canterbury or his senior theological advisor, whoever he is, and the collection agencies for once taking a back seat. The collaborating countries, too, need to be advised of this development and perhaps we all need to get involved in some sort of conference. Secondly, we need to draw up recommendations for studying the space bible in depth. What we want to emerge is nothing short of a dictionary that can be used, say, with the medical pages, or with any further documents that come our way. And I have a strong feeling there will be more."

"I think we also ought to involve Father Mac as soon as he feels able," said Tim forcefully, "not only for his linguistic slant on the space bible, but in case a theological input is needed. I mean, it's not as if we're exposing him to ELK data. He's known about the Christian dimension entirely through his own efforts much longer than us. If you're happy, Nick, I'll pursue that as soon as we break up today."

"Please do," said Nick. "And I think we've got to the stage where we need to meet briefly most days. Things should begin to move fast soon, and the only secure way to keep you and Hugh in the loop is by personal contact. How about a daily phone call to one or other of you every day to say come or don't come. How about you, Hugh, at 9 am every day?"

Hugh nodded vigorously. "And I'll phone Tim."

"Now see what I've done," said Kathy, still a little weepy.

*****

When Tim got home, Lucy said, "Oh, Tim, can you pop over to the presbytery? Norah's got something to show you."

"To show me?"

"Well, me too. It's something Doc Campbell brought back from the hospice."

"Oh, of course, he and Megan were going there to see Father Mac. I thought that was a few days ago. I meant to ask them for their assessment of him. They must have popped down there again today. It would have been a brief visit. It's barely noon now. All right, then. Are you ready to come?" Lucy nodded.

At the presbytery they rang the bell. Norah opened the door and guided them into the sitting room. As they approached they heard voices. Tim's antennae began quivering. "I know that voice," he cried. Sure enough, there in the room stood Father Mac leaning on a stick and with him Sister Winifred.

A few hugs and hand-shakes later Tim said, "We need you, Father. With some urgency. In the next few days. And I don't mean for parish work."

"Will you not let the good man wipe his feet on the mat before you begin making more demands on him?" said Sister Winifred vehemently. "It was this other business that made him unwell in the first place."

"Nonsense, Wiffie," said Father Mac in a strong voice. "No, not quite nonsense, but things are different now. There is no threat. And anything of importance can be shared. Not bottled up, as before."

"I'm staying here with him for a while," said the nun. "So I'll be overseeing his well-being. I just don't want him to be seriously challenged too soon. Donald will try con-celebrating on Sunday and see how that goes. He'll also make a short address. And I do mean short. Not a homily. Just a few thank-you's, I believe." Father Mac nodded.

"Yes, and I'd be delighted to speak to Tim's colleagues," he said.

"Just for an hour or so," said Tim. "It really is important. In fact, it's of – national importance. I wish I could explain."

"There's no need," said Sister. "I know more than you could guess. Very well, I know it's important. So you can have him. But bring him back in one piece!"

"Well, let me just tell Father something in confidence immediately," said Tim, steering Father Mac away from the others. "We won't need to read your extra comment. The one you gave Mike McGuire. I can destroy it now, unread."

Father Mac's eyes lit up. "I knew that's what you were talking about. So they made a breakthrough."

"Yes. That's all I wanted to say. We'd better join the others."

"Oh, don't let Wiffie intimidate you, like she does me." They both laughed.

As soon as Tim got home, he phoned Hugh, giving him the good news of Father Mac.

"That's terrific," said Hugh. "I'll let Nick and Kathy know. If Father Mac can be there, it will make our session with Debbie more meaningful."

*****

Later that day, when he was sure Mike McGuire would be back from work, Tim called round.

Mike was in, though obviously busy on some household improvement, as his paint-daubed overalls suggested.

"I would think you get enough of this at work all day," said Tim, grinning.

297

"Ah, this is different. It's a labour of love. Anyway, how can I earn the respect of the missus if I get someone in to work in my own house. And I enjoy it. I don't do painting on the day job. I build what's basically a shell and let others do all the extras, all the tarting up. Anyway, what can I do for you? I gather Father Mac's raring to go."

"Not quite," said Tim, "but he's getting there. And speaking of Father Mac, I understand you're holding a sheet of paper intended for me."

"Password?" said Mike. "Sorry, pass-phrase, I believe."

"Hang on," said Tim, "what's this? Father gave me no pass word, or pass-phrase, as you call it."

"Then you're not the right fellow. Good night."

"Wait a minute, Mike, if you say he should have given it to me, I have to believe he did. Give me a minute to think." Tim closed his eyes and thought his way through his last sessions with the Priest. Ah, yes. Dawn broke in his mind.

"Dominus vobiscum," he said with a broad grin.
"Et cum spiritu tuo," said Mike, grinning himself. "My God, 'tis a few years since I've said those words in anger. Wait there and I'll get you the envelope. I suppose this is all to do with that business at the presbytery and that foreigner we arrested. I'm sure you and Father between you will save the world."

He disappeared for a minute or so, then returned with an envelope.

"Thanks, Mike," said Tim. "I can't wait to read his words of wisdom, but I rather think I know what to expect. I'll see you around."

"Dominus vobiscum," laughed Mike.

"Et cum spiritu tuo. Oremus."

"Yes, indeed," said Mike, "We all need a few prayers!"

****

Back at home, Tim tore open the envelope. The message was terse.

> Dear Friend,
> I suspect that the "Roman" characters on the single sheet are Cyrillic and, if so, might even form part of an Easter, repeat Easter, greeting.
> Dominus vobiscum,
> Donald McNulty

Tim chuckled and went to screw up the paper, but thought better of it. He'd give it to Nick or Kathy as a souvenir.

That night, sleep eluded him. He tried to wrestle with all the implications of a Christian Bible being handed over by a civilisation presumably tens or hundreds of millennia in advance of his own. Or were they that much in advance? Technologically, yes. But, on the other hand, it only took one or two major breakthroughs to revolutionise the technological status quo. It had taken man millions of years to devise the wheel, a millennium to develop uses for it and a mere handful of centuries to revolutionise life as it was known at the time. In the fifteenth to the seventeenth centuries it was largely the turn of the arts for a major make-over, while the next two centuries were dominated by scientific discovery, precipitating the Industrial Revolution. The next century in turn had seen remarkable progress in the fields of flight, the automotive industry, radio, TV, nuclear power, computers, and miniaturisation of circuits leading to chips of ever-decreasing size. It was almost inconceivable that all this could have been achieved in a few hundred years. But it had. Clearly, progress fed progress down an irresistibly exponential path. So it might take very little time to learn the secrets of near-instant space travel. In evolutionary terms, however, the humanoid Father Mac had met had looked just like people here on Earth. A touch smaller, perhaps, but then so were millions of humans below average height. The thing was there were no obvious evolutionary changes. Where were the tiny creatures of science fiction with their huge heads, large slanting eyes, and minuscule ears, a description supposedly backed up by personal encounters? To reach that physical state would surely need several million more years. That is, if there were truth in the description in the first place. Besides, didn't God make people in his own image and likeness – another good reason for Father Mac's visitor to look as he did.

And speaking of God… But that was it. Tim couldn't. As he would often say to Father Mac, when some point of liturgy arose, "I'm not a professional Catholic, like you. I'm just an amateur." And if that held true for Church ritual, it held true a fortiori for matters of theology. He was an absolute duffer. He had not the faintest idea where to begin on that side of the argument. In his own lay manner, all he could do was pose a few Noddy questions. Like: did God populate other planets with people in his own image and likeness? Did the composition of the atmosphere have to be conducive to their looking like God? How many planets did he populate? Was it two or three, or two or three million?

Were they all in the Milky Way, or were some in other galaxies? Did Man commit original sin everywhere and get chucked out of whatever garden God had made for him? Did this happen on all these planets, or only some? Did God then send His only Son to them, to bale them out by suffering death on a cross (or some other instrument of torture and death in use on that planet at that time) in redemption of their sins? How many deaths had Our Lord endured? Was his birth accomplished in the same way on every planet? Was a virgin selected to be the mother? Was it (somehow) Our Lady every time? After the Annunciation, did she always say the Magnificat (stop it Tim, you're being childish. I know, but …). OK, were there any planets where there was no original sin and thus no redeeming death by the Son of God?

When did these particular Christians set out? And why? A mission of evangelisation? But why here?

Did they not realise this could cut both ways? Yes, but only if the story were released. What would be the advantages of releasing the story? Assuming the story were believed, it would surely produce an enormous revival in Christianity throughout the world. That was a given. But what about the depth of feeling in other camps? They would surely not believe a word of it. They would not see beyond a typical Western Christian conspiracy. What would they do, if anything? Aye, there's the rub. Perhaps some diplomatic move would be a good idea? Take any potential aggressors into their confidence before a general revelation? Hmm. Dear God, he prayed, we thank you for the knowledge You have given us of your work among other peoples not of our planet. Bless that civilisation we know nothing of. Guide our leaders to use this new knowledge wisely and for the benefit of all. Through Christ Our Lord, Amen. Tim always sought comfort in prayer when he … Dear God, was that Charlie? He seems to get earlier. No, it's just that dawn is getting later....

Tim did finally drop off, and actually woke refreshed. It was as if he'd had a great mental clear-out. Now all he had to do, to avoid it being a wasted exercise was commit his thoughts to memory, or at least sit at the computer and try to go back over things. After taking Lucy a cuppa, he booted up his terminal. Ten minutes into his labours, the phone rang. Oh, hell, I'm still in my pyjamas and that'll be Hugh.

It was Hugh.

"No need to go in today, Tim," he said. "Nick has been in touch with Debbie by secure Email – just the bare bones. She's totally bowled over and will discuss this with her seniors. There's no doubt a few

300

meetings are in the offing. It's a question of when and where, who to involve, et cetera. The first meeting is sure to be in Benhall and will benefit enormously with Father Mac there."

So, that was that. The message was "wait to be summoned."

*****

How it came about, Doc Campbell was not sure, but he found himself on that Tuesday chairing the meeting with Professor Lewis's "experts," not in some hospital or research establishment, but in Oakley – in fact along the corridor from Kathy's office. He suspected someone had put their foot down. This material from outer space seemed suddenly to have become even more sensitive and they didn't want someone who was not even a member of GCHQ roaming the countryside with photocopies of such a large bundle of the pages, albeit sanitised versions. He'd only learned of the change of venue yesterday evening. Well, that was OK. He knew his lines and could do his stuff anywhere. The one most affected was Megan, who had been looking forward to a day in Oxford.

There were three visitors. Kathy met them and Doc Campbell, saw them into the premises and showed them into a small, rather austere room. Business got underway by 10 am, and after introductions were made, Campbell ruled that notes could be taken as long as they were totally non-attributable. He displayed the pages they had come to examine and explained that their provenance could not be revealed. He then talked them briefly through the various pages, bringing in his own opinions and those of Professor Lewis. He had earlier labelled each of the illustrations involving a use of metal cladding with the relevant atomic numbers. After his opening remarks, he invited comments.

The debate was totally free-flow, high-spirited and, on occasions, hilarious. They were in no doubt where the pages originated. "The six fingers give the show away, old boy," said one of the three experts, a consultant clinician. The other two were a consultant cardiologist and a metallurgist with experience in medical applications of metals. The three-way discussion was fascinating, and Campbell was full of admiration for Professor Lewis for selecting the trio so wisely and predicting how well they would complement each other, and simply gel professionally. His big problem was that no-one had thought to provide a secretary to take notes, and he found himself cast in that role as well

301

as that of chairman. In fact, after his initial remarks, he barely acted as a chairman.

After about two hours, he decided to reduce the meeting's findings to a series of bottom lines, realising that these were likely to be only the opening salvoes to further debates that were sure to be requested. Whether Professor Lewis liked it or not, the birth of a medical working party might have just occurred. On the whole, Doc Campbell was pleased with the list of statements and conjectures that came out of the meeting, especially as they were very much on the lines already suggested. In the form he later put them for Professor Lewis, these were:

a. that the diagrams of parts of the body were not helpful without any text. While all the internal organs were readily identifiable, it was not clear with no text, what point, if any, the diagrams were seeking to demonstrate.

b. that the illustrations of limbs and torsos partly or fully encased in metal were extremely interesting and potentially very helpful. The metallurgist said nothing as extensive as the treatment depicted had been attempted anywhere as far as he knew, and the mix of several metals for the one treatment was unusual.

c. that caution should be exercised in simply copying wholesale the sort of techniques depicted. They may be targeting diseases or conditions existing elsewhere, but not here. Nevertheless, funding should be sought to launch a progressive series of experiments, the precise nature of which would need careful planning.

Doc Campbell invited his guests to lunch, but all declined, pleading other appointments or a full caseload. He was not unduly sorry, as he could get on and write up his notes in a secure environment. Perhaps, he reflected, other meetings would take place at which he would be required as a continuity man, especially if the cast of players changed.

*****

Tim found it hard to contain his impatience over the next few days. Lucy sensed his impatience (it was hard not to do so), but welcomed a brief return to normality. Shopping for Groutwhite was not Tim's idea of fun, any more than using the bloody stuff. A visit to mama was a welcome reprieve. Finally, on the Friday, the summons came.

"They've arranged with security for Father Mac to come in with us today," said Hugh. "We couldn't give him any notice. We've only just got the details. I do hope he can come."

Tim phoned the presbytery. Sister Winifred told him Father was saying his Office and could not be disturbed. Tim was to come over in about half an hour. He smiled. Good old Sister, getting things into perspective for him.

Tim collected Hugh and, then went back for Father. They hurried over the hill to Oakley.

"Impressive building, this," said Father Mac. It was. Built to resemble a giant conservatory with a predominance of glass in its structure and large palm trees in the atrium, it still commanded the hillside, despite the encroachment of houses right the way up the slope from the new Sainsbury's.

"This was just one building of the old complex here at Oakley. It's still in limited use, but nearly everything is now in the Doughnut over at Benhall," said Hugh. "You wait till you see that."

When they had arrived and signed in, Kathy got Sharon to organise coffee, then Nick held the floor.

"It'll be next Tuesday in Benhall at 10:30, and our Director will kick things off," he began. "Then it's our show. The five of us. It's purely a briefing. I think questions will be allowed, but no organised discussion. It will be quite an eclectic gathering, too, from what I understand. Apart from the five of us, there will be a small group from JIC – Debbie, of course, and perhaps even the Chairman, JIC, among them. SS will be there, but not SIS. There'll also be a group of Americans, mostly from NSA. SUSLO and CANSLO will be there, possibly Director, CSE, and at least one other, unspecified, delegate."

"Now who are all these people?" asked Father Mac. "If I'm to talk to them, I need to know who I'm talking to."

"Just pretend it's a congregation, Father," grinned Tim. "I bet you don't know who all of them are."

"True," conceded Father Mac, "but I don't want to know their names. Just their allegiances."

Nick took over. "Ah, well," he said. "Let me start with ourselves. I'm Head of GCHQ's Cryptanalytic Division, and Kathy here is one of my senior analysts. Hugh had my job before he retired about the same time as Tim, I believe. The JIC is the Joint Intelligence Committee. It produces all-source assessments on whatever it is tasked with by the major intelligence customers, the Foreign Office, the Home Office, the

Ministry of Defence and others. It also produces prioritised requirements papers for the collection agencies, by country or by international subject. SS are the Security Service, or MI5. They're responsible for identifying and countering any threat to the UK from within, as distinct from SIS, the Secret Intelligence Service, or MI6, who, together with GCHQ, are responsible for foreign intelligence that might affect the safety or well-being of the UK. SUSLO is the Senior US Liaison Officer in the UK. He's from NSA, the National Security Agency, GCHQ's American counterpart. Several other Americans will also be there, though not all from NSA. I don't know where the non-NSA-ers are from. The Canadian Senior Liaison Officer in the UK, CANSLO, will be there. He's from CSE, the Canadian Security Establishment, where your brother Andrew used to work. Their Director may be there, too, and it sounds like there'll also be a mystery guest. Our Director will have a tricky time skating round the introductions."

"Thank you, Nick, that's very helpful," smiled the priest.

"Now, it's apparently up to us to get our act together. We're told this is a very important occasion, so we have to give them a very full briefing. Our chief performers will be Kathy and Father Mac. I will have to do a bit of scene-setting. I understand one of the Americans will also make some contribution to the proceedings. Father, it will be helpful if your briefing can cover both your analysis of the so-called fragments, as well as some of your lurid adventures. Tim can chip in here, too, on the activities of Misha and co. The Security Service will be represented but they're quite happy for Tim to cover this aspect, in view of his close involvement. OK, I think that's the basic outline. Now we need to sort out the best order, get some idea of timing, decide if there are any pitfalls to avoid or, conversely, points to emphasise. One basic question, I suppose, is do we need any visual aids, apart from the fragments themselves, which will be on view. If we do, does this mean PowerPoint?"

"God, no!" said Hugh, emphatically. "PowerPoint is to help discuss the production figures for widgets. I think a straight chronological narrative is what we want. That would leave no room for ambiguity."

"OK," said Nick. "A straight chronological narrative, though remembering not to stint on our description of the analytic bits. I'm not quite sure what you plan to say, Father. We've been waiting for you to recover sufficiently. Apart from your adventures, I assume you'll be discussing that single sheet of paper."

"Yes, but there's not really much to say," said Father Mac. "I won't bother you with it now. My solution to what this is all about nicely complements Kathy's. Two approaches, one common solution, if you like. To be honest, I was so overwhelmed with what I was seeing and its implications that I was sure no-one would believe me. Some might think that, as a Catholic priest, I had a particular axe to grind, so I felt the best course was to let you come to your own independent conclusion. Besides, coming from an official channel would invest our startling discovery with authority and credibility. By the way, I'm still not sure our visitor was a human and not an angel. Or some spiritually advanced being approaching that status. As you can see, the whole thing needs airing on so many fronts."

"I'm sure you're right, Father," said Nick. "Anyway, we're very happy to leave the content of your contribution in your capable hands. We're only too delighted you're up and running again. By the way, Debbie will be here Monday afternoon just to make sure we're happy with what's being asked of us. I can't see any need for the Bourton contingent to come in. I'll let you know of any oddity that crops up. The other delegates will arrive on the Tuesday morning. Speaking of which, I'm intrigued to find out who our mystery delegate will be."

They spent an hour or so going over the major content of the presentation and the point at which one speaker would give way to the next, and at the end felt pretty satisfied with their efforts.

"Right, then," said Nick. "I'll see you in church. Oh, sorry, Father, I wasn't thinking."

"Think nothing of it," said Father Mac.

"It's true for me, anyway," said Tim. "It is actually Father's big day on Sunday – his first stint on the altar for nearly five weeks. His progress really has been meteoric."

"Yes, no more skiving now," smiled Father.

*****

Father Mac's comeback on the Sunday went well. He had to move about the altar with a stick, but used the lectern to lean on when he thanked the congregation for all their kindnesses to him, and for keeping the parish ticking over so well. Tim, Lucy, and Norah came in for special mention, to their dismay. Father Danny followed with a few words, saying how pleased they all were at Father Mac's swift

305

recovery, and thanking members of the parish for making him so welcome.

Tea and coffee followed Mass, as usual, and Mike McGuire wheeled in a "Welcome Home" cake made by Norah. Everyone cheered.

CHAPTER 33

Tuesday soon arrived. Tim worried about the occasion. Would Father Mac be up to it? Would he be up to it himself? He didn't particularly want to get involved. The hard work that had brought about the meeting had been done by Kathy and Father Mac, though the full extent of Father Mac's contribution would perhaps become clearer this morning. Tim picked up Hugh and Father Mac and drove over the hill. The priest was not in clerical garb.

The morning was crisp and clear. The Malverns, 30 miles away, looked close enough to touch, while the Welsh mountains stood out starkly a further 20 miles to the West. They arrived at the Doughnut in good time, and Tim found at security that they were on a special list for the meeting. Nick was there to meet and escort them.

Tim was always impressed with the Doughnut. The group strolled along the long circular corridor, Tim and Hugh nodding and smiling to the former colleagues and acquaintances they ran into, hastily excusing themselves for being unable to stop. Nick guided them to the Directorate conference room, where tea, coffee, soft drinks, and biscuits were laid out. Kathy was waiting, chatting to CANSLO, Jim McKenzie, and Professor Alan Lewis. Father Mac was introduced to them and, not surprisingly, soon discovered that Jim had worked closely with Andrew. GCHQ's Deputy Directors were also there and a flurry of activity a few minutes later announced the arrival of several others – SUSLO with three Americans in tow and Debbie with two men, presumably, like her, from JIC. An MI5 Director followed them in, and the Director of GCHQ appeared last, leading in an exquisitely groomed lady, whom he introduced to the Americans. He chatted briefly to the JIC contingent, then walked across to Nick's group, shaking hands with his former colleagues and with CANSLO. Nick introduced him to Father Mac, with whom he dealt most graciously, saying how honoured they were to have him with them.

After the Director had made the rounds, Nick and Kathy fussed around the refreshments, making sure everyone was properly catered for before business began.

"I always know I'm getting old when people in the highest authority, like your Director, look so young," said Father Mac.

"In his case," whispered Tim, "He actually is young."

Conference chairs with arms had been deployed fairly randomly around the room, and everyone sat. The Director stood at the front and addressed them.

"I would like to welcome you all. This must be a first. Most of us would never have dreamed those of us here today could possible assemble under the same roof." There were a few chuckles. "We are here simply to be briefed on a series of unusual events and to report back to a higher authority in our respective countries, knowing that they, in turn, will also confer at their level, as we are doing at ours. We are conscious that the briefings that follow will be unusual in the working-level detail offered. Some may think, why don't they cut to the chase, but we need to convince you today, for onward and upward transmission, that the basis for future deliberations is totally sound. Momentous decisions will hinge on those deliberations."

The Director continued, "The events central to today's briefing involve a very brave man, Father Donald McNulty." There was some gentle applause. "He will be the first to speak, followed by Tim Sullivan, a retired member of GCHQ and a parishioner of Father McNulty, who also found himself caught up in events. Kathy Webb will then address the analysis of the material we're all so interested in, and the progress so far made. We'll then hear from Jim Brogan, who has flown in from Rome and who will introduce himself more precisely when he speaks, right Jim?" One of the Americans smiled and nodded all round. From Rome? thought Tim puzzled, while Father Mac stared at the visitor.

"I know him," whispered the priest, "or at least, I recognise him from a photograph somewhere."

"The final speaker will be Professor Alan Lewis, a senior scientific adviser to the government, mainly to the intelligence community. Those are the speakers. One other special guest we are privileged to have with us is Larissa Kiranova, who has travelled here from Moscow, and who is our Russian contact on material exchange." The elegant lady smiled and gave a little wave. "The rest of us here are from the American, Canadian, and British intelligence apparatus, including, on the British side, officers from our all-source assessments staff. We, of course, are used to collaborating on intelligence and conferring together. It took, in my view, a degree of imagination and one might even say courage to widen this particular gathering to include the other interested parties. After the briefings, questions will be permitted, though please shout out during a briefing if it's a really important point. You will hear a good deal about some so-called fragments. These will be on display after the briefings. Nick, would you like to get the ball rolling?"

"Thank you, Director," said Nick. "Good morning. My name is Nick Watson and I'm Head of GCHQ's Cryptanalysis Division. This will not be a formal presentation with technical aids. We prefer an informal, narrative approach and the only props we have are a whiteboard and pen. Right, are you ready Father?"

Father Mac nodded and walked to the front, where a chair had been placed, to face the audience. He did not, however, sit in it, but threw his stick into it, went behind, and supported himself by leaning on the back of the chair. He paused, looking all around those gathered there. His gaze dwelt for some time on the Americans, who were sitting as a group. There was absolute silence.

"My name is Donald McNulty. I am the parish priest of St Nicholas Roman Catholic Church in Bourton-under-Wychwood, a town of some 5,000 residents about eight miles from here. Most years I fly to Ottawa to visit my brother Andrew and his family. I now know that Andrew works for CSE, the Canadian Signals Intelligence authority. Every time I visit, we fit in a few days camping, often in Algonquin National Park. Though he is retired, Andrew is on-call in the event of a crisis. This time we set up camp near Smoke Lake down in the southwest part of the park, and two days later Andrew was recalled to Ottawa. I stayed on, as I had driven down there in Andrew's second car. The following night, a Friday, I went to bed, slept soundly as usual, then was woken at about 5 am on the Saturday by a very bright strobe light. Shortly after, there was an almighty roar and something passed low overhead and crashed into the trees not too far away. I assumed it was an aircraft, but not a large one, as the area affected did not seem to be extensive. Small fires had started all around.

"When dawn came shortly afterwards, I went to the crash scene to see if I could do anything. Perhaps there were survivors. I saw the crashed vehicle. It was not a light aircraft, as I had expected, but a circular craft about fifteen or sixteen feet in diameter – just under five metres. It was a dull silver and had a distinctive logo in two places, two green crossed lines with a star in red above. I thought 'a U.F.O.?' Did such things exist? Or some sort of research craft? As I inspected the vehicle, the door opened, a gangway automatically descended and a small figure in startling white appeared through the smoke. He wore what was clearly a space suit, but seemed to glow, so intense was the light emanating from him. He wore no helmet and looked exactly as we do, though a little smaller than average. He walked unsteadily down the staircase, then approached me, offering something he had in his hand. He spoke one word to me, that sounded like 'Molly's' or 'Mollees.' He said this twice. Was this an introduction? I gave my name and he repeated it. He then gave me some documents." You could have heard a pin drop in the room.

"He then went back up the staircase, though the door, waved and indicated I should leave the area immediately. I did so, somehow made aware of what was about to happen. As I fled, there was a massive explosion, and fiery debris rained down through the trees, some lodging there and setting fire to branches. By now, a military rescue party had arrived in five helicopters and I decided not to risk being detained and getting embroiled in a question and answer session. So I packed up and left for Ottawa. On the way back, two attempts were made to ram my car. I choose the words carefully. These were not accidental events. They were quite deliberate, involved the same vehicle on both occasions, and, in light of later events, were without doubt aimed at relieving me of the documents. I arrived back at my brother's house unharmed, but considerably shaken." There were a few stirrings among the audience, some delegates exchanging glances.

"Back in Ottawa, I decided to report the incident to the Department of National Defence and to offer the documents I had been given, but the officer I saw sought to assure me that what I had witnessed was no more than a simulated air crash and rescue exercise. I clearly could not argue with him and concluded there was no point in offering him the documents I had. I then reported the incident to the British Defence Liaison Staff at the High Commission. I understand that by some mysterious process my report reached the interested authorities in the UK." There were a few smiles.

"A quick glance at the documents suggested they could be important. They were in a script totally unknown to me, and not even vaguely resembling anything I had seen before. I decided to keep them and follow up on them in the UK. When I returned home, I examined them more closely." Tim couldn't help but notice that Father Mac had made no mention of catching Andrew red-handed photographing some of the documents, and considered this a wise decision. What did these people need to know about actions involving a close Sigint ally, which, with hindsight and given the context, were completely justifiable?

"There were four types of document. First, there were several fragments of a map and a few dozen pages from what was clearly a medical book with diagrams of the body and textual portions in the unknown script. Then there were several substantial chunks from a large book that had literally been blown apart. For want of any better label all those that became involved in this study agreed to call this a 'reference book.' Finally, there was a single, large sheet of paper, about poster size and covered with the unknown script on one side, while on the reverse side were what I first took to be letters from the Roman alphabet. All these items will be on display after our briefing. Incidentally, the logo or insignia on the space vehicle also appeared on the large book.

"My parish duties left me little time for any in-depth study of the fragments, though I did manage to find a few hours on three or four evenings. I succeeded in piecing together the map fragments and found the map was of the Black Sea, with much of the Crimea present." A soft murmur arose from the listeners. "What were obviously place names in the strange script were scattered over the map. Using a map I had, I found it was not difficult to match some of the place names with their alien counterparts.

All I discovered from my own look at the medical pages was that the bodies in the diagrams were of beings in every way resembling humans, but with six fingers on each hand." There were several gasps from the audience. "The large book yielded nothing from the text, but with all the pages numbered, it did allow me to reconstruct the alien numerical system. Not surprisingly, a civilisation with twelve fingers counts on a base of twelve." There were more gasps. Nick and his boss, the Director, were clearly pleased with Father Mac's performance. He was gradually building up credibility.

"Finally, the single sheet. As I mentioned, on one side were a few apparently Roman characters." Father Mac moved away from the chair supported by his stick, went to the white board and grabbed a red pen. "This is what I saw." He wrote in red OC BOC. "Underneath were another two letters BO. Almost miraculously, I instantly understood the significance of the letters. May I digress for a short while?" What on Earth is coming now, thought Tim. "Many years ago I studied Russian. This was during my compulsory military service. Our instructors included many who had suffered great hardship during the war. Most were middle-aged, some elderly. Two or three were younger, including a man who took my conversation class. At the outbreak of war he was living right on the Russian/Polish border, just inside Poland. Not surprisingly, he was totally bilingual. He was training for the priesthood. When the Russians came, he left the seminary and went home to be with his elderly parents. However, he was arrested and sent to mine gold in Kolyma, up in the Arctic. When the Russians later changed sides, he and those with him were released and left to their own devices. His own plan was to find his way across Siberia and help fight the Germans. He eventually reached North Africa, where he joined the Polish Army mustering there under General Anders. My teacher saw action in Italy, including at Monte Casino."

Tim shifted uncomfortably. What was the point of all this? What was Father Mac saying now? "We found we both had a strong Christian faith, and after my course we kept in touch for many years at the two main Christian festivals, Christmas and Easter. At Easter, we would exchange cards and his would always contain the traditional Orthodox Christian greeting. This greeting became engraved in my mind. This is it." Father Mac seized a blue pen and added several more letters to the board, so that the top line now read ХРИСТОС ВОСКРЁС. He limped over to the elegant lady, smiled at her and said the words "Khristos voskrios". She immediately replied "Voistinu voskrios." Father Mac smiled all round. "Christ has risen!" he said, "And the response 'He truly has risen!'" He then wrote the response in Cyrillic on the board ВОИСТИНУ ВОСКРЁС. "Yes, the words were in Cyrillic, and the little man I saw was a Christian or at least had knowledge of Christianity. Indeed, in his brilliant white suit and with his small stature and friendly disposition I took him for an angel, and who is to know whether I was right or wrong?" He looked long and hard at the American contingent.

Tim emitted a long sigh. So that's what the old priest was sitting on. A clever piece of extrapolation leading to a way-out solution, one he felt reluctant to offer without some sort of corroboration he felt sure the "reference book" would eventually yield if studied by the right people. Father Mac had only had eight characters to work with from what he deduced to be two phrases of twenty eight characters – and in Cyrillic! What vision!

Father Mac continued. "I realised I was sitting on a time bomb. If it became generally known that somewhere in outer space was not just another civilisation similar to our own, but a Christian one, the consequences would surely be immense. Think of the possible political and military implications of such a disclosure, and as for the theological implications, goodness only knew what these would be. It is not for me to speculate. There are others much more qualified. I felt weighed down with the responsibility of having this knowledge and, after a further attempt was made to cause me to crash, I realised I must confide in someone I could trust and who might be able to advise me on who to approach. Meantime, I decided to hide the fragments, and to write a full account of events, rather as I am giving you now. This became a matter of urgency as I began to feel unwell. I hid the fragments, but did not get beyond leaving my account of events on my computer and entrusting my thought on the single sheet with a trusted friend. These have now been destroyed as they have outlived their usefulness.

The next day I found myself in hospital without the power of speech, and little feeling down one side. I'd had a stroke. It transpired it was only a mild stroke, though my speech was quite badly affected for a week or two. As you can see it has fully returned." He smiled and the audience responded.

"Father, why don't you let Tim take up the story now?" said Nick, "I think we've reached a logical stage in the narrative. Thank you. And, as the Director has said, the famous fragments have been brought here today and will be on display following these briefings." As Father Mac resumed his place, there were murmurs of approval at his performance. Tim stood at the front.

"Good morning. My name is Tim Sullivan. I'm a former employee of GCHQ. I retired two years ago.

"My role in this story is as Father Mac's confidant. I should first mention that no sooner had Father Mac been taken to hospital than two strangers, identified later as Russians, came to Bourton and asked searching questions about his illness. Also, the first night Father Mac was away, there was a break in at his presbytery. Father Mac's sister, a nun from a hospice south of here, had moved in ready to look after Father Mac upon his discharge from hospital. She disturbed the burglars who were soon apprehended. They had been hired, clearly by the two strangers, to search the presbytery for any documents in a strange alphabet. Father Mac as a keen and skilled linguist had a collection of reading material in several languages. All that the intruders could offer their employers were novels in languages such as Greek and Russian." There were a few smiles.

"I visited Father Mac in hospital the next day. Though he could not speak, he got me to understand there was something urgent for me on his computer. He became very agitated about this. I managed to locate Fr Mac's account of his adventures in Canada, and knew my priority must be to locate the fragments he had referred to."

Tim went on to recount the kidnapping of Father Mac and himself, the interrogation in the cottage and the subsequent arrest of the two Russians. It became evident there was a third Russian involved – a more senior accomplice named Misha. Tim recounted discovering the fragments, examining them, and reaching his own, modest conclusions on the numbering system and the area depicted on the map. He soon concluded he should take a former colleague from GCHQ into his confidence in case the papers were in some way important or sensitive, quite unaware of the chain of events they would unleash, including the briefing session he was to be involved in at the safe house. He described his absence from home as an opportunity to leave some bait, confident it would be taken by Misha and passed on to his local contact. The bait took the form of a spoof CD, purporting to contain photographs of the documents.

"Imagine my distress when I discovered I had left the genuine CD to be found. Imagine my relief when I found that, far from data on weapons or propulsion systems, we had donated to some foreign power extracts from a Christian bible." There were a few chuckles. "Following an operation not relevant to the work of GCHQ, in which a Special Branch officer was badly injured, the address of Misha's contact was identified, though what that contact may or may not have revealed is beyond the scope of this briefing. I'll now pass you over to the next speaker."

Tim sat down and Kathy took his place at the front of the audience. "Good morning. I'm Kathy Webb, a senior cryptanalyst at GCHQ. So far, I've been pretty well alone in examining the fragments in an effort to resolve the alien language. This problem is quite unlike our normal remit and some may query why the task fell to me and not some academic versed in ancient tongues. But it was argued that their training and aptitude would not necessarily equip them to make inroads any better than my own experience and training in cryptanalysis. Also, I have some advantages over him, namely unlimited computer power if needed, and a large body of colleagues whose corporate flair encompasses pretty well every approach possible. Finally, the provenance of the material is very sensitive, and we're geared up from security considerations to handle and store material of this sensitivity better than anyone else in the country. So rightly or wrongly, I was tasked with studying the material." Why is she seeking to justify our involvement? wondered Tim. Perhaps the audience included a few sceptics, he concluded, though, if so, he wasn't sure who those were.

"Hugh Frobisher, Nick Watson's predecessor, first drew my attention to the fragments and to the work Father Mac and Tim Sullivan had done on them. As Father Mac mentioned, I did not recognise the message on the single sheet as an Easter greeting in Cyrillic, so I could make no immediate assumptions that what I was dealing with had some relevance to Christianity. After checking the conclusions on the map fragments and the numeric system reached by Father Mac and Tim Sullivan and agreeing with them, I then began to study the alien orthography. This led to the isolation of 40 discrete symbols or letters and a separator, as well as the fact that some words were in a larger typeface. I then assigned an arbitrary binary label to each symbol, scanned into the computer the pages of what we now know to be the bible, and produced an equivalent binary text, noting which equivalents represented the words in larger text.

"I realised the way forward was to attempt to recognise these words in larger type. They were obviously important, and might well represent names of places or persons – proper nouns, in fact. The stepping-stone here had to be the alien map. I had to assume the place-names were true phonetic equivalents of the Russian. So I armed myself with some maps in Cyrillic and set to work. I soon found that my assumption was correct, when several place-names with letters or syllables in common could be seen to have the same alien symbols. This quickly allowed me to produce a list of alien letters and their phonetic values. I then studied what we were calling the reference book, looking one by one at the words in the larger type in order of their frequency of occurrence, in case anything meaningful emerged. The second most commonly occurring word was a hit, and very much so. It occurred well over a thousand times. This is it." She turned to the white board and wrote "Iesus."

A voice came from the audience. "Did you say over a thousand appearances?" It was the visitor from Rome.

"Yes, over twelve hundred, in fact. I don't have the precise figure with me. I'm now working to match up precise parts of our own Bible with precise parts of the alien bible, based on the patterns of occurrence of the word 'Iesus.' Oh, I forgot to mention, some of the occurrences are followed by another word in large type. This transliterates to 'Khristos.' So, our reference book turned out to be a Christian bible.

And that's as far as I've got." General conversation now broke out in the audience.

"I think we've finished this part of the briefing now," said Nick, standing, "other than to state the obvious. That the work in matching precise bits of text will be extremely time-consuming, but the result, if we can ever achieve it, will be some sort of dictionary."

"Let's pause for now before the next part of the briefing, and invite questions," said the Director, "Or general points."

"NSA," said a voice. "We'd be happy to share in the building of a dictionary. Perhaps you can spare Miss Webb for a few days, Director, to get us up to speed, if we've not got to this point under our own steam." The Director nodded at Nick.

"I'm sure that can be arranged," smiled Nick.

Kathy spoke again. "One thing I haven't mentioned. My overall impression at the moment is that the book we're dealing with is actually bigger than its Earthly counterpart." That caused a stir in the audience. "If you want something more than a dictionary, such as a full reconstruction of the bible we have, you're looking at a truly monumental task."

"May I add something, too?" said Father Mac. "I have almost certainly identified the text on the reverse side of the large single sheet. You'll recall I mentioned this. There are two groups of sentences, or whatever they are. One of about ten propositions, if you like. The other of about nine. Now what could they be? If you wanted to sum up the Christian faith in a few succinct words to appear on the back of a statement boldly proclaiming 'Christ has risen,' what would you write?"

"Ten, you say, followed by nine?" said the American from Rome. Father Mac nodded.

"Then it's no contest," he said. "The Ten Commandments and the Beatitudes from the Sermon on the Mount."

"Beatit...?" stumbled the elegant lady.

"Blazhentstva," supplied Father Mac. "And yes, I would agree with you."

"Could this be a book produced on another planet, but somehow reporting Christ's life here on Earth?"

This came from a member of the Assessments staff. No-one was rushing to answer.

"I think that question takes us very appropriately to the final part of this morning's proceedings," said the Director. "I mentioned that one of our guests has flown here from Rome. He's a theologian and an astronomer – an invaluable combination in these particular circumstances. I'll leave him to introduce himself."

The American who had mentioned the Ten Commandments rose, and walked to the front. He was a short, jolly-looking man in a black suit that, far from being a cunning civilian disguise for the occasion, could well have been the garb that served him in his everyday life. All he lacked was the dog-collar.

"Good morning," he smiled, "I'm Jim Brogan, my family is called the Society of Jesus, and my Boss is the Holy Father." There was a sharp, collective intake of breath. "My day job is to serve on theological committees, if and when required, to contribute to the record of our proceedings, and produce an occasional monograph. My night job is far busier: I'm a member of the Vatican Observatory Research Group, which is part of the Mount Graham International Observatory in Arizona, not too far from Tucson. I'm here today mainly to put a theological slant on what to many will be pretty Earth-shattering news: that somewhere out there is an alien civilisation who, like millions of people on Earth, are Christians. In fact, the news is not Earth-shattering to me or many of my colleagues. Indeed, we have been waiting for definitive proof of what, in Vatican circles, has actually been suspected for about 600 years. That we are not alone in the universe as a thinking civilisation capable of acknowledging a divine creator." He grinned. "All we have to do is sort out the theology. Mind you, there has not been total agreement within the Vatican. Of course there hasn't. How could there be? Perhaps now there will be agreement.

"My contribution this morning will not be a scholarly speech, or a very long one. There are so many facets to the theology of extra-terrestrial life, it would take a long time to examine them all. And that's not what this is about. By the way, I'm well aware some of you may be of other faiths or of no faith. You might be moved to reconsider your positions in light of this current development. I do hope so.

Anyway, it might help to recap on where things have stood among scientists and churchmen for many years. Before we get into theology, let's play the numbers game: give or take a few, our Sun is one of 200 billion, repeat billion, stars in the Milky Way, and the Milky Way is only one of 10 billion galaxies. If you assume only about half of these stars have a planetary system, with an average of, say, six to ten planets per star, then in calculating the number of planets you begin to run out of zeroes. To believe we are the only planet capable of supporting life as we know it among such an abundance of candidates is surely the most supreme arrogance. As a distinguished Cardinal put it as early as the fifteenth century, 'It would be folly to consider all the worlds that surround us as uninhabited deserts.'" Tim recalled that he had heard these numbers somewhere before. Of course, Brother Simeon had quoted the same figures, perhaps not surprisingly, though. Both he and Monsignor Brogan may be clerics of different standings, but both were astronomers, both clearly believed in extraterrestrial life, and both would have accessed the same literature. He expected a few other points Monsignor Brogan would make would also ring the odd bell.

Brogan continued, "OK, so that's the logic based purely on numbers. I find that pretty persuasive on its own, but this logic has been backed up consistently with sightings of space vehicles – thousands of them by sane and sober citizens. And by physical encounters: Father McNulty's experience was one more of the hundreds of live contacts already reported. Now, put all that to one side and consider the theological debate. For example, there is the argument that says, 'Since God created the universe, He would have created aliens, too.' Well, heck, He sure created us. Would He really have created an immeasurable number of other planets, intending nothing more for them than a totally sterile existence forever? I don't think so. God is the supreme creator. Surely He would have populated more than one planet with life forms. What life forms are we talking about? People just like us? In most cases, I say why not? We're led to believe that Man was made in God's image and likeness. But does that hold true everywhere? Well, it was certainly true in the case of Father McNulty's contact. But life forms evolve, then branch, and continue along one or more paths, as Mr Darwin has reminded us. On the planet where Father McNulty's friend originated, somewhere along the evolutionary path six fingers were found to be more useful than the five we have. But that was the only visible difference. There may be other planets, perhaps millions of them where, while the basic likeness to our concept of God holds good, small evolutionary differences are also present. Whether these extend to little green men, or the popular depiction of beings with large heads, huge almond eyes and puny bodies, or reptilian features, I have no way of knowing.

"So, given that there are innumerable planets potentially capable of supporting a reasonable facsimile of Man-on-Earth, what about the real theological questions? The tough ones. The toughest of all, certainly at the present time, is the Incarnation. The argument goes: Do you mean to say that God has sent His only son to all these planets to die in whatever cruel way was the fashion there in order to redeem the sins of the locals? We don't know the answer. Some theologians argue that because these are aliens and not humans, then *ipso facto* there is no original sin to be redeemed on their planet, *ergo* no Son of God appearing and no crucifixion. In other words, on every planet where the version of Mankind diverges significantly from the Earthly model, there is no need for redemption, because, surely, these guys don't have a soul, as we understand it. Another theological argument put forward is that there is no need for Jesus to be crucified time and time again. Surely, one single act of redemption would serve to redeem all men everywhere and at all times. Certainly this is backed up by St Paul. In his letter to the Jews in Palestine, the Hebrews, he says that Jesus appeared on Earth for the destruction of sin by the sacrifice of himself, and since men die once only, He was offered once only to exhaust the sins of many. But if this is so, why did that single act of redemption take place on our planet Earth when the series of space vehicles that have been visiting us are clearly from a civilisation immeasurably more advanced than ours and therefore in existence considerably earlier than us? Why then did they not stage that all-embracing act of redemption on their own planet and spare Earth the shame of organising a crucifixion? We don't know. But this is a question we could barely have asked last week.

"Going back to evolution, some theologians believe this has also occurred spiritually, and that on some planets there exists a race which, in purity of soul, is a long way along the path to being angels."

Father Mac exclaimed, "Mine was one such being. I'm in no doubt."

"Well, certainly the gift he and others like him have repeatedly brought here for us puts that possibility on the agenda. I'm in no position to say whether your contact was a humanoid or an angel. We are in absolutely no doubt of the existence of angels, as servants of God, dispatched to carry out errands for Him In fact, all three major Abrahamic religions, Judaism, Christianity, and Islam believe in angels. Unlike mankind, which is made up of flesh, blood, and the spirit, angels are purely spiritual beings. They have uncannily appeared at the brink of a disaster and have somehow caused it to be averted, or, if a disaster has already struck, have helped mitigate the consequences in some way. They appear where God directs them. All three religions have suggested that in their normal form angels may exist as light or fire but they can manifest themselves as beings with flesh and blood, if

319

their errand calls for this. Witness the three men who visited Abraham. These were angels, but they even shared a meal. Think of the Annunciation. The Angel Gabriel, who appeared to Mary, took on bodily form. Think of Moses and the burning bush, when he was told he had been chosen to lead the children of Israel to the land God had promised them. Father Mac saw a being cloaked in white, who glowed. I am suggesting, Father, that what you saw, and indeed, met, was either an alien from a civilisation well advanced along the spiritual path, or, if the alien occupants of the craft were dead, an angel who appeared on the scene in order to ensure that the transaction intended by the occupant or occupants, namely the handover of the documents, took place." Brother Simeon again, thought Tim. And, again, not surprisingly. In fact, it was very likely that some of what he'd read had actually been written by Monsignor Brogan.

The Jesuit priest was listened to in respectful silence. If there were cynics present, they did him the courtesy of hearing him out without interruption. "You're all very polite in the face of some pretty contentious stuff. By the way, I understand you are guinea pigs. I'm to appear in London some time soon to cover the same ground with the politicians. Hey – maybe they'll let me go on tour," he smiled. There was ripple of laughter. "Do you have any questions before I give way to the final speaker?"

"Do you get given particular theological tasks to perform?" This was Hugh.

"We are aware of the major questions. Some of these have been around a long time. But generally we are not given specific areas of study. We are allowed much freedom of action and thought. If some new reasoning occurs, we might get together and confer. Some of the English-speaking staff, with an eye to a good pun, regard us as a bunch of loose cannons." Laughter broke out.

"What about your astronomy? Does this inform your theology, and vice versa?" asked Nick.

Brogan looked inquiringly at the Director, who nodded, and said, "We've reached the point in these briefings where, for some of you, we'll be breaking new ground. There are aspects of these alien visits that are dealt with in another working party. Technically, these fall outside the ELK ONE briefing most of you were given, but we will mention them here. This is because the events in question might well reach the public domain quite soon. Others will be discussing the question of release into the public domain. I think, Monsignor Brogan, if you and Alan Lewis can now do a double act, that might work out best."

Jim Brogan nodded. "My astronomy? It's extremely relevant to the question of this particular series of visits. You see, we've been tracking them pretty well since the series began." The audience looked at each other and whispered among themselves. "We've had – what? – sixteen so far. Alan?"

Professor Alan Lewis walked to the front to join Jim Brogan. "Yes, the Canadian crash occurred on the sixteenth visit. I know this will come as a shock to some of you, but we think these small spacecraft travel here from a point somewhere between Saturn and Jupiter. They come from an enormous mother ship and are assembled on board from what I can only describe as a kit. They could have dozens of these on board the mother ship. The small craft arrive here in about three days. They probably home in on Evpatoriya. Jim?"

"Thank you, Alan," said Monsignor Brogan. "Yes, there's a warning blast of white noise from them by radio to say they're on their way. That's incoherent noise. They send this about 36 hours away, with another blast about 6 hours away. We pick them up visually from Mount Graham about a day out. Because of their likely destination, we've lately been advising Evpatoriya immediately. They no doubt tell their own authorities. The same information is also released to the world at large on an international network."

"Any questions so far?" asked Prof Lewis.

"I wouldn't know where to start," said a bewildered Nick Watson, "I suppose the main ones would be firstly, 'Whatever speeds are we talking about here?' and secondly, 'You spoke of a mother ship, where does that originate?'"

"I must ask you to accept some facts on trust," said the Professor. "This is not the place to back them up with scientific argument. We know a great deal about the propulsion system of these vehicles. The technology is surprisingly simple. There is just an extra critical step or two to discover. If our visitors are purveying nothing more than a Christian bible – incredibly important though that is – there will be nothing in it to assist countries hostile to us to in their own studies of high-speed flight. We do not know precisely the highest speed attainable by these vehicles, but from our understanding of the technology involved we believe that they could approach the speed of light, though, of course, the closer they get the more their mass increases to prevent them attaining it. As you know, light travels at

186,000 miles or 300,000 kilometres per second. Maybe they could be aiming at about half that speed, to prevent these other problems. Major assemblies, such as the mother ship associated with this current series, might not quite attain such a speed, but it would not be far short. The very small bible-bearing craft launched from the mother ship, which incidentally I think are one-person vehicles, can probably attain only a few thousand miles per second." The Professor paused. He knew full well that data of this sort, endlessly tossed around among those within his own scientific ambit, would present a bunch of laymen (was that the word with a company that included two clerics?) with a mind-bending experience, and that time to chatter excitedly was required before they simmered down. He was right. After a full two minutes the chatter subsided.

Nick Watson pursued his theme. "You say we're close to understanding the propulsion system of these vehicles?"

"Only theoretically. There's still a significant amount of work to do, and some key materials involved may not be easily obtainable."

"So how did you manage to make a start?"

Professor Lewis looked a little uncomfortable, but after a slight hesitation he continued. "You will probably know that over the past sixty years or so a few extraterrestrial vehicles have crashed. I'm not talking about the small ones in our bible-bearing series launched from a mother ship – they don't carry quite the same technology. Nor the huge mother ships themselves. These surely cannot crash with so many fail-safe measures installed. No, I'm talking about large, circular craft, the serious space-explorers that cover prodigious distances at what we call flash speed. Some have suggested they nip down the odd black hole or two, but I certainly don't want to go down that path. Anyway, a couple of these explorer vehicles have been of value to us. I won't say where these crashed, but it proved possible to apply reverse-engineering to some of the components recovered. This has assisted in the fields of integrated circuits, transistors, fibre optics, and laser technology, for example." The Professor was clearly not too happy to progress further down this path. "But we're beginning to get too far away from our briefing. I believe you were asking where the vehicles originate, Nick. The short answer is we don't know. To even begin calculating possibilities, much would depend on knowing when they started out, and that in turn would depend on how long it took to build the mother ship. You must understand this is a huge structure, about the size of a small town with living accommodation for hundreds, if not thousands.

I'm not sure what other facilities it offers, but I'm quite sure Jim will convince us there is at least one church." There was some subdued laughter.

Nick persisted. "I'm not sure I understand what it is that prompted one planet probably light years away to embark on what by any standards must have been a highly ambitious project, even for them. And why they chose to do so when they did."

Jim Brogan took over. "We're getting to the real heart of things now. The really contentious part. I want to say right away that some of what I'm going to say now is not new. But it has taken on an added significance with the recent events. When this series of visits began just over a year ago, the first two or three vehicles ended up in North America. By then we were able to detect and track their passage through space over the last day. We then had a spate of visits to Russia, and gradually formed the opinion that was really their target area and that the earlier destinations were aberrations, as was one visit to the UK, where the spacecraft was detected on radar and buzzed by two fighters. According to a farmer, it jettisoned something, then made off at an incredible speed. The incident was never allowed to trouble the media. Maybe our visitors hadn't discovered the value to them of the Evpatoriya transmitter until after several visits." There was a subdued buzz around the room.

Monsignor Brogan continued. "Now, the gentleman there – Nick, is it? – was asking about what prompted these Christian space travellers to embark on this project. I think the answer can be summed up in one word – evangelism." The murmur among his audience broke out again. "If you'll bear with me, may I give you a short history lesson. Do you remember what significant event took place in October 1917?"

Nick said, "Unless you mean some particular action in World War I, then I assume you mean the Russian Revolution."

"Correct. That's certainly one answer. Not the only one, but certainly the usual one, though the Russian Revolution actually began with an attempted uprising in the February, but that was a shambles. When Lenin returned to Russia in the summer of 1917 after lying low overseas, he took charge. He came to a crucial decision on 17 October: that the revolution would begin exactly one week later, on 24th. This time, Lenin was careful to ensure that troops loyal to the Bolshevik Party moved into key positions in St Petersburg – the main telephone and telegraph offices, the post offices, the railroad stations, major bridges. Within a day the Bolsheviks had control of most of the city. It was all over bar the shouting. As you probably know, there was then a period of civil war until eventually Lenin formed a government, and on his death in 1924 was succeeded by Stalin. A regime of unimaginable cruelty followed that was to last nearly thirty years. Millions starved to death in famines, millions more were slaughtered for perceived opposition to the regime, further millions were exiled to the labour camps, the practice of religion was banned upon penalty of death. I could go on, but won't. Now, there was another event, significant to some, which also occurred in October 1917. Any takers?"

One voice spoke. "Fatima," said Father Mac.

"You had an unfair advantage," grinned the Jesuit. "Yes, Fatima. The appearance of Our Lady to three peasant children in Portugal on the thirteenth day of six consecutive months in 1917 ending in the October. On every occasion she was bathed in the most radiant light and spoke to them. You may not believe this happened. Millions do. Belief in the phenomenon has the blessing of the Catholic Church. On her last appearance in October 1917 Our Lady is said to have passed on to the children certain warnings, known as the Three Secrets of Fatima. One of these concerned Russia. She said it was God's wish to establish in the world devotion to her immaculate heart, and the consecration of Russia to her immaculate heart. If these requests were met there would be peace. If not, Russia would spread her errors throughout the world, causing wars and persecutions of the Church. The good would be martyred and some nations annihilated. The present war would end, but another would begin. During Our Lady's final appearance, the sun is said to have changed colours and rotated rapidly – a miracle said to have been witnessed by 70,000 people. I firmly believe in the miracle of Fatima.

"Now it seems to me, in light of the visits by these bible-bearing spacecraft clearly targeting Russia, that they might just be doing so in response to Our Lady's plea for the conversion of Russia." There was a stunned silence. Even Nick was silent.

After a while he found his voice. "But the timing's all wrong, Monsignor," he interjected, still determined to play Devil's Advocate for the assembly, sensing that he was not the only listener experiencing some cynicism towards the Jesuit's propositions. "We're talking about them responding to some request allegedly made over ninety years ago, therefore being in transit for well over ninety years and arriving here twenty years too late. And in any case, the alleged appearances of the Virgin Mary were here, not on some planet light years away."

"Your last objection can easily be countered," said Father Brogan. "Just as angels can be where they want to be at any time, so, of course can Our Lady, in spades, if you like. There wouldn't be the slightest difficulty in her appearing above the planet our visitors hail from, advising them of the problem affecting our planet Earth, and giving guidance on its location. What might she have said? I don't know. How about 'A country on a small planet, third from its sun, in a solar system n light years away is poised to spread evil around this planet. Go. Remedy this in the name of Almighty God.' As to the timing, goodness only knows what the duration would have been in their own time. I could sound off about time dilation and I'm sure Professor Lewis could give a thoroughly learned lecture on the subject and fill the board with equations if we had a day or two to spare, but I really don't want to go down that road. And who knows what short cuts might be available to them with their level of technology? As we hinted earlier we don't know how long it took to assemble the mother ship. You can bet it didn't come off a production line ready made. No doubt it's modular, but each module could be no more than a shell waiting to be filled with specialist contents. So – a huge job and a time-consuming one. Then there's the whole question of their location. On this we just haven't a clue. With these unknowns, I can comfortably rationalise they acted in response to their own manifestation of Our Lady and her request that Russia be converted, even though, in our terms, they arrived twenty years too late for that purpose. But would that matter? There would be plenty of evil somewhere on the planet that needed combating and the effect on the world at large of their arrival here bearing bibles, once publicised, would be unimaginable. Everywhere would be affected, not just the pockets of evil."

"May I respectfully put something to you, Monsignor?" said Father Mac. "It may occur to some people to say, "What's the use of sending a load of bibles in a totally alien language? How can that convert people?" I think we have to remember that use of one of their own languages was the only course open to our visitors. They had no knowledge of our own planet and its languages. But that's academic. No-one needs to read the book they keep leaving for us. The requirement was simply to identify it as a Christian bible. The bible was intended as a gesture to part of a planet that they had perhaps been told was Christian and was in danger of losing the faith. As far as they were concerned, the bibles were readily identifiable as such by what was presumably their own Christian logo stamped on to the cover.

However, after many visits they began to realise that we might be failing to recognise this logo for what it was, and that some prompt would be useful. They were right. Both the map fragments and the poster with the Easter greeting in their own way contributed to the identity of the bibles. Both would have been easy to put together on the mother-ship. That's all I can think of. Is all this feasible, Monsignor?"

"I think that's a first-rate piece of deduction, Father," said Brogan. "Offhand, I can't think of anything to improve on your theory, though it does beg the question of how they came by the Easter greeting."

My only suggestion is that for one of the Crimea visits a second crew member was brought on board and left behind to find something that might serve as a hint. The Orthodox Easter was not too long ago and Easter cards may still have been available in churches. The second person could have been picked up later. I know it sounds a bit unlikely, but I can't think of anything else."

"In fact, two of the Russian visits did occur within two days of each other," said Professor Lewis. "This was the only time this happened. The normal interval was about three or four weeks. They could have put together the poster on the mother-ship, with the Cyrillic greeting one side and the Beatitudes and Ten Commandments in their own orthography on the other, ready for all future visits."

"So it's not totally out of left field," said the Monsignor. "I think I'll add this conjecture to my briefing tomorrow. My final thought is that if it is agreed to release this news to the wide world, our visitors will soon become aware that the publicity they were seeking has sure been achieved. Perhaps beyond their wildest dreams. If we're right about why their visits took place, these should then cease."

The Director intervened. "I think at this point we'll have to draw proceedings to a close. We came together here today mainly to hear an account of how we came by the bible, and how we're responding technically to recovering the language, in the expectation that this knowledge will serve us if, in the future, any other documents from a similar source come to hand. These events will be summarised tomorrow for those who will be involved in key discussions and decisions on what to do about this amazing development. The technical and theological insights by Monsignor Brogan and Professor Lewis were the icing on the cake. They will be present, together with JIC representatives, at the government-level meeting. Inter-governmental discussions will also clearly be needed. I really must thank on behalf of us all those who presented the briefings. I suggest we now adjourn and take a look at the fragments, which Kathy Webb will set up. I understand these will be copied and forwarded to our collaborating agencies, right Debbie?" Debbie nodded. "Fresh tea and coffee are on their way."

The Chairman, JIC, leapt to his feet. "Before we break up, I would like to thank GCHQ for hosting this briefing, and for the unique opportunity this has given us to meet in common cause some of those we would not normally get to meet. The Director spoke of imagination and courage to get this meeting agreed. I fully endorse that, and trust we can repeat the formula, if it proves necessary." There were several cries of "Hear! Hear!" and some gentle applause.

The audience then broke up into smaller groups. Father Mac made a beeline for the Americans and singled out the Jesuit. Tim followed.

"God bless you, Monsignor," said Father Mac, grasping his hand. "I thought it was you. Your picture was in the Tablet."

"Probably to do with the Vatican's collection of meteorite remnants," chuckled the man. "My word, you and Tim Sullivan here really had a few adventures."

"I suppose we did," said Tim. "I was intrigued to hear about your job. It sounds really interesting, the more so because I recently had a briefing on your work from a young Benedictine."

"From Prinknash, no doubt," said Monsignor Brogan.

"Yes," said Tim. "This was when Father Mac was in hospital."

"I'm hoping to visit the Abbot one day soon," said Father Brogan. "We briefly studied together at one time. Anyway, show me these famous fragments."

As they moved off, Tim saw the Director in earnest discussion with one of the other two Americans – possibly Deputy DIRNSA or a group chief, speculated Tim – and with the Director of CSE and the Chairman, JIC. The Russian lady was also a member of the group. The other American was with Nick, Hugh, and Kathy. They were all sharing a joke. There seemed no doubt he was the chief of cryptanalysis, Nick's counterpart, though with many times the resources.

As they examined the fragments, the Russian lady joined them.

"We have some of these in my organisation," she said, "But not the map, the medical pieces or the 'blazhenstva' – the beatitudes I think you called them. We would like to have a copy please." She had a low, husky voice, which, together with her elegant appearance, made her one of the sexiest ladies Tim had seen in a long time. "By the way,

327

Father, are you quite sure your angel friend said 'Molees'?" That could suggest he thought he was on Russian soil."

"Yes, you're right," said Father Mac thoughtfully, and was about to develop the theme, when Tim, not understanding the significance of the exchange, intervened.

"Do you agree with what Monsignor Brogan said?" asked Tim. "That these vehicles are being targeted at Russia? We've had one, the Americans and the Canadians two each, I think, but you've had – what – nine or ten?"

"Oh, there's no doubt Russia has been targeted," she said. "I found his history lesson most persuasive and I couldn't have said that twenty or so years ago. Someone would have reported me. I expect these N.L.O., these space vehicles, are attracted by the radio broadcast from Evpatoriya. You know, the transmitter. Like, like ночные бабочки? to the light."

"Moths," smiled Father Mac.

"Yes, moths."

"What does N.L.O. mean?" asked Tim.

It's Russian for U.F.O." said Father Mac, "Neopoznannjy Letayushchiy Ob'yekt."

Larissa went on, "But they don't all land in the Crimea. Some do. But others come towards Evpatoriya then continue on towards Moscow or on into central Russia. In fact, only five I believe have landed in the Crimea." She paused. "But be careful, that piece of information, like my name, Larissa, is top secret." She laughed at her little joke, a high, tinkly sound in contrast to her husky voice

"You don't look a bit like Rosa Kleb," joked Tim.

"Ah, yes, James Bond," she said, "All our ladies love your James Bond." She turned to Father Mac. "But you, Father, where did you learn to speak Russian so well?"

Father Mac and Larissa launched into a torrent of Russian, much to the amusement of SUSLO, who happened to be passing.

"Gee, you guys," he laughed. "I've seen everything now."

Nick and Kathy were collected together by Professor Lewis, who then found Debbie and manoeuvred the group to one side.

"Just to make sure you are all in the loop," he said. "As the Director said, all the fragments on display today will be photocopied. But not everything is on display. I have safely in my custody a few of the so-called medical pages, so everyone will have to wait for a while. It may prove necessary to withhold them altogether, at least from dear Larissa.

328

On the other hand, it may not. I can't say anything else yet. I'll let you know my recommendation as soon as I can."

"Very well," said Debbie slowly. "Speaking of Larissa, she is a bit of a stunner, isn't she?"

"I wish I could afford to dress like that," said Kathy.

"Why?" said Lewis. "It would only spoil that natural English rose look you wear so well. A rose with brains, too."

"Oh, go away, Alan," said Kathy, colouring.

The meeting disbanded. The Director shook hands with everyone and escorted the Americans and Larissa along the corridor and outside the Doughnut, where they were discreetly joined by others – the minders, thought Tim. A sign of the times.

Nick and Kathy joined their colleagues in the building, while the Bourton contingent made its way back over the hill, to await developments. Tim had no idea if he was now out of the loop entirely as the politicians took over.

CHAPTER 34

COBRA is as much a concept as a location. It is essentially an ad-hoc committee that meets in response to a national crisis at home, or events overseas that could seriously impact on the United Kingdom. It meets in one of the Cabinet Office briefing rooms – hence the startling acronym. It is often summoned in haste, and usually pre-empts every other appointment the delegates might have had. The meeting can be called by a head of department, a cabinet minister or even the prime minister, as was the case the day after the historic briefing in GCHQ. Crises leading to the activation of COBRA usually involve terrorism or occasionally threats to public health. Never before had there been an emergency where the central issue was religion. The question before the committee was simple: do we, or don't we?

The Chairman, JIC, held the floor. "We had the most excellent briefing hosted by GCHQ yesterday, Prime Minister. Two of the speakers are here today. With your permission, I'll briefly summarise the first part of yesterday's briefing, then invite you to hear Monsignor Brogan and Professor Lewis. The evidence is irrefutable, Prime Minister. As you know, over the past year or so, spacecraft from some distant civilisation have been visiting the Earth with the express purpose of handing over to us copies of a book. Most of the visits have been to Russia. The craft have briefly alighted, deposited their ... er ... gift, then made off. In three cases, the space vehicle has exploded and only remnants of the book have been recovered, as was the case with the most recent visit, where the vehicle crashed in Canada, though whether this was its intended destination or not is not known – on balance, probably not. We haven't heard from the Canadians yet on what, if anything, the wreckage reveals."

"Are we absolutely sure that wasn't the intended destination, Jim?"

"Pretty certain, Prime Minister. There are a number of clues to suggest their intended destination was again Russia. Now, as you know, we have been sharing specimen pages of the books with others, even though each new copy of the book appears superficially the same as previous ones. No-one has succeeded in reading the material. Until now. The Canadian incident was unique in that, for the first time, contact was made with the occupant of the spacecraft. For the first time, too, other materials were handed over, perhaps to assist with exploiting the contents of the book."

"Yes, a priest was involved, I understand."

"That's right, Prime Minister. He witnessed the explosion, then the occupant struggled out of the vehicle and handed these other materials over to him, together with some charred fragments of the usual book. The priest was able to form a few views on these various fragments, then fell ill without revealing these views to anyone, though he did leave an account of the events on his computer. A friend of his, fortuitously a retired member of GCHQ, found the account, and later the materials the priest had brought back. He recognised the likely importance of them and handed them over to GCHQ. Both the priest and GCHQ, quite independently, concluded the book was a Christian bible. The priest. by his own admission, had an advantage over GCHQ. He recognised a few symbols on a fragment of paper the alien gave him as part of a Christian greeting in Cyrillic. He's a Russian linguist. And also a priest. In this case, a telling combination. So he made the instant deduction, but had no time to follow it up before illness struck. GCHQ, on the other hand, had to follow analytic procedures. They have actually been able to recover a few words from the book. For example, the name 'Jesus' occurs over a thousand times, as it does in our own bible."

"I'm convinced," said the PM. "And so, I understand, were the others at the briefing. By the way, how did the Holy See get involved? They weren't part of our sharing agreement, were they?"

"No, as soon as the nature of the book was recognised, we told the Americans. They in turn, with our agreement, tipped off the Vatican, realising they would have to be involved at some point anyway on the theological sense of it all. But curiously the Vatican expressed no great surprise at the disclosure. Monsignor Brogan will explain this."

"And things have happened very quickly. That's a credit to the system."

Chairman, JIC nodded. "We felt we had to act quickly, Prime Minister. In fact, it was an inspired thought on the part of the Americans to get someone from Rome to the briefing. Monsignor Brogan, as you will hear, is both a theologian and an astronomer. He works at the Vatican Observatory in Tucson, Arizona. He's also a home-grown boy, right, Jim?" Jim Brogan chuckled. "The approach was through the Papal Nuncio in Washington via the State Department.

It was quite a coup getting Monsignor Brogan here in the first place, particularly at such short notice."

"That's fine," said the PM, "I'm more than happy. So, the big question is: do we release or do we not? If so, how? What do the Americans say? Bill?"

"As far as we know, they're still deliberating," said the Foreign Secretary. "This is a pretty momentous decision, Prime Minister."

"John?"

"I'm not convinced the release would automatically lead to violence," said the Home Secretary. "There would be plenty of refutation, dark mutterings of a conspiracy, that sort of thing. But it's not the sort of thing to go to war over."

"We're already at war," said the PM. "I'm thinking more of communal relations on the home front. It's just the sort of thing an extreme right-wing group here can hijack as their own cause célèbre and use to taunt the Muslim community. Invoke the spirit of the Crusades. That sort of thing. We can do without that. Get the American view on release. Nothing on this from our Ambassador in Washington, I suppose? Or their man here?"

"They're both in the loop, Prime Minister, but nothing so far," said the Foreign Secretary.

"Well, my own view is we should make this public knowledge. Though we're a multicultural society these days, our core values reside in Christianity. If there are others out there in space who share these values, more power to our elbow. And theirs. I don't think there's anything intrinsically threatening in that, though I'm damned sure some will think so. We now need a careful assessment of the likely reaction, rather than gut feelings. I understand Monsignor Brogan has an appointment this afternoon with the Archbishop of Canterbury and the Cardinal Archbishop of Westminster. They will need to consult with their theologians, but only in a hypothetical context for the present. There may already be an Anglican position on alien contact. I've no idea. Anyway, all this secrecy can be dispensed with if and when we go public. I'm sure the Americans will be doing the same sort of thing. Can you keep talking to the ambassadors, Bill? Find out what's happening. I'll be talking to the President, but first I want to allow time for both sides to get their act together. Hell, this thing is important. More important than anything in its potential for conflict. Right. Anybody have any other points to make? No? Now, I'm very much looking forward to hearing from Monsignor Brogan and Professor Lewis. Welcome, Monsignor."

Monsignor Brogan largely repeated the points he had covered the previous day, Professor Lewis joining in from time to time. Chairman, JIC had heard it all before, but sat riveted to his seat again. He could not help but be impressed, especially with Brogan. The man was so natural, charming, and persuasive. Others might have been tempted to move the deference gear up a notch given the distinguished audience, but not the Jesuit. He was saying what you see is what you get, whoever you are. The Jesuit spared his audience nothing. There was no doubt the Prime Minister was impressed. At the end, he said so.

"We are so grateful to you, Monsignor, and you, Alan. That was a tour de force. You've not made our job any easier on the question of general release but you've certainly given us an excellent grasp of the credibility of our evidence and just what will hit the general public. "

"I certainly hope our announcement will shake them out of their traditional apathy, Prime Minister," said the Foreign Secretary. "But I'm afraid the response might well be, 'Aliens with a bible? Oh, yeah? But how did United get on?'"

There were a few smiles and chuckles. The meeting adjourned, the PM and his ministers shook hands all round, then departed.

*****

The following day Monsignor Jim Brogan met with the Archbishop of Canterbury and the Cardinal, Archbishop of Westminster. Both expressed little surprise at the fact of an intelligent civilisation elsewhere in the universe. They readily accepted the evidence that the aliens were Christians, both agreeing that "if people very much like us exist elsewhere, they will inevitably be believers in God." Both enthusiastically favoured release of the news to the general public and both backed the Jesuit's assertion that the visitors were basically space missionaries, clearly targeting Russia. The Cardinal was very receptive to the Jesuit's suggestion that they were originally motivated by Our Lady's request at Fatima, which, through another miracle, they also witnessed. The Archbishop was less convinced. The Jesuit priest then flew to Rome, satisfied with his own missionary work.

Things continued at an increased tempo: only a day later, out of the blue, the Papal Nuncio sought a meeting with the Prime Minister to advise him that the Holy Father would be most grateful if he could

333

graciously consent to seeing him in audience, together with the Presidents of the United States and the Russian Federation. There were some urgent matters the Holy Father wished to confer on. Appointment schedules on both sides of the Atlantic were discarded. A date with the Holy Father of only a week away was agreed by all three leaders.

The Chairman, JIC, orchestrated a flurry of activity that led, early the following week, to a consensus paper assessing the threat that disclosure might bring. The paper recommended release into the public domain of news of the bible after the PM's visit to Rome, but only if his meeting there produced a consensus. Knowledge of sensitive news had a tendency to spread in Whitehall circles as more and more members of staff would be put forward for clearing. Some time or other someone, somewhere, would fail to keep the lid on such a startling development. So, disclose and meet any risk head on. As to the risk of trouble, this was assessed as twofold: immediate, but sporadic disturbances at the local level, and a more considered response from leaders, condemning the disclosure as a cheap, sensational attempt to discredit Islam, though urging restraint. Reluctantly, the PM decided not to satisfy the curiosity of cabinet members not directly involved. It was against his natural inclination, because he believed in full cabinet involvement, or at least awareness through a briefing note, of all developing issues. At the same time, he was only too aware of the need-to-know principle and if he, as Prime Minister, could not observe this, what hope was there for the security of the country? In any case, assuming general disclosure would soon follow, he could brief them on the eve.

*****

Meanwhile, in Oakley, Kathy had resumed her work on translating the bible. She was finding it a daunting task, with well over two thousand pages confronting her. It was not in the least straightforward. Passages that seemed to be analogues in the two bibles responded only here and there to the recovery of specific words as equivalents. The beatitudes from St Matthew's gospel, identified by Father Mac on the back of the single sheet, were exceptions. This was fertile ground, and she was able to add, unambiguously, about three dozen words to her slim dictionary. But most of the other passages she examined seemed to have been edited in some way. There also seemed to be a large body of text for which she could find no apparent equivalent. She soon concluded that a whole army of analysts would be needed. Moreover, it was questionable whether this work should legitimately fall to GCHQ. It was only the blanket of secrecy surrounding the whole business that prevented the work being farmed out somewhere. Other urgent work would suffer if the work remained GCHQ's alone to pursue, especially if more resources were allocated.

Kathy made her thoughts known to Nick Watson. He entirely agreed and said he had already voiced his concern. Some joint working group was probably the answer. If the problem became de-classified as a result of public disclosure, one of the universities might host the project, supported by government money, and with joint GCHQ/NSA supervision. Kathy thought she might fancy a secondment to an American campus.

As a courtesy, Tim, Hugh, and Father Mac were invited in to the office on the Monday to view the progress, and Father Mac, in particular, was able to suggest a few solutions.

"You should be doing this, Father," said Kathy. "You have so much more instinct on purely biblical matters."

"I'd be delighted to pop in from time to time when you're really stuck and you think it would help," said the priest. "But only if no-one took it into their head to remunerate me in any way."

Nick sucked his teeth. "I'm sure the rules don't permit that sort of arrangement," he said. "Today has to be an exception. Any more visits and you're a consultant. You can't keep being a friendly uncle!"

"Friendly grandpa," laughed Father Mac.

*****

Two more days rolled by, and on the Wednesday Doc Campbell called on Tim and Lucy while they were eating a leisurely breakfast of warm croissants straight from the baker.

"You're up bright and early," said Tim, "but then you always were an early riser. Have you had any more of your planned meetings yet?" asked Tim. The doctor sighed.

"Just the one so far. The problem is Professor Lewis is still unavailable. He teed everything up, then I can't get hold of him to give him the feedback. I think he's been tied up in London and is likely to be tied up for a while longer. All he will say is he's been bitten by a snake, whatever that means."

That was a bit indiscreet of the Prof, thought Tim, though there was no reason Doc should have heard of COBRA, and if he had (it had been discussed with some ignorant levity in the national press), he was unlikely to make a connection. Anyway, things were now clearly moving along quickly. But after forty years in intelligence, he shouldn't be surprised. In some parts of the world coups followed coups and there were usually instant meetings if only to decide which side we were on.

"Anyway," said Campbell, "as I was passing I thought I'd pass on something of interest you probably don't know. Young Jenkins has applied to join the police. Actually, his application has been accepted and he's waiting now to go to some assessments centre, I think it's called."

"Oh, I'm so glad," said Lucy, "but it doesn't surprise me. Has he left the paper yet?"

"Well, yes and no," said Campbell. "Apparently, after taking a load of crap from his boss, he told him to stuff the job, and marched out. The boss then managed to talk Brian into staying on, and Brian agreed, but only until he knew he had been accepted by the police, and only doing assignments he agreed to. To be honest, I think Brian is glad he and his editor have cleared the air. He can't really afford to be out of work."

"Well, that's great news," said Tim. "Give him our best wishes when he does the assessment bit."

*****

Just after breakfast, Tim had a call from Nick.

"Look, sorry about the short notice, but Kathy may have stumbled on something – er – interesting, to say the least. I wonder if you and Father Mac could come in for a short while."

"I can't answer for Father," said Tim. "I do believe he's saying Mass about now. He's phasing daily Mass back in. I think it's every other day now. I really should make more effort to go to weekday Mass. I'm afraid I got out of the habit when it was discontinued. It's no good phoning him. I'll pop over and lay in wait for him." And he did.

Father Mac, in theory, was supposed to have a short rest now, then do some light physio, but an intellectual summons could never be ignored. He did, at least, stop for a quick coffee before leaving with Tim.

Kathy met them at the security desk.

"I've got this name I've been toying with," she said on the way to her office. "I can't find it anywhere in my copy of our own bible. Of course, there are many such words, but this one occurs frequently in the large, completely unidentified chunk. I wondered if it had ever come up in your own study of the scriptures."

They reached the office, where Nick was waiting for them.

"Perhaps you'd better translate the name for yourself," he said, "to make absolutely sure."

Father Mac pored over the phonetic equivalent table. "Let's see, we have m, oo, s and a. That's Moosa, or Musa, as we would write it." He looked rather excited, but at the same time bewildered. "Pity I didn't bring my copy with me," he added, "I've long wondered if it might be needed."

"Your copy of what?" asked Kathy, catching some of his excitement.

"My copy of the Koran," said the priest. "If I remember rightly, this is the Islamic name for Moses."

Everyone else looked stunned.

"I thought this was a Christian bible," said Nick. "This throws a spanner in the works. We'll need to pass this up the chain right away. And to the collaborating countries."

"Hold on for a little while," said Father Mac. "We need to test things out a bit more before we spread the news. You said, Kathy, that the name was confined to the large unidentified chunk?"

"Ye-e-s."

"How large is it?"

"Ooh, several hundred pages, I suppose."

"And how is it organised? Are there chapter numbers? And how many of them?"

"Yes, there are headings in their numbering system. Look, here we are. Here's the last numbered chapter or whatever."

"Don't show me. Let me hazard a guess. How about 144? I'm right, aren't I?"

"Wait a minute, Father, they're on a base of twelve. I'll need my conversion list." She quickly found it.

"Yes," she breathed, "That's their 120. You are right, Father."

"This has really thrown the cat among the pigeons," said Nick, concern written all over his face.

"Not necessarily," said Father Mac. "We really don't know why God, in his infinite wisdom, has caused our visitors to unite the two

337

holy books into one book. Many learned people will be discussing that."

"Meantime," asserted Nick, "as I was saying, we must get the message passed up immediately, and to the highest level. Goodness only knows what plans the Prime Minister has for discussing what he has been led to regard as a Christian bible." Even as he spoke, the Prime Minister was being briefed on the logistics and security of his forthcoming trip to Rome, now only two days away.

*****

A frenzy of communication followed, involving the UK, the US, Canada, Australia, Russia, and the Vatican. It was decided that the wisest course for the PM, in light of the new dimension that had arisen, would be simply to defer to the Holy Father and his advisers, who would surely include Jim Brogan, SJ. There might well be some underlying theological rationale that escaped the PM and his advisers, as mere laymen. He was flown out by the RAF under conditions of strict secrecy on the Thursday night, ready for his joint audience the following day. Everyone in the know held their breath.

CHAPTER 35

The PM returned on the Friday night, following the audience. He summoned his three Secretaries of State (Home, Foreign Affairs and Defence) for discussions over the week-end, then reconvened COBRA on the Monday. Among those also present on this occasion were the directors of the three intelligence agencies, as well as the Chairman, JIC and the Scientific Advisor, Alan Lewis.

The PM was all business. "Right. Three important decisions were arrived at by the two presidents and myself, guided by the Pope. First, we release. Both bits, the fact of both Christian and Muslim texts. We also mention the medical pages. We delay for two weeks to give time to reconsider the decision, and to allow any more startling findings to surface. As the ones that broke the news in the first place, the UK will start the release ball rolling, with something rather low-level to test the water. We've suggested a leak to the press, involving just one paper initially, perhaps even a provincial rag. The two presidents wouldn't hear of that for their own release. The penalties for unofficial disclosure of government-held data are very severe in both countries. But we're rather good at that sort of thing here. So, we make the running, then build on it over a day or so. To start with, there is government silence here. A day or two later other elements of the press, the big dailies here and in the States and Russia are involved, as well as radio and TV. Somewhere along the line, the media in many other countries will have joined in, including Islamic ones. Any questions, or comments?"

"So much for the media," said the Home Secretary. "When do governments get involved? And how?"

"I'm not sure when. It will probably differ around the world. You will probably be the anchor man here, John, for official statements. We can also count on PM's questions to raise the issue. Sooner or later, this will get on the UN agenda. The Security Council. We'll not make the first move there, but will play ball if and when. Now let me move on. The second item of agreement concerns the study of the book. At the moment, this is in the capable hands of one analyst in Cheltenham, though I was told the Americans are now contributing some effort. After disclosure, we want a team of about twelve scholars of various disciplines involved. The Americans thought about twice that number.

We said it would be overkill. The larger a team, the more potential for it to get a bit out of hand. Different personal agendas can develop. Little mini-alliances. You know the sort of thing."

"So who will be in the team, and where will it be based?" inquired the Foreign Secretary, who had been over this ground with the PM the day before, but was raising the issue for the sake of the meeting at large.

"There will be very careful selection. We can see the need for linguists, cryptanalysts, and theologians, a national mix, UK, USA, Canada, Russia, the Holy See. We would like at least one Islamic scholar involved. We may start small, establish a modus operandi, then expand. The final composition of the team will be the subject of some debate, as will the base. The Americans made an immediate offer, but I think Rome will be hard to beat. It's central for most purposes. Christian theologians are on hand, it's near enough to the UK and Russia, as well as centres of Islamic scholarship. Hebrew scholarship, too, if needed. Only the Americans and Canadians might feel a bit isolated."

"And the third agreement, Prime Minister?" Again, the Foreign Secretary.

"Simply that Monsignor Brogan will be doing the rounds to summarise the considered theological arguments just before release. From the Christian standpoint, obviously. As the team of scholars develops its findings, he will make periodic feedback visits here and to the States, Canada, and Russia. Perhaps, in the fullness of time, even accompanied by an Imam. Who knows? That's really it."

"Can you put a precise date on release, Prime Minister?" asked the Chairman, JIC.

"I said two weeks, but that meant two working weeks. So we're looking at two weeks today."

"And if you're looking for a provincial rag, I know just the one," said Director, GCHQ with a smile.

Everyone stood as the Prime Minister left, and those attending the meeting continued with their own discussions, laying down the first markers, now they knew what would be required of them.

*****

After Nick Watson had been told of the Prime Minister's audience in Rome, and apprised of its outcome, his director sprang a surprise. He wanted Nick to ensure that the Regent reporter who had written the earlier articles on the episodes involving Father Mac and Tim was also briefed on Kathy Webb's work and her findings, and encouraged to produce a further article summarising them.

In fact, a developing series of articles, starting with the Christian bible, then disclosing the presence of the Koran, and perhaps another article or two mopping up anything else that seemed relevant. Moreover, said the Director, if the help of Father Mac or Tim Sullivan were needed in drafting the articles, that would be perfectly acceptable. After their close involvement in the whole affair, he felt certain they could be relied on to keep the lid on things for two weeks.

Nick was astounded. Never in his long professional life had been asked to be party to such a blatant breach of security. At the same time, despite the risk involved, he could see the longer-term wisdom of the move.

"This goes against the grain, but I think it's a good move, Director," he said. "So is the involvement of Father Mac and Tim. They actually know the reporter very well."

Nick wasted no time in summoning the two of them and Hugh Frobisher to the office.

"Jenkins knows much of this already," said Tim. "Not the precise source of the material, nor its precise nature, but I think he may even have guessed some of that. I'd be very happy to be the one to talk to him about the disclosure, and to draft something for us to consider before giving it to him. We should, of course, let him be free to put his own gloss on it – his own choice of words here and there. He is a reporter, after all, and style for him is all. Besides, it's no more than a courtesy in exchange for a favour. It's quite a risk, though, isn't it? The assumption is that once the first bit surfaces, the disclosure about the Christian bible, there may be some disturbances, but that the second disclosure would serve to quell them. But once disturbances begin, they can develop a momentum of their own, and suddenly influential people get involved and fan the flames. Then when the second disclosure appears, it might even look as though we manufactured it to appease the rioters. Why not release both secrets together?"

"I'm sure those making the decisions were not short of expert advice," said Kathy Webb, "but I'm so glad you're here. The Americans have got their own effort going on the book. Small by their standards. About six of them, I think. But it's paid off. Someone made an assumption and may well have been proven right. She said suppose

Islam isn't the only additional source represented. How about Judaism? 'She' is Sally Goldman, a friend of mine in NSA. We've met at conferences. I've been concentrating on the New Testament, especially the Gospels and the Acts. She's been looking at the Old Testament – only over the last few days, mind, and only structurally, if you like. They only started their effort last week. So she hasn't got into a comparison of text, only chapter headings, or, more accurately, the titles of the books. What she seems to have found is that all the books in our Old Testament are indeed there. But more importantly, after the first few books, the order in which the books are presented appears to go haywire. In fact, it's not haywire. It's the order the books appear in the Tanakh, the Hebrew bible."

"I thought the Jewish bible was called the Torah," said Hugh.

Father Mac intervened. "No, the Torah is only the first five books of the Old Testament, what are sometimes called the Pentateuch."

"So, if the general content of the Tanakh and the Old Testament are the same, both the Christian and Jewish faiths are there in the one chunk of the book. With the New Testament also present later on for the Christians."

"Yes, you're right," said Father Mac, "and perhaps that's what they set out to achieve. But the different order each faith has adopted for the books of the Old Testament is important to both of them. You see, the Hebrew bible is considered complete in itself. The cycle has been fulfilled. All is ready for the coming of the Messiah. Christians, on the other hand, regard the Old Testament as a prelude to some further activity, and this is described in the New Testament."

"So," mused Tim, "perhaps the thinking was – the Christians have got their message across in the New Testament, so we'll give some prominence to the Jews in our order of presentation of the Old Testament. We'll present it as the Tanakh." Tim looked pleased with his analysis.

Father Mac said, "There is some merit in that, Tim. And, of course, Muslims also accept the Hebrew bible. You, know, this book of ours is looking less and less like a bible, as we know it. I suggest we leave it at that, for the moment. I would think this finding is every bit as important as the Koran. Have you had any formal notification yet of the NSA finding?"

"No," said Kathy. "It's just been an exchange of emails, and a promise on Sally's part to go back over her work. Nick and I only heard from her late yesterday."

"Don't worry, Father," said Nick. "I'll pass this on. If validated, this has to reach the highest level as soon as possible, including the theologians. What we must be careful to avoid is getting our wires crossed with the Americans. I'll sort this one out and let you know how this affects things."

"Right," said Tim. "Well, if you're happy I'll start drafting something for Brian Jenkins. It looks like this new development should go in on Day 3 of his series, as long as it's confirmed and no-one says don't do it."

*****

That evening, Tim struggled with his draft of the first article for Jenkins. He decided not to mention anything to him yet. There were one or two things awaiting confirmation. The more he thought about the task he'd offered to perform, the more the reality of what he was trying to achieve sank in. The responsibility of it! At the stroke of a pen, he could trigger riots all over the place. People could be, correction, would be killed. So he must do it gently. But not too gently, or the article would lack any authority. And it must not do that. The government, the church, everyone in The Establishment wanted it to be known that henceforth things would never be the same now that we knew an alien civilisation not only existed, but went to church (or mosque or synagogue) every Sunday (or Friday or Saturday) to worship the same God we did. Should he refer back to previous articles about Father Mac and himself? Perhaps he should. He surely needed something to anchor the new disclosures on to. The most important thing was the headline, though, wasn't it? That either grabbed or did not grab a reader's attention. He remembered his college magazine once ran a competition for the most arresting and improbable headline in three words or fewer. A friend of his had won with "Pope Has Abortion." He could see Jenkins' headline up there with it.

Tim picked up a pencil and began doodling. For some reason, he always used pencil to think with. It was the instrument of contemplation, the instrument of ideas, most of which he would reject. How about the headline? What had actually happened? A spacecraft from a civilisation probably light years away had landed – no, not one, but a whole series. No, leave that for the detail. One is enough for the initial impact. Aha, says the reader, I always thought there were little green men out there. We must get rid of the little green men idea,

343

thought Tim. It reduces a serious (deadly serious!) story to comic book stuff. Again, what these visitors looked like is for the story itself. So, why did they land? Are they benign, or are they a threat? That's for the headline, too. Or perhaps for the subhead? Now, the next thing to consider – why did they come? Very important. This is the real shock news so it must be right up there with the fact of their existence and arrival here. After going over these thoughts again Tim picked up the pencil and wrote, "Alien Spacemen Visit Earth. Donate Christian Bible." The subhead could proclaim something like "Several visits recorded over past year. All assessed 'Peaceful and Benign'" Peaceful and benign? Tautology? No, one word builds on the other. OK. As a working draft, it will do, thought Tim.

Now for the text. About two hours later, after much chewing of the pencil and much trial and error, Tim considered his draft text.

"Whitehall sources close to the Cotswold Regent (*Brian's editor will love that!*) have revealed that alien spacemen have been visiting Earth frequently over the past year. In an exclusive interview for the Regent, our sources acknowledged that over a dozen such visits have occurred, at least three of which ended in the vehicle crash-landing. Batches of documents were recovered at the crash sites. On other occasions similar documents appear to have been deliberately jettisoned for the benefit of Earth, including, on several occasions, a complete book, now known to be the source of the smaller batches. The documents, written in the language of the aliens, have defied all efforts at translation by experts in this field, until a breakthrough was achieved recently by staff at GCHQ.

Amazingly, this shows quite clearly that the book is a Christian bible, though one that appears to contain some additional sections. No theologian was available for comment, but our sources have indicated that leading Church figures are aware of this development and are assessing its implications.

Readers may recall an earlier story in the Regent reporting the hijacking of an ambulance and its subsequent use for the kidnap of Father Donald McNulty, Parish Priest of St Nicholas Roman Catholic Church at Bourton-under-Wychwood, and of his parishioner, Mr Tim

Sullivan, a retired member of GCHQ. Father McNulty is thought to have found some documents on a recent visit to Canada, which, it is now thought, might have been related to the space visits. There is an unconfirmed report that the most recent vehicle to visit crashed in a remote region of Canada."

That will do for now, thought Tim. It probably would not survive in that form, as events moved on and perhaps even more startling revelations surfaced. There were still, after all, another thirteen days to the agreed release date. Twelve, really. Today was just about over. But it was a start!

*****

Nick was informed that Monsignor Brogan had promised there would be a considered statement on the theological implications of the space bible/Koran/Tanakh in less than a week. The Jesuit would be in Washington DC over the coming week-end, jointly briefing the Americans and the Canadians, who would fly down there. He was hoping to fly to London on the Monday, have discussions almost upon his arrival with the Archbishop of Canterbury and the Cardinal, Archbishop of Westminster, before speaking to the PM and his coterie the next day.

"Sounds like you'll miss out," said Nick when Father Mac, Tim, and Hugh called to review the progress of Kathy and her US colleagues, led by Sally. "Though I'm hoping the Director will be present and will pass on at least to me the substance of Monsignor Brogan's comments. I'll let you know what I'm allowed to. You may need the gist of it, Tim, for the news items."

"We may not miss out," said Father Mac. "I had an email from Brother Simeon at Prinknash on behalf of the Abbot. He said that if time allowed, Jim Brogan was hoping to call in to see his friend the Abbot later that same day, the Tuesday. The Abbey would feed him and give him a bed, then get him to Birmingham Airport the next morning for a flight to Frankfurt, where he would then board another for Moscow. It sounds a bit hectic, but, in fact, there was no urgency in his getting back to Rome as long as he briefed all four major players well before news-release day."

"So, are you saying they'll ask you to join them?" asked Tim, eagerly.

"Not only me, but those of you who wish to be there. Doc Campbell, too, if he wishes. Though they can't promise to feed us all."

"That's great," said Tim enthusiastically. "But how will this sit with Father Brogan's official briefing? What do you think, Nick?"

"I can't see it will affect it," said Nick. "This is a friendly chat between the Abbot and Father Brogan to which we have been invited as guests. I feel sure the powers-that-be will not be unhappy at the prospect of people at the sharp end receiving the feedback from Rome outside official channels. How can they be, when it can enhance their ability to do their own job, at least potentially. But I will mention it to Director. I suppose technically we are exposing uncleared people to what are at present classified facts a few days before release, but the fact that the decision has been made to release has to make it OK in the interests of progress. Anyway, what have you got for us, Kathy?"

In fact, Kathy had very little new, but she was able to confirm Sally's first impressions of the Hebrew bible. All the books were there and all under the same names as their Old Testament equivalents. The Americans had added a few words to Kathy's dictionary after studying the early part of Genesis. The dictionary was now held on a computer file in both agencies, and a daily enciphered email from each agency contained new recoveries in three categories: Tentative, Probable, and Confirmed. For every entry in the Confirmed category, a chapter, verse and line reference was provided for the source. The hard slog of work at the coal-face was underway. Tim could see how important it was, but how much more could be achieved with a larger, multi-disciplined workforce. When that came into being, presumably all interested parties would hold a copy of the dictionary and receive electronic updates.

They left, encouraged by these recent developments.

*****

Tim spent the next few days toying with the text of a further two articles for Brian Jenkins to include in the Cotswold Regent. There was plenty of time left. He planned to approach the reporter the following Wednesday, the day after Father Brogan visited the Abbey. Meanwhile, Lucy had expressed interest in the visit, and wondered if she could join the party going there.

"I'm not sure if you're entitled to," he said. "There's a form you're supposed to sign when you have knowledge of what this whole thing is about."

"And you don't think I do?" said Lucy incredulously. "Father Mac's little green man."

"Please don't call him that, darling. You're just making the whole thing sound silly and fictitious. This is a serious development and the world will never be the same again."

"I'm sure you're overestimating the great British public. If this business makes the national dailies, readers of the serious papers may pause for thought. The others will turn over to assess the boobs on Page 3."

Tim sighed. "I expect you're right," he said. "All right, I'll find out."

Lucy continued. "I know it's not a stag do," she said brightly. "That Kathy girl will be going, won't she? She could probably do with some female support."

That argument persuaded Tim to make a phone call the next day. "I know someone who'll be sympathetic, anyway, and that's Nick Watson. He was arguing that the old rules barely apply now, as this will all be in the public domain in another week or so." In fact, Nick did suck his teeth for a short while, but then relented.

"The old clearance forms will probably end up by the wayside, though there may be a new one relating to progress achieved in building the alien dictionary. I can understand that Lucy would be one of your inner circle and cannot help but be exposed to what's been going on. Technically, she would probably have had to sign the Inadvertent Disclosure thing, but it's pretty well academic now."

First thing on the Friday, while they were both floating about in dressing gowns, they had a visit from Doc Campbell, bending Tim's ear about the medical pages.

"I just can't get hold of Alan Lewis," he said. "It's as if he's completely gone to ground. I realise this bible thing is coming to boiling point, but surely there's nothing he can do about anything now. The immediate spotlight will be on three things: theological insights, if any; progress on Kathy's dictionary, if any; and public reaction upon disclosure, if any. The medical questions are slow-track issues, but it would be nice to give him a bit of feedback."

"We don't know exactly what his remit is," said Tim, slightly irked by the doctor's attitude. Campbell had at least had his meeting. "I mean, he is an important chap and I'm sure his fingers must be in a dozen pies." He sought to change the subject. "How is Mary? And Brian Jenkins?"

"Oh, fine," said the doctor. "Everything is on hold at the moment, while his application for the police is being processed. If he's recruited, then after training they'll move wherever he's posted. They want to move in together, but good old-fashioned Megan tells Mary to wait a little, then get married and set up home together properly. She's never accepted this business of living together. Strike a blow for commitment, that's what she thinks. Set a new trend. Bring back the old. Good old Megan."

"I couldn't agree more," said Lucy walking in and overhearing, "Girls should stay virgins until their wedding night." She grinned. "I did. Oops, I'm giving our secrets away."

"So did Megan," said Campbell. "Though I can't say I did."

"Men are such a bunch of hypocrites!" said Lucy with feeling, "Though I suppose medical students are surrounded by temptation all the time. Dozens of adoring nurses."

"Hundreds!" said Campbell with a grin.

The good doctor left and Lucy said, "That man gets up at six every morning and expects everyone else to do the same. Look, it's not much after eight now. Come on, this is one of the days Father Mac has a weekday Mass. We've been very lax lately. Let's get to church."

CHAPTER 36

Suddenly, another week-end was upon them, bringing the usual routine – shopping on the Saturday, church on the Sunday. Father Mac was clearly stronger now, though he still needed a stick, and would probably continue to need it indefinitely. He still felt a bit tired preparing for and celebrating only one of the two week-end Masses, but hoped to manage both in another month or so. He had been saying Mass twice in the week, but, again, hoped to add at least one more soon. They took less preparation as there was no sermon, just a few words on the saint of the day.

On the Monday evening Tim dug out his second article for Brian, and fiddled with it until he was pretty well satisfied.

KORAN FOUND INSIDE CHRISTIAN BIBLE
DONATED BY SPACEMEN
THEOLOGIANS PUZZLED

Further revelations by Whitehall sources close to the Cotswold Regent indicate that among the additional material printed with the Christian bible donated by spacemen from an alien civilisation is the Koran, the book sacred to Muslims. All 144 chapters, or suras, appear to be present. Those analysing the donated material, including staff at GCHQ, cannot reveal how the identification was achieved, but are confident of its authenticity. It is understood that leading theologians are puzzled by the co-existence within the same publication of two sets of text sacred to two separate communities. As work continues, further disclosures are possible, the sources have indicated.

The sacred texts have been found over the past year at three sites where space vehicles have crashed, and some have been deposited, apparently deliberately, by the visitors, who are believed to have briefly alighted for this purpose. One of the crash sites may have been in Canada and is thought to have been the source of material found and brought back with him by Father Donald McNulty, Parish Priest of St Nicholas Roman Catholic Church in Bourton-under-Wychwood. The priest, who suffered a mild stroke two months ago and was then involved in the incident in which an ambulance was hi-jacked, is understood to have made a good recovery and has returned to his ministry.

Not bad, thought Tim. Essentially correct, and full of the weasel wording necessary in these circumstances.

*****

Next morning, Tim received a call from Nick to confirm that Monsignor Brogan had arrived safely and would be briefing COBRA at 10 am. He would be lunched, then driven to Prinknash Abbey by an official driver. Good, thought Tim. VIP treatment. And he certainly was a VIP. He would also be collected the next morning by the same driver and taken to Birmingham airport for a 10 am check-in.

Tim doubted that a professional chauffeur would take much more than an hour or so to get there – head towards Cheltenham down the long hill to Brockworth, a couple of miles from there pick up the M5 northbound for thirty-odd miles, and the M42 near Bromsgrove for another twenty.

They were asked to get to the Abbey by 7 pm after Vespers. The Abbot and Father Brogan would probably wish to attend Compline at 9 pm, so bearing that in mind, and taking account of the Jesuit's punishing itinerary and resulting tiredness, it clearly would be inconsiderate to take up much of the good man's time.

So, at about 6:20 pm Tim set off with Lucy, went back through Bourton to collect Father Mac and Doc Campbell, then picked up the Stroud Road in Cheltenham. Meanwhile, Hugh had arranged to drive Nick Watson and Kathy Webb, both of whom lived in Cheltenham, more or less on his way. Both cars arrived at the Abbey within a few minutes of each other, a little before 7 pm. Waiting there to meet them in his off-white habit was Brother Simeon, with his mop of red hair blowing around and a large, toothy grin on his freckled face. Tim introduced everyone to him and they were led into St Peter's Grange, down a stone-flagged corridor and into the comfortable lounge Tim was familiar with.

"I'll let them know you're here," said the monk. After he disappeared, a friendly face peered round the door. It was Father Danny.

"I heard you were coming," he said, "but I can't join you. It's good to see you looking so well, Father."

"Thanks so much for standing in," said Father Mac, "I'm almost firing on all cylinders again."

"That's wonderful," said Father Danny. "Ah, I think I can hear them coming. 'Bye for now. God bless." He withdrew his head.

In walked the Abbot, accompanied by Monsignor Brogan. As the one who knew everyone, Tim handled the introductions.

"Now, I remember you, Tim, and Father McNulty and Kathy from your briefing," said Monsignor Brogan. "I guess the boot's on the other foot now."

"We're not only grateful to you for sparing us your valuable time, but for allowing us to be party to the same opinions you've passed to our prime minister and cabinet members. We'd no doubt have got some sort of feedback from Whitehall, but it's not the same as the horse's mouth." God, I hope that's an American expression, too, thought Tim in a panic. Will he think I'm calling him a horse? "It's important for all of us, either because we're attempting to resolve the alien language, or to understand the medical papers, or, in my own case, to compose items for the local press."

"Yes, I heard of that," said Brogan. "I understand they're doing something similar back home, based on disclosures in the UK. I think some of the city papers will be involved – pretty big circulation, but not exactly the nationals. So, there are various needs to address here."

The Abbot looked puzzled. "Medical papers? You mean there were other things found as well as the bible?"

"Sorry," said Nick. "But yes, you're right. Along with the bible Father McNulty was also given some other pages, many of which appeared to come from a medical textbook. There were also fragments of a map, apparently depicting part of the Black Sea, but they're not really relevant to this present discussion. Anyway, Monsignor, please don't tire yourself unduly on our account. You must be feeling travel-weary."

"Oh, he's a tough old nut," said the Abbot. "Anyway, we've had a good old natter, and I know now how important it is for you to hear what he's been up to. So how exactly do you want to play this?"

Tim looked around. Nick picked up the ball. "Why not just pick up from where you left off in GCHQ. Your briefing there was very comprehensive. You made it clear what you yourself felt. Your colleagues in Rome, though, would probably only know so much. They would know of the series of visits to Earth by an alien civilisation over the last year. What they would not have been aware of is the recent evidence that these visits seem to have been for the purpose of Christian evangelisation, that they certainly pose no threat and that they appear to be targeted against Russia. At least, that was the initial assessment. There is now evidence of an Islamic dimension, and probably a Jewish one. What can that mean? Now that you've dropped this enormous bombshell among them, what do they think? Are thoughts divided on what it all means, or is there a consensus?"

"We need a bombshell now and then," said Monsignor Brogan. "But you're right. They were shocked. At present those tasked with venturing an opinion fall into two camps. Some – the majority, in fact – agree with the suggestion that these visits have been for evangelisation."

"But I thought the Koran and Hebrew bible put the kybosh on that," said Nick.

"Not a bit of it." said the Jesuit. "In some ways, you can even argue that they strengthen it."

"But, what about your Fatima theory? Surely the Virgin Mary would not guide our alien visitors to urge use of the Koran to aid in the conversion of Russia?"

"Why not? There are millions of Muslims in the south of Russia. And a few pockets of Jews." He could see everyone looking a little confused. "Look," he continued, "We here on Earth only know what Our Lady said to three children in Portugal. We do not know if Our Lady also appeared to those on a distant planet, and, if so, what instructions were given to them."

Father Mac joined in the discussion. "So this presupposes that the three monotheistic religions are active on that planet?"

"I don't know about that," said Brogan, "but it certainly indicates that the other civilisation is aware these three monotheistic religions are active on our planet, and that by some means or other our visitors hold sacred texts associated with all of them. We know for certain there have been landings on Earth before this latest series. Some of them long before. And I can well rationalise that our visitors set off with the broad aim of converting what had become an atheistic society, namely the

Soviet Union, to a theistic one, and more specifically, a monotheistic one, even if this belief expressed itself in three different faiths. That in itself would represent tremendous spiritual progress."

Brother Simeon cautiously entered the fray, with one eye on the Abbot in case he signalled disapproval. "What does the other camp consider a more likely explanation?"

"They think the bible our visitors have been donating is more in the nature of a history book," said the Jesuit. "They think these aliens are so far ahead of us in their spiritual development that whatever sects there may have been on their planet at one time, these have all coalesced into a single monotheistic faith that has overridden previous divisions. In other words, a supreme ecumenism has eventually evolved, and prevailed."

"I really can't see that happening here," said Father Mac. "Our three traditions are as different as can be: all three more or less align themselves behind the Old Testament, which is full of hints that God will send his chosen one into the world to deliver Mankind. They then disagree on the fundamental issue of the Messiah. You're saying that somehow the traditions in force on the visitors' planet at some time managed to become reconciled. Whereas in Bourton, for example, we've just about got the Anglicans, the Methodists, and the Catholics to meet a few times a year, worship together and share a cup of tea. And these are all Christian to start with. I don't want to belittle our own efforts. It's a great achievement and one that would have been unimaginable a couple of generations ago. But some of your colleagues are saying that these space people have achieved the impossible. If so, they surely are more angels than humans or humanoids. I'm convinced that the person I saw was as much angel as person. No-one will talk me out of that conviction. So maybe your colleagues are right."

"If they are right, remember it has probably taken thousands of years to reach their stage of ecumenism."

"So, it all ends up very similar," said Lucy, who had so far maintained a modest silence, as might be thought to befit a lady in a male bastion, and a holy one at that. "Whatever you call this book from space, it's basically a monotheistic Bible based on three religions now practised on Earth, which they can cart round the universe and donate to those they know could use it. Or they keep it on their coffee table as a nicely presented history book. It can serve either purpose. So where is the division among your colleagues, Monsignor? As far as I can see, they're all singing from the same hymn sheet."

353

They all stared at Lucy, then Monsignor Brogan burst out laughing and before long all the others joined in. Tim was always worried at Lucy's capacity for rushing in where angels feared to tread, but she usually ended up on the right side. Serious people took to her bold interventions.

"You must come and work in the Vatican," said Brogan. "We can use people who can go right to the heart of things."

"Funny you should mention a coffee table book," said Doc Campbell. "That's exactly what Professor Lewis said the medical pages came from." He looked at the Abbot. "He's the government scientist involved in all this. The professor wondered if the book was nothing more than an illustrated summary of the use of metals and minerals in various fields. A people's textbook – the sort of thing *Readers' Digest* might put out here."

There was a knock on the door, and an elderly lay helper in an apron arrived, pushing a trolley. Brother Simeon went over to help.

"Thank you, Charley," he said. "We'll take it from here."

Two pots of coffee and a large plate of biscuits were on the trolley, together with milk and sugar. The company found it was easiest to help themselves.

"Charley is an institution here," said the Abbot. "He's the brother of one of our community, long deceased. He has no family ties, and cannot look after himself for reasons I won't go into, so we took him in. If we hadn't, he might well have ended up in prison again, where he'd probably have suffered at the hands of the inmates. He helps in the kitchen and does various odd jobs for us. Anyway, where were we?"

"As far as I'm concerned, I've got what I came for," said Tim, "a general feeling among the theologians I can base a headline on. Just the fact that the experts are thinking about all this and that Rome is consulting with the Protestants is news in itself. But do you think, Monsignor, that the story of the bibles from outer space really will be considered as sensational as we regard it?"

"My own view is that it may take a few days to hit home that we're in earnest about it. I think once the big newspapers get in on the act, they won't let it go, and TV and radio will then stage interviews galore."

"Then I'll look out for you, Monsignor," said Doc Campbell with a smile.

"May I ask you if you think the series of visits will end now that we know their purpose?" This was Kathy. "I mean, we haven't resolved everything by any means. The aim now is to build a dictionary and the formation of this special study group addresses that. We can then feed our recoveries into the text of the medical pages, for example. What else is there to achieve? Surely the visitors will realise that."

"That's an excellent question," said Monsignor Brogan. "We simply don't know what their level of knowledge is on conditions inside the former Soviet Union. With the collapse of Communism came an end to institutionalised atheism and to the persecution of the different faiths. These faiths have now reasserted themselves and overt worship is not only tolerated, it is a feature of life in the new Russia."

"But Christianity, for example, was not totally suppressed," said Father Mac. "There was still religious observance, of a kind."

"There was indeed," said the Jesuit, "but it was strictly on terms dictated by the state to serve their own needs. Leaders of the church became channels of communication between the government and the community as and when required. They were tolerated as long as they were useful. That's all changed now, of course, though we mustn't be complacent."

The conversation turned to the work of the Mount Graham Observatory, and Brother Simeon blossomed. He seemed to know exactly what went on there, spoke of stars in terms of the mysterious labels the experts attached to them and tried to elicit from Monsignor Brogan a view on the planet of origin of the visitors. Brogan would not be drawn. "Your guess is as good as mine," he said. So, much to the surprise of the Jesuit, Brother Simeon gave him his own guess. Monsignor Brogan promised he would pay special attention to that part of the sky.

"I really think we must let the good Monsignor go now," said Nick Watson. "You have a long journey tomorrow, and I understand you're planning to attend Compline before you retire this evening. This has been really stimulating, Monsignor. Not only has it provided us with an insight into current Church thinking on these visits, but we feel privileged to share the thoughts previously communicated only to our leaders. We wish you a safe journey tomorrow."

The others echoed these sentiments in their own way, then left for the return to Bourton.

*****

On the drive home, Tim asked Doc Campbell when he thought would be a good time to get hold of Brian Jenkins.

"You could try when we get back," said Campbell. "It won't be much after nine. I know he's not out with Mary this evening. That usually means he's got some assignment or other on. Probably an evening meeting somewhere. I've an idea it's the monthly meeting of Bourton Town Council. I know he covers them. Try his home number first. If there's no reply, try his mobile. I'll tell Mary you're anxious to get hold of him in case you don't get him. When you drop me off I'll give you his phone numbers."

Tim was in luck. It was exactly as Doc Campbell had predicted. Brian had been covering the Bourton Town Council meeting and was just leaving the Town Hall when Tim caught him on his mobile. Not only was he in Bourton, but on the Cheltenham side, where Tim lived. Jenkins was round at the house inside five minutes.

"Come in," said Tim. "I would have thought you'd be popping in see Mary, as you're already in Bourton."

"The night is young yet," said Jenkins with a grin. "Anyway, what can we do for you?"

"Can you use a coffee?"

"Certainly. Milk only please."

Lucy popped her head round the door. "Hello, Brian," she smiled. "I heard Tim mention coffee. I'll get it."

"Now then, Brian," said Tim. "You remember your stories in the Regent a few weeks ago? One was about the use of the ambulance for the kidnapping of Father Mac and me."

"Of course. Then there was the sequel about the shooting in Pittville Park."

"That's right. Did any of the nationals pick the story up?"

"No. We were surprised. The editor touted it around a bit to our contacts, even put it on a wire service but there were no takers, so he concluded that everyone thought it was too improbable to be true. I wanted to use their lack of interest as another front page story, naming some of the papers that had ignored it. You know "The Regent names and shames the papers who quote know best unquote." The editor thought our jobs would be on the line if we did. Not that I cared anyway. It would have been a great story to leave on."

"I've got a story for you that's even more improbable. What's more, like the other two stories, it happens to be true. In fact, I've not only got a great story for you, but a sequel for a day or two later. And you can carry on milking it for a few days after that if you want. All front page stuff. Read these two articles slowly. You are, of course, at liberty to put your own stamp on the articles. I understand that. Every journalist has his own style and likes his own work to be recognisable as his, even without a by-line. On the other hand, if you'd prefer, you can leave the wording exactly as it is."

Tim passed the first article across to Jenkins, just as Lucy appeared with two steaming cups of instant.

"I won't join you, you'll be relieved to know," she said, with a smile. "I must phone mama before she gets to bed. We're organising a shopping orgy for Saturday." She disappeared.

Jenkins slowly read the article, then looked up and whistled.

"This is an amazing story. And you say it's true?"

"It's undeniably true," said Tim. "Totally bomb-proof."

"These sources in Whitehall," he said with a grin. "Who's that? Some typist called Tracy?"

"No, Brian," said Tim. "Actually it's the PM."

"What!?" cried Jenkins, raising his voice.

"Yes, Brian, the PM. He wants the story disclosed and the Regent has been selected as the vehicle for doing so. He simply wants a little-known provincial rag to drop the bomb in the first instance in an article that sounds pretentious, with its claim to have sources in high places. You know – who do they think they're kidding?"

"Do you remember when we had lunch in the Royal Oak, and I told you what I thought was going on? I almost said then I suspected something like this, but I thought, 'No. If I mention it, and I'm wrong, that will totally destroy my credibility.' So I kept mum."

"Well, no need to keep mum any longer."

"There are actually two stories here, each sensational in its own way. There's the fact that U.F.O.s have been regularly visiting us, and the fact of the occupants being Christians."

"Personally, I think the Christianity story is by far the more important," said Tim. "If people are really honest, well over half of them would admit to a sneaking belief in U.F.O.s. I mean, it's to be expected that they exist. It's only logical, and films and TV have reinforced the belief. These recent visits and official admission of them simply confirm what most people have suspected. But the Christianity thing is totally unexpected."

"I suppose it is. But won't that trigger an angry reaction in some parts of the world?"

"Yes, but probably not until the tabloids scream if from their front pages. So it's important they act upon your story this time. And quickly."

"You mean you want to spark off a load of riots?"

"I don't personally, but – yes. Not exactly riots, but some sort of reaction."

"Why, for God's sake?"

"The thinking, as I understand it," said Tim slowly, "is to start whipping up passion, and then to cause this to be replaced by pause for thought when a second article appears. In other words, draw their fire. And from that point on, things will take on a much more measured progress. Reason will replace rhetoric. Here, read this item we want the Regent to print the following day, or the one after, depending on how long it takes for the initial reaction to get started." He handed over the second article. Brian read it slowly, sucking his teeth, then took a swallow of coffee.

"And you think this will draw their fire? Riots, once initiated, quickly generate a momentum of their own."

"Yes, I know. So does the PM and those at the top who are party to this. It's a gamble."

Jenkins gave a low whistle. "I'll say. Timing will be crucial. The nationals must pick the first story up pretty quickly, but they must pick up the follow-on article instantly. If you're hoping to put a fire out, you have to get the fire brigade – in this case, the nationals – there immediately."

"You're absolutely right," said Tim. "But my bet is that someone in Whitehall will be at the heart of things, orchestrating them. It won't just be the press. There'll be interviews on the radio and TV, questions in the House of Commons. The Lords, too. They've actually got bishops there if we can get some of them to turn up. That sort of thing."

"OK, Tim. I'll try it on my editor. When do they want the first article in?"

"Next Monday."

"It's slightly awkward, holding the entire front page all week-end, but we can do it. I'll just have to convince the editor. He hates having his authority undermined. All editors do. They start ranting on about a police state and manipulation of the press. Which, I suppose, in a way this is."

"Not exactly," said Tim. "There's already a bit of control with the D Notice thing. And you should have seen what went on in World War

358

II with suppression of news, and infusion of propaganda into the news. What we now call spin. Long before your time, of course. If you like, this is a D Notice in reverse. It's a request to publish. It's not even a leak. They can be nasty, furtive things, often about bedroom scandals. No, this is a request for disclosure with the government's blessing."

"Well, I hope the editor will buy it. He may have to come in on Sunday to nurse it through, or I will, if he lets me. I'll let it stew for a day or two and broach it with him on Thursday or Friday, though I will hint that there's something big brewing, which is likely to break at the week-end."

Brian Jenkins finished his coffee and moved to the door. "I must go now if I'm to see the fair Mary tonight. She knows I'm in Bourton, so she'll expect at least five or ten minutes with me. Lucky me."

"Lucky you, indeed," grinned Tim.

"Goodnight, Tim." He raised his voice. "Goodnight, Lucy. Thanks for the coffee."

He drove over to the Campbells' to see his beloved, but he was quiet and preoccupied as they sat holding hands in the lounge. Mary knew full well something important was brewing.

"It's that Father Mac business, isn't it?" she said. That's how she usually referred to the complex web of events she had found herself in the midst of several times.

"Yes, love," he admitted. "Look, I'm really sorry, but I think I need to get home and work on some copy I've got to produce. Do you mind? I might have a hard time with the editor."

"No, of course I don't mind. It's a good job you'll be leaving the Regent soon."

*****

Back at home, Brian mulled over what he had learned from Tim on handling the disclosure. The Cotswold Regent would initiate the story on the Monday, then about 12 hours later several papers in the US, Canada, and Russia would pick up the story from a wire service, attribute it to UK government sources and reproduce it pretty well verbatim. Whatever the UK article said, so would all the others. It was vital that everyone sang from the same hymn-sheet. Those measures, and a few radio and TV interviews to fan the flames, would be the limit of the contrivance. By 24 hours, it was predicted all the major papers, including many from the Arab press, would be carrying the Regent's first article, or the substance of it. The second article would follow fast on the heels of the first. Thus, a crisis would arise, be immediately quashed, and everyone would live happily ever after.

The more Jenkins thought things over, the more his misgivings. He felt keenly the responsibility being entrusted to him and the Regent. He had set to work on the articles as soon as he got home, tarting them up a bit, putting his own stamp on them as Tim had said was not only permissible, but expected. At last he felt better able to broach things with his editor the next day. He'd cleared his mind, and he had some decent copy.

*****

"Sources close to Whitehall, Brian?" said the Boss next day. "What's this nonsense? The copper who stands outside No.10?"

"No. It's something devastating. I know precisely what the story is, but I've been asked not to release it to the world at large until Monday. It's big."

"Even bigger than that warehouse robbery in Ashchurch?"

"A little."

"Look, ever since you began hobnobbing with the police over that story about the priest, and the so-called foreign agents, you've never been quite the same. You've even been threatening to leave the paper."

"Just hold Monday's front page. I promise you, the Regent will become known and respected throughout the world. Or at least the story it's about to unleash. And, incidentally, a follow-on for the next day. And more of the same over the next day or so. Think of the kudos for the paper."

"You mean for you, if I let you go ahead."

"No. I don't need the by-line. You grab the credit yourself, if you like. You're the boss."

"Then I also get the shit and derision if it's all a load of cobblers, like I think it is. Go on, tell me the story now."

"I can't now. I'm just waiting to see if there's any reason to change anything at the last minute. I'll let you in on it tomorrow. And please. You must agree to publish it on Monday. Important people need us to."

The editor huffed and puffed a bit more, but ended up agreeing to consider including this mysterious article on the Monday. That was as much as Brian had expected.

*****

Why? Kathy Webb asked herself as she stood in front of the mirror in the ladies' loo, patting her hair.

Why should that tall, distinguished genius want to spend so much of his time looking over her shoulder? Hanging on to every new word or phrase recovered. If she were to be honest, Professor Alan Lewis was becoming something of a nuisance. He was an unwelcome intrusion into her thought processes. She had complained to Nick Watson, who now spent much of his time at the other site, and hadn't witnessed how intrusive Lewis had been.

"He's really intrigued with those medical pages," said Nick.

"Oh, I know that," said Kathy, "though I thought they weren't all medical, but something to do with the many uses of metals and minerals. You probably heard Doctor Campbell say that Professor Lewis has described the publication they came from as a coffee-table book."

"Well, whatever," said Nick.

"He's coming in again this morning. He wants to get hold of the daily update signal from NSA that comes overnight. He seems to think he's more likely to get what he wants from the bits they're studying."

"He's probably right. They're looking mostly at the Old Testament, where you should encounter a more comprehensive range of vocabulary, whereas much of the New Testament is a narrative, either of Christ's life or the adventures of the apostles. Plus the letters, of course. But I'm certainly no expert."

Kathy sighed. "I suppose what you say is true, though. But I think what he should do is task us much more specifically. He needs to draw up a list of buzz-words that might help him. Or he could even read the bible looking for things that could lead him somewhere – individual words, or whole passages. Then we could try to match them up. He could try the Psalms, for example. Why, here he is now. I must ring off, Nick. Talk of the devil, Professor, how are you?"

"Jolly puzzled," he said with a sigh.

"Are you still working on those DNA pages?"

"Yes, if you like to call them that. In fact, please do keep calling them that. I feel sorry for Debbie. I'm giving her a bit of a hard time. She doesn't really like me traipsing around the country with those sheets." He didn't realise he had touched a nerve.

"And do you think we do?" asked Kathy severely. "We're the official custodians. Just because you're so brilliant, you think you can break every rule in the book. We're working against the odds to try to recover some text for you, and you take the edge off our work by giving us a permanent headache. Good old Debbie." Kathy knew she'd overplayed her hand. Lowly principals just did not speak like that to people who had the PM's ear.

Lewis's face was comical. He coloured, looked both guilty and contrite, yet somehow tried to convey that he didn't mind being spoken to like that.

"Look, Kathy, I'm sorry. You're absolutely right, but it'll only be for a few more days. I understand Debbie will be giving you the go-ahead to get the new material photocopied and sent to our collaborators in what? Four countries. Debbie knows I'm still hanging on to four pages and that I do not want them copied – probably ever. My worry is that someone will be writing a covering letter with the photocopies, I expect. It's important that none of the recipients knows there are bits missing."

"Don't worry," said Kathy. "It'll probably be me. And ..." she looked a bit hurt. "There was really no need to remind me."

Lewis looked distressed. "Oh, I'm so sorry, Kathy. Of course I trust you. I was only worried someone less closely involved might ... you know. Oh, God. I'm just digging a great big hole."

His flustered look brought a squeeze on the arm and a smile from Kathy.

Reassured, Lewis pressed on. "There was another favour I wanted to ask you, Kathy. I've decided to move into a hotel near here for a week or so, so I'll be eating out more than usual. I'll need some guidance on the best places. Perhaps you could show me some. We could start tonight, if you're free."

CHAPTER 37

Thursday dawned. With a certain amount of reluctance, Brian Jenkins prepared to confront his editor. He had to get agreement to publish the article. The task of informing the world at large depended on it.

"OK, Brian, I'm all ears," said the editor. "Convince me."

To Brian's amazement, he had no trouble at all.

"U.F.O.s," he said eagerly. "I've been waiting for something like this. Did you know, there was a spate of sightings over Cleeve Hill in the 1970s? There was even one at Smith's factory. Before your time here. Before my time here. They're back!"

"No, this is nothing local, apart from the involvement of that priest, Father McNulty."

"Oh, you mean that earlier stuff's tied up with it?"

"Indirectly. But listen, here's the real, underlying story." Brian went over everything with him, then pushed the first article over to him. The editor read it carefully, then nodded.

"And we've been selected as the first ones to break this to the wide world? I wonder why that was?"

"It might have had something to do with your decision to publish those two stories about Father McNulty. I mean, of all the newspapers in the world, we are actually the only one to have carried those stories. We knew they were important, but weren't sure why. Now we know. We put them on the wire, but nobody picked them up. Look upon this as our reward."

"Yes, perhaps you're right," mused the editor. "OK, we'll do it. If this is the real thing, it's the coup of a lifetime and we haven't had to wave a cheque book. Not that we ever do. We'll steal a march on the nationals without paying a penny. Leave the copy with me, Brian, and now get on with your other work."

As Brian left, the editor re-read the first article, thought a minute, then pencilled in on the subhead: *Spy Base Breakthrough*.

*****

A relieved Tim put the phone down later that day.

"Brian's boss has bought the bits I drafted for the Regent," he told Lucy.

"You really get through socks at a rate of knots," she said. "I must add those to my list for Saturday. You wouldn't like to join us would you?" she added anxiously.

"No, dear, I'm quite happy for you to choose some socks for me."

"I always have done, together with your pants, your shirts, and your trousers. About the only things you buy for yourself are shoes. You have to try those on."

"Anyway, I need to get on the garden. I've been neglecting it. Things to do with Father Mac and the bible have reached the point of no return. Important people have reached decisions, and a course of action has been mapped out. All we can do is wait. I hope to God things work out for the best."

"You worry too much," said Lucy. "I can't really see the ordinary people suddenly taking to the streets."

"They probably wouldn't if they had a choice, but in many places people do what they're told. And they'll be told that the so-called evidence was planted by the Americans."

"What, when most of it's in Russia?"

Yes, the Russian government isn't too popular either. So it's a clear case of collusion, with the UK another party to the conspiracy. I'm sure everything will calm down when the second bit comes out. You see."

.

*****

As soon as Brian got to work on the Friday, he found the editor pacing up and down.

"Come in here a minute, Brian," he said, a worried look on his brow. Uh-oh, thought Brian, he's had second thoughts about the UFO story. That little matter that we've been entrusted with telling the world about. He went into the editor's office, and stood there holding his breath.

"I'm going to have to send you to Ashchurch. That warehouse story is about to break. Apparently, it's not quite what we thought. One of your mates in the police asked if he could meet you there. He didn't want to talk over the phone. Are you happy?"

"Yes, Boss, no problem. I was doing that thing on the dig near Bourton. They've found another part of the town's defensive rampart against attack from the Danes. Why not send Cindy to cover that? A good opportunity for her to diversify." Cindy was the newest cub. She'd been with the *Regent* all of three weeks.

364

"Good thinking, Brian, can you brief her before you leave. Don't take long though, I said you'd get there by ten."

Brian gave Cindy about three minutes on the background and left her his notes.

"I don't know anything about the Danes," she said, "except that Abba came from Denmark."

"You even got that wrong," said Brian. "They're Swedish. The Danes were Vikings. They used to raid Britain and carry off young women just like you."

"What for?"

Brian told her.

"Ooh."

"Anyway, I'm off."

Minutes after Brian's departure, there was a phone call for him. The caller declined to leave his name, saying the matter was confidential. He also declined to leave a phone number.

"Who was that?" asked Cindy.

"No idea," said Geoff, another reporter. "If he won't leave his name and number, he can't expect me to give him Brian's mobile. Some pretty dim Welsh boyo. Perhaps they didn't teach him the psychology of quid pro quo in the Valleys."

But the dim boyo had another means of getting in touch with Brian. He phoned Doc Campbell.

"It's Alan here," he said. "I'm sorry I've not been around to get your feedback on the meeting. You'll be reassured to know, though, that one of the consultants has been in touch and said how well the meeting went, thanks in no small measure to your handling of it."

"Oh," said Campbell, clearly pleased. "That was an easy meeting to chair. They were the sort of people I like. You just wind up a spring, press a button and they'll go at it hammer and tongs. Actually, there's no need to arrange a special meeting. I've typed something up for this special group of yours, so it'll be waiting in your office. Anyway, what can I do for you?"

"I need a quick word with that journalist, Jenkins. Do you know how I can get in touch with him? I tried his office, but he's out somewhere."

"Yes, I can give you his mobile number. It's just here on the wall." He gave Professor Lewis the number. "Did you know, that American Jesuit chappy Tim was telling me about came to Prinknash Abbey. I was invited. Fascinating. Anyway, don't worry about the medical bits. I think your friends will be recommending another meeting, but in my view, now that we've had a jolly good session, it can wait a bit. I can't see any great urgency."

Nor can I, thought the professor. That's not the problem.

After a bit more polite chit-chat, Lewis rang off and tried Brian's mobile.

"Jenkins," came the reply. "I've just pulled over to answer. Call in about twenty minutes, when I get to my stop but if it's really urgent, I'll get out now. There's a better signal."

"Please do," said Lewis. A few seconds later Brian told him to go ahead.

"I don't think we've met. My name's Alan Lewis."

"The government scientist? Oh, I know all about you, from Doc Campbell. How can I help you, sir?"

"To start with, you can help by calling me Alan. I need to see you urgently about the articles you're preparing for next week. This has to be face to face. Can we meet somewhere for a coffee. Or even lunch?"

Brian thought. "I'll tell you what. I'm on my way to Ashchurch, near the M5 Junction at Tewkesbury. Can you meet me at The Hobnails in a couple of hours? Say 12:30. I only need a sandwich and a swift half. Do you know the pub?"

Lewis confessed he had had no previous acquaintance with the charms of The Hobnails.

He received directions from Brian. If he could pick up the Evesham Road out of Cheltenham, he should turn right at Teddington. Alternatively, he could pick up the Broadway Road, go through Bourton, and turn left at Toddington. Teddington or Toddington? There was a song there somewhere, he thought.

*****

Brian was delighted to see Norm Hobbs at the crime scene in Ashchurch.

"You scratch my back," he said, "and you know the rest. The important thing here is that this isn't your run-of-the-mill place. Yes, it's another warehouse robbery. But in this case it's not a dedicated warehouse. You know, stuffed with one company's carpets, or furniture, or washing machines and other white goods. Just one company renting the space. This warehouse is different. It acts as a redistribution centre for dozens of companies. Smaller, and by definition, more expensive goods.

366

Wholesale lorries come north or south on the M5, take the exit that's just up the road there, unload here, and after a few days or weeks a fleet of smaller lorries, or vans more likely, would put together a load for more local consumption. Several small vans could service the whole region. And there are quite a few companies that use this place."

"And what you're interested in is the sort of products involved?"

Yes. One or two in particular. Automotive bits. Spare parts are very expensive, especially for the more exotic models. Same with computer bits. Then there's beauty products. Perfume and cosmetics. Another luxury market. And our old friend, pharmaceuticals."

"But the drugs would all be over-the-counter stuff, surely?"

"Not a bit of it. Some of the consignments are for dispensing chemists."

"Phew! So what can I say and what can't I say?"

"You can say exactly what I've told you. What you can't do is name names. Companies. There's to be a police statement tomorrow. Around noon. All I'm doing really is jumping the gun a little so that you can have your copy written and ready to go, but obviously you can't release anything until the afternoon. Mind you, between you and me, I don't think they took very much. Some lines of goods weren't touched at all. And there was no evidence of a van to load stuff into. If it was just a carload, then it's barely worth bothering about, except that drugs could have been involved. We're still waiting for the wholesaler to come and do some bean-counting."

"How did they get in?"

"Seems one of them was dropped off and managed to hide on the premises after closing time. He disabled the alarm and opened up when his mate arrived. But so little appears to have been taken it was hardly worth the effort unless it was a few particular drugs. They may have been interrupted – or were just jumpy and only planned to stay about five minutes."

"Still, it'll make an interesting story. We can catch the late edition. Thanks very much." Brian paused a minute. "There's something I'm tempted to tell you, but for God's sake don't breathe a word about it. All I can say is look out for some startling news next week. On Monday and Tuesday, certainly, and perhaps on later days, too. I can't even hint at what it's about, but I believe chief constables in certain areas will be given this same tip-off probably on Sunday. Just in case of trouble. You know, public unrest. Now I've told you, forget it!"

367

Hobbs chuckled. "OK, mum's the word. But I'm really intrigued."

"Mum certainly is the word," said Brian. "For both of us."

*****

Brian's rendezvous with Professor Lewis in The Hobnails was duly effected. After extensive flood damage in 2007, the 15th-century pub had been refurbished and boasted a pretty good carvery, but the two of them settled for a baguette and a half of bitter.

Lewis came straight to the point. "I've obviously not seen the articles that will be going in the Cotswold Regent next week. I understand Tim Sullivan drafted something for you and your editor to play with, if necessary. I've got something else that needs to go into one or other of your articles. I know it won't have been included, because I've been dealing with this aspect on my own. It's really important that it gets included though, and I'd greatly appreciate it if you didn't discuss it with Tim Sullivan or anyone else. He may try to exercise a right to exclude it, and he may well be within his rights to do so, but he's not been closely involved in some of the other fragments. The medical ones. You did know about them, didn't you?"

"Tim gave me a general briefing on all this, to put the articles into context for me. He mentioned there were a few extra bits of this and that, map fragments for instance, but all the focus has been on sacred texts, and this is what will be reported."

"Good. Well, there were some medical extracts and some were very interesting. There were some illustrations. They showed there were a few slight differences in the physique of the visitors. The obvious one was six fingers. I expect you knew that."

Brian looked astounded. "Good God, no!" he exclaimed, unable to keep the excitement, or the volume, out of his voice. Diners at the next table looked at him in alarm.

"Yes, it is a little startling at first to anyone unaware of it," said Lewis. "Now, I don't want you to get very specific in your article, but I do think a brief mention of the medical pages would be of great interest and might help deflect some attention away from the main thrust of the disclosure. All we need say by way of detail is that the medical pages included, for instance, what were clearly diagrams of the visitors' DNA, and these showed some minor differences from our own Earth-based DNA. Here, I've scribbled a few words out for you. It might even be worth including it in the first article. That's really up to you, though." He handed a small piece of paper to Brian, who quickly scanned it.

"This looks pretty straightforward," he said. "It certainly enhances our story and, as you say, might deflect some attention away from any religious controversy. Is that it?"

"Yes. There could be something later on treatment techniques if we can ever understand the alien text." He pointed to Brian's glass. "Would you like the other half?"

"Not for me, thanks. I've got to get back and work on some copy. It's not true what they say about reporters spending most of their time in pubs waiting for something newsworthy to happen. That may be the London scene, or the way of life in a war zone. I wouldn't begrudge a reporter a tot or two when he's in danger, but some of the war zones are dry."

"Perhaps they send the teetotal ones there," said Lewis.

"Are there any?" said Brian wryly. "Must go. I've enjoyed meeting you, Alan, and I promise we'll get your bit inserted. Bye for now."

He left Lewis in the Hobnails, contemplating an age-old problem: should he have the other half or not? Could he compare himself with someone in a war zone? Perhaps there were similarities. After mulling things over with that razor sharp brain of his, he ambled over to the bar for the other half.

*****

The plan on the Saturday was for Tim and Lucy to drive over to mama's in the morning, bring mama home with them, then have a light, salad-based lunch before shopping. Lucy would put some chops in the oven on the timer and prepare a few veg. Tim would then get on with some gardening and come in at 5:30 to put the veg on. The plan worked out pretty well. Mama seemed a little tired, but nevertheless keen to have the outing. She waved a shopping list at Tim, when they got to her house.

Tim knew they wouldn't be doing grocery shopping, so it must be all clothes. He couldn't think what a lady in her late-80s could possibly want in the way of clothes.

"Of course I don't need clothes," she said. "But I do want to change the ones I've got occasionally. They'll all end up with Sue Ryder, anyway. They always do."

Mama declined the invitation to sleep over, and so it was that, after a tasty dinner, Tim helped mama into the car and set off towards the

Stow road. When they arrived back at her home, she was clearly quite exhausted.

"You look very tired to me, Mother," said Tim.

"I'm all right," said mama, not very convincingly. "Don't fuss. I'll get a hot drink, then go straight to bed."

"You go on to bed now and I'll get you the drink. I'll bring it up in five minutes or so. What would you like? Horlicks? Chocolate? Bourne Vita? Ovaltine?"

"Don't be daft. I'll have a nice cup of tea."

Fifteen minutes later, having ensured the old lady was comfortably tucked up with a hot drink inside her, Tim gave her a peck on the cheek and left her.

A phone call the next morning confirmed that she'd had a good night, and felt well and rested.

Father Mac was virtually his old self again, certainly in terms of his speech, and his ability to say Mass and deliver a decent sermon. His limp was still there, of course, and always would be now.

In the Sullivan household Sunday Mass was followed by Sunday roast and when this had been devoured, it was time to devour the Sunday papers, and perhaps watch a bit of cricket on the box. Both Tim and Lucy were keen cricket fans, going back to their childhoods. After college, Tim had played for a local club and when he started going with Lucy, he found she had long mastered the complexities of scoring, so she became the team's scorer. They played sides all over the Cotswolds and the Forest of Dean. The fixture list was based more than anything on the quality of the tea and the friendliness of the pub. In those by-gone days before most young men could afford a car, travel had been by coach, and this allowed them to make an evening of it in the pub and have a sing-song in the coach coming home. Ah, those most certainly were the days!

Almost before he knew it, Tim found it was time for supper. Before going up to bed, he went on the computer and reread the two articles he'd given Brian. He hoped upon hope they would come out right and that they'd do the job they were designed to do. He knew prayer would help. So he prayed.

CHAPTER 38

Tim was dreaming. It was the usual mix of unrelated themes the mind seemed capable of serving up.

The mind was like a computer. It went back over the previous day's experiences, and processed them, committing some bits to his long-term memory store, assessing others as too ephemeral to be worth retaining, briefly enjoying them again, then discarding them. It was an exercise in mental housekeeping. Thus it was that he saw Father Mac limping around the altar and reading one of the articles Tim had prepared. The Communion bell rang. It rang and rang and rang. Why was nobody answering it? Tim and Lucy had no answer service, so it kept on ringing and ringing. He woke with a start. Lucy was still fast asleep. His clock alarm glowed 4.20. His head quickly cleared. A phone call at this unearthly hour? Bad news. It must be. One of the children or grandchildren? Mama? Yes, mama. He staggered downstairs to the phone.

"Tim Sullivan."

"Mr Sullivan? This is Jennifer Osborn."

Who the heck is Jennifer Osborn? His mind raced. Yes, of course, mama's next door neighbour.

"Hello, Mrs Osborn. I suppose this is about mama? My wife's mother?"

"Yes, her panic button went off and the centre in Hereford got no reply from her, so they phoned me as keyholder. I've been into the house. I'm not sure what happened, but she was on the floor in the upstairs bathroom. I've called the paramedics."

"Is she conscious?"

"Yes, but she's not really coherent. And she's breathing badly."

"You're very kind, Mrs Osborn. I'm so sorry you've been disturbed. We'll come over. We'll be ready to leave in five minutes or so. One more favour. Could I give you my mobile number so that you can phone me to let me know what happens when the paramedics come."

"Yes, of course. If I were you I'd go via Moreton-in-Marsh. If they take her to hospital, that's the most likely place they'll take her."

"Good thinking. Here's my mobile number."

Tim rang off and dashed back upstairs to find Lucy half dressed.

"I heard bits of that," she said. "I knew it must be mama. How is she?"

"We'll go into all that in the car," he said. "She's alive and could be heading for Moreton-in-Marsh hospital."

Five minutes later they were speeding off as the first signs of dawn heralded a new day.

The phone call came after about fifteen minutes. Lucy answered then turned to Tim.

"Yes," she said as she switched off. "She is on her way to Moreton. She seems OK, but she's not able to talk properly."

"Sounds like Father Mac all over again," said Tim. "So what will they do with her?"

"Oh, they'll keep her in for observation once they've stabilised her," said Lucy. "It could be one day, or two or three. It depends on how many tests they feel they need to do. If it's several days, I'll stay in mama's house and you can get back in case there's any problem with those articles of yours. This is the big day, isn't it? I don't mean yours personally. I mean all those people this business has touched in one way or another. Even little me." She smiled.

*****

At the hospital they heard the story of mama's little drama. She had collapsed on her way to the loo, briefly losing consciousness and losing fluency of speech. Typical TIA said the reception doctor, a bright young woman with glasses on the end of her nose and a cheeky smile. Tim warmed to her instantly. Her Irish brogue helped. Observation probably until tomorrow unless the standard tests showed something untoward. In that case, more tests would be needed and that would delay her release. There would be more news later in the day – perhaps mid-afternoon.

The day wore on. At about nine, Tim popped out for a couple of packets of sandwiches and some bottled water. They agreed to have a decent meal about noon or just after, then hang around a bit longer in the hope they could see her.

They found a cosy restaurant on the Stow road and had a very acceptable pensioner's lunch of two courses for only £7.95, then resumed their vigil in the hospital. At 3 o'clock Tim's mobile phoned. It was Brian.

"Where are you, Tim?" he said. "I've been trying to get you at home. Doc Campbell gave me your mobile number."

Tim explained what had happened.

"I'm so sorry," said Jenkins. "I do hope she's soon recovered. Did you see the article? Sorry about the slight changes here and there. I'm sure they're for the best."

Changes? What changes, thought Tim. "No, I've been stuck in the hospital. I'm not sure I can even buy a Regent out here. And I've not heard any news, though I suppose I could go out and listen to the car radio."

"Don't worry. Everything's fine," said Brian. "I must go now." And he rang off.

Tim was mystified. Why the phone call at all if everything was fine? He might have to wait until tomorrow to get his hands on a copy of the paper. Meantime, all he could do was catch the news and hope there was nothing nasty happening anywhere.

As a first step, he went to the car, climbed in and spent a frustrating time trying to find a news broadcast. He realised he'd probably have to wait till 4 pm. Most channels offered news "on the hour." A thought occurred to him. He went back into the hospital, found the patients' TV lounge and put his head inside. There were three elderly ladies staring blankly at the antics of a chef. Tim didn't have the heart to switch channels. In any case, they probably didn't even have satellite, where the full-time news channels were. He walked back to Lucy.

"We'll be seeing someone soon," she said. "A nurse came by and said Dr. Amir would be ready for us in ten minutes or so." She looked at her watch. "That was ten minutes ago."

Soon after this, a young woman in a white coat came up to them. "Mr and Mrs Sullivan?" she said. It was not the Irish doctor. This one was Asian. "I'm Dr Amir. Could you follow me please, to my office?"

They followed the doctor and sat opposite her across her desk.

"Your mother is fine," she said. "We've stabilised her and there are no adverse signs. She probably had an ischaemic attack, a mini-stroke."

"There's a lot of it about," said Tim. "Someone else we know has had several of them."

"You're right. We get a lot of collapses by the elderly. If it's not a heart attack or a stroke that brings them here, it's likely to be a TIA. This one is not severe, and her speech is almost normal again, but we need to keep her here overnight, just to be sure. The thing about TIAs, especially in the elderly, is that once you've had one, you may well get others. So you should think seriously of your mother's future. She's what? Eighty-six? And living alone? If other arrangements can be made, it would be better all round."

"Don't we know it," said Lucy with feeling. "But she's just a stubborn old woman."

"She values her independence," smiled Dr Amir. "They all do. You will at her age."

"I know," sighed Lucy. "Well thank you very much, doctor. Can I see her?"

"Yes, afternoon visiting has ended, but there's a shorter one after tea. Six till seven. She's in cardiac."

"Look, Tim, you get back home. I know it's important that you do. I'll stay overnight in mama's house and you can pick me up some time tomorrow. I'll phone you. Mrs Osborn will get me to the hospital and back this evening, I'm quite sure. There's some ham in the fridge. Sorry, doctor. I mustn't waste your time on our domestic arrangements. Thank you again. You've been very kind. Now if you could frighten a stubborn old lady in wanting to move in with us, I'll be eternally grateful. Goodbye."

They left and walked to the car. Tim opened the door for Lucy.

"I'll wait to make sure Mrs Osborn can get you to the hospital and back this evening," he said.

This proved to be the case, and an hour or so later Tim was back in Bourton. The newsagent was closed, but the Co-op was open, and still had a few copies of the Regent left. Changes? thought Tim. That's what Brian had said, somewhat apologetically. He looked with some foreboding at the front page and almost reeled when he saw the headline

ALIEN SPACEMEN VISIT EARTH
DONATE COPIES OF KORAN

The subheads had expanded slightly:

Several Visits Recorded Over Past Year
All Assessed "Peaceful and Benign"
Spy Base Breakthrough

Oh, my God, thought Tim with a sinking feeling. Whatever have they done? Was this Brian's work, or that of his editor? There would be hell to pay! This was not just some provincial rag trying to be too clever. There were international implications. Several nations were party to the decision to make the disclosures, and (he assumed) in an agreed sequence. The press in other countries were about to take their cue from the UK press. People in high places would surely be – what was the diplomatic phrase – he was pretty sure the phrase was not 'pissed off' but that's what it would amount to. He'd be much in demand for an explanation. He couldn't put the blame on the editor and a reporter from a small-time provincial paper. He'd still get blamed for not getting the message across persuasively. He'd have to carry the can. He'd have to accept responsibility and concoct a rationale for his maverick action. He looked round furtively, half expecting people to be looking at him. He'd have to get back home quickly and read the article thoroughly. Would there be any redeeming feature in the text? Any hint of justification?

He left the Co-op, got in the car, and drove home in a daze. He made a large strong coffee, poured a splash of Scotch in, and read the text:

Exclusive

"Whitehall sources close to the Cotswold Regent have revealed that alien spacemen have been visiting Earth frequently over the past year. In an exclusive interview for the Regent, our sources acknowledged that over a dozen such visits have occurred, at least three of which ended in the vehicle crash landing. Batches of documents were recovered at the crash sites. On other occasions similar documents appear to have been deliberately jettisoned for the benefit of Earth, including, on several occasions, a complete book, now known to be the source of the smaller batches. The documents, written in the language of the aliens, have defied all efforts at translation by those expert in this field, until a breakthrough was achieved recently by staff at GCHQ.

Well, that at least was how he had started off his own version. What came next?

Amazingly, this shows quite clearly that the book is a copy of the Koran (or Qur'an) a book sacred to Muslims, though

375

many additional pages of text are also present, possibly
also of a sacred nature. No Islamic scholar was available
for comment, but our sources have indicated that this
development has aroused great interest and its
implications are under urgent study.

They would have to say this, thought Tim, given the headline. That
makes it consistent. And given that the Regent had gone down this
path, it was good thinking on their part to mention additional text
"apparently also of a sacred nature" – no doubt teeing up later
revelations of a Christian bible. Now, what about the last paragraph?
He read on.

Readers may recall an earlier story in the Cotswold
Regent reporting the hijacking of an ambulance and its
subsequent use for the kidnap of Father Donald McNulty,
Parish Priest of St Nicholas Roman Catholic Church at
Bourton-under-Wychwood, and of his parishioner, Mr Tim
Sullivan, a retired member of GCHQ. Father McNulty is
thought to have found some documents on a recent visit
to Canada, which, it is now thought, might have been
related to the space visits. There is an unconfirmed report
that the most recent vehicle to visit crashed in a remote
region of Canada."

Exactly the same as his original. So virtually no changes. In effect – for
Christian read Muslim and for bible read Koran. But God, what
changes! Earth-shattering!

But were they? What would the man in the street react to? The
Koran? Possibly. But the main impact on him would surely be the fact
of the space vehicles, the U.F.O.s, the flying saucers. So that growing
army of what were long thought of as cranks were vindicated. There
was now a government seal of approval. A few foreign governments
poised to take their lead from the UK would be puzzled, but would
their feelings run to a sense of betrayal? Tim could not guess, and he
could not alight on any sensible course of action for himself, other than
to lie low – and the lower the better. He must remain incommunicado
and see what happened. There was almost a case for going back to join
Lucy in mama's house. Go to ground. He certainly had what would be
seen as justifiable grounds for absenting himself from the front line.

But no. He knew there was no reason for him to clear off into a void. He must stay around and face the music.

Having reasoned out his course of action, he felt better. It was his only possible course of action. To involve himself in no action. To do nothing. There was no sense in courting disapproval by making a few ill-judged phone calls. Right, that was it. He would do nothing. He put his policy into immediate practise by making a plate of sandwiches, sipping a hot chocolate, and having an early night. Despite the ache of intense worry he felt deep down, his rude awakening at 4:20 am that morning, the waiting around in the hospital and the driving here and there had together built up a fatigue in him that won the battle for command of his consciousness. He slept like a baby until 7:30 the next morning.

*****

This was it, he thought. Today would be the crunch. He put Radio 4 on and kept it on, listening carefully to the news and to those penetrating interviews the channel was famed for. Nothing. Nil. Rien. Nichts. Nada. Nichevo. Zip. To name but a few. This kept up throughout the morning. The TV 24-hour news channels said nothing. His phone was silent, too. He slowly reached a conclusion. Whether it was right or wrong, he had no idea, but was it plausible? Definitely. The world was holding its collective breath! What would the Regent reveal today? The story of the bible that should have preceded everything? Well, he'd soon know. The main edition came out at noon.

Meanwhile, Lucy phoned with an update on mama. Essentially, there was nothing much to say. There were no more alarms and excursions, mama's condition remained stable, her speech and all her other functions were normal, but in view of her age, they would keep her in one more night. All being well, she could go home the next day after doctor's rounds. No need for Tim to make a special journey in the morning. Mrs Osborn (bless her!) would pick mama up, then Tim could come for Lucy later in the day. Tim felt relieved on several counts.

He made a dash for the newsagents, head bowed, in the early afternoon. He saw a few people he knew well and could not avoid greeting them. Everything was perfectly normal. No-one accosted him. Why should they? He picked up a *Regent* and looked at the front page. The headline was not at all what he expected.

SPACEMEN: MEDICAL PAGES SHOW MINOR DNA DIFFERENCES WITH HUMAN RACE COMMON ORIGIN LIKELY MORE DISCLOSURES EXPECTED

What on Earth were they going down that path for? And where did they get this from? Doc Campbell wouldn't have gone over everyone's head. Only one person would feel he had the authority to do that. Alan Lewis. When would they publish the disclosure about the bible? The medical bits were interesting, in fact very interesting given that spin on the DNA, but they weren't in the same league as the religious disclosures. Back home, he made a coffee and read the article, which was short, but clearly enough to keep the space visits on the front page.

Cotswold Regent Exclusive

Further information from official sources close to the Cotswold Regent has revealed that among documents donated by visiting aliens are medical texts, which contain a number of illustrations, including a DNA diagram. This is said to show several differences with the DNA signature of our own human race, but these are not thought extensive enough to weaken the conclusion that the two races are a common species. Our sources have commented that, following this exploratory finding, further study of the medical texts will be temporarily set aside until all other texts have been examined.

In yesterday's edition we reported that the space visitors have donated copies of a book containing an entire copy of the Koran (or Koran) as well as other, possibly sacred, texts. Other disclosures are thought to be imminent.

What was going on? Had the revelation about the Christian bible been deliberately held back by the Regent a further day, given the lack of reaction the previous day? But where were the radio and TV bulletins? And the national press? The foreign press? He had no idea if they had fulfilled the promise made, but did it still hold good if the UK played silly buggers? Brian Jenkins and his editor had completely thrown everyone. The government had presumably teed up a small army of radio and TV commentators and various interviewees to discuss the donation by an alien civilisation of a Christian bible, and found they could not quickly replace this structure with a Muslim one when required unexpectedly to do so. Whom should they call on? Could one spokesman be found to represent all Muslims everywhere? This was a waiting game for everyone. Everything would surely hinge on tomorrow's edition.

At last. A phone call. It was from Nick Watson.

"Tim? I guess you've been lying low for a day or two. I think we all have. Let me say right away that none of this is being laid at your feet. Seems this Jenkins chap persuaded his editor to go down this different path. I had a brief word with the editor. I invited him to the Doughnut. He was over the moon. His 'spy base' took on a bit of flesh. Anyway, nobody upstairs seems to be unduly concerned. Director had a call from the co-ordinator, who simply said "Well, it's different!" I gather the PM hasn't been involved. The Secretaries of State have agreed to wait and see. Reading between the lines, I get the impression there was tacit support for the change, even admiration at the 'sod you' attitude of a simple journalist. The co-ordinator has been squaring all this with the Americans, Canadians, and Russians. I've had a brief exchange at desk level with NSA and CSE. Everyone's relaxed, Tim. Tomorrow's edition should square a few circles. By the way, the foreign press have been playing ball and there have been a few mentions on local US radio stations, none taking the claims made in a small-time UK newspaper seriously, but at the same time not deriding them either. So the ball is now just about in play."

"Nick, you can't imagine how relieved I am. I should have known people at the top would take this different approach in their stride, weighing up its merits and not looking for a villain. I've been putting my life on hold."

Nick laughed. "You can relax now. At least until we see if there are any more surprises tomorrow, but the editor thought Jenkins would behave himself now. He'd make sure he did. Bible next, then the Jewish bit."

When Nick rang off, Tim made a series of guarded phone calls to the others who would be avidly reading the Regent and wondering what was going on – Father Mac, Hugh Frobisher, and Doc Campbell. Father

Mac was very interested in the way things were turning out. He had been trying to get hold of Tim, but heard through Norah of mama's illness and assumed Tim and Lucy were still away. Hugh had himself phoned Nick, and had been told the bare bones. Tim was able to add a few bits for him. He left Doc Campbell until last.

"It doesn't surprise me one bit," said Doc. "I have a high regard for Brian. He's an independently minded young man. He follows his instincts. Perhaps he's right in this case. As for the DNA story, this must be Professor Lewis's work. As you know, I've chaired one medical meeting for him, but this excluded DNA. All he's told me is that he's hoping something in Kathy's language study might coincide with the text surrounding the DNA diagram. He's an odd chap. Out of the blue he's suddenly become obsessed with this one topic."

"Perhaps that's why he's a senior scientific advisor," mused Tim. "He identifies subjects worthy of some attention, and which it might be in the national interest for him to pursue, then worries them to death. He's obviously one of those terriers that won't let go."

"That's Lewis all right," agreed Campbell.

"Have you spoken to Brian about things?"

"No," said Campbell emphatically. "He's disappeared off the face of the Earth. Apparently he told Mary he planned to lie low for a few days, because his work might attract some adverse comment. She said he's staying with a friend, and so that he won't get waylaid on his way into the office, he's been emailing his copy in on his laptop."

"He's not the only one that's been lying low," said Tim with a sigh.

The rest of the day passed peacefully. Tim treated himself to a nip of Black before retiring, then lay in bed, wondering what Wednesday would bring.

*****

On the Wednesday morning, Tim felt he'd better order a copy of the Regent.

"You're the third one to do that apart from the regulars," said Caroline.

"There's a rumour that you're in there. They've started doing a Page 3 girl."

"That'd be enough to guarantee a few cancellations," she laughed.

Later in the day, when Tim went back to the shop, he was amused to see Father Mac and Hugh already waiting there for the delivery of the Regents. They all agreed today's revelations would be the crunch. The van arrived and Caroline could hardly cut the string from the bundles before anxious hands plucked a copy off the pile and handed over their money. All three glanced at the headline on the front page:

CHRISTIAN BIBLE FOUND WITH COPY OF KORAN DONATED BY SPACEMEN
SPY BASE "POSITIVE"
THEOLOGIANS PUZZLED

"At last," breathed Tim.

"But will it still cause trouble?" wondered Father Mac. "I wish that angel had said something. Not that I'd have understood his speech. Perhaps he could have got some message across with signs."

The trio read on.

Further revelations by Whitehall sources close to the Cotswold Regent indicate that among the additional material printed with the Koran donated by spacemen from an alien civilisation is a Christian bible. Both books appear to be fully intact. Both the Old and New testaments of the bible appear to be there in full, while in the case of the Koran (or Qur'an) all 144 chapters, or suras, appear to be present. Those analysing the donated material, including staff at GCHQ, cannot reveal how the identification was achieved, but are confident of its authenticity. It is understood that leading theologians are puzzled by the co-existence within the same publication of two sets of text sacred to two separate communities. As work continues, further disclosures are possible, the sources have indicated.

The sacred texts have been recovered over the past year at sites where space vehicles have crashed, and some have been deposited, apparently deliberately, by the visitors, who are believed to have briefly alighted for this purpose. One of the crash sites may have been in Canada and is thought to have been the source of material found and brought back with him by Father Donald McNulty, parish priest of St Nicholas Roman Catholic Church in

381

> Bourton-under-Wychwood. The priest, who suffered a mild stroke two months ago and was then involved in the incident in which an ambulance was hi-jacked, is understood to have made a good recovery and has returned to his ministry.

"You've got to admire his lateral thinking," said Tim.

"As well as his chutzpah," said Hugh. "Speaking of which reminds me the Hebrew dimension should appear tomorrow."

"I'm not sure." said Tim. "Brian waited two days to allow time for the Koran to sink in. He may do the same this time."

"Isn't it amazing how one journalist has the whole world by the balls," said Hugh, adding belatedly. "Sorry, Father."

"Don't worry. I share your sentiment completely, and I think that would be my own choice of words."

Tim invited the other two for a coffee, but they had other pressing things to get on with, so the group dispersed. Tim went home and phoned Lucy to fix a time to fetch her.

"I assume mama's home now," said Tim.

"Yes, love," said Lucy, "but despite her getting the all-clear, I really do think I ought to stay here another night. She looks rather frail. She managed to dress OK, but she still seems a bit wobbly. Mrs Osborn said she'd look in several times tomorrow and for the next few days, and cook for her if necessary. I would like you to pop over though. I'd be interested to hear how things went today. And I could do with a change. Wearing mama's is out of the question. It's all very well washing the ones I came here in, but I have to go without until they dry."

"Oh, stop it, you tease. You're exciting me. Yes, of course I'll come over. Just knickers?"

"No, bring a nightie, too. I can manage without a bra."

"There you go again, talking dirty," he laughed. "I'll be over about six thirty, after tea. I'll bring today's *Regent* with me. 'Bye love."

*****

Tim did as he promised, setting off after tea with a bag of flimsies. He listened to the 6 pm news, but there was nothing on the space visits. Just as he neared mama's house, however, the announcer said.

382

"Here is a late item of news. The BBC has learned that reports by a Gloucestershire newspaper that extraterrestrial vehicles have visited the Earth several times over the last few months appear not to have been ruled out by official sources. This afternoon a government spokesman refused to deny the claims, stating that reports of this nature were nothing new. Here is our science correspondent, Luke Aherne."

(New voice): "The Cotswold Regent began publishing these claims as early as Monday, attributing the disclosures to what they referred to as "Whitehall sources" close to the paper. No other newspaper in the UK picked the stories up, but some foreign publications have repeated the claims, including several in North America and in Russia. The Russian press have gone so far as to state that most of the space vehicles have landed briefly in the Crimea and other parts of the country. A spokesman from the Ministry of Defence has admitted the government finds the claims "interesting" but at this stage is unable to comment further. Interestingly, while this statement does not confirm the claims, it does not completely rule them out either. This is Luke Aherne at the Ministry of Defence."

It's started! thought Tim. It's really and truly started, though there was nothing about the religious overtones of the visits. No doubt that would come the next day.

Mama seemed much better than when he last saw her, though she was pretty subdued. Lucy said that was inevitable. Apart from the odd broken limb and sniffly cold, Mama had had no real health problem throughout her eighty six years. It's when a vital organ lets an old person down that they begin to lose confidence and realise they are not immortal, after all.

"I've had a chat with mama about moving in with us. She's not impressed with the idea, but she might settle for the next unit that comes up in Abbey Court." This was a sheltered accommodation complex in Bourton with a warden service and a communal lounge for socialising.

"But I'm not getting involved in any disgusting knees-ups," she said fiercely.

"Don't be silly, mama," said Lucy soothingly. "They don't have those there. It's very refined," she added, putting on a posh voice.

Tim showed Lucy all three copies of the Regent, without comment. Instead of saying "Oh, poor Tim, you must have been worried out of your mind" she could not see beyond the boldness of Brian. Tim became a little irritated.

"Brian was a disobedient newshound," he said, "He could have landed several of us in deep you-know-what. The whole thing had been thrashed out at the highest level and he drives a coach and horses through policy that had the PM's approval."

"Oh, stop being childish," she said. "Of course he's right. He's got more nous than the lot of you put together, Prime Minister included. Just think how lucky you are to have him correcting your policy for you."

Tim couldn't help laughing then. There had been times at work during a crisis when he'd felt he was carrying the whole world on his shoulders until Lucy would say, "Oh, lighten up for heaven's sake. I don't know what the world problem is this time, but get back to basics. I love you and you love me, and that's more important than any crisis." She was right, of course. The old mantra was always true: "Today is the tomorrow you worried about yesterday, and all is still well." He drove home, trying various radio channels, but there was nothing more until he got home when he heard essentially the same item, pretty well word for word, tucked at the end of a TV news broadcast, almost as an afterthought, as had been the case earlier.

Tim made sure he had another early night.

CHAPTER 39

Thursday brought with it the sort of radio exposure Tim had been expecting earlier. The news was full of the space visits and the religious dimension, but there was very little in the way of discussion. The presenters clearly hadn't managed to get their ducks lined up. They were probably still wondering who the ducks were. The "Today" programme was usually the best informed of the news channels and their interviewers the most incisive, if not abrasive, but the best they could do was a junior defence minister and an Anglican clergyman who happened to be around after giving a live "Thought for the Day." John Evans began sensibly enough by saying there were two obvious headings under which to discuss these space visits, the vehicles themselves and their technology; and their apparently religious mission.

"May I begin with you, Minister?" said Evans. "Are you telling the British people that alien space vehicles really do exist?"

"There have been many reports in the past that suggest that conclusion, some more plausible than others."

"We know that, Minister, but what about these latest reports? They carry all the hallmarks of a carefully engineered government disclosure. Is that what happened?"

"The reports are certainly more convincing than some."

"Of course they are. That's why we're here discussing them. But there is no way a small provincial newspaper nobody has ever heard of outside the Cotswolds would have the ear of the government. So is it an official leak? Yes or no?"

"I wouldn't exactly call it that."

"What would you call it exactly? Oh, never mind. Answer me this. What do we know about the propulsion system of these vehicles?"

"Anything that might have been discovered in the past, which incidentally I've not seen even if anything did exist, would be highly classified and could not be discussed."

"But three of these vehicles are said to have crashed. Was anything recovered? I mean, any hardware."

"I have no knowledge of that."

"You don't seem to have much knowledge of anything. All right, let me have a word with the Reverend Stephen Bond, who was with us earlier in 'Thought for the Day.' What do you make of the claim that copies of both the Koran and the Bible were left for us by these aliens?"

"Well, of course, it is only a claim."

"Yes, that's what I just said. Let's be daring and assume it's true. The question is why would sacred texts from two quite different faiths appear together in the same publication?"

"I'm not a theologian."

"I know, but you're the only show in town at the moment, Reverend. The question remains: why, in the opinion of an Anglican non-theologian, would a Koran and a bible appear together in the same publication donated by an alien civilisation?"

"I have no idea. It would be wrong for me to hazard a guess. Theology is a complex discipline and when a comment is called for, this is best left to experts to provide."

"Fair enough. Thank you both for your time. This debate is only just beginning and will be with us for some time, perhaps even years. Listeners are invited to leave their comments on our website. Now for the recession…"

Tim swallowed the last of his toast and headed for the shower.

*****

"Dave," said Kev.

"Yeah?" They were in Kev's garage.

"Do you know anyone who wants 11,500 Aspirins?"

"No, I bleedin' don't. You and your 'Don't worry, I know that warehouse.'"

"Well, they must have switched stuff around. Anyway, I did get a bottle of 'Homme Sausage.'"

"That's 'Sauvage.' That's the one ponces wear."

"Now he tells me."

"You'll be chased all over the place."

"What's the one that makes girls tear their clothes of?"

"Well, if you chat them up properly, they all do. Except that one. What about taking it to the tip?"

"What, the after-shave?"

"No, you berk, the Aspirins."

"They'd be suspicious. We'd be better off fly-tipping. After dark."

"No. Too dodgy."

"I know. I'm going to take them back. Say we were given the wrong consignment. That's the word they use. There's only ever one bloke there and he's working his arse off. There's vans coming and going all the time. You saw that when we went. We may not even have to see the bloke. We just dump all them boxes outside somewhere. They do that all the time. One company sends several vans. The bloke goes off in his fork-lift, then when he's put the order together they split the load up into different vans. Organised chaos they call it."

"OK , let's at least suss it out. Fancy you having an idea, Kev."

*****

They succeeded beyond their wildest dreams. They pulled over to one side and watched the action. It was, indeed, organised chaos, with vans of all shapes and sizes milling around, drivers or their mates yelling at the warehouseman about their turn in the queue, and loads being divided up between vans. There were even two pharmacy supply vans that had just finished. The drivers disappeared.

"They've gone for a piss," said Kev. There's a couple of portaloos round the back. Quick. Half in each van. Then scram."

Their bold action blended in with the general pattern of activity, and they were not challenged.

"What's that?" asked Dave, pointing to something in the boot.

"Oh, it's something that got left behind when we gave them books and stuff to them foreign blokes."

"Do you want to take a look?"

"Not now. We've got to get the hell out of here."

And so they did. As they went round the first bend, they didn't see two van drivers regarding their loads and scratching their heads.

*****

Back in Bourton Kev's Mum made them a coffee and Kev gave Dave the item that had caught his attention. It was a map.

"It's in one of them foreign alphabets," said Kev.

"I think this one's Greek or Russian," said Dave, nodding his head, knowledgeably.

Kev was impressed. "We've got a shredder," he said. "I can put it through there."

387

"No," said Dave. "This belongs to the priest. He's back now. It belongs to him and it may be something he really likes. I want to get it back to him, 'cos he was beaten up by them foreign blokes."

"All right," said Kev. Dave sometimes surprised him by going a bit soft, but all them things had happened weeks ago. Water under the bridge now. "I don't think I'd give it to him direct, like. Give it to someone to give to him."

Dave thought. "That's your second good idea today, Kev," he said. "But who? That McGuire bloke? The builder? He knows him." He considered. "No. No way. I can't stand him."

"There's old Mrs Walsh," said Kev, "and the doctor that retired. Now he's a nice bloke. Or that Sullivan man. He's all right, though he did ruin that game of darts for you, when he brought that nun in the pub. Remember that?

"Well, that's over and done with. I've got nothing against him now." They sipped their coffee and thought about the possibilities.

*****

Tim had a call from Lucy, excusing herself for one more day, and asking him to pick her up the next day. Mama was stronger and coping well, but clearly not quite back to normal. One more day would help all round, mama for simply having help around, and Lucy for her peace of mind.

On the space side, Tim was delighted that Brian had followed the script and quietly mentioned that the order of presentation of the Old Testament books suggested that of the Hebrew bible, though it was stressed that very little work had been done in this area. It was not revealed that that was largely because NSA and CSE were working on it under their Division of Effort. NSA were also examining the Koran.

The nationals had now got hold of the story under the sort of headlines that might be expected. One of the popular tabloids screamed "Little Green Muslims and Little Green Christians." Underneath, the subhead read "Government Disclosure Bungled." The spin in the article was broadly along the lines that in using a "nothing" paper read by yokels as the vehicle for leaking a story of this magnitude, assuming it were true, the government had risked losing any possible credibility. The paper clearly felt its status had been impugned, so largely lost sight of reporting the actual story itself.

388

"Flying Objects No Longer Unidentified. Government Concedes They Exist" was the more measured headline of one of the broadsheets. The subhead read "Donations of Sacred Books Pose Dilemma for Theologians."

"It's All Happened Before" ran another headline and underneath (unwittingly hitting the nail nearer the head than the others), "Alien Plan to Convert Russia?"

"Aliens Devout But Flat-Chested" advised another tabloid, letting imagination run riot. The subhead read "DNA of Spacewomen Shows Halo But No Boobs." Spacewomen? thought Tim.

Tim made a note of all the headlines and phoned his close friends to share them. He could not bring himself to phone Father Mac, so emailed him instead.

The space story continued to dominate the news broadcasts and, sadly, there were reports of disturbances in a couple of northern towns. Both sides felt they had been insulted or "dissed" in the press reports, though their rationale for this assessment was not entirely clear. There were a few scuffles, but much worse happened at football matches and these were quickly quashed. There were no reports of demonstrations anywhere in the world.

*****

Curiously, Bourton was not entirely unaffected by the reports in the media, though only at a reasonably friendly level. One of the most distinguished residents of the town and its environs was an Iranian surgeon, who lived in a big old house just outside the town. His son attended the prestigious Cheltenham Boys' College. Term time had recently finished so he was now home, waiting to fly off on a family holiday. Kev and Dave knew him well by sight and would try to wind him up. They had no idea what his first name really was and always addressed him as Abdul. Abdul, the same age as Dave and Kev and a keen sportsman, was quite capable of looking after himself. If anything, both sides enjoyed their little exchanges.

"Look, Kev," said Dave. "There's Abdul. All right, Abdul? How you doin', mate? I'm thinking of changing over to your lot. Muslim. I'm C of E. No stop laughing. I am really. Someone was saying if you're Muslim there's like lots of virgins waiting for you when you get to heaven."

"I think you are misinformed. I don't think that applies to everyone. Certainly not former members of C of E."

"Listen, is it true they chop your hands off if you nick stuff?"

"Well, if they do, you'd be the first to get yours chopped off. You'd better change your ways. Anyway, you can't do much with a load of virgins if you've got no hands."

"You'd be surprised," said Dave. "See what the papers are saying? It's all supposed to be one big thing, and we're all mates now. Whether you're C of E or Muslim. Right, so come on in the Plough and have a pint with us. OK?"

"You prat," said Kev in contempt. "They don't drink alcohol."

"What, not even Australian lager?"

"No," said Abdul. "We have to keep a clear head for all those virgins." He strode off, athletically.

*****

The best TV coverage by far came with the "Question Time" programme in the late evening. The BBC had by now assembled an intellectual and articulate group who should know something about the topic which, by now, was on everyone's lips.

"Welcome to 'Question Time,'" intoned the chairman, "which tonight comes from the University of Mid-England. Our guests are the Right Honourable John Cavendish, the Home Secretary, the Right Honourable Hugo Martin, the Shadow Defence Secretary, Dr Jamilla Hussein, Director of Middle Eastern Studies at the University of Hartlepool, and the Abbot of Prinknash. I think there's no doubt what topic will be at the forefront of our debate this evening. Indeed, this may be the first programme that has concentrated on one subject to the exclusion of all others. What form these questions will take exactly we shall see. Now can we have our first question, please?"

"Edna Furness. Do flying saucers exist and have they visited Earth?"

"Home Secretary."

"Yes and yes are the short answers."

"And what are the longer answers?"

"The longer answer is that almost certainly for several decades extraterrestrial vehicles of various shapes and sizes have flown above the Earth, perhaps for reconnaissance purposes, and some have probably alighted. A few appear to have crashed. Many alleged sightings have been made of these vehicles and some contact with the occupants has been claimed. These reports have included so many by entirely credible witnesses that they have come to be believed. It has been the policy of successive governments from the 1940s, when the first reports in the modern age began to trickle in, not to publicise them for fear of causing widespread panic. That was the policy from the start, and has remained the policy by successive governments down the years, even though, so far as we know, none of the visits reported is known to be of a hostile nature. However, as the number of these incidents has greatly proliferated and many more members of the public have some personal experience of them, it has become less and less attractive to couch them in a cloak of secrecy. The recent series of visits, reported first in a provincial newspaper, was in fact known to the government from the time of the first such visit and for several months we have been weighing up the merits of going public. The paper has perhaps pre-empted us a little."

"Hugo Martin."

"This is not a party political issue, and so, amazingly, I find myself in agreement with the Secretary of State. The fear factor is not to be overlooked. There have been several occasions to my knowledge when some particular incident or other has sparked a debate on the possible release of information to the general public, but no overwhelming case could be made for it. In the present circumstances, we were well aware of the visits, and we knew that other countries around the world were equally well aware, certainly our allies and probably some countries that are hostile to us, or potentially so. Whether use of a small newspaper in the Cotswolds was the best channel for incremental disclosure or not is another matter."

"Dr Hussein."

"I find some interesting euphemisms flying around. When Hugo speaks of an incremental disclosure, he means a blatant, carefully orchestrated leak agreed with the official Opposition. In other words, a conspiracy. But that's all right. The result is a sneaky, furtive attempt to impart a story, but with a handy escape channel. If something backfires, they can always argue the disclosure was unauthorised, the source was unidentified and if it were that important, surely a major national newspaper would have been approached in the first instance. If the government were sure of their facts, why not share them with everyone? Why not stand up in the United Nations assembly and state their conclusions, with a full disclosure of the evidence leading to them.

There is a good deal that is known behind closed doors, but is being shared only among a favoured few nations. Other countries are being excluded, including the whole of the Muslim world."

"Abbott."

"Surprisingly, I know a little bit about this. I found recently that most people were not aware of two facts about the Vatican. Firstly, that it has long had an open mind about the existence of other civilisations in the universe, but I won't dwell on that now. I expect it will come up later. The other fact is that the Vatican has operated its own observatory since the late 18th century. This has been moved around parts of Rome, in order to optimise viewing, but in 1993 a much more powerful telescope was commissioned on Mount Graham in Arizona. Those who operate the telescope and study the results are known as the Vatican Observatory Research Group. Now, I could not tell you what they get up to precisely, but in light of the Vatican's great interest in extraterrestrial life, I'd be very surprised if they were not able to detect the vehicles involved in this series of flights before they reached Earth. So to answer the question, I agree with the Secretary of State. Yes, they do exist and yes, they have visited the Earth, not only over the past year, but probably on several occasions in the past, going back many years. Incidentally, I understand this latest series are detectable while they're still some distance from the Earth." The Abbot smiled benignly all round.

The chairman allowed a couple of questions from the audience and a little sparring among members of the team, then asked for the second question. This was from a retired Air Force officer, who asked if anything were known about the space vehicles' propulsion system. The Shadow Defence Secretary made most of the running here, but would not or could not go beyond admitting that some general assumptions had been made, but that nothing at the practical level had been developed or was even close to being attempted. There was certainly no prototype sitting somewhere in a lab. He added that if and when any country developed the capability to progress beyond the hypothetical, it was to be hoped that that country would not be among those hostile towards to the UK. The propulsion system that enabled what was known as "flash speed" – that is instantaneous motion – to be achieved by space vehicles, could in theory be harnessed to propel weapons of mass destruction to a target thousands of miles away in seconds. On that sobering thought, the Chairman moved on.

The third question brought a bit of light relief. An elderly lady asked what features they would like to have, or to see in a partner with a different DNA structure to their own. The Abbot said that as he was not allowed a partner, he would attribute the desired differences to his own body, and wish for an infallible short-term memory. Dr Hussein wanted a partner with a programmable compartment to his brain, so that he could be controlled to bring her a cup of tea in bed, or to drive with more caution. The Home Secretary for some reason felt he would like an extra pair of hands, while Hugo Martin wanted two extra brains, which invited the retort from the Home Secretary that that would therefore result in his having two. Everyone was in good humour as the next question was put to them.

"Charles Cooper. Are the three great monotheistic religions practised on several planets?"

The question master intervened briefly here, probably superfluously bearing in mind the kind of audience the programme attracted: "For those unfamiliar with the term 'monotheistic' I should explain that the question relates to the three great faiths that hold there is one single Almighty God. These are Islam, Christianity and Judaism. Dr Hussein. Are the three great monotheistic faiths practised on several planets?"

"I would like to think that Islam is practised universally. When the Archangel Jibril, or Gabriel, appeared to Muhammad, this was not his first appearance to a prophet. He had previously appeared to Abraham and Moses, for example, and Jesus was also inspired by his teachings. Oh, yes. Muslims very much believe in Jesus Christ as an important prophet, though reject his claimed divinity as the Son of God made man. The Archangel's teachings, however, became sullied and distorted over time and a further appearance was necessary to supersede the previous ones. This last appearance on Earth was to Muhammad and restored the purity of the message.

If these multiple appearances on Earth are true, and we believe they are, one other truth must follow: if God created other intelligent forms of life and placed them on other planets, the Archangel would have appeared to them also. And since we happen to believe that such intelligent forms of life do, indeed, exist elsewhere in Creation, then the answer to the question is 'yes' as far as Islam is concerned. This certainly has been taught on other planets and, therefore, practised."

"Abbot."

"I am no less certain that Christ's message of redemption has been preached on every planet where it has pleased God to create intelligent life forms. In fact, only yesterday guidance was issued by theologians in the Vatican on what these recent disclosures might mean, but bear in mind these are only initial conjectures. The debate continues even as I speak. The prevailing suggestion about the existence of what would appear to be a monotheistic bible embracing all three faiths is that the mission of these space visitors is evangelical, and targeted specifically against Russia – that our visitors had been instructed by divine means to return God to the Russian people, who had been deprived of practising their faith under atheistic communism. One means of doing so would be a series of dramatic landings with donations of sacred texts. The fact that all three monotheistic faiths are represented in the texts recognises the reality of the religious heritage of the vastly diverse Russian peoples."

There was a loud murmur in the audience, and the chairman said, "This is fascinating, Abbot, but I think I'll take a few questions from our audience at this point. You, sir, yes, you in the green shirt." He pointed to a member of the audience, a young man.

"If, as you suggest, our space friends have been sent to re-convert Russia, they're about twenty years too late. Religious practice has been restored."

"We don't know where they came from, and how long the journey took. But you're right. They may well be late for their original purpose. All we're trying to do is seek some fundamental motive that may have driven them to evangelise Earth, and more specifically Russia at this time."

"Yes, you. The young lady in red."

"What you're suggesting sounds awfully like the message attributed to the Virgin Mary at Fatima, if Fatima actually happened. Is that what is really involved here? Or rather, is that what you're trying to make us think this is all about?"

"I would certainly not try to make anyone think one way or another. I did not bring Fatima up."

"It was only a question of time!" shouted the lady in red. "I just got there before you." There was laughter at this. The chairman seemed content to let things flow.

"I really had no intention of bringing Fatima up, but I was well aware someone else might. OK, since you have raised it, I do believe in Fatima. I do believe Our Lady manifested herself to three peasant children every month on the 13th of the month from May to October 1917, and I do believe she made a number of requests, including

394

prayers for the conversion of Russia. This request may have been imperfectly understood at the time, but within days of her last appearance the Bolshevik Revolution broke out and within a few years religion was crushed. Whether or not this had anything remotely to do with the mission of these space vehicles I haven't the faintest idea. But I'll tell you one thing: if Our Lady can appear to three children in a rural part of Portugal on Planet Earth, she's equally capable of appearing to another group of people on a different planet at some other time?"

"Yes, madam. Lady in the blue dress."

"You said the appearance of sacred texts representing the three great monotheistic faiths all appearing in the same publication recognised reality – the fact that these were all practised in Russia at this time. But does it not also mean the three faiths were also being practised on an alien planet?"

"I don't think so. It has been suggested that since these aliens are perhaps many millennia in advance of us in their evolution, they may have evolved much more spiritually than physically and have become creatures more resembling angels than people. Angels capable in their worship of reconciling monotheistic differences while not compromising individual beliefs."

"Mr Chairman," said Dr Hussein angrily, "the Roman Catholic Church does not have a monopoly on theological debate, though from what I've just heard, I'm inclined to say 'theological waffling.' Who does the Abbot think we are? How can the three faiths in question somehow merge? This is not possible."

"How can we tell?" said the Abbot gently. "Incidentally, one thing I have not mentioned. While the Archangel Gabriel may have appeared to different people at different times both on Earth and on any number of other planets and imparted his teachings, Jesus has done the same, but has not had to be crucified many times over. Christians believe that one single act of self-sacrifice, namely dying an agonising death on the cross, has the power of redeeming the sins of all, for all time and in all places."

"I think we must move on now," said the chairman. "Remember, you can have your say in 'Any Answers.' The lines are open immediately after the programme. Now, still on the same question. Shadow Defence Secretary."

Hugo Martin grinned. "I cannot match the eloquence of our previous two speakers," he said. "I'm afraid I've always taken religion lightly. I have no strong allegiance to any faith, though if pressed I will admit on official forms that I am a sort of woolly C of E, though in times of danger my belief in God increases enormously. But most of the time I really can't be bothered to get involved too much. I'm vaguely aware that there are these three major monotheistic faiths, and each of them pairs off in some way against the other one. The Christians and the Muslims agree the saviour of the world has come, but disagree who it is, while the Jews are still waiting for him. Whoever he is, the Muslims and the Jews don't believe he's Jesus, while the Christians and the Jews don't believe he's Muhammad. And so, Mr Chairman, here endeth today's lesson." The audience gave him a resounding round of applause.

"Secretary of State."

"I'm Jewish. My family and I observe the domestic disciplines to some extent, though I'm seldom at home at the right times. I must say, I find it difficult to accept that all three great monotheistic faiths will somehow merge in the future. We did have some input on the theological implications of these donations of what certainly does appear to be a monotheistic bible, for want of a better term. One other theory put forward not mentioned by the Abbot, but one which I find reconciles the facts much more happily, is that the bible does not, in fact, indicate current worship practices on the planet our visitors come from, but is more in the nature of a history of monotheistic worship down the ages on their own planet, or a description of current practise on Earth. In other words, a sort of coffee-table book, and it was actually called this by one of our number."

There was scattered applause for this contribution. Tim was glad the Home Secretary had mentioned this alternative suggestion. It was a welcome escape route for those who did not want to see one faith pitted against another. Tim was a committed Christian, but had long accepted that God Himself had pointed out other roads that led to Him, and that, therefore, He would know how these were to be reconciled.

The last question had spawned a great deal of audience reaction, and the Chairman permitted many more comments from the audience than normal, but it made for good television. These were serious issues that had got the whole nation talking and this was the first really good airing they had received.

At the end, Tim felt relieved. There were differences of opinion expressed, naturally, but no nasty confrontations. In other words, nothing that might be seen as capable of inciting violent action. He went thankfully to bed.

CHAPTER 40

Kathy Webb was doggedly making inroads into the alien bible. She now had four intelligence analysts to assist her, all of whom were also first-rate linguists, two Russian, one Chinese, and an Arabist. The New Testament did not seem to offer as much scope for adding to the dictionary as did the Old Testament, many parts of which were contemplative in nature and therefore likely to contain similar word usage. At any rate, most of the recoveries were coming from Sally and her party in NSA.

Nick stuck his head round the door.

"Could you pop in for a moment, Kathy?" He said.

Nick closed the door behind him. This was an unusual gesture.

"I'm not sure who was negotiating with whom, but it went to a very high level. I was asked for an input in the first instance, but that's all. There are still some posts to be agreed, but the joint study party that was mooted now has official blessing. There are to be twelve in the team initially, with an option to expand. The team leader will be a Russian. We would like you to be his deputy. The team will be based in Rome. What do you say?"

Kathy blushed with pleasure. "I suppose I should say 'May I think about it?' but I'm pretty sure what my answer will be. I'd be delighted. Do you know any more at this stage. Duties and so on?"

"It's still being thrashed out, but it looks as if there will be two study parties, one of six people plus a supervisor, probably your friend Sally Goldman, and looking at the Old and New Testaments, and another of three people looking at the Koran. I don't have a name for the Muslim scholar who will be in charge of that little group, and as for the members of the study parties, they have yet to be decided There will certainly be a member of the Vatican staff involved. By the way, for convenience you'll be diplomats accredited to the appropriate embassies with, in your case, First Secretary status."

"And what will my terms of reference be? What exactly will the job consist of?"

"It will, in my view, be the most important job of all. Consolidation. Studying the suggested recoveries across the board, adding to the dictionary, suggesting the order of study, and perhaps playing the recoveries against other texts, such as the medical book or whatever it is."

Kathy pondered. "Ye-es, I can see that would be an important job. And best done across the board by someone not bogged down by one narrow bit of text. Hmm. Yes. The more I think of it, the more it appeals to me. Thank you for your input to the decision."

"It was backed very forcefully by Professor Lewis. He's the one with the clout. By the way, he'll be in later."

"He's a bit of a nuisance sometimes, but at heart he's a dear."

"Then I'll pass your reaction on as a positive maybe," grinned Nick, quoting his favourite mangler of the English Language, Sam Goldwyn. "Right, you can carry on the good work now."

*****

While Kathy was ensconced with Nick Watson behind closed doors in M Block that Friday morning, Alan Lewis was just arriving for a meeting with a fellow scientist also in the pay of HM Government but with a somewhat different remit. Although they had seen each other from time to time at various scientific gatherings, they had not previously had any close dealings with each other.

"Good of you to see me," said Lewis, shaking hands, "especially as I was so vague on the phone."

"Your status and reputation speak volumes," said Dr Phil Ramsey. "It's a pleasure to meet you properly. Do sit down. I saw you arrive so took the liberty of arranging coffee. Now, what can I do for you?"

"The fact is I need to fly a kite and not be shouted down in derision," said the professor, "and, as I said on the phone, you seemed just the chap to approach. You have the right professional credentials, and although you're not a member of the ELK TWO Committee, you're on the ELK TWO list. You've been cleared for receiving their reports. You also come under M.O.D. and you have close contacts with the right bits of industry, like British Aerospace. By the way are we Tempested?"

"Yes, no problem," said Ramsey, confirming that the room had been electronically swept and found to be free of hidden monitoring devices. "Coffee is about to arrive, so we'll wait for that before we get started."

Even as he spoke, a knock on the door signalled the arrival of coffee.

After a few sips Lewis began. "I'll get straight to the point. This is an ELK matter, but strictly ELK TWO, so it has nothing to do directly with the so-called multi-faith bible from outer space, several copies of which have come to us over the past year. There could be a tenuous connection, I suppose. Much depends on what the translators find. Anyway, that is largely ELK ONE stuff.

"I'm probably not making myself terribly clear so far. Let me press on. Now, you'll know that the last alien visit, which resulted in the vehicle crashing and exploding in a remote region of Canada, was unique in that contact was made by a Catholic priest with the pilot of the vehicle."

"Yes, I heard that," said Ramsey. "I got a short summary of this encounter from the ELK TWO Committee."

Lewis smiled. "Good. Anyway, going back to the pilot. So far as we know, he was the sole occupant. As you will know, it's the view of both the ELK ONE and TWO Committees that if a vehicle crashes and the pilot survives, he must ensure the propulsion unit is destroyed. There would almost certainly be a self-destruct mechanism that is easily activated. We assume there is a time-delay that can be set to allow the occupant to enter a preservation chamber. Now, shortly after this last vehicle crashed, there was evidently an on-board explosion, though probably not the propulsion unit at that time.

The priest was by now approaching the vehicle, and saw a hatch open and the occupant emerge through the smoke, carrying the charred remnants of a large book – the bible, of course, though completely unidentified at the time. There were also some map fragments and a separate single sheet of paper, poster size. He gave all this to the priest, who on impulse gave the visitor a sheet of paper containing prayers for the dying he had brought to the site. The two of them tried to converse, but with only limited success. The visitor looked at the priest's paper with great interest and became very animated. He even tried, unsuccessfully, to pronounce some words. Then, apparently as an afterthought, he re-entered his craft, and came out with another bundle of papers. He handed these to the priest, then returned inside, urging the priest with signs that he should leave the crash site as quickly as possible. Shortly afterwards, there was a huge explosion, this time presumably the self-destruct mechanism of the propulsion unit.

Examination of the additional documents showed that the map fragments ..."

"Contained bits of the Black Sea, wasn't it?" said Ramsey. Lewis nodded.

"Russia appears to have been the target for their evangelising," he said.

"Now, I hadn't heard that officially, but I'd assumed that was the case, in view of the large number of space visits with Russia as the apparent destination. Evangelising, eh? This is fascinating."

"The single sheet," continued Lewis, "contained on one side a mass of alien writing, organised into two groupings of ten and nine sentences, or propositions as they have been called. Leaping ahead, I can tell you these have been confirmed as the Ten Commandments, and the Beatitudes from the Sermon on the Mount."

Ramsey whistled. "I'll refrain from an expletive here, in view of the context," he said with a grin. "The ELK ONE lot get all the fun, don't they? You've no idea the gaps you're filling in."

"Much of it is down to the priest and a very clever lady from GCHQ," said Lewis. "The priest had an insight into this right from the start, because on the back of that single sheet were a group of letters not in the alien script, but evidently in Roman script. In the event, they turned out to be in the Cyrillic alphabet, some of whose characters are similar to Roman. The priest is a Russian linguist, and was able to reconstruct the group of letters into the Easter greeting used by members of the Orthodox Church. Indeed by many Russians now, I would think. The greeting is simply 'Christ has risen' and the response is 'He has risen indeed.' So the priest guessed right from the start that he had a Christian bible on his hands, though later this turned out to be only a part of the book. Anyway, all that is largely by the way. The matter I really want to involve you with is the other thing he was given by the alien. You'll have heard about that."

Ramsey nodded. "The medical pages. Yes, I've seen a copy of these, though mainly the diagrams of the body and the possible DNA structure. There were other diagrams I didn't understand. There had obviously been a good bit of surrounding text but this had largely been obliterated as unintelligible to mere scientists and engineers. I believe you've made some progress on these medical diagrams."

"Yes. I involved in the first instance a GP-friend of the priest. Nice chap. He had a meeting with some medical consultants and a metallurgist and they're pretty sure some of the diagrams depict various conditions being treated with electro-magnetic fields, either using the natural electro-magnetism of the planet or generated with an outside power supply. For some conditions, the patient lies prone or supine, for others he is suspended various distances from the floor or bed. The different variables involved – choice of metal conductor, strength of current, way the patient faces, height of suspension, if any, and particularly the choice of body parts to cover and to what depth together seem to add up to a menu for treating all sorts of conditions."

"How amazing," said Ramsey, impressed. "It's almost like acupuncture. But I would urge caution. What works on one planet may not work on another."

"You're absolutely right," said Lewis. "But I'm getting near the crux of the matter now. What seemed at first sight to be part of a medical textbook may not be exactly that. You just said that you didn't understand some of the diagrams. Well, I'm not surprised. After closer scrutiny, it has become apparent that other themes are also present: there were illustrations that seemed to suggest, for example, construction work, and various modes of travel, including a vehicle with a configuration similar to those that crashed. Indeed, someone has suggested that the pages come from what we would call a coffee-table book describing the different uses of metals in general or perhaps of certain conductive metals in particular."

Ramsey grinned. "Well, it's one view. Do you agree?"

Lewis went on. "I'm not sure. There were not many pages to go on, no more than about forty. These were perhaps all that survived the first explosion. With our knowledge of the alien numbering system we were able to conclude that the forty-odd pages came from all over what was evidently a much larger book, certainly one of approaching three hundred pages. As you now know, we have come to some pretty reliable conclusions about some of the genuine medical illustrations."

"You say 'genuine medical illustrations.' Were there others that were not genuine?"

"There was one in particular we first took to be medical, or rather physiological, in nature, but which I now think was anything but. This is the apparent DNA diagram you referred to just now. Based purely on page numbering, we found it was separated by more than a hundred pages from the genuine medical pages, and that the travel portion of the book came just before the apparent DNA diagram."

"So are you saying they're linked?"

"I'm very tempted to think so. Take another look at that so-called DNA diagram." He fished in his briefcase. "I've got a better version here than you will have seen. Study it."

Ramsey studied the diagram long and hard, as he knew Lewis would wish him to.

"Well," he finally concluded, "It's certainly a double helix, though not the stick and ball DNA representation we're used to. It's confined in a sort of tube with just a few lines sticking out and leading into what looks like some sort of box. But there's only the top of the box showing."

"Good," said Lewis, warming to his theme. "Leading into a box, yes. Now turn over a page. What do you see?"

"It looks like the lower part of the same box disappearing into something else. This seems to go through some sort of wall, then gets swallowed up in a series of concentric rings." Ramsey turned to Lewis. "We didn't receive this picture."

"No, we only sent sample extracts to most people, just to give them an idea of what we were talking about when we referred to 'medical pages.' I deliberately kept back the ones you're looking at now. Now turn over one more page."

Ramsey did so. "Yes. We didn't receive this one either. Well, this shows the whole assembly, I suppose. This time the double helix is glowing and ...... Good God! I think I can see what you're suggesting."

"So, where else have you seen something configured as a double helix?"

"Theoretical papers on propulsion systems employed on alien space vehicles. But these are purely speculative. A beam of electro-magnetic energy is projected ahead allegedly as a propeller for the craft to ride on. It's said to consist of revolving pulses of hot ionised gases...."

"Plasma," said Lewis.

"Exactly," said Ramsey, "Plasma. A double-helical plasma flow propelled ahead and said to be thousands of times more efficient than a source of power thrusting from behind. Each pulse is no more than about half a kilometre in length and is renewed hundreds of thousands of times a second. This system supposedly permits speeds approaching that of light, or what some people call flash speed or hyper-drive."

"I knew I could count on you, if anyone."

"But has no-one else made the connection?" asked Ramsey. "I mean, I've no idea if your conjecture is right or wrong. There's a huge difference between the imaginings, however brilliant, of a group of scientists and the reality of it. Now what about all the the text surrounding those diagrams? There's text on every page. I don't suppose you can make anything of that?"

"Ay, there's the rub," said Lewis. "We have recovered the sounds of the letters, or at least approximations of them, a few proper nouns and even a few possible translations of single words. By 'we' I mean small groups of people in the UK and USA. Obviously, I can't read the text that goes with the diagrams, but I think I can guess what sort of text it is. I know, for instance, that many of the characters are numbers. Some of the others are letters, occurring singly or in small groups, but there are yet others we've seen nowhere else. They appear to be neither numbers nor letters. Look, I've converted all this text to the extent that I can with the help of my friend at GCHQ. Of course, it's all totally meaningless, especially as numerically our visitors are on a base of twelve, and the letters can only be represented as possible sounds based on Cyrillic place-names. Also, as I said, there are bits that are neither one thing nor another." He fished in his briefcase and came out with a dog-eared sheet covered in rows of text, with underlining at intervals. "There. What do you make of all that?"

Ramsey studied the paper at some length.

Take your time," said Lewis, "this is important."

"If I were to make a wild guess ..." began Ramsey.

"Oh, please do," urged Lewis. "In a way, the wilder the better."

"So," mused Ramsay, "we've got letters, numbers, and some characters that are neither, all mixed up together. Well, I'd say that with that sort of structure, these are formulae, or scientific equations."

Lewis emitted a long sigh. "Good man!" he enthused. "Oh, you wonderful chap. I know you're bang on target." He clapped Ramsey on the back. "So then, how do you assess the bits that are neither numbers nor letters?"

"They've got to be mathematical symbols – plus, minus, roots, and so on, and physical constants, some perhaps rendered in another alphabet, as we do on Earth with Greek."

Lewis's face was wreathed in smiles. "I'm so glad I came to see you. Your assessment exactly parallels my own. Arrived at totally independently. We must be right."

"And you think this study of the language in GCHQ and by the Americans will help you resolve these equations or whatever?" said Ramsey doubtfully. "Two small groups of analysts, I think you said. I mean it sounds like a very small hammer to crack an enormous coconut."

"You're right, but all that will soon change. There are plans to increase the effort with the addition of several others, and basing the team in one location. The plan is to make it international and inter-denominational."

"So there'll be Christian, Muslim, and Jewish scholars all rubbing shoulders. And these will include Brits, Americans, Russians, Canadians, Arabs, and what, perhaps Aussies. Whew, that will take some controlling. It will also take some special skills to prevent the wrong people from learning what you and I believe is the true significance of the so-called DNA pages. If our conjecture is anywhere near the truth, of course."

"Well, fortunately, only the so-called multi-faith bible will be there. Several copies of it. We will, of course, carry on with our study of the so-called medical pages here as, no doubt, will those countries involved in the data-exchange arrangement using the feedback that will come from the team. The only difference will be that we will also have the four pages that I removed before the remnants of the book were copied. To be honest, although the huge increase in effort may well help in the compilation of some sort of dictionary, which in turn might assist in the understanding of the medical pages, I can't really see it helping with the formulae we have here. So that's where we stand. We're on our own. I hope you don't mind me including you in this. You've been an enormous help, and I do hope you can spend more time with the problem. Why don't I photocopy my converted version for you. If that's all it is with no labels, I can't see it being classified. But I'll get the proper permission, of course. Mind you, I've still got to sell these suspicions to the powers-that-be, but you've given me the confidence to go ahead, and I really do appreciate it."

"You're most welcome," said Ramsey. "I'm glad to have been of help, and I feel privileged that you chose me as a sounding-board. I really do think you're on to something. I look forward to seeing you again, after we've both had a long hard look at this stuff. Good luck with the powers-that-be!"

"If we really are on to something," said Lewis, "one day you and your colleagues will be modelling something clever in the lab."

The professor bade farewell to Phil Ramsey, and set off for Cheltenham to see Kathy and/or Nick before the working day ended, to check on recoveries. En route, he got hold of the office of the Secretary of State for Defence.

"He won't thank me for this, but could you please tell him it's urgent. I want about ten or fifteen minutes with him tomorrow, in his shirt-sleeves in the garden if necessary. Nothing formal, and any time to suit him."

The professor got his wish, then called into M Block, where Kathy brought him up to speed and agreed to have dinner with him.

CHAPTER 41

The next day, Professor Lewis was shown into the Secretary of State's study at his private residence near Buckingham.

He went through the sequence of reasoning leading to his conclusion about the propulsion system. He inevitably had to take things a little more slowly than with Phil Ramsey the previous day, but the Minister had a good mind, and soon appreciated the importance of Lewis's conjecture.

"So if you're correct, we could even crack the problem of flash-speed travel. But then, so could others. We'd work with the Americans, anyway, and the Canadians, but what about the Russians, for example? They will have the medical pages, as we're calling them. We may have to bring them into the circle, as we did with the original sharing agreement, especially as we've agreed for the team in Rome to be headed by a Russian. Some of the others in that team may be a problem, too. We'll need to make sure there's no loose talk when we get that thing going."

"I have to confess to a small oversight, Secretary," said Lewis, looking suitably contrite. "The page with the double-helix was copied to everyone, but not the four pages that followed. They were omitted. Incidentally, I'm in hot water with Debbie on the JIC staff for hanging on to these pages. She's right of course, but it is these four pages that suggest the diagram is not related to DNA, and might instead have a bearing on propulsion. Moreover, I ensured that the local paper in Cheltenham that first carried the story of the space visits included the reference to DNA. This was to leave the impression that that's what we were assuming the diagram was portraying. If our removal of the pages were to come to light, it could be argued that we were reluctant to give wide exposure to what might well prove to be a crack-brained idea by a mad scientist. If we prove to be right, we can then decide who to bring into our confidence."

"Don't feel guilty, Alan. That's a perfectly sound course of action. Now, thinking about that last visit, the vehicle that crashed, it would seem that our space friends were pretty relaxed about giving the medical pages to the Russians. After all, they had no way of knowing they were not in Russia."

"On the contrary, Minister, I think they knew they were not in Russia, though not until after they had crash-landed. They had made several successful landings in Russia, dropping off the multi-faith bible, but one thing they could not accurately gauge was how effective their visits were. They were hoping the visits would lead to a revival of religion. They must have been aware of the fall of communism and felt this would now automatically occur. But, of course, their bibles were unintelligible. They might as well have been textbooks of some sort. Those finding the bibles needed a bit of help. So for what turned out to be their ill-fated landing in Canada, the visitors had included on board what they thought was a crib to recognising and understanding the bible, namely a poster containing the Russian Easter greeting on one side and the Ten Commandments and Beatitudes on the other. And the map fragments, of course."

"And that was exactly what led the priest to recognise that he had been given fragments of a Christian bible or missal perhaps," said the Secretary.

"Exactly," said Lewis. "Kathy in GCHQ had to work harder, but got the same result. In fact, she was able to go a lot further, because she had a bit of computer assistance. And in any case, by now the priest was in hospital. But back to the crash in Canada. After the occupant had studied the priest's prayers for the dying and had also seen the park notices, then and only then was he moved to go back inside and bring out the so-called medical pages, which actually included what was probably a brief summary of flash-speed propulsion. He did this because of the writing in the priest's prayers and on the park notices. He may not have recognised these as being in English, but he at least knew by then he was not in Russia, a country with an evil reputation, which he had no way of knowing was or was not still justified. Yes, I'm sure that was it. The occupant and his colleagues were clearly uncertain about Russia and her intentions. Did she still pose a threat to world peace? Perhaps it would be prudent to give someone else a leg up technologically and this was the opportunity. He stopped short of technical manuals. In any case, they probably existed only as computer-held data and within the propulsion unit itself. All he had was this popular science book, a sort of technical encyclopaedia, perhaps one of a series. Even though it contained various formulae or equations, it could still have been regarded as a recreational item. We're dealing with a civilisation so far in advance of us technologically that they have probably been travelling at flash speed for thousands of years, and their children learn these sort of equations in kindergarten. Like our kids learn their tables, or at least used to in my day. I'm sure this general science book was not intended to be destroyed, but in the event it was badly damaged, so he simply handed over what few pages had survived."

"And this was to help the West develop a capability that would enable them to retain control?"

"That's right. Mind you, Minister, I really have no idea how much grasp our alien friend had of the geo-political position here on Earth, but I do think he was also impressed by the priest's general demeanour. Here was a gentle person, a compassionate person, someone from a society he could trust. All this is pure speculation, of course."

"No, no. It makes sense, Alan, insofar as any theory does. So what you're saying is that we in the West ought to be able to develop this technology based on the help we've been given?"

"Possibly, though to be honest, I don't think anyone can do much with three or four Mickey Mouse drawings. The surrounding text is the key."

"Look, Alan, the more I think about this, the more I'm convinced you should be there with them."

"Do you mean with British Aerospace, or whoever?" said Lewis, surprise written all over his face.

"Good God, no, man! Rome."

"Rome?"

"I think we need you on the spot. We can replace you here in your present duties. Perhaps not so ably, but different advisers bring different skills to the post, all of which are welcome."

"But where will you put me?"

"Possibly in the Embassy. You're too senior and almost certainly too well-known to be one of those ubiquitous First Secretaries that masquerade as all sorts of things, but who manifestly know sod-all about their alleged job. So we won't go down that road. British Council? Perhaps. Or tucked away somewhere in academia? There are many possibilities. Yes, Alan, my mind's made up. Will that be difficult domestically? I – I understand there's no longer family at home."

"I've been a widower many years now, Minister. My wife was an early victim of cancer. No, no, don't commiserate. It's been over ten years now. The children, of course, are grown up. My son and his family live in the States. I visit them every year. My daughter is a lecturer. She has a great partner. Unfortunately, no kids. So, really, no ties. May I think about this? I must say I'm tempted. An inspired thought on your part, Minister. Thank you."

Professor Alan Lewis did think about it. All the way home. Yes. It would certainly help the government. It would suit his own plans, too. He'd already decided on frequent visits to Rome. This would be even better.

*****

Even though it was Saturday, Kathy went in for a few hours, mainly to look at the latest top-up from NSA. Her mind was still full of her "date" with Professor Lewis the night before. Against all the odds, she had really enjoyed herself. She had recommended a little Italian restaurant at the top of the Promenade in Montpellier. The food was excellent (if you like Italian, and both of them did), and the general ambience was delightful – candlelight giving a warm, romantic glow, and the faint strains of Italian music. The wine, too, was just right. So here they were: on the one hand a somewhat gauche scientist touching fifty, who had brought her a single rose still bearing its price tag; and on the other a 41-year-old lady in a smart suit, still not quite recovered from a six-year relationship with an actor. She had not laughed, not really laughed, in the three years since it had ended. Now here she was laughing her head off, as Alan Lewis told her jokes about (would you believe) the particle accelerator at Cerne and the sexual practices of microbes. At the end of the evening, they walked arm-in-arm around the town enjoying the warm, balmy air. They called into the Queens for a nightcap, then Alan had gallantly escorted Kathy home (mother had gone to bed). A peck on the cheek for him, and Kathy was gone.

*****

Tim drove out the same day to collect Lucy. When he got to mama's he found the old lady surprisingly contrite. This was not like her.

"I'm such a burden to you," she said mournfully, with even a hint of a tear in her eye. "I'm so sorry, Tim. I keep wanting Lucy here, and I keep dragging you over here."

"You're not a burden, mama," said Tim gently. "Though I must admit it would be handier if you lived round the corner, but we can't make you do that."

410

"I've been thinking of that," she said. "But it's so hard to leave. Your father and I moved here nearly thirty years ago when he retired. We saw this place and fell in love with it. It's full of memories."

"But, mama," said Lucy, "They can't have been very happy ones. Daddy only lived about seven or eight years into retirement, and for the last five of those he was ill much of the time."

"Yes, you're right. And you were always coming over then, as you do now. Where exactly is this place?"

"What, the sheltered housing?" said Tim, sensing mama was weakening. "Look, come back with us for a few days before fending for yourself again. You can have a good look round. We know one or two people who live there. Mostly widows and widowers, like you. You can meet the warden, too. She'll tell you how to get onto the waiting list."

"Waiting list?" cried mama in horror.

"Mama," said Tim. "There are over fifty small apartments and there's quite a regular turnover. I mean …" He broke off, horrified, as he realised what he was saying to a very old lady recovering from a mini-stroke.

"Of course, dear, there would be," she agreed, clearly taking no offence at Tim's faux pas. "All right," she said sweetly, "I will come for a few days."

*****

News of the space visits continued to dominate the press around the world, though the news of the multi-faith bible clearly took back seat to the official admission of the existence of the space vehicles themselves. There was no shortage of comment on the vehicles, particularly their configuration and capabilities. Archive pictures galore were dusted off. Personal reminiscences were trotted out. There were accounts galore of sightings and of close encounters, including abductions. Some of the tabloids contained lurid details of minute physical examinations aboard a space vehicle, and there were the inevitable claims of sexual encounters with the occupants of the vehicles. The label "wishful thinking" could well apply to those accounts that featured a large, beautiful goddess surrounded by tiny males, one of whose duties it was to find a supply of healthy Earth men for her insatiable appetites. A sort of adult "Snow White and the Seven Dwarves." It was not difficult for the layman to pick his way through all these offerings separating the

411

informed comment from the ramblings of the many cranks and fantasists who crawled out of the woodwork.

The religious dimension did get some coverage in the serious press and both the Times and the Telegraph conducted surveys on the topic. Both asked passers-by in cities what they thought of the news of the space visitors and of their belief in God. The results were almost identical for both papers. About 70% of all those interviewed expressed no surprise at the existence of the extraterrestrial space vehicles. Most of the others said they did now believe they existed. Given that these vehicles, then, did exist, were they surprised the occupants believed in God. Over 90% expressed no surprise. The reason most commonly given was that they had seen such a large part of the universe or the Milky Way that they knew it couldn't just be there by accident. A few percentage of the population considered the whole thing was a conspiracy by the government/the Vatican/the Chief Rabbi/the Archbishop of Canterbury/Islam. The flights never happened. They were fabricated to get more believers. A group of 8-year-olds (weaned on a diet of space wars or whatever) had no doubt these vehicles existed even before this was officially acknowledged. Also, 100% of them expected the aliens to believe in God "because they come from somewhere near heaven, and pass by it every day." Some thought they probably knew God pretty well, because they were neighbours.

Radio and TV offered generally higher quality fare, screening out the cranks and the fanatics. It was the BBC that decided to cut to the chase. The programme planners thought hard about the best, most informative, content for a programme. The BBC came to the conclusion that whoever else contributed, one guest was indispensable: Father Mac. There was a regular series they could use that featured people in the news. This moved around the country, depending on where the story was centred. In this case, most of the action had happened in the Bristol region's backyard. The priest was tactfully approached and to their relief agreed, but only on his terms. He was to be asked only about his encounter with the space visitor, and in view of his recent health alarms, he wanted two others with him – his sister, who was a trained nurse, and one of his parishioners to help him with his memory, if necessary – assuming, of course, they were willing and able to help in this way. These conditions were readily agreed to. He was required to come to the Bristol studio at 7 pm in three days time. The programme began at 8 pm.

"And I want to hear nothing more of this until I roll up," he said. "I don't want any stupid rehearsals. Give me a list of questions to agree to beforehand and don't try to slip extra ones in. I admit that in an interview there might be the odd supplementary. That's OK. It promotes natural dialogue. So that's fine, as long as it's on the same topic." These stipulations were, in fact, a normal part and parcel of many an interview and were, again, readily accepted. Father Mac gave them his email address, then phoned Tim and broke the news.

"Please come and hold my hand, Tim. Intervene where necessary. You know all about what's secret and what's not. I'm not good at all that stuff and I'm worried they might try to trick me into revealing something I shouldn't."

"I'd be glad to," said Tim, "But it's your show and I don't want to intervene unless absolutely essential. I'll get Hugh or Nick Watson to let Debbie in London know, as a courtesy."

"I hadn't thought of that."

"I'm sure there will be no problem. They certainly won't oppose the interview, especially as we have control over the line of questioning."

"I'm going to ask Wiffie to come with us, too," said the priest.

Sister Winifred also said she would be pleased to help him. "The sisters will give me a hard time. 'Star of stage, screen, and radio' – you know the nonsense. Even Sister Matron will suggest I've succumbed to the sin of pride and should go to confession. I'll tell her I'll mention it in my next confession. We've got a lovely priest. He's been on radio and TV, as Sister Matron well knows! So she can put that in her pipe and smoke it. By the way, Donald, why can't these TV people come to you?"

"I thought of that, but there's a small fee involved, so I thought I'd better do what I'm told. The fee's for the hospice."

"That's very kind, Donald. And that's one more in the eye for Sister Matron!"

*****

On the Sunday morning, because Father Mac now felt able to conduct two masses, Tim, Lucy, and mama went to the 8:30 am service. Who should be there but Sister Winifred, fussing with the flowers on the altar. Tim immediately introduced her to mama.

I'm so glad you're here, Tim," said the nun. "The more I thought about this TV thing, the more I thought my place was here with

Donald, so I've come to stay for a few days. I can take Donald to the television studio on Tuesday. I was going to suggest a little get-together with you to go over what he should say. You must remind him of what he can't say, because of all this top secret nonsense."

"Oh, we'll steer well clear of that," said Tim. "The people in London have been told about the interview and are very relaxed about it. They say they have every confidence in me to keep things from branching out in the wrong direction. So I'd jolly well better. Anyway, it's very good of you to come up, Sister," said Tim. "As a matter of fact you've pre-empted me in every way. I was going to email you to say I'd be picking Father up, then stopping off for you on the way to Bristol. I was also planning to go over the ground with Father and have a chat with you on the car journey."

"What we'll do is come into the presbytery after Mass for coffee and biscuits," said Sister Winifred decisively. "Toast and marmalade, too, if you've had nothing this morning. Then if we can all travel to the studio together on Tuesday, that would be marvellous, and we can go over things again on the journey."

"Fine," said Tim. "I see it's almost time for Mass. We'd better sit down." They all sat together. A 10-year-old boy in a white surplice came out of the vestry, and moved to the rear of the church to check that the gifts of bread and wine were all ready to be brought up, while the reader moved to the lectern, welcomed everyone, asked for prayers for those unable to attend Mass today through illness, then resumed her seat. All was now ready, and Father Mac limped on to the altar.

After Mass, they all went into the presbytery, where Sister Winifred and Lucy put together a light breakfast, while mama and Father Mac exchanged health stories and hospital experiences. Tim looked at the questions. When they were all sitting round the table, he said, "Perhaps it would be easiest if we simply considered events chronologically, Father, starting with your visit to Canada. Yes, you went there. Yes, you went camping. Yes, you were left on your own."

"We now know that was because Andy was called in to work," said Father, "Is that OK?"

"I think so. What we mustn't say is that he was called in because another in the series of space visits had been predicted. There was no way anyone knew this visit would actually terminate in Canada itself. Andy would come in for all of them. Anyway, if you just say he was called in, not specifying why, let those who wish to speculate on why, do so. OK, then the crash."

Father Mac smiled. "Well, we're on pretty firm ground here. Loads of articles have covered that aspect, more than any other, and they all seem to have got the facts more or less right. The vehicle came crashing through the trees. There were two explosions. One shortly after the crash, and a second one after I'd spoken to the angel. Can I describe the space ship?"

"By all means. You're not giving away anything that's not generally known. Yes, talk about the size and shape, the logo, the gangplank automatically lowering, and talk about the occupant greeting you."

"I want to emphasise that he was not a little green man, nor did he have a lizard head or scales. He was smallish, but otherwise looked like anyone's neighbour. Except that, as I spoke to him I became aware of an aura, a sort of glow."

"That's wonderful, Father. They'll lap that up."

Father Mac became a little cross. "Tim, I'm not doing this for effect. This is the truth. This is what I saw. Why should I exaggerate when the truth itself is so wonderful, and at the same time – humbling?"

Tim felt chastened. "Sorry, Father. That was silly of me. Now what are you going to say about the bible and other pieces?"

"There's no point in hiding anything, is there?"

"No," agreed Tim, "It's all been in the papers, though if you do get on to the medical pages, I think you should simply say there's not much to say, because they're being studied by experts. You probably don't know, but for some reason Professor Lewis has gone all coy over the DNA, so the least said the better."

"What about the attempts to run me off the road in Canada and here?"

"The public and the media don't know about them. They only know there was something nasty involving a hi-jacked ambulance and some foreigners in a cottage, but that was after you had your stroke."

"That's right," intervened Sister Winifred. "Now, if we're into the medical side of things, what is there to say? Precious little I would have thought. Medical stuff is all confidential. The TV people won't want to pry. You can say that you were fortunate and the stroke was less serious than had first been feared. That's about all."

"I agree," said Father Mac.

"Well," smiled Tim, "I think that's about all there is. Everything that followed concerned deductive processes we can't get into – they don't involve us, anyway – and decisions by the government. I suppose they might get into the theological side."

"And what's your advice on that, Tim?" asked Father Mac mischievously.

"Heaven forbid I should presume ..." he began, then realised he was being had. Everyone laughed.

"I suppose one thing we might need to consider," said Lucy thoughtfully, "is who else is going to be on the programme. You may have your thunder stolen here and there."

"As far as I know, it's just me. It's that series they run called 'Centre of Attention.' You must have seen it. It's about someone in the news, discussing things from their point of view."

"Hmm," said Lucy, "Though not exactly from their point of view, because some BBC person devised the questions."

"True," said Father Mac, "but I was asked to comment on the list of questions they emailed me. So there was some input."

There was a bit more chit-chat. Plans were made for the journey on the Tuesday and Tim took Lucy and mama home.

*****

Later that morning, when Tim was engaged in his most loathsome chore – whitening the grouting in the shower – there was a ring at the door. Lucy went. A young man stood there.

"Er – Could I see Mr Sullivan? Tell him it's Dave." Lucy went upstairs to Tim.

"Is this really who I think it is? Dave? The boy who ... you know?" Tim went to the door and shouted back, "Yes, love."

"Dave, what a surprise," he said. "How's your mate? Kevin, isn't it?"

"Yeah. Look, I know you've got no reason to want to talk to us, but the other day Kev was clearing out his boot, a thing he does about once a year. He's a lazy bastard. Anyway, we found something that must have fallen out of that bin-liner when we – err – borrowed them books from the vicar."

"Father Mac? The priest?"

"That's the bloke. It's some sort of map with foreign words and stuff on. Can you give it back to him? He must have been using it. There's all sorts of scribble on it." He handed the map over. Tim briefly glanced at it, registering Cyrillic place names and pencil jottings.

416

"Tell him I'm sorry about what we done, and I hope it made a difference them foreigners not having this one, like. Now I gotta go. Cheers."

Dave trotted off down the garden path and retrieved a bike he'd propped against the fence, leaving Tim staring thoughtfully at the map. He went inside and took the map to his den. He could just about read the Cyrillic place names. Lucy walked in.

"Was that really Dave at the door?" she asked.

"Yes, it was our Dave. Kevin's mate. They found a map of Father Mac's in Kevin's car. It must have fallen out of the bin-liner they used when they took those books and things from Father Mac. I'd like to take a look at it before I give it back to Father. Here, take a look."

"No, it's all right, love. I can see from here it's in Russian, or 'Acrylic' as Norah calls it. I'm making coffee. I'll bring you one in."

Lucy went off and reappeared shortly after with the coffee. Tim studied the map again. Father Mac had clearly made some progress in playing the phonetic sound of the Cyrillic place-names against their alien equivalents. He'd got nowhere near as far as Kathy Webb in drawing up an alien alphabet with their phonetic equivalents, but in the limited time available he'd managed to isolate several frequently occurring proper nouns – names or people or places, identifiable as such by the fact that they were in larger letters. Across the large empty expanse of the Black Sea appeared small clusters of alien letters and attempts at a Cyrillic version. As Tim could see, Father Mac was proceeding on the right lines, but, though he was not to know it, time was against him. A stroke was waiting in the wings, minor, as it happened, but a little more serious in its effects than a TIA.

Tim was ready to fold the map back up, when he noticed a doodle down in the bottom left-hand corner. An alien word was there, and next to it were a few Cyrillic letters: Ие-у- Two of the letters were unrecovered. Looking at the alien version, Tim could see the two missing letters were identical.

Closing his eyes, he tried to relive the occasion in Kathy Webb's office, when she had dissolved into tears. This was the word, wasn't it, though complete on that occasion. Иесус. Jesus. Any analyst in a foreign intelligence agency receiving this map with all its doodling would have made short work of the message the map offered: that the book they were so interested in was nothing more than a Christian bible. Or at least a load of sacred texts including references to a prophet many considered to be their saviour, Jesus Christ. The foreign agency might well have set up a study party and eventually found evidence of teachings from the Koran, too, but they would also sure as hell find there was nothing on propulsion systems buried away there.

What was it Dave had said? He hoped it made a difference by them foreigners not having it. Well, yes, Dave, it might have stopped one man possibly being killed, two men crippled for life, a priest beaten up, an ambulance hi-jacked. You know, that sort of thing. Otherwise no, not much difference, Dave.

*****

On the Tuesday, Tim and Lucy collected Father Mac and Sister Winifred in good time, went over the hill to Cheltenham, then picked up the M5 on the Golden Valley. When they reached Bristol, they headed towards the Clifton district and picked up Whiteladies' Road. They were at the studio in good time and were conducted to an ante-room. There they met the producer, a bright, attractive woman called Sue Cooper, probably in her late 30s.

"I'm glad we've agreed the questions so easily, Father. Between you and me, some of our guests are – difficult. Your interviewer is our usual one, Helen Bloomfield. She'll put you entirely at your ease, and not spring any surprises. Towards the end, though, Helen might slightly accelerate the exchange between the two of you, making it appear a little more – intense. At the same time we may bring your face into closer view. This is a well-known TV technique. Presentationally, we're aiming to build up to a sort of crescendo, though interviews don't always lend themselves to that. Are you happy with that, Father?"

"Provided I can have my two minders with me."

"Yes, of course. We'll introduce them along with you. Better still, let you do that. Now, let's get you all to make-up."

"Shall I wait here?" said Lucy.

"You can watch," said Sue. "In fact, you can stay with your party the whole time, except for the interview itself. By the way, there's no audience, though I think you suspected that. It's not really that sort of programme." They all nodded.

I'm not sure if I should do this," said Sister Winifred. "Get made up. I'm in uniform. I forgot to get advice. What do other nuns do?"

"They stay quietly in their convents," said Sue Cooper, "instead of gallivanting around, parading themselves in public." She smiled. "I'm sure in the interests of the arts, you would be permitted a few touches

418

of make-up, Sister. It's not as if we're applying cosmetics to help you lure men into your wicked clutches."

"Anyway, I'm too old now for that sort of thing," said Sister with a sigh, at the same time winking at Lucy.

Twenty minutes later, they were all back in the ante-room, waiting for their interviewer. Helen Bloomfield bustled in. She was about the same age as Sue, but while Sue was in jeans, Helen was more formally attired in a smart, black suit with a red scarf at her throat and a neat pair of drop earrings. She was attractive and friendly. They all warmed to her, even Sister Winifred, who generally reserved her judgment on people until longer acquaintance.

While Father Mac and his two minders were being prepared to appear on television, a number of viewers in and around Cheltenham were making themselves comfortable, ready to watch the programme. In Bourton, Doc and Megan were sitting expectantly with Mary and Brian, Norah made herself a cup of tea and sat down in front of her set, and the McGuires and Hugh Frobisher in their households were also making themselves comfortable. In Cheltenham itself, Kathy had asked Alan Lewis to sit with her and her mother, the Nick Watson household was making ready, while down in the Whaddon district Lennie Gill sat waiting with his wife and Colin. He still winced every now and then from the attentions of Misha.

A few minutes before 8 o'clock, Helen Bloomfield and her party all trooped into the studio, and arranged themselves as directed. They chatted informally to allow the sound engineers to get their levels right.

"When you hear a buzzer, there are ten seconds to go," explained Helen. "Then that big red light there will change to a display saying "On Air." OK? I'll begin by introducing the programme, of course. When I introduce you, Father, a smile and a nod would be about right. All this will occupy the first couple of minutes. Then off we go." She smiled encouragingly all round, and squeezed Father Mac's hand. She knew all too well that being interviewed live on TV took a certain amount of courage, and some, probably most, would find it an ordeal.

"There goes the buzzer," said Helen and smiled all round. The red light changed to "On Air." Helen was off.

"Good evening, this is 'Centre of Attention' and I'm Helen Bloomfield. At the centre of attention this week is a man who a few months ago would never have imagined for one minute he would be cast in that rôle. Father Donald McNulty is parish priest of St Nicholas Roman Catholic Church at Bourton-under-Wychwood in the

419

Father Mac

Cotswolds, near Cheltenham. He unwittingly set in progress a whole
chain of events that culminated in the story that's still on everyone's
lips – official government admission of U.F.O.s, and evidence that we
on Earth worship the same God as our space-visitors. Welcome,
Father." Father Mac gave the camera a beatific smile. "Now you have
two other people with you. Who are they?"

"This is my sister. In fact she's a sister three times over – my own
sister, a nun known as Sister Winifred from a convent near Stroud, and
a trained nursing sister. And this is Tim Sullivan, a parishioner, who
helped me through some difficult times." Both Sister Winifred and Tim
dutifully nodded to the camera. Tim gave a broad grin, but Sister
remained solemn.

"Now tell us, Father, how did you personally set in motion this
chain of events?"

"Well, I'll abbreviate this. Your listeners won't want to hear what
colour socks I was wearing. They want to hear about the angel I met."

"Angel?" asked Helen, clearly not expecting this.

"Yes. I went camping in the wilds of Ontario with my brother and
his wife. They had to return home suddenly, to Ottawa, so there I was
on my own, counting the chipmunks and watching out for bears. On the
second night, an hour or so before dawn, I was woken by a powerful
strobe light, something dark passed low overhead, and whatever it was
crashed near my camp-site and pockets of fire sprang up. I tried
approaching the crash scene in case I could help, and to see what had
happened."

Father Mac took her over his decision to explore the wreck, his
initial retreat, then his second attempt as dawn began creeping in. As he
approached the shape in the woods, he became aware of a group of
helicopters coming in low, searching for a suitable area to land. They
eventually did so, about half a mile away. No doubt they were a rescue
party of some sort. While he was watching them, there was an
explosion from inside the crashed vehicle. He waited a little longer and
this time was able to examine it. He went on to describe its size and
rounded appearance and the portholes dotted about in two rows. He
described the logo, then the opening of a door.

"Were you not frightened throughout all this?" asked Helen, visibly
shaken by all this detail.

"I don't know," said Father Mac. "I don't think so. I was drawn to
it. It was very odd. I knew I was on the brink of something wonderful.
Some wonderful revelation. But I didn't know what. I was completely

420

transfixed. Soon after the door opened a sort of gangway automatically dropped down, then a figure emerged through the smoke and began slowly descending."

"And what did the figure look like?"

"It was a small man, a little over five feet in height. He was clothed in white. Though he came from another civilisation, he looked just like a human being from Earth – in fact an amalgam of several racial types. His skin was slightly tanned and his eyes had just the hint of the Asian. He had no trouble breathing in our atmosphere."

"Did that surprise you? The way he looked?"

"Not in the slightest. I've long believed there were other civilisations out there, and that when we meet them, we would find they were similar in appearance to us, not tiny people with large heads and huge almond eyes, or with reptilian features. I believe all people are made in the image and likeness of God, wherever they live. The only feature I wasn't expecting was the aura that surrounded him. He seemed to glow."

"What are you saying, Father? Can you explain this aura."

"Oh, easily. The man I saw was nearly an angel."

"You mean …"

"I believe he was from a race that had evolved way beyond the human race, but their evolution had been spiritual rather than physical. Intellectual, too, of course."

"And you firmly believe that?"

"Oh, yes. I have no doubt. Anyway, this man was clutching something in his hand. When he reached the ground, he approached me. We tried to exchange greetings. I gave my name. We embraced and he uttered one word."

"And what was that?"

The word was 'Mo-lees.' I took this at first to be his name. It was some time later that I recognised what he was saying. I'll come on to that later." He paused, as Helen made a note of the word, then resumed. "The man gave me a book from the space craft. It had obviously been damaged in the explosion. It was badly charred in places, and clearly not complete. There were also some other fragments, including parts of a map. I happened to have in my pocket a copy of Prayers for the Dying, part of my emergency kit for use with the dying. Prayers, oil, and the sacred host."

"A communion wafer?"

Yes, the sacred host. I gave the prayer sheet to the man. He looked at it and became very animated. He then pointed to two park notice boards about camping regulations and disposal of rubbish. I understood then what had excited him. He recognised English, and knew he had come down somewhere where English was the normal language. Or at least he recognised the language as not being the one he expected."

"And what was that?"

"Russian."

Uh-oh, thought Tim, we're getting on to thin ice. But Father Mac was on autopilot now. Words flowed from him.

"Russian?" said Helen gently. "Oh, of course, some of the other landings had been in Russia, hadn't they?"

"Yes, and my new friend might well have landed there himself."

"How could that be?" Helen was genuinely puzzled.

"Well," said Father Mac conspiratorially, "and this is top secret, so don't tell anyone." He winked at Helen. In the wings, Sue was ecstatic. Tim groaned. He's going to be indiscreet, God help us.

Father Mac resumed. "Well, surely you don't think the little space craft I saw was designed to fly for several years over a distance of several light years with a crew of one, and expect to reach Earth intact. No, there's a mother craft somewhere in the solar system, where they knock these things together and launch them – a whole series of them. And recover them for re-use, too, I'll bet. Or most of them."

"Father, you're projecting a cosy image of a group of small men, all glowing, struggling with components from a flat-pack."

"You've got the picture. Or at least an approximation. Now, after my little friend became excited, he went back up the gangway into the craft and emerged with another bunch of paper, gave it to me, embraced me and went back up into the craft. By now the rescue party from the five helicopters had made their way through the forest hacking a way forward. They were very close. I got the impression they were military. The alien reached the door again, turned and waved, indicated I should make myself scarce as soon as possible, and disappeared inside the craft. I hurried away and shortly after there was another explosion. The whole craft trembled and burning debris was flung high into the trees, some of it subsequently dropping to the Earth. More papers. That's it, really. I packed up and returned to Ottawa."

"What a fascinating story, Father. There was so much detail that I and I'm sure most of our listeners were not aware of. What happened then? You completed your holiday, and came back, bringing the book and papers you were given with you as souvenirs. Didn't you report any of this?"

Father Mac looked at Tim. What, if anything could he say?

Tim breathed a sigh of belief. "Let me come in here briefly," he said. "We're moving into the realms of officialdom. Father Mac did, in fact, report this to the Canadian military authorities and, as a British subject, he also mentioned it to the Defence Liaison Staff at the High Commission. Both claimed no knowledge of the incident, perhaps because they were not prepared for a public disclosure at that stage. They thanked Father, and soon after this he returned home, where he immediately prepared a record of events on his computer. He intended to involve me, but wished to clear his mind first. He also hid the fragments of the book and the other papers, with clues where to find them. But then he had a stroke. The paramedics came and took him to Cheltenham General Hospital."

"And I came rushing up to Bourton to be near him," interposed Sister Winifred. "He lost his speech and some use of one side. His speech returned after a couple of weeks, but he's left with a limp. So, fortunately, it turns out he was a bit of a fraud, weren't you?"

"May God forgive you," said Father Mac.

Sue Cooper was in raptures.

"A few questions, Father, if I may," said Helen. "What happened to your angel?"

"I understand there may have been a survival chamber. I hope he survived."

"And why did you address your account of things to Mr Sullivan?"

"I knew that when he found the fragments of books and things, he'd get them into the right hands. After all, they were in an alien script."

"You've recently retired from GCHQ, Mr Sullivan. Did your experiences there permit you to decode the papers you found?"

"Personally? No. But, as they say, I knew a man who would, or at least might, be able to make something of it. Though, in fact, the man was a woman."

"I believe there were problems with people trying to steal the fragments, Father."

Sister Winifred leapt in here. "Yes, poor man. He was run off the road twice on the way back from camping, and again when he got back here. On the M5. Then when he was moved from the hospital in Cheltenham to my convent near Stroud, he was kidnapped along with Mr Sullivan. Poor Donald. He was badly beaten up."

"You're a brave man, Father," said Helen admiringly.

"You should see the other fellow," he grinned, then became serious. "No, I suppose I should try to imitate the angel. He would feel deep compassion. There were several casualties."

"Most of this been released to the media," said Tim.

"Yes, so I believe," said Helen. "But now, the really big issue. What did those papers consist of? We know there was a book, or fragments of a book. We'll come on to that in a moment. What else were there?"

"Let me come in here," said Tim. "To be honest, these other fragments are still under examination."

"Some of the papers mentioned medical textbook extracts, with DNA diagrams."

"Yes, I've heard that, too," said Tim innocently, "But I don't know if it's based on fact, or speculation. It could be the sort of reference book any space-craft might carry in case of on-board illness. I know there was probably only one person aboard the craft, but it could be standard issue. It makes a good tabloid headline, I suppose."

In Cheltenham, Professor Alan Lewis squeezed Kathy's hand. "Good old Tim," he breathed.

"Now, about the book itself, the main one," Helen continued. "What is it, a multi-faith bible, or perhaps a coffee-table book tracing the history of religion on their own planet, or even on Earth? We've heard both descriptions. Is either true? Father?"

"I'm not sure a precise label is helpful. Remember, a study of the book has only just begun, but at first sight it does seem to present the sacred texts of the three monotheistic faiths."

"Monotheistic?"

"Belief in a single God. Islam, Judaism, and Christianity are all monotheistic. And they don't just believe in one God. They believe in the same God. Whatever the purpose of the visits, Russia was clearly the country targeted. Therefore, this series of visits might have been a call to the people of Russia to practise their faith. But, you may ask, if that is so, are they not many years too late? As I expect you know, after years of religious suppression, all three faiths are again practised there. But are these visits really too late? Are these angels, or what ever they are, exhorting not only the people of Russia, but perhaps the world in general, to practise their faith now, today, really practise it – their belief in the same God – and not slide into complacency, or be seduced into fanaticism. Be good to people. Love each other. For God's sake, love each other. And this doesn't just mean 'don't blow them up.' It means do things for them, and not to them. Be like the angels. Start now, even if you are many years too late, all of you."

Sue Cooper held her breath, as Father Mac turned and looked deep into Helen Bloomfield's eyes. "Let me tell you something, Helen," he said in a soft voice, "there is no such thing as a Christian angel, or a Jewish one, or an Islamic one. God knows, the scriptures of all three great faiths are teeming with accounts of the works of angels. These angels are still with us. There are angels everywhere and they belong to everyone. Everyone." The camera closed in on his face.

"And will there be any more visits, Father?"

"No. They've fulfilled their mission. Our own government and other governments have recognised these visits as a wake-up call, and I hope they will show the lead. The visitors will soon be embarking on their next mission, steering to where Our Lady points them."

"Finally, Father, tell me what that word was the angel said to you. I have it here 'Mol-ees.' What is that?"

"It means 'pray' in Russian. I then knew instantly the book I was given was sacred." He seemed to project his gaze somewhere ahead of him, as if trying to see his visitor in white. A wonderful smile came over him. Some viewers claimed they even saw a faint glow surrounding him. "I knew then that my visitor really was an angel." As the priest continued in a beatific trance, the camera moved in still closer, then the picture slowly faded.

"They do it with special lighting," said Mrs Gill in her house near the Robins' football ground.

"Not in this case," said Colin. "That was genuine. It came from inside the priest." He hesitated. "Er – Dad, shall I go and get you a 4-pack from Sainsbury's to help with the pain? My treat."

SIX MONTHS LATER

Father Mac's prediction was correct. The visits by the space-craft with the distinctive logo ceased. News of the multi-faith bible seemed to have a calming effect in those parts of the world where possible conflict had been anticipated. A remarkable increase in attendance at Christian services was registered. This was less noticeable with Jewish and Muslim worship, where attendance was already high. Another result was a sudden surge in candidates for the Christian priesthood, though the Church would have to wait several years to reap the benefit of this.

Father Mac himself suffered two more mini-strokes. Neither was serious, but the Bishop insisted he now retire. A married deacon was assigned to the Deanery and took up residence in Bourton presbytery. Norah was thrilled. His wife was a teacher and their children were grown up. Father Mac again took up temporary residence in Sister Winifred's hospice. He knew his days of globe-trotting were over, and was delighted when his friend Father Ambrose came to visit. Only weeks later, a conference in GCHQ brought Andy over, together with Chantelle. Father Mac was permitted to write a book about his experiences. This would become a best seller. With the agreement of all parties, he would divide the sum of money he received three ways: a third for the diocese, a third for Sister Winifred's hospice, and a third for himself and Sister to set up home together. Quite coincidentally, they were to find themselves living a few doors from Lucy's mother.

Tim and Lucy reverted to a normal domestic routine, as did the Campbells. Doc was quite content that he was no longer required to work with the little band of experts recruited by Professor Lewis. No more interesting meetings to chair. Never mind, there was plenty to interest him in helping Mary to plan her future. She had become almost a surrogate daughter. Brian Jenkins, meanwhile, was now in the police, and would soon be ready for his first assignment. He and Mary were to get married at Easter, then move to wherever Brian was posted. Mary's plans to get into teaching were placed on hold until she knew where they would be living.

The ELK ONE Committee as such was disbanded (allowing Bob and Hugh Frobisher to slip gracefully into full retirement) but was superseded by another committee, which operated at no higher than the Confidential level. This met from time to time under the chairmanship of Debbie, who, together with GCHQ and the competent agencies in other countries, received a regular service of recoveries from the team in Rome. The team gelled surprisingly well and compilation of the dictionary continued apace.

It was again Kathy who initiated a major breakthrough. She arranged for the medical pages showing treatment involving the total or partial encasing of body parts in metal to be scanned, and the words assigned a digital value based on the same digital labels assigned to the letters forming the words in the multi-faith bible. These results were added to the bible, and comparisons were made across the entire book. Over time it became possible to identify words for hand, arm, leg, foot, eye, ear, heart, and many more. It was a revelation how many times parts of the body were referred to in the bible. It was also a revelation how many times the choice of body parts to be encased in metal bore no apparent relation to the body part being treated. Plans were laid for an experimental programme of treatment to be conducted in one of the large hospitals, though these did not extend to use of a gantry in the first instance.

Professor Lewis had a very loosely defined role within the British Council, promoting scientific liaison between the UK and both Italy and the Vatican. He paid several visits to the observatories in the Vatican and near Tucson. He also had Phil Ramsey over to visit him, and the two would be seen dining together and scribbling on the backs of envelopes. Their meetings seemed to be getting more and more intense. Could they be getting somewhere? Every so often he came back down to Earth. After all, he mustn't forget his date with Kathy – his wedding date!

Iguana Books
iguanabooks.com

If you enjoyed *Father Mac*...
Look for other books coming soon from Iguana Books! Subscribe to our blog for updates as they happen.

iguanabooks.com/blog/

You can also learn more about Mike Rafferty and his upcoming work on his blog.

mikerafferty.iguanabooks.com/blog/

If you're a writer...
Iguana Books is always looking for great new writers, in every genre. We produce primarily ebooks but, as you can see, we do the occasional print book as well. Visit us at iguanabooks.com to see what Iguana Books has to offer both emerging and established authors.

iguanabooks.com/publishing-with-iguana/

If you're looking for another good book...
All Iguana Books books are available on our website. We pride ourselves on making sure that every Iguana book is a great read.

iguanabooks.com/bookstore/

Visit our bookstore today and support your favorite author.

IGUANA